THERE'S SOMETHING ABOUT SCARLETT

HOPE COVE BOOK 8

HANNAH ELLIS

Published by Hannah Ellis
www.authorhannahellis.com
Postfach 900309, 81503 München
Germany

Cover design by Mario Ellis

THERE'S SOMETHING ABOUT SCARLETT

CHAPTER 1

He almost walked straight past her. If it hadn't been for the sun dazzling him, he might never have turned in her direction. Pulling his sunglasses down from the top of his head, Fraser spotted the girl sitting on a bench, who was grinning as though she was the happiest person in the world.

"You've dropped something," she shouted.

It took him a second to realise she was talking to him. The rolled-up University of Exeter brochure had slipped from his back pocket.

"Thanks," he called as he scooped it up. "Are you thinking of studying here?"

"Maybe." She closed her eyes and lifted her chin to the sun, radiating joy.

Fraser looked ahead to the car park, then back at her. Taking advantage of the fact that she had her eyes closed, he let his gaze travel over her black leggings and blue T-shirt dress that came to the middle of her thighs. Her long brown hair was tucked behind her ears. There was nothing particularly striking about her. She had that girl next door thing going on, but it was the joy on her face that was mesmerising.

"Are you lost?" she asked, opening her eyes and catching him staring.

"I … erm … no … I was just …" *Crap.* Pretty girls didn't usually turn him into a jabbering idiot. "You've got a nice sunny spot." He indicated the bench. "Do you mind if I join you?"

Her shoulders twitched. "I don't own the bench. It belongs to the university."

"Right." He sat beside her. "What do you think of the campus?"

"I like it. And they have the course I want to take. I've already been offered a place. As long as I get the A-levels I need."

"Which course?"

"English with Creative Writing."

"Do you want to be a writer?"

"I *am* a writer." The corners of her mouth twitched upwards. "I've written two novels and I'm in the middle of a third."

He nodded approvingly. "So you want to make a living from that?"

As she shifted to look at him, a ray of sunlight caught the piercing below her bottom lip, making the red stud sparkle. "I'm going to publish my books one day. I also plan on having my own publishing company to publish books for other authors."

"That's ambitious."

"I know." Her eyes sparkled. "I'm going to do it though. I can do anything I want."

"It's really cool that you know what you want to do."

"Yes. It's *very cool*," she agreed.

Her confidence was unnerving, and for once Fraser found himself struggling for conversation. Casually, he pulled off his sunglasses and hooked them into the neck of his shirt. Then he ran a hand through his hair. Women always loved his thick blond hair, which fell in a soft wave.

"Does that annoy you?" she asked, staring at his hairline.

"What?"

"The way your hair falls forward. It would drive me crazy."

"Most people like my hair," he said, wriggling his eyebrows. "I get a lot of compliments for it."

After staring at his hair for a moment, she gave a small shake of the head and looked away.

"The sports facilities here are impressive." He cleared his throat when his voice came out a pitch too high. "The gym's brand new."

"The library's new too."

Racking his brain for something intelligent to say, he came up blank. "Do you live far away?"

She looked thoughtful. Was he coming across as such a weirdo that she was worried about disclosing where she lived?

"I live in Hope Cove," she finally said.

"It's beautiful there. We used to go for day trips when I was a kid."

"It's a nice place." She checked her watch. "I have to drive back there now."

"Maybe I'll see you in September. Are you definitely coming to Exeter? Or do you have other offers too?"

"I only applied to Exeter."

"Cool. We'll probably bump into each other then." Except he wasn't even planning on accepting his offer at Exeter. He was going to university in Manchester with his two best friends, so he had no idea why he'd said that.

"I doubt it." She ran a finger over a groove in the wood of the bench. "One day I'll study here, but not in September."

"I thought you'd got a place?"

"I'm going to turn it down."

He opened his mouth to speak but struggled to find words. "I don't understand."

"I don't have the money for the tuition fees." A breeze dragged strands of hair across her face and she swept them aside.

"Get a student loan," he said, confused.

She shook her head. "I can't. I'm not eligible because my parents can afford to pay. But they won't."

"They won't pay for you to go to uni?"

She looked at him impatiently. "That's what I just said."

"Why not?"

"They don't think I should go." Her gaze was fixed on the gravel under her shoes, but he caught the flash of sadness in her eyes.

"That sucks."

"I'll work for a year and save up. One day I'll get a degree and then I'll start a publishing company. I'm definitely going to do it."

"Can't you tell the loan company that your parents refuse to pay? Surely there's a way around it."

"No. I emailed and asked." She closed her eyes again, bathing her face in the sun's warm rays. With her features relaxed, she had that look again, as though she didn't have a care in the world. Which was impressive considering it obviously wasn't true.

"That doesn't seem fair," he said. "Is there really no other way to get the loan?"

"Not unless I get married. But that's pretty unlikely since I don't even have a boyfriend."

He blinked a few times in quick succession. "If you were married, you could get a loan?"

"If you're married, the loan company looks at the income of you and your spouse rather than your parents. It's a bad system if you ask me." She stood and picked up her bag.

"Do you want to get a coffee or something?" he asked quickly. "My treat."

"I have to leave before rush hour. I don't like driving in traffic."

She didn't look at him as she called goodbye over her shoulder. Automatically, he shot off the bench and hurried to catch up.

When his brain failed him and he lost the power of speech, she cast him a suspicious sideways glance.

"Are you following me?"

"No." He pointed ahead. "My car's parked over here."

When she quickened her pace he matched it and made an inane comment about the weather. She didn't reply and only looked at him again when she reached her car – an old blue Micra.

"It was nice to meet you." She looked around. "Where's your car?"

He raised his chin as he looked across the car park in the direction of his prized possession. The silver Audi had been a gift from his parents for his eighteenth birthday. Pulling the fob from his pocket, he pressed the button, making the lock pip and the lights flash.

She didn't even look, just climbed into her car. Standing taller, Fraser raked his fingers through his hair again, but apparently she was swoon-proof and only rolled her eyes slightly as she reached to close the car door.

Instinctively, he put a hand on it to stop her. "What's your name?"

"Scarlett Mercer," she said, looking uneasily at his hand.

He smiled at the way she said it so formally. "I'm Fraser Graham."

"Goodbye, Fraser Graham." She reached for the door handle.

"Do you want to swap phone numbers?" he asked, tilting his head and raising an eyebrow in a way that usually made women flutter their eyelashes and giggle.

"Why?"

He looked blankly down at her. Occasionally, if it seemed as though a woman might not fall for his charms, he acted completely indifferent. It always got their attention. Now he had the feeling he was being played at his own game.

"I don't know." He wasn't usually so tongue-tied. "Maybe we could be friends?"

"I've got two friends already," she said confidently. When he laughed, she looked at him with an intensity that made his smile fall away. "Can you please let go of the door, Fraser Graham? I need to go."

He removed his hand. "We should swap numbers anyway," he said, the words tumbling out as she pulled on the door. "You might not need a friend but you said you're in the market for a husband." His eyes widened. Where the hell had that come from?

The car door stopped just before it closed. "Pardon?"

"You need a husband, right? We could get married. Then you could get a loan and accept your place on the course."

She tapped on the steering wheel and stared straight ahead. "You're offering to marry me?"

"Well …" That did seem to be the case. It wasn't as though he was actually *going* to marry her. He just wanted her phone number. No one ever turned him down when he asked for their number. "Marriage is just a piece of paper, right? At least let's swap numbers. We can think it over, then get together and chat it through."

The silence that followed felt like torture. He'd offered to marry her and solve all her problems and she was casually mulling over the proposition as though it was the sort of offer she got all the time. She should have snatched his hand off so fast that he got scared and ran away. Or maybe she knew that was what would happen. Maybe he'd met his nemesis when it came to playing hard to get. And it was bloody working because he was fairly sure he'd resort to begging for her number if she didn't give it to him soon.

She thrust her phone at him. "Put your number in there, Fraser Graham."

He tapped away. "I don't know if getting married would really be a possibility, or if you could actually get a loan that way, but we should get together for a drink sometime and chat it over."

When he handed the phone back, he swept his hair aside and gave her his most dazzling smile. She rolled her eyes again and closed the door with a bang.

Watching her drive away, he had a sinking feeling that she wasn't going to call.

CHAPTER 2

"How was it?" Auntie Verity asked when Scarlett walked into the kitchen at the back of the cafe. The place was already closed and Verity was busy cleaning up.

"Okay," Scarlett replied, leaning against the counter.

"I'm still not sure why you went to the open day when you're not going to accept the place on the course. I'd have thought that would be depressing."

"It was motivating. I'll defer my place on the course and save up to go next year. I'm going to have my own publishing company one day."

Verity switched the dishwasher on. "I don't know where you get these big ideas from."

"I can do anything I want." Or so her friend Emily had told her. Meeting Emily had been one of the best things about moving to Hope Cove. It was the first time she'd met another writer in real life. "After Emily told me I could publish my books, I got thinking about what else I'd like to do. I want to have my own publishing company. I know all about publishing so there's no reason why I can't."

"It's very ambitious."

"Don't start telling me I can't do it. You'll sound like Mum. I came to live with you to get away from her."

Verity put her hands on her hips and sighed heavily. "I'm inclined to think you probably will do it. If you could do it on sheer determination alone you wouldn't have any problems at all. It's not going to be easy though. You need to make sure you get the grades you need in your A-levels. Then you need to save up. Getting onto the course is only the first step. It'll be hard work getting a degree ..."

"I know!" Scarlett said impatiently. "But Emily and Lizzie have been helping me study. I'll get the grades. And I'll go to uni and get a degree."

"Setting up your own business won't be easy either."

"I don't like it when you're negative."

"I'm being realistic. You've a lot of work ahead of you."

"I know!" she said again. "Can you just be a bit more positive?"

"Sorry." She put a hand on Scarlett's shoulder. "I want you to achieve everything you want. But I don't want you to be disappointed if you don't. And I'm sorry I can't help you more." Her chin wobbled and Scarlett hoped she wasn't about to cry. "You know I'd give you the money for uni if I had it."

"Yes," Scarlett said, unsettled by the intensity of the conversation.

"You're a good girl," Verity said, patting Scarlett's cheek.

She sidestepped to get away. "You're making me uncomfortable."

"I'm sorry." Verity chuckled. "Run away upstairs if you want to get away from me."

"I've got some revising to do. I've got two exams next week." At the doorway, she paused and looked back. "Thank you for letting me live here."

"I like having you around," Verity said, kindness shining in her eyes.

Scarlett hurried up the stairs at the back of the building. The flat above the cafe was small but cosy. Verity kept it neat but wasn't obsessed with everything looking perfect like Scarlett's mum. The flat felt more like home than her parents' house ever had. She could relax without wondering what she was going to get into trouble for next.

Flopping onto her bed in the small back bedroom she felt wiped out. The visit to Exeter University had been stressful. New places and people always felt daunting, and even the drive there and back had been a challenge. Hopefully by the time she went to uni she'd have saved enough money to live on campus so she wouldn't have to drive there every day. It was just over an hour each way, so it would be possible for her to keep living with Verity, but not ideal.

Taking her phone from her pocket, she scrolled through the contact list until she reached the latest entry. She'd been on a bit of a high after the university tour when the weird guy had disturbed her peace. She supposed meeting all sorts of different people would be part of the university experience. It definitely wasn't something she was excited about. She wanted a degree, not a social life. Especially not if it meant hanging out with creepy guys like Fraser. The way he'd kept touching his hair as though he had a nervous tic put her on edge. Not to mention the way he'd followed her to her car.

His joke about getting married sprang to mind. She presumed it was a joke. Sometimes other people's humour went over her head. It was true what he'd said about it only being a piece of paper. She wished he hadn't mentioned that. Not being able to get a loan hadn't bothered her much before, but the idea that it would be possible if she had a marriage certificate made it seem almost within reach. Some words in front of an official and a few signatures and the money would be hers. She'd be able to start uni in September and not have to spend the next year working in the cafe and saving every penny she could.

He'd been joking though. She was sure of it.

CHAPTER 3

The Thorverton Arms was reasonably busy when Fraser sauntered in on Saturday evening. He knew half the people in there and smiled and nodded greetings while he waited to be served at the bar. Friends of his parents were seated near the fireplace, and he had a quick chat with them before wandering to the side room where the younger crowd hung out. He spotted his two best friends at a table by the window and pulled out a stool to join them.

Immediately, he was distracted by fingers trailing across the back of his neck. Craning to look up, he grinned at one of the girls he'd gone to school with.

"Hey, Millie."

"Hey, yourself. I've been messaging you all weekend. Where were you last night?"

"I went into Exeter with the lads."

"I was in Exeter. We could've met up if you'd replied to my messages."

"Sorry. You know what I'm like at keeping track of my phone." He flashed a wide smile. "Next time we'll definitely hang out."

"I'll talk to you later," she said and wandered away.

"Pathetic," Allie muttered opposite him, while Liam raised a hand and high-fived him. "Don't encourage him!" she chastised.

"Oh, come on. It's fun to watch women falling all over him. It's an interesting study on human behaviour." Liam took a long sip of his drink. "Who were you out with last night?"

"Ian and Pete. You should have come. It was a good laugh."

Liam draped his arm along the back of Allie's chair. "We went out for dinner, then the cinema."

"Sounds like a wild night," Fraser said mockingly, earning him a kick in the shin from Allie. "Anyway, I've got a funny story for you …" He was interrupted by a hand on his shoulder and automatically smiled as he looked up. "Hi, Monique."

"I haven't seen you all week," she said, her dark eyelashes batting against the delicate skin below her eyes. "Maybe we can hang out later?"

"Yeah. We should catch up."

"My parents are away for the weekend so I have the house to myself. You could come over tonight and keep me company if you want."

"I'm not sure what I'm doing later but I'll let you know." He gave her hand a quick squeeze and she went back to her friends.

"I thought you broke up with her?" Liam asked.

"Yeah, I did."

"Oh my God!" Allie shook her head. "She's a disgrace to women. *You* broke up with *her* but she still wants to sleep with you?"

Fraser caught Liam's eye and suppressed a laugh. "I made it very clear that I'm not in a place to commit to a relationship. If she wants to use me for my body, I'll just grin and bear it."

Allie snatched at a beer mat and threw it at his head. "She's not using you, you pig. She's hoping that if she hangs around, you'll realise you're madly in love with her. Don't string her along."

"I'm not!" He pulled his phone from his pocket and checked

the display before sliding it onto the table. "Can I tell you my story now?"

"As long as it doesn't involve you treating women like crap," Allie said. He was sure most of her outrage was an act. She just enjoyed telling him off.

"I went to look around Exeter University," he said, checking his phone again.

"Why?" Liam asked. "I thought you were definitely going to Manchester. The three of us together. You can't break the threesome."

Allie aimed another beer mat at Liam's head. "How many times do I have to tell you not to use the word threesome in relation to us? It creeps me out."

Fraser leaned towards Liam and wrapped his arms around his shoulders. "Any time you guys need to spice up your sex life, let me know and I'll jump right in there. It's what friends are for, right?"

"You're so generous," Liam said in a jokey tone. He put his arms around Fraser and rubbed his forehead against his.

"Will you two get off each other!" Allie pulled them apart. "That joke's worn out. And it makes me nervous how comfortable you two are with the conversation."

"Any time," Fraser said, winking at her.

She shuddered. "Just tell us the story. Why did you go and look around Exeter?"

"It was something to do. Mum was on my back about … I don't even know what it was this time, but I needed to get out of the house and it was the open day at the uni so I went to check it out. I thought there might be some talent around the place."

"I can't believe you went to look around," Liam said. "We're going to Manchester. The three of us living together is going to be such a laugh."

Fraser distracted himself by taking a few slow gulps of his beer. The three of them had met on the first day of primary school and had been best friends ever since. When they were eight, they'd decided they'd live together when they grew up. Somehow they'd stuck with the plan and had decided to share a house together in Manchester. Liam was the one who was driving the idea now. Fraser couldn't bring himself to say it, but living with a couple didn't align with his vision for uni life. He suspected Allie wasn't thrilled by the idea either.

"I was only having a look," he said. "The sports facilities are mint."

"Are you considering going there?" Allie asked in surprise.

"No, but the weirdest thing happened. I was about to leave and I spotted this girl sitting on her own."

Allie groaned. "If you had sex with her in your car I don't want to hear about it."

"As if he'd risk messing up the seats," Liam said, deadpan.

"I really wouldn't," Fraser agreed.

Liam chuckled. "What happened then?"

"Nothing." Fraser tilted his phone to check the screen. "It was as though she was immune to my charms. I pretty much had to force her to take my number."

"You're really sad, you know?" Allie said.

He shook his head, remembering the look on Scarlett's face as she'd smiled into the sun. "There was something about her. I can't put my finger on it …"

"Was it actually two things?" Liam asked. "And were they attached to her chest?"

Fraser gave him a playful shove. "It wasn't her looks … I mean she's pretty but it wasn't that. She was confident to the point of being aloof. And she did that thing where she pretended not to be interested. I always wondered why that works, but when you're on the other side of it it's hard to resist."

Allie grunted a laugh. "Did it ever occur to you that she just didn't find you attractive?"

"Are you serious?" He pointed to his face. "That definitely didn't occur to me."

"Pig!"

"Is this the first time this has happened?" Liam asked. "That you've tried to chat someone up and they've had none of it?"

"We all know it's not a regular occurrence. She did take my number in the end." He winced as he remembered how desperate he'd felt in the car park.

"Has she called?" Liam asked.

He shifted in his seat. "Not yet."

Allie's eyes sparkled with amusement. "Is that why you keep looking at your phone?" She squeezed her shoulders towards her ears. "This is brilliant. A woman is making you wait for her call. How exactly does your own medicine taste?"

Fraser wished he could say he didn't care that she hadn't called. Instead, his gaze fell to his phone. It had been almost a week. Why the heck *hadn't* she called?

"She's not going to call," Allie said smugly.

"She'll call," he said.

"No, she won't. She doesn't like you!"

Fraser reached for his pint. "She's definitely going to call."

That's what he kept telling himself the following week. Every time his phone rang or a message came through, he felt a flash of anticipation that was quickly dashed. He'd even found himself distracted in his biology exam on Thursday. It would have been just his luck if she'd called during the only two hours of the week when he didn't have his phone beside him.

On Friday evening, he hoped meeting Allie and Liam would take his mind off the fact that she still hadn't got in touch. Arriving at the pub before them, he nabbed a table in the courtyard at the back of the building to make the most of the bright spring evening. A bunch of people he went to school with had taken over a couple of tables inside, but the bustle didn't appeal and he was happy sitting on his own for a while.

When Liam and Allie turned up they chatted about the

exams they'd sat that week. Allie was complaining about her little sister when Fraser drifted into a daydream.

"What's up with you?" Liam said after a while, leaning in front of Fraser to get his attention.

"Nothing." He contemplated heading home to play video games. Staying in at the weekends wasn't his usual MO, but he wasn't feeling sociable.

"Did you ever hear from that girl?" Liam asked.

"No." He took a swig of his pint, then looked at Allie. "I think you've earned yourself an 'I told you so'."

She pressed her lips together, teasing in her eyes. "I'll say nothing."

"That would be a first," he said lightly.

"Okay then. I will say something …"

Of course she would. Allie had been giving a running commentary on his life for as long as he could remember. Little Miss Perfect told him everything he did wrong. It should have been far more annoying than it was.

"Can you take a moment and realise this is exactly how you make women feel when you lead them on and then leave them hanging?"

"I don't lead anyone on. If I take their number but don't bother to get in touch, I think I'm making myself pretty clear." Fraser winced as he realised that was exactly what Scarlett had done. She'd made herself very clear and yet he still had a ridiculous spark of hope that she might contact him. "Okay, fine," he said to Allie. "I can be a bit of a dick sometimes. But you make me out to be some sort of monster when I'm not."

His friend Ian appeared at the door to the pub and raised a hand to get his attention. "I'm ordering a taxi into town. Are you coming with us?"

"No, thanks. Have a good night."

"That's not like you," Liam remarked.

"I just don't feel like a big night. I'm going to head home soon."

Allie stared at him, clearly dying to comment. She probably wanted to make some quip about how he must be ill for not wanting to go out.

"I've got another exam on Monday," he said, before she could get a word in. "I need to get some revision in over the weekend."

"That wouldn't normally get in the way of your partying," she said flatly.

He sipped his pint, then shifted his weight to get his phone when it buzzed in his pocket. As the screen lit up, notifying him of a message from a number that wasn't in his contacts, all he could do was stare at it.

"Is it *her*?" Liam asked with a grin.

"Oh, it better not be!" Allie said.

Fraser clicked into the message. His heart was thudding furiously and he grimaced when he read the message.

"What did she say?" Liam asked eagerly.

"Erm … well … I think I might have forgotten to tell you one tiny detail from when I met her …"

"Give me that." Allie snatched the phone from him and he drew his chin to his chest in readiness for a verbal bashing.

"This doesn't even make sense." Allie tilted the phone to show Liam. Then she read the message aloud. "Were you serious about getting married or was it a joke?"

Liam took the phone, peering at the screen. "Please tell me the thing you forgot to mention wasn't that you asked this girl to marry you."

"It just sort of slipped out," he muttered. The verbal assault didn't come. It seemed as though he'd finally managed to leave Allie speechless. "But I can explain … it's not as bad as it sounds …"

"So you didn't try and get in her knickers by asking her to marry you?" Liam asked.

He winced again. "Well, kind of. But there's more to it. She can't get a student loan because of her circumstances. So she needs to get a job for a year and save up for uni. The only way she'd be able to get a student loan and go to uni this year is if she gets married. I sort of vaguely suggested I could marry her." He hopped off the bench and out of reach when Allie launched herself at him. He held his hands up. "I was offering to do her a favour, so I don't know why you're attacking me."

"Because you're not actually going to marry her! You said it to get a date."

Fraser took his phone back and began typing a message. When he glanced up, Allie was staring at him.

"Please don't do this," she said. "It's cruel. Leave the poor girl alone."

"All I'm doing is taking her out for a drink so we can discuss the matter further."

Liam leaned on the table. "You don't actually have any intention of marrying her, do you?"

"Of course not." He smiled wickedly. "But I do intend to find out the colour of her underwear."

That time he wasn't quick enough, and Allie's punch landed heavily on his bicep.

CHAPTER 4

Fraser hadn't actually answered Scarlett's question when she'd messaged him. Annoyingly, he'd just invited her for a drink. But she supposed if he was going to marry her he'd probably want to get to know her better.

She drove into Exeter in the afternoon to give herself plenty of time to find a parking space and locate the pub he'd suggested. After she'd sussed out the location, she wandered around the town to pass the time. Shortly before it was time to meet him, she returned to the pub and waited outside a shop across the road. The busy street in the heart of Exeter was a hive of activity. From the number of people coming and going from the pub, she guessed it was a popular spot for Saturday night drinks.

Several times it crossed her mind to abandon the plan and go home again, but after working in the cafe more than usual that week she was feeling decidedly unenthusiastic about having to work there full-time for a year. If there was any chance this guy would marry her, she'd take it.

Taking a deep breath, she went through a mental checklist of things she needed to remember – the things she always forgot when she was nervous. Eye contact was the main one. For some reason, it made people uncomfortable when she didn't look at them. *Don't fidget*, she reminded herself. Remember to smile; she always forgot that one. She should laugh when he did, even if she didn't understand the joke. And she should ask questions to keep the conversation moving. What else? With the number of times her mother had drilled these things into her, she should be better at remembering them. While she'd been living in Hope Cove she hadn't needed to remember so much. Most people didn't seem to mind if she didn't make eye contact or if she couldn't think of anything to say when they tried to chat to her.

It was important now though. She needed Fraser to like her. As her mind raced, she almost missed him arriving. She just caught sight of him walking into the pub and quickly moved to cross the road.

"Hi," she said, standing beside Fraser at the bar. It was noisy and the smell of sweat and stale beer hung in the air.

"Hey!" He smiled widely. "Perfect timing. I just got here."

She felt slightly dizzy as she tried to remember her checklist of how she was supposed to act. When she couldn't think of anything to say, she at least remembered to smile. And look at him.

He swept his hair back. "What do you want to drink?"

"Lemonade, please."

"Aren't you drinking tonight?"

"I will be when I get the lemonade."

He chuckled. "You're funny. I meant anything alcoholic."

"Oh." She felt her cheeks heat up. "I have to drive back to Hope Cove later, so I can't drink alcohol."

"Shame," he said, then turned to order the drinks.

Once he handed her the lemonade, she followed him across the room and sat opposite him at the table that had just been vacated.

"Do you come out in Exeter much?" he asked.

"No. Never." She watched the condensation run down the side of her glass. "Do you?"

"Most weekends." He was looking at her intently and it made it hard to keep her eyes on him. The impulse to look elsewhere was hard to override. "I'm really glad you got in touch."

"I didn't know if you were serious about getting married ..."

His smile slipped. "I'm not sure either. To be honest, I said it without a lot of thought."

"I looked into it, and to get married you have to give notice at the registry office a month in advance. There's only six weeks before I need to accept or decline the offer for my course. So I need to know soon. We'd need to be married before I accept the offer so I'd know for certain I can get the loan."

"Right. Yeah. That makes sense."

"So will you do it?"

He scratched at the back of his head. "I thought we might get to know each other better before I decide."

That made sense. "What do you want to know?"

"I'm not sure." He took a sip of his drink. "What do you do when you're not writing books and making plans to take over the publishing industry?"

"I work at my aunt's cafe. And study for my exams."

"What about your social life?"

"I have two friends: Emily and Lizzie."

His eyebrows drew together. "Two friends?"

"Yes."

"That's ... nice." His cheek twitched as he stared into his pint, and she had the feeling he was getting bored of the conversation.

"Since I moved out of my parents' place I've been focusing on studying and writing my books," she said, hoping he'd think she was just too busy to socialise rather than chose not to.

"What happened with your parents?" he asked. "How did you fall out with them so badly that they're refusing to pay for uni?"

"I fell out with them *because* they wouldn't pay for uni."

"Can't they afford it or something?"

"They can. They just think it's a waste of money. I'm dyslexic, so they don't think I'd manage to get a degree."

He leaned forwards. "Are you serious?"

"Yes." She wasn't sure which part he was questioning. Maybe she shouldn't have mentioned the dyslexia. "I'm not stupid. I just get words mixed up and stuff. I can definitely manage the course."

He shook his head. "Your parents really won't pay for you because you're dyslexic?"

"Yes."

"What kind of people are they?"

"Annoying ones."

Fraser smiled. "Are they rich?"

"Not really. They have enough money but not loads. Mum was complaining that they'd have to cut back on holidays if they were paying for me to go to uni. And they might not be able to get the new car they want."

His mouth hung open. "I can't believe you're serious."

"I am. I promise." She rarely lied.

"Sorry. I didn't mean I was questioning it. I just mean … that's awful."

"Mum kept saying I could get a job in a shop or a restaurant or something. I got annoyed and moved in with Auntie Verity. She's really nice. She lets me use her car and she said she'd pay for uni if she could, but she doesn't have a lot of money. I don't have to pay her any rent so that's good."

Fraser seemed to have lost interest in the conversation and was looking over her shoulder, frowning.

"That's really shit," he said, his eyebrows pulled so tight they were almost touching.

It took Scarlett a moment to figure out he was still talking about her parents. "It is a bit. But I'll still have a publishing company one day. Just because my parents won't help me doesn't mean I can't do it. And maybe when I publish my books I'll send them a copy."

"With a note telling them that they're the stupid ones and not you?"

She laughed. "Yeah, maybe."

"I feel really crap now," he said after a moment. "To be honest, I'm not even sure I'm going to Exeter uni. I wish I could help, but I don't think I can marry you."

Scarlett blinked back tears. It shouldn't have been a surprise. "We definitely couldn't get married if you're going to be living in a different city."

"I'm sorry," he said, reaching over and touching her hand.

She pulled away. "It's okay. I thought you were joking when you suggested getting married, but you also said it's only a piece of paper so I wasn't sure."

"I didn't really think it through."

"Never mind." Scarlett just wanted to get away from him. "Thank you for the drink. I have to go now." Standing abruptly, she pushed her way through the crowd.

Fraser caught up to her outside. "You didn't *really* think I was going to marry you, did you?"

She swallowed hard and kept her eyes on the pavement. It seemed stupid now, but she actually had thought he might.

"It would only be a bit of paperwork," she said. "And you were the one who suggested it. If you hadn't spoken to me the other week and hadn't mentioned it, then I wouldn't have got my hopes up about going to uni in September. And I wouldn't have driven all the way here to meet you." Pulling her bag off her shoulder, she fished out the papers. "I wouldn't have wasted my time researching what we'd need to do and filling in these forms." She thrust them at him. "I don't know why you came here if you weren't even considering it. You just wasted my time."

She kept her head up, refusing to cry as she marched away. One day she'd go to uni and get a degree. If no one would help her, she'd figure it out alone.

Fraser's head pounded as he lay on his bed the following lunchtime. He'd heard the doorbell ring half an hour earlier but hadn't paid much attention to it. The gentle knock on his bedroom door came at the same time as Allie pushed it open.

"Have you been here ages?" he asked, not bothering to move.

"I had a coffee with your mum."

"Cosy," he said, not sure why he was so annoyed.

Allie closed the door and moved further into the room. Sunlight flooded in when she pulled the curtains back, making him shield his eyes. "She said you arrived home a couple of hours ago, stinking like a brewery."

He sat up and glared at her. "Have you been sitting downstairs slagging me off with my mum?"

She didn't reply, just stared out of the window. The fact that she couldn't even be bothered to deny it said a lot about what their relationship had come to.

"I take it you had a fun night with the girl who wants to marry you?"

"Not really." After Scarlett had left he'd returned to the pub, certain that alcohol would erase the image of how upset she'd looked when he'd told her he couldn't help her. Alcohol didn't have the desired effect so he'd called Monique. She'd been eager to hang out and had invited him to her place since she had the house to herself again.

"So you didn't spend the night with her?" Allie asked.

"I stayed at Monique's, if you must know." He looked away to spare himself from seeing the disgust in her eyes. "Did you come here for a reason?"

The silence seemed to stretch on. "I can't live with you at uni."

The way she said it made it seem as though she expected him to be surprised by the revelation. He snorted a laugh. "I'm not keen on living with a couple anyway. You can find a cosy place with Liam. Don't worry about me."

"It's not because I want it to be just Liam and me. I don't want to live with you because I don't like you."

Swinging his legs off the side of the bed, he smiled up at her. He'd forgotten what a joker Allie could be. Except she didn't look amused.

"I don't know what's happened to you over the last couple of years," she said, her tone deadly serious. "I thought it was just a phase and you'd get back to being your usual self, but I'm sick of watching you hurt people. It seems to be just what you do these days."

"Is this about Monique? Because she knows the score and it's up to her whether she wants a casual relationship. If she's upset it's not my fault."

"And what about telling a girl you'll marry her just to get a date?"

His headache increased and he rubbed at his temples. "Clearly I was never going to marry her. It's not my fault she thought I might."

"You really believe what you're saying, don't you?" Tears shone in her eyes. "But it's not just the way you treat women that bothers me. It's Liam too."

"What?" Now she was talking in riddles and it wasn't helping his hangover.

"You know his dad's been really ill, don't you?"

"Yeah. But the chemo went well. He's going to be okay."

"That's not the point." Allie's chin wobbled before tears spilled down her face. "The point is, Liam's had a shit year and you've not been there for him. You're too busy drinking and partying and chasing women."

"I invite Liam out all the time."

"But he doesn't want to go out!" she snapped. "And the worst of it is that he feels like crap for being a bad friend to you. Every time you ask him to go for a night out, he feels as though he's letting you down. You should be asking what *he* wants to do. And if it's a quiet night in listening to what's on his mind, you should do that. But everything has to be about you."

"That's not true," he said weakly.

"You need to tell Liam you don't want to live with us at uni. He's worried about upsetting you, so it needs to come from you."

"That's fine. I'll talk to him."

"Your mum's worried about you too."

He wiped his hands over his face. "Did you just come here to lecture me? Because you've made your point. I'm a terrible person. You can leave now."

"You can't keep on like this," she said, then left without a backwards glance.

Crashing back on his bed, Fraser closed his eyes, desperate for sleep. Allie was being melodramatic as usual. Admittedly, he hadn't always been there for Liam, but it was difficult with Allie constantly hovering around him. She was much better at that sort of thing anyway. Fraser never knew what to say. That didn't make him a horrible person. Pushing the thoughts aside, he relaxed into a deep slumber.

When his phone rang, jolting him awake, he had no inkling of how long he'd been asleep. He grasped at his phone and answered without even looking at who was calling.

"I just wanted to check you have the wedding date in your calendar," Monique said as he answered.

"What?" he said, rubbing at his eyes.

"My cousin's wedding. Thank you for agreeing to come. It'll be fun, I promise."

"I agreed to come to your cousin's wedding?" He racked his memory but came up empty. There were definitely a few gaps in his recollections of the previous evening.

"Very funny! It's on the 18th of November. In Bristol."

"I'll be at uni," he pointed out.

Her voice changed, losing brightness. "You said it was fine

because it's on a Saturday. You said we could make a weekend of it."

"Right ..." He squeezed the bridge of his nose. "I don't think it's a good idea."

"Why not?"

"Well... we're not together any more."

"We're together when it suits you," she said tersely.

"I told you I can't be in a relationship at the moment." He wasn't sure why she was annoyed when he'd been very clear about things.

"You said you wanted to cool things down a bit," Monique said.

"Yeah. Exactly. A relationship is too much for me at the moment."

"So what exactly is going on between us?"

"I dunno ... nothing really."

"Oh my God." She made a weird sound, something between a laugh and a cough. "Are you serious?"

"Yeah, we talked about this."

"So you were just using me?"

"No."

There was a pause and he wondered if she'd hung up until she sniffed loudly. "People tried to tell me you were using me and I defended you."

"I wasn't using you."

"What was last night then?" Her voice was thick with emotion. "Did you just agree to come to the wedding to get me to sleep with you?"

He couldn't actually remember why he'd agreed to go to her cousin's wedding, but he guessed sex probably was the reason. "I'm sorry."

"Are you?" She was crying properly now. "Do you even have a conscience about this stuff? Do you care about anyone but yourself?"

"I care about you," he muttered.

"Really?" She sniffed. "In that case, can you do me a favour?"

"What?" he asked softly. He wasn't going to go to any family weddings, but he really wasn't a bad person. He'd help her out if he could.

"Stay away from me."

He swallowed hard, shaking his head. "We can still be friends."

"I don't need friends like you," she said angrily. "No one does."

When he opened his mouth to argue, the line went dead. He wasn't sure he had much of an argument anyway.

CHAPTER 5

It was two weeks before Fraser managed to catch up with Liam and Allie. Whenever he'd tried to hang out with them they'd said they were revising for their exams. He tried not to take the excuses personally, but after his roasting from Allie it was hard not to.

Finally, he got them to agree to drinks in the Thorverton Arms on Friday night. The beer garden had newly planted flowers in raised wooden beds and the burst of colours gave the place extra warmth. Also extra wasps. He swatted one away from his pint and took a long swig to give himself the courage he needed to break the news to his oldest friends.

"I've been thinking," he said, drawing their attention across the table. "I'm not going to live with you at uni."

Liam's eyebrows shot up. "Don't be daft. It's the three of us together, like always. You can't change the plan now."

"Sorry," Fraser said.

"What's going on?" Liam asked. "Do you want your own bachelor pad or something? Are we too boring for you these days?"

"No." Fraser batted another wasp away, then covered his pint with a beer mat. His friendship with Liam and Allie had been on rocky ground for a while, so he wasn't sure why the thought of them going their separate ways affected him so much. Plus, it was inevitable. Just because they'd been friends since childhood didn't mean they'd stay friends forever. They were hardly the same people they'd been when they were four years old. "I'm not going to live with you because I'm not going to Manchester."

Allie leaned onto the table, surprise wrinkling her forehead. "What are you talking about?"

"I'm going to uni in Exeter."

"Are you joking?" Liam asked. "I can't tell if you're messing around. Why would you go to Exeter?"

"The course is really good, and they have great sports facilities. It feels like the right place for me."

"But it's twenty minutes down the road," Liam pointed out. "You've been saying how much you need to get away from here."

Allie was staring at him. "Is this because I had a go at you?"

"No. Well, yes, partly." He made a display of repeatedly swatting another wasp away, mainly to stall for time. "I've been talking to Scarlett …" Not actually talking, since she seemed to have an aversion to answering her phone, but they'd been messaging back and forth.

"The girl who wanted to marry you?" Liam asked.

"Yeah." His throat was dry and he took a sip of his beer. For two weeks he'd been telling himself that what he was doing was perfectly logical and reasonable, but he suspected that saying it out loud might make him realise it was insane.

"Oh God." Allie put her hands to her mouth. "Please don't say it."

"I'm going to marry her." Surprisingly, saying it aloud just made him smile.

"No way," Liam said. "You're having us on. Ha-bloody-ha!"

The skin around Allie's eyes crinkled. "You can't marry someone you don't know."

"I know it sounds ridiculous, but when I met her for a drink she was telling me about her parents refusing to pay for her course because she's dyslexic. Can you imagine? Your parents just write you off and don't support you at all."

"It's not your problem," Liam said.

Fraser chewed the inside of his cheek. "She's also only got two friends."

"You shouldn't feel sorry for her lack of friends," Liam said in a rush. "You should be wondering what's wrong with her that she's only got two friends!"

"It wasn't like that. She wasn't looking for sympathy. But both times I spoke to her she mentioned having two friends … and there was something about the way she looked when she said it …"

Liam sighed. "Did she also get a violin out and play a sombre tune?"

"She wasn't giving me a sob story. It wasn't like that … I can't explain it but I felt this weird connection to her. She needs help and I can help her." And maybe if he helped Scarlett, it would make up for the fact that all he seemed to do recently was hurt people. "It's only a matter of signing a few papers and saying a few words at the registry office."

He'd also need to live with her. That had almost made him back out. When he'd accepted the fact that he wasn't going to be living with Allie and Liam for his student years, his plan had been to get himself a bachelor pad on campus for the first year, then find a like-minded group of lads for a house-share after that. Living with Scarlett felt like his penance for all of his bad choices, but once he'd made the decision to help her he wouldn't back out, even if the living arrangements would seriously cramp his style.

Liam was staring at him. "Mate, are you serious about this?"

"Yeah. If I can help her, why not?"

"Is this because of what I said?" Allie asked, her shoulders tensing. "All I meant to say was stop being such a shit, not marry some needy girl to redeem yourself!"

Liam frowned. "Did you two meet up without me?"

"Never mind," Allie said, patting his leg. "We need to focus on Fraser and talk him out of ruining his life."

"It's not going to ruin my life! You're really dramatic sometimes."

"I can't believe this is a serious conversation," Allie said. "Who the hell is this girl that she's managed to wrap you around her little finger?"

"She hasn't!" Fraser said through a laugh.

"Has it occurred to you that you're being played?" Allie put a hand on his arm. "She needs money and she's charmed the first flashy rich kid she could find."

"I'm not a …" It didn't seem to be worth getting into that. "She doesn't even know I'm rich."

Allie thumped her chest as she choked on her drink. "Is she blind? Everything about you says bratty rich kid."

"You're really not my biggest fan these days, are you?"

Her features softened. "I'm sorry. You know I love you. Otherwise I wouldn't care enough to have a go at you. But you can't get married."

"We've already filed the paperwork and booked the registry office." He couldn't help but smile at the looks on their faces. "I was wondering if you'd be our witnesses?"

"No!" Allie snapped. "We will not. No way. We're not going to be a part of this."

He'd known that would be her initial reaction. He also knew it wouldn't take long to talk them round.

~

Three weeks later they were standing outside the registry office waiting for Scarlett.

"It's not too late to change your mind," Allie said. "You can back out now and there's no harm done."

"She wouldn't be able to go to uni." Fraser fingered the rings in his pocket and glanced up and down the road. They were a bit early, but he'd expected she might be too. He'd messaged her that morning and she'd replied to confirm that she'd meet them in front of the registry office.

"I don't know why you look so twitchy," Liam said. "If she doesn't turn up, you're off the hook."

"She'll turn up," he said, not sure why he seemed to be trying to reassure himself. After all, Liam was right; it wasn't any skin off his nose if she stood him up. There was nothing in the marriage for him, so it absolutely didn't matter.

"You really like her, don't you?" Allie asked.

"No." When they'd met up to buy the rings he'd realised that she absolutely wasn't his type. Actually, he'd already figured that out when they'd gone for a drink. "I mean, yes, I like her. But not like …" He shifted his weight and wondered why he was being so inarticulate. "She's nice but it's not like … I don't know. I've never really met anyone like her before." For a start, she hadn't bothered to laugh at his jokes. He'd found it oddly refreshing. They'd been lame jokes that didn't really deserve a laugh, but he was used to girls who giggled at everything.

"Oh, you like her!" Liam said with a wide smile.

"I think this makes the situation worse," Allie said. "Are you marrying her so you can sleep with her?"

"No!" He shook his head. "It's not like that." Not that he'd have any objections if she wanted to consummate the union, but that wasn't why he was doing it. "There she is," he said as he caught sight of her. He brushed his hands over the front of his white shirt to smooth it out.

"Which one?" Allie asked.

"Brown hair," he said, not taking his eyes off of her. "She's wearing a white summer dress with blue flowers on it." It wasn't over the top, but she looked cute. Her fingers tapped against her thumbs as she neared them.

"Hello," she said, stopping in front of him.

Fraser told her she looked nice and she nodded in reply. She barely acknowledged Allie and Liam when he introduced them.

"We'll have to hold hands to make it look convincing," she said. "And when they pronounce us married you'll have to kiss me. Be very quick. Don't put your tongue in my mouth. Okay?"

"Yeah, okay." He had an inkling they wouldn't be consummating the marriage.

"Have you got the rings?"

He patted his pocket, then offered her his hand. "Shall we go?"

Reluctantly, she took his hand and they moved into the building. She seemed so nervous he was sure the registrar was going to get suspicious. Fraser kept smiling at her, but the only times he managed to catch her eye she scowled in response. No one would have guessed it was him who was doing her the favour.

Thankfully, the exchange of vows and rings didn't take long. Before he knew it, they were married and standing on the street again.

"Should I take a photo?" Allie offered, holding her phone up.

"Why?" Scarlett asked.

Allie's smile was more of a grimace. "To remember the day."

"We have a marriage certificate. We don't need wedding photos, it's not that kind of wedding." Scarlett turned squarely to Fraser. "I need you to fill in a form about your income to go with my loan application. I'll email it to you. You can email me anything you need me to fill in, and I can send you a copy of the marriage certificate."

"I don't think I need it for anything," he said vaguely.

"You'll have to apply for a loan as a married person now."

He shook his head. "I'm not getting a loan. My parents will pay for uni."

"Oh." She looked puzzled. "What about money for your rent and food? Will you get a job?"

"My parents will pay for it."

Her eyes rolled upwards as though she was processing the information. "Okay. But we need to find a house to rent. If we apply to live on campus we'll be offered accommodation as a married couple, which will mean only one bedroom, so that's no good. I did a search and found the cheapest student houses available. I'll email them to you and you can decide which one you like most. They're not nice, but I need it to be cheap."

"Your loan will cover rent too," Fraser pointed out, panicking that he was going to end up in some crappy accommodation in a dodgy part of town.

"I know, but the less I pay for rent, the less debt I'll be in when I finish uni."

"Right." He rubbed at his jaw. "I'll talk to my parents. They'll probably just pay the rent for both of us so you won't have to worry about it." Telling his parents he'd married some girl he barely knew wasn't going to be a fun conversation, but they were generally very relaxed, and he was sure that once they got over the shock they'd be okay with it.

"I can't do that," Scarlett said, shaking her head fiercely. "I have to pay my own rent."

"They really won't care."

"*I* care." She glared at him. "I can pay. We just have to find somewhere cheap."

"Okay." He touched her arm, hoping to reassure her. "Send me the places you found. I'll do my own search too and see what I can find. We'll figure something out."

"Good." She shifted her weight and stared at his hand on her arm until he withdrew. "Thank you for marrying me."

"You're welcome. Do you want to get some dinner?"

"When?"

"Now …"

"No. I've got stuff to do. I have to go." She took a couple of steps backwards. "Goodbye."

"Bye," he said, then remained rooted to the spot as he watched her hurry away.

"That was awkward," Liam said as he and Allie came and stood at either side of him.

"Yeah," Fraser replied.

Liam slapped him on the back. "Just to make sure I've got it right … you're going to spend the next three years living in a shit hole with a girl who hates you?"

"She doesn't hate me."

"I'm fairly sure she does." Allie leaned her head on his shoulder. "But I kind of like her."

Fraser managed a half-hearted smile. What the hell had he done?

CHAPTER 6

Breaking the news of his marital status to his parents was even harder than Fraser had anticipated. Telling them his plans incrementally seemed like a good idea, so he started with the fact that he was going to Exeter uni rather than Manchester. He got the feeling his mum was pleased he wouldn't be so far away. Next, he dropped a few comments about wanting to rent a house rather than live on campus.

Now all he had to do was mention that he'd be living with his wife. His parents had been for a two-week holiday in the south of France, so that had bought him some time, but he couldn't put it off any longer. Scarlett was getting more and more anxious about organising a place to live and he'd told her he'd sort it out. His plan was to find a decent two-bedroom house and tell her that his dad knew the landlord so he was giving them mate's rates. Scarlett could pay a token amount and think she was paying half. She didn't need to know the actual cost.

It was a Saturday morning in July when he decided he had to bite the bullet and tell his parents. After mentally running through possible ways to drop the bombshell, he made an effort to relax his jaw, then pulled his shoulders back as he strode into the living room with his laptop open in his arms. He'd show them the houses he'd been looking at, and when they inevitably remarked on the fact that he didn't need two bedrooms he'd tell them about Scarlett. Easy.

His dad was sitting on the couch, watching golf on TV.

"Do you want to go for a round this afternoon?" he asked Fraser.

His mum's voice drifted from the dining table, where she was sorting through a pile of post. "I thought you were going to mow the lawn and tidy up the garden today?"

"We'll do that tomorrow. Golf today." His dad winked at him. "Fraser's earned a break after his exams."

His mum let out a humourless laugh. "Fraser needs a break? I hope that's a joke."

"I've been looking at places to rent," he said, redirecting the conversation before his mum got into a full rant about how lazy he was. "I found a few potential houses. I thought I better see what you think since you'll be paying for it." He flashed his mum a dazzling smile. She wasn't looking at him, though. Her eyes were on the post in her hand.

"Fraser Graham!" she growled in a tone that made him wince.

"What have I done now?" he asked, rolling his eyes at his dad.

"The credit card bill," she said, waving it in the air. "What the hell is all this?"

"I dunno." He reached an arm out and made a grabbing motion until she stood up and brought it to him. His eyes scanned the list of charges. "Clothes," he said. "More clothes. Trainers. More trainers. Football kit… Oh, I bought a mountain bike."

"Why did you buy a mountain bike?"

"A few of the lads were going out for a ride and it sounded like a laugh."

"So you bought a bike on a whim?"

"I was bored."

"Leave the lad alone," his dad said. "He worked hard for his exams. A few treats aren't a big deal."

His mum sighed heavily, taking the bill back. "Did you buy another watch? How many watches can you possibly need?"

"I like to match them to my outfit. But I haven't bought a new one in a while."

"There's a charge for a jewellery shop. It must have been your sister. Has anyone seen Hattie today? Is she back from Philippa's yet?"

"I don't think so," his dad said.

"The jewellery shop was me," Fraser said sheepishly.

"What were you buying, if not a watch?" his mum asked. "I hope we're not paying for expensive gifts for your girlfriends. You're only supposed to use the credit card for essentials."

He briefly wondered how many girlfriends she thought he had, then decided he didn't want to get side-tracked. "I bought wedding rings."

His mum loomed over him, behind the couch. "Wedding rings?"

"Yeah. I've been meaning to talk to you about it. I sort of got married."

His dad reached for the remote and turned the TV off. "You sort of did *what?*"

"I got married." He smiled up at his mum, but she just stared back at him open-mouthed.

"I think I mis-heard you," she said.

"No, you didn't. I got married." He'd have held his hand up and showed the ring as proof, but since it wasn't a real marriage he wasn't intending to make use of the ring.

"Bloody hell, Fraser," his dad said on a long exhale. "Don't say you've knocked some girl up."

"No." He laughed. "She's not pregnant. We just got married. It's actually a funny story."

"A funny story?" his mum said through gritted teeth. "You got married and it's a funny story?"

The front door opened and his sixteen-year-old sister burst in.

"Can you go up to your room please, Hattie?" his mum said shrilly. "We need to speak with Fraser."

"You're not going to believe what happened!" Hattie said, ignoring their mum's request. "I was hanging out with Philippa last night. We were just chilling out and having a couple of drinks. Nothing crazy. But I knocked the bottle over and spilled red wine on the cream rug in the living room."

"Hattie!" their mum snapped. "Go upstairs. You can tell me later."

"I need to tell you now because Philippa's mum's probably going to ring you. That woman's mental. She flipped out about the stain and made us scrub it with some disgusting chemical foam stuff." She held up a hand. "Look at my nails. I got acrylics put on two days ago and I've lost one thanks to her making me scrub the floor like Cinder-bloody-rella."

She dragged her fingers through her blonde hair and tied it in a ponytail as she continued to witter away. "I don't understand what she was so upset about. It was an accident. She'll make herself haggard stressing about stuff like that. It's only a rug for God's sake. All she has to do is go online and order a new one. She could get a same-day delivery. Problem solved."

"Oh my God!" Their mum put her hand over her eyes. "I don't know where I went wrong. You're horrible human beings, the pair of you."

"Me?" Hattie shrieked. "All I did was spill a bit of wine."

"Go to your room, Hattie!" At their dad's request she stomped away.

"I honestly despair," their mum said, pacing up and down. "Maybe it's because you worked such long hours when they were little." She looked at her husband. "If you'd have been at home more, they might not be so out of control now."

"The marriage isn't such a big deal," Fraser said. "If you'll let me get a word in I can explain."

"Who the hell have you married?" his mum asked. "Monique? I thought you'd split up with her."

"I did split up with her. It's not her."

"Thank God." His dad quirked an eyebrow. "Don't get yourself lumbered with one of those high-maintenance types."

"Apparently it's a bit late for fatherly advice on choosing a wife!" his mum shouted.

Fraser blew out a breath. "Her name's Scarlett and I met her at the open day for the uni."

"You've only just *met* her?" his mum asked, sinking onto the couch beside him. "What on earth were you thinking?"

"She needed to get married to be able to get a student loan. So we did it for the paperwork. As soon as we graduate, we'll get divorced."

They both stared at him. He was aware of his heart thudding as the silence dragged on.

"Well that's the stupidest thing you've ever done," his dad said. "And that's saying something."

Beside him, his mum started to cry.

"It's not so bad." Fraser put an arm around her shoulders, wishing she'd shout at him. It would be far preferable to the tears. "I actually did a nice thing. She wouldn't have been able to go to uni otherwise."

"So you're not together?" his mum asked, sniffing.

"No. It was just for the paperwork. We'll have to live together. We need to be living at the same address to get the loan and make it look real, but we're not a couple."

"Why did she need to get married?" his dad asked.

"Her parents refused to pay for uni because she's dyslexic. They thought it would be a waste of money or something."

His mum dabbed at her eyes. "The poor girl."

"Yeah. It was pretty crap for her."

"This is why you changed from Manchester to Exeter?" His

dad looked dubious. "So you could help out some girl who you just met?"

"Yes." He should probably be regretting the whole thing already, but he felt pretty calm about it.

"You'll have to bring her around for dinner," his mum said.

He spluttered a laugh. "Did you miss the part where I said it's not a real marriage?"

"I want to meet her," his mum said firmly. "We may be relaxed about rules in this house, but we keep some standards. If you get married, you bring your spouse around for dinner."

"I'll ask her," Fraser said on a sigh. "Don't hold your breath though."

In the end, he didn't even bother to ask. The fact that she refused to meet up with him over the summer was a good indication of how she'd react to the suggestion of meeting his parents. She even turned him down when he invited her to look around the house he'd found. It was between the university campuses, so the location was perfect. He'd thought she'd want to check it out, but she'd said she was busy and told him it looked fine from the photos. He didn't encourage her too much as it meant there was less chance of her finding out that the rent was about three times as much as he'd told her.

She didn't turn up for freshers' week but messaged and said she'd arrive on the Sunday evening before the course officially started on the Monday. By Friday, the insane alcohol consumption was taking its toll, and Fraser thought she might actually be quite sensible to skip the notorious week of partying. He'd signed up for the university football club, and most of his week had been spent at training sessions and playing friendly matches and drinking with the team.

A few of the lads from the team were going out on Sunday evening, and he was glad to have the excuse of needing to stay home and wait for his housemate to arrive. He didn't want to be hungover for his first day of uni.

It was just before eight when the doorbell let out its short, shrill ring.

"Hi," he said when he opened the door. He took a step forward, intending to kiss her cheek, but she swung her suitcase between them in what seemed to be a deliberate blocking manoeuvre.

"Thanks," she said when he lifted it into the hallway.

"I can help you carry your stuff from the car if you want."

"That's everything."

His eyes flicked from the suitcase to the backpack on her shoulder. When he'd arrived, his car had been packed full. His parents had brought more stuff in their car too.

"I'll show you around. The kitchen's through here," he said, walking along the hallway to the back of the house. "It's pretty well equipped. I went shopping yesterday, so feel free to raid my food until you have chance to shop. I don't know what you want to do about food generally. I guess it makes sense to share basics … bread and milk and whatnot …" He rubbed the back of his neck and finally stopped wittering.

"I don't know," she said, her gaze sweeping around the kitchen.

"We'll figure it out." He moved out of the kitchen and back down the hall to the living room.

"Was all this here already?" she asked, staying at the doorway as she looked into the room.

"Yes." He'd already told her the house was furnished. "The furniture anyway. The TV and games consoles are mine. My mum bought the rug and the lamp. She wanted to make it homely. You can add anything you want."

"Can you show me my bedroom?"

He picked up her suitcase and carried it up for her. At the top of the stairs, he set it down and opened the first door. "That's the bathroom."

She stepped inside. "Is there just one bathroom?"

"Yeah." He'd thought she'd be happy with the house, but she seemed to be scrutinising everything with a frown. If he'd have stayed within her budget she'd really have something to frown about.

"Are they your clothes?" she asked, pointing at the floor.

Sliding past her, he scooped up the pile of washing. "Sorry."

"If we share a bathroom, you can't leave your dirty clothes on the floor. It's gross." Stepping back onto the landing, her gaze flicked to a towel hanging over the bannister rail.

Fraser grabbed at that too, apologising again. He wasn't actually sure what the problem was with hanging a towel over the bannister to dry. Hopefully she wasn't obsessive about tidiness. "That's your room," he said, tipping his head at the next door, then continuing on and slinging the pile of clothes into his own room. Scarlett was dragging her suitcase into her room when he joined her again. "The bedrooms are about the same size so I just picked one. I hope that's okay."

"It's fine." She stood in the middle of the room for a moment, then moved to the window, which looked out onto the small back garden. "I think we should have some rules."

He scratched at his earlobe. "What kind of rules?"

"Don't come in my bedroom," she said, turning and dropping her gaze to his feet.

He shuffled back until he was outside of the room. "Anything else?"

"No. I don't think so. You stay out of my bedroom and I'll stay out of yours. Do you have any rules?"

"Not that I can think of."

"Good." She smiled at him as she crossed the room. Then she closed the door in his face.

He opened his mouth a couple of times before he managed to formulate words. "Do you want a drink or anything?"

"No," she called through the door. "I have to unpack and make sure I have everything organised for tomorrow."

Again, he did a goldfish impression but couldn't think of anything to say so retreated to his own room.

CHAPTER 7

For the first two weeks of uni, Fraser barely saw Scarlett at all. She only spoke to him to have a go at him for leaving clothes in the bathroom or damp towels hanging over the bannister. When challenged on it, she'd told him that it wasn't the fact that he hung his towels there that bothered her, but that he didn't always spread them out correctly. She'd grumpily explained that the air couldn't circulate if he left them scrunched up, so they wouldn't dry. It had been hard not to laugh as she'd grumbled about it. If she didn't look so bloody cute while she ranted, he'd have cut out his annoying habits by now.

He'd jumped straight in the shower when he'd come home from football training that Friday evening. As he stepped out of his room ready for drinks with some of his teammates, he heard Scarlett moving around in her room and backtracked to fetch his towel. He listened intently as he spread it over the bannister. At the click of her door handle, he swiped at the towel to crumple it and moved quickly to the top of the stairs.

She noticed it immediately and sighed as she spread the towel out across the bannister. He felt oddly disappointed that she hadn't bothered to have a go at him about it.

"I've got a few friends coming over in a bit," he said. "I hope you don't mind."

"It's your house," she said as she followed him downstairs.

"Yours too."

"You still need to give me the bank details so I can transfer the rent money."

He waited at the bottom of the stairs, letting her overtake him and following her to the kitchen. "I told you my parents got a good deal, so they're happy to pay. You don't need to worry about it."

She got a glass from the cupboard and held it under the tap. "I can't let your parents pay for my rent. Please just write down the bank details for me."

"Yeah, okay."

"Now!" she said, glaring at him.

He stood for a moment, wondering what to do. His parents were expecting to pay all of the rent. The token amount he'd mention to Scarlett wouldn't make any difference to them, so she may as well keep it.

"What are you waiting for?" she snapped.

He walked away to find a pen and paper. Then he scribbled down his own bank details. It wasn't as though he wanted to profit from her living there, but she clearly wasn't going to drop the subject. He could transfer it back to her when they moved out or something.

"Thank you," she said when he handed her the paper.

"How's uni going?" he asked.

Her forehead creased. "It's difficult, but it's okay."

"Have you made some friends on your course?"

"No. But I don't need to make friends."

He leaned against the doorframe, smiling. "You've already got two, right?"

"Yes. I think so."

"You think so? What does that mean?"

She paused and seemed to be debating whether to go on.

"Now that I'm at uni, I won't see Lizzie and Emily so often, so I'm not sure what will happen. I think they'll still be my friends."

Fraser thought of Liam and Allie and felt a heaviness in his chest. "Sometimes friends drift apart. Especially when your circumstances change."

"That's what worries me. Lizzie asked Dotty to babysit last week. I'd told her I could go back to babysit any time, but she didn't ask me, she asked the neighbour instead. What does that mean?"

"I have no idea. I don't really understand."

"Lizzie has two kids: three-year-old twins. Usually I babysit for them, but now she's found someone else."

"I wouldn't worry about it," he said. "She probably didn't want to bother you."

"It feels as though everything is changing. I don't like change. Verity is moving in with Bill tomorrow."

"Your aunt?" he asked, struggling to keep up.

"Yeah. She's got a boyfriend. He's got a really nice dog called Perry. Anyway, I thought they were just friends, but they're not, and when she moves into his place she's going to rent out the flat above the cafe, so I'll be homeless."

"You live here," he pointed out.

"I know. But it's not my home." She took a sip of her water and seemed to be deep in thought. "I need to figure out a way to get Verity to keep the flat."

"You're very resourceful. I'm sure you'll think of something."

"Why do you think I'm resourceful?"

He couldn't help but laugh at how genuinely puzzled she looked. "You seem to be very good at getting what you want. You need to get a degree to start a publishing company, so you figured out a way. Even if we hadn't got married, I'm sure you'd have found a way."

She nodded. "You're right. And you've given me an idea." It

didn't seem as though she was keen to share it as she waltzed past him.

"I'll try and keep the noise down this evening," he called after her. "But if it disturbs you too much let me know."

"I'll just put my earphones in if you're loud."

"You could also come down and have a drink with us. Meet some of my mates."

"No thanks," she shouted from the top of the stairs.

He hadn't expected to see her again for the evening, so he was surprised to hear her call his name across the living room an hour later. It wasn't exactly a big party but the music was pretty loud. Scarlett was smiling widely, so he presumed she hadn't come to tell them to keep it down.

"Do you want a drink?" he asked.

"No." She spoke loudly over the noise and didn't move further than the doorway. "I'm going home now. I'll see you next week."

"How come?" He tried to get closer to her, but the couch and a load of people blocked his path.

"I had an idea," she shouted. "If I can get Emily and Lizzie to go into business with me, I won't need to worry about them not being friends with me any more. They'll have to be. And we can rent the flat from Verity so I won't lose my home."

"Wait." He shook his head, confused. It took him a moment to reach her. "What are you talking about?"

"I'm going to get Lizzie and Emily to start a publishing company with me. We can use Verity's flat as the offices. It's perfect." She was still shouting and seemed oblivious to everyone in the room staring at her.

"I really like the name Scarlett Ink," she went on. "It sounds like a company name. Which it is, but not inc like incorporated, ink like the printing material. I hope Lizzie and Emily like it."

"It sounds cool," he replied, feeling self-conscious as everyone listened in on the slightly bizarre conversation.

"I have to think about it more before I speak to Lizzie and

Emily. But I realised I don't need to be here at the weekends. I was going to help Auntie Verity move tomorrow, but I'll go now and see if Lizzie wants me to babysit tonight."

"Yeah, okay. Whatever you want."

"I'll go back to Hope Cove every weekend. Then I don't have to listen to your loud parties."

"Sorry," he said.

She didn't seem bothered. "I'll see you next week."

"Yeah, bye." He turned and smiled, causing everyone to get back to their conversations.

"Who the hell was that?" his teammate Simon asked, stepping beside him.

"Scarlett. My housemate."

"What a weirdo!" he said, laughing.

Fraser finished his bottle of beer in a few mouthfuls. "She's all right," he said, then went to get a fresh drink.

~

Just as she'd said, Scarlett started spending her weekends in Hope Cove, so Fraser hardly saw her at all. During the week, he had a hectic schedule of lectures and football training and socialising so he usually didn't get home until late in the evenings. As far as he could tell, Scarlett spent her evenings hidden away in her bedroom.

After two months he felt completely settled into uni life. He'd exchanged a few messages with Liam, who seemed to be enjoying life in Manchester. Apparently Allie was enjoying it too but he hadn't had any contact with her directly.

On a Saturday in late November, Fraser was hanging out with friends in the halls of residence at St Luke's campus. A bunch of them were in Simon's room playing video games and drinking beers. It was a relatively quiet night after a rowdy one the previous evening when there'd been a party in the halls.

Fraser had been dodging questions about a girl who'd been

all over him at the party and was contemplating leaving when a group of them left to hit some bars in town. At Simon's encouragement, he hung around for another beer. Two other guys were there too. Brett was on the football team and the other guy, Tarak, lived in the halls and often hung out with them.

When Brett brought out a bottle of whisky, Fraser half-heartedly declined. He was given a glass anyway and winced as he took a swig. He still had a beer on the go and would rather have stuck to that.

"So are you going to tell us what happened with you and Charlotte now that the rest of them have left?" Simon said when they finally gave up on Mario Kart.

"Nothing happened." Fraser could feel his eyelids getting heavier and sat up straighter on the uncomfortable plastic chair that had been brought in from the communal kitchen.

"Yeah right." Tarak raised his eyebrows. "Last time I saw you she had you pinned against a wall and things were getting pornographic."

"Get stuffed! It wasn't that bad."

To be fair, he had a bruise on his shoulder blade as a reminder of how she'd slammed him against the wall as she'd stuck her tongue down his throat. Her hands had roamed a bit too freely considering they were in a public corridor in the halls of residence, and he'd put a stop to that but probably not before a few people had seen.

"So how was she?" Brett asked. "I'd say she's pretty energetic. Did you go back to her place or did she come to yours?"

"I didn't sleep with her."

Simon stared at him. "She's hot as hell and was practically begging for it. What's your problem?"

"I don't have a problem." He sipped the whisky and wished he'd left an hour ago.

"Is it a medical thing?" Brett asked, nodding towards his crotch.

Fraser swore at him while the three of them fell about laughing.

"Are you gay?" Tarak asked. "It's all right if you are. You can tell us."

Fraser suspected it probably wouldn't be okay with them at all, but he wasn't going to find out. That definitely wasn't the reason why he'd turned Charlotte down when she'd asked if she could come back to his place. His first thought had been that Scarlett might be at home. Just because she usually wasn't there at the weekends didn't mean she definitely wasn't. There'd never been any mention of him not being allowed to bring women home, but the thought of bumping into Scarlett made him uncomfortable.

"I'm not gay," he said. "I'm just not that into her."

"Have you got your eye on someone else?" Tarak asked. "Women are always flocking around you."

"Nah." He sipped the whisky and cursed himself. Why was he still drinking? "I don't have my eye on anyone … but …" He stopped talking and shook his head.

"Spill!" Simon said. "What's the issue?"

"It'll sound crazy." He glanced at the door to check no one else could be listening in. "I'll tell you but it stays in this room… No one else can know."

The three lads nodded eagerly and he launched into telling them about Scarlett and their marriage of convenience. He had their full attention for the next ten minutes and was only interrupted a few times as he rambled on.

"But if it's not a real marriage and you're not together with her, what's the problem?" Brett asked. "You can still see other people, right?"

"Yeah." He massaged the muscles at the back of his neck. "But when Charlotte was all over me last night, I kept thinking about Scarlett. It just felt wrong somehow."

Simon leaned forward in his seat. "I guess having *her* pop

into your head would put you off your game. She's proper weird, isn't she?"

"Scarlett's all right." He put his empty glass aside and stood up. "She's pretty cool really. Easy to live with."

"She's got the crazy eyes," Simon said. "Always beware of a woman with the crazy eyes."

"Shut up." Fraser's head was woozy, but two thoughts were very clear.

The first was that he wanted to leave immediately. The second was that he should never have told them about Scarlett and him.

CHAPTER 8

The first term absolutely flew by. Suddenly it was December and there was only a week of uni left before a four-week break. When the doorbell rang late on Sunday afternoon, Fraser wondered if Scarlett had forgotten her keys. He checked his watch as he set the game controller aside. It was a bit early for her to be back. She worked in her aunt's cafe on Sundays and wasn't usually back until later.

"Hi!" he said with false cheer when he answered the door to his parents. "This is a nice surprise!"

"Try and sound like you mean it," his dad said, amused.

"I wasn't expecting you."

His mum moved along the hallway, looking all around. "We've got a table booked for dinner in town and we thought we'd call and say hello. How are you?"

"I'm fine," he said, following her through to the kitchen. "You know I'm fine because you messaged me this morning." He gave her a pointed look. "She's not here, so your surprise visit is a waste of time."

"I don't know what you mean," she replied with a small smile that said she knew she'd been caught out. "Is Scarlett really not here?"

"No. I told you she goes back to Hope Cove at the weekends and doesn't come back until late on Sunday. Sometimes not until Monday morning," he added quickly. It was a lie but he didn't want his mum to get any ideas about hanging around to wait for her.

"I wish we could meet her," his mum complained. "Will she really not come over for dinner sometime?"

Fraser had an attack of guilt over the fact that he'd been lying to his mum, saying that Scarlett didn't want to when that wasn't entirely true. "I haven't actually asked her," he confessed, as he filled the kettle. "But she definitely wouldn't be up for it. She's not really a people person. She keeps to herself. And she doesn't have a lot of time since she works at the weekends."

"You could invite her over for Christmas," his mum suggested.

He shook his head. "No."

"Where are the mugs?" She didn't wait for a reply, but opened the cupboard nearest to her. Fraser caught the surprise on her face and he reached to close it again quickly.

"That's Scarlett's cupboard." There wasn't a lot in it; the bottom shelf contained a row of tinned tomato soup and the next shelf was packets of pasta and jars of pasta sauce. He'd seen her eat toast too, and sandwiches, but from what he could tell her diet wasn't exactly varied. Opening another cupboard, he got mugs out and ignored the twitch of his mum's eyebrows. He'd thought the cupboard looked weird when he'd first seen it too, but it was one of those things you got used to.

They sat together in the kitchen, chatting about mundane stuff as they sipped their drinks.

"What time's your meal?" Fraser asked, then finished his tea in a long gulp.

"Trying to get rid of us?" his dad asked.

"I've got some coursework to finish. I need to hand it in before the end of term." That wasn't really true. He was just aware of the fact that Scarlett might be home soon, and he'd rather they weren't still there.

"We'll leave you to it then," his mum said, standing and hugging him tightly.

"You'll see me soon," he said when she didn't seem keen to let go.

"Did you decide how long you'll come home for over Christmas?"

"I'm not sure," he said as they moved towards the front door.

"I presume Liam and Allie will be back?" his mum asked.

"Yes. They'll be back for two weeks."

"It'll be nice for you to catch up with them." His mum took her coat from the bannister and pulled it on. "It must be the longest you've ever gone without seeing them."

"Yeah." Part of him was looking forward to seeing them, and part of him was worried that the time apart might have served to emphasise the cracks in their friendship.

He stood on the doorstep and waved his parents off. A few snowflakes fluttered on the breeze, and he shivered before closing the door and retreating back to the warmth of the living room.

Scarlett arrived half an hour later and he wandered into the hallway to greet her.

"How was your weekend?" he asked.

"Busy." She dropped her backpack at the foot of the stairs and walked swiftly to the kitchen.

"How's everything coming along with the publishing company?" The last couple of times he'd seen her, she couldn't stop talking about her plans. Her eyes lit up when she spoke about it and he found it quite mesmerising.

"Really good. Everything's been moving quickly. Lizzie and Emily both work from the flat now. They call it the office but I still think of it as Verity's flat. Did I tell you they didn't like my idea for the name of the company?"

He nodded vaguely. She'd told him at length, but he didn't mind hearing about it again. "I liked the name Scarlett Ink," he told her.

"Hope Cove Press is a pretty boring name." She filled a glass with water. "It was two against one though. Anyway, it doesn't really matter. At Christmas we're going to discuss which authors we want to take on first. We'll start small, but it's still exciting."

"It's really cool."

"Yeah, it is." She hovered for a moment, her eyes dropping to the floor as though she was suddenly shy around him. "I've got work to get on with," she said, moving to the door.

No doubt she'd hide away in her room for the rest of the evening and he'd hardly see her all week. Then it would be the Christmas break and he wouldn't see her for ages.

"I was thinking of inviting some people over on Friday night," he said quickly. "To celebrate the end of term. That wouldn't be a problem, would it?"

"No. But I was thinking of staying here on Friday and going back to Hope Cove on Saturday."

"And you'll be there for the whole of the break?"

"Yeah. I'll be busy with the cafe and setting up the publishing company."

He followed her into the hallway since she seemed determined to get away from him. "You could invite people over on Friday too, if you want. Friends from your course or whoever."

"There's no one I'd invite." She paused on the stairs. "But maybe I can have a drink and celebrate making it through the first term."

"Great." He smiled up at her. "I'll look forward to it."

~

Fraser invited the usual crowd around on Friday – guys from the football team and a few people from his course. Unsurprisingly, extra people turned up, and he wasn't quite sure who they were.

Scarlett was up in her room. He'd knocked on her door when he'd got home from uni and asked if she was still up for joining the party. She'd seemed indifferent but said she'd probably come down for a drink later.

By 9 p.m. the living room was full of people. The kitchen was the same, and more spilled out into the hallway.

"You made it!" Fraser said, when he walked into the kitchen to find Scarlett sitting at the table with some of the guys from the football team.

"I live here," she said.

He moved to stand beside her. "And you found a beer."

"I know where the fridge is." She rolled her eyes, making everyone around her laugh. Including him.

Simon wandered in and slapped him on the back. "I didn't know your wife was joining us."

"Scarlett's my housemate. Simon doesn't understand the concept of two friends living together," he explained when everyone around the table stared at him. "He thinks there must be more to it."

Scarlett looked annoyed as she sipped her beer.

"Do you really have your own publishing company?" Matt, sitting beside her, asked.

"Yes."

"That's impressive," another of them said, nodding approvingly.

"Do you publish any authors we'd have heard of?" Matt asked.

"We haven't published anything yet. We're only just starting up." She spoke fast and stared at her beer bottle while the guys around her exchanged amused looks. "I wanted it to be called Scarlett Ink because it's a play on words, but my business partners wanted to call it Hope Cove Press. I was outnumbered. It's fine though. I can stay at the flat at the weekends, so that's another good thing about having a publishing company."

The doorbell rang and Fraser craned his neck to look down

the hall as someone opened the door. "I don't know who they are," he said, slightly concerned that the house was packed and people were still turning up.

"I invited them," Simon said. "The blonde one's mine. Met her last week. You're welcome to the brunette."

"I'm all right, thanks," he muttered.

"At least come and say hello." Simon pulled on his arm, but he refused to budge from his spot beside Scarlett.

Matt leaned close to her. "What's the book about that you wrote?"

"I don't want to tell you because I haven't published it yet and you might steal my story."

"That's a good point," Matt said mockingly.

When someone called to Fraser, he looked down the hall to see Brett standing in the living room doorway. "I thought you were getting beers?"

"Hang on," Fraser replied, then moved to the fridge and loaded up his arms with bottles of beer. "Why don't you come in the living room?" he said to Scarlett.

"Don't steal her," Matt said with a smirk. "We're enjoying her company." As laughter rippled around the table, he tried to catch Scarlett's eye so he could telepathically tell her to follow him, but her eyes were cast down. He'd take the beers and come straight back.

Simon grabbed at his arm as soon as he offloaded the beers to outstretched hands in the living room. "What do you think?" he asked, raising his voice over the music and casting a pointed glance at the two girls he'd invited.

"I dunno," Fraser said, preoccupied by the fact that he'd left Scarlett surrounded by wolves.

"Come on …" Simon slung an arm around his shoulders and turned him towards the two girls, who were giggling in the corner. "They're hot. I'll introduce you."

"Maybe later."

"What's wrong with you?" There was a slur to his words. "Is it that freak of a wife? Are you one of those guys who are attracted to crazy girls?"

"She's not crazy." Fraser forcefully pushed Simon's arm away.

"Are you shagging her or what?"

Fraser's hands curled to fists. "Shut up," he growled.

"You may as well. She is your wife, even if she *is* mental." Simon looked over Fraser's shoulder and flashed a leery grin.

He knew before he turned that Scarlett was standing there, but he hadn't anticipated how much the look on her face would feel like a punch in the gut. When she turned and fled, he followed her but didn't catch her until she was up the stairs.

"Wait," he said, pulling on her elbow and swinging her around to him. The pain he'd seen a moment ago had been replaced by indifference. So much so that he wondered if he'd imagined the hurt in her eyes. Maybe she hadn't even heard anything. "Are you okay?"

"Yes." She stepped into her room and began to close the door.

"Are you sure?" He put a foot in the door and she glared at him.

"You're not allowed in my room. We have rules, remember?"

"Yeah, I know. I just … I'm sorry about Simon. He's an idiot sometimes."

"Why did you tell people that we're married?"

"I was drunk and it slipped out. But it was only a few people."

"I don't think we should tell people about it."

"Yeah, I know. I didn't mean to."

"Enjoy your party," she said before softly closing the door.

Trudging downstairs, he completely lost enthusiasm for the party. He definitely wasn't going to make a cheerful host, but most people seemed to be drunk enough that they wouldn't notice or care. He'd give it another hour and start suggesting they move into town and hit the bars and clubs. Once the party was over, he'd check on Scarlett. Though she probably wouldn't even open the door to him.

As it turned out, he caught sight of her slipping out of the front door ten minutes after he'd left her in her room.

"Where are you going?" he asked, stepping out into the cold. She didn't look at him, and he suspected she was averting her gaze because she'd been crying.

"Back to Hope Cove," she said.

"I thought you were going tomorrow."

"I changed my mind."

"But it's dark. And you've been drinking."

She shook her head. "I only drank two sips of beer, so I can still drive. I'm going now. See you next year."

"Wait." He held the car door open. "I don't want you to leave when you're upset. Simon's an idiot …"

"I'm not upset. I'm annoyed because you're holding the door open when I want to leave. That's all."

He let go of the door and she immediately slammed it shut.

"Bye," he muttered as she drove away.

Walking back inside, he felt a heaviness in his gut. He hadn't done anything wrong though. It was Simon who'd offended Scarlett. In an attempt to avoid him, he wandered back to the kitchen.

"What's up with you?" Chris asked. They were on the same course.

"Simon was talking shit about my housemate and she heard."

"I can't stand that guy," Chris said. "I don't know why he's so popular."

"I'm not much of a fan either. Although he's not so bad when he's sober."

Chris picked at the label on his beer. "What's the deal with your housemate anyway? What's her name? Scarlett?"

"Yeah." He realised it had been optimistic to hope that word wouldn't get out about them being married after his drunken rambling. It seemed as though Chris had heard something. "We're just friends."

"Yeah, but I mean … you know …"

"What?"

He poked his tongue into a tooth as though he had food stuck. "Is she autistic?"

Fraser stared at him, trying to gauge if it was a joke. Part of him wanted to laugh. But at the same time his heart rate kicked up a notch and his stomach clenched uncomfortably. "I don't actually know her that well."

"My cousin's autistic," Chris said. "Asperger's syndrome. Except they don't class it as that now. It's high-functioning autism. Scarlett has the same awkwardness. The way she can't make eye contact and she's completely lost in social situations."

Fraser's heart continued to pound and he couldn't think of anything to say. "I don't know if she is or not."

"I suppose you can't really just come out and ask. But I thought she might have mentioned it since you're living together. How did you meet her anyway?"

"We got chatting at the open day. She was looking for someone to share a house with."

"You'd think she'd have preferred to share with another girl."

"We just got on well …" Fraser closed his eyes as he felt a wave of nausea sweep through his stomach. "Could you help me out with something?"

"What?"

Fraser's eyes scanned the room and he felt completely exhausted. "Can you help me get rid of everyone?"

"You're joking, right?"

"No." It felt like an impossible task but he wanted everyone gone. Immediately.

Chris looked at him sadly. "We could hide the booze, I guess.

A lack of alcohol is your best bet for encouraging people to go elsewhere."

Fraser nodded. "Good plan."

CHAPTER 9

Hattie was walking out of the house when Fraser arrived home on Sunday afternoon. He felt a lot more affection for his bratty little sister when he hardly saw her.

"I thought you weren't coming home until later in the week," she said as she hugged him.

"Change of plan. Where are you off to?"

"Cinema with Philippa. Did Mum tell you I passed my driving test?"

"Yep." He craned his neck in the vague direction of the road. "Get off the road, people!"

She laughed and gave him a gentle poke in the ribs. "I'll have you know I'm a great driver. I passed my test three months after I turned seventeen, which was faster than you. But I suppose you can't help your gender. Women are naturally better drivers."

"Is Mum letting you use her car?" he asked, clocking the key in her hand.

"Yes. I can't wait until I'm eighteen and I get my own. What do you think I should ask for?"

"Don't know. Don't care!"

"Why would you when you have a beautiful Audi?" She

glanced over at it and frowned. "It needs a wash. Poor car. Don't tell me the novelty has worn off already?"

"I've been busy with uni." He had been neglecting his car, but he had plenty of time to wash and polish it over the holidays. "Are Mum and Dad in?"

"Yeah. Mum's in a bad mood but what's new?" She smiled at him as he moved towards the door. "It's actually quite nice to see your ugly mug!"

"Same," he said with a gentle smile.

After dropping his bag by the stairs, he walked across the entrance hall and found his dad sitting with his laptop open on the dining table.

"You're back early," he said, glancing up.

His mum came out of the kitchen, pushing her hair from her face. "Everything okay?" she asked as she hugged him.

He sank into her embrace and rested his head on her shoulder. "Just felt like coming home. Something smells good."

"I'm cooking a roast. And I'm glad you're here because your sister decided to go out without warning so I've got far too much food. Did you see Hattie?"

"Yes." The smell of roasting chicken made his mouth water as he took a seat opposite his dad. He asked him about work and listened to him fill him in on what was new in the hotel business. He owned a chain of luxury hotels that Fraser had very little interest in, but he nodded along and asked a few questions. As they ate he answered their questions about his course and the workload.

"You look tired," his mum remarked as he pushed his empty plate away from him. "You're pale too. You need to have a good rest while you're here. I'll get some home-cooked food into you."

"Thanks." He chewed on the inside of his lip and felt a cool flutter in his chest. He'd hardly slept the past couple of nights and was looking forward to curling up in the comfort of his old bedroom.

"Is everything okay?" his mum asked.

He wiped his hands over his face, debating whether he should discuss Scarlett with them or not. "I think I messed up," he finally whispered.

"What did you do now?" his dad asked wearily, while his mum rested a comforting hand on his shoulder.

"I should never have married Scarlett."

"Well, we know that," his mum said. "But what's done is done."

"She's autistic." He hadn't been able to stop thinking about it since the party, and he was certain it was true. On Saturday morning he'd gone into town and bought a couple of books on autism. He didn't have to read much before everything became really obvious. By the time he'd read to the end, he had no doubt. It explained so much: from the way Scarlett didn't make eye contact and how uncomfortable she was in social situations, to her sleep issues and lack of friends. He wasn't sure how he hadn't realised before.

"Autistic?" his mum echoed.

He nodded slowly. "She has autism spectrum disorder."

"What does that mean?" his dad asked.

"It means her brain is wired differently to other people's. She has difficulty in social situations and … I don't even really know what it means."

"But what does it mean for you?" his mum asked. "You said you shouldn't have married her."

"I feel as though I did something wrong. Like she's vulnerable and I took advantage of her or something."

His mum glared at him. "Well, did you?"

"No. I was trying to help her. But now I feel as though maybe she didn't really understand what she was doing. I don't know … I just have this feeling that I did something wrong."

"She's an adult," his dad said. "Does she seem as though she's not capable of making her own decisions?"

"No." He smiled. "Not at all. She's one of the most capable

people I know. She set up her own publishing company and she works in a cafe and writes books. And she's studying for her degree."

"She has a publishing company?" his mum asked.

"Yeah." He felt oddly proud of that. "It's a new thing. She's doing it with a couple of friends."

"She definitely doesn't sound incompetent," his dad said.

His mum's eyes lit up. "I watched a film a while back about a woman with autism. It's based on a true story … what was her name … Temple something."

"Temple Grandin," Fraser said. He'd read about her.

"Yes. That's her. She was quirky but kind of a genius. Is that like Scarlett?"

"Like *Rain Man*?" his dad added happily.

"I don't think she's a genius. I don't know."

"And you didn't know she was autistic before you married her?" his mum asked.

"I had no idea." Looking back, it was blindingly obvious. But he hadn't known much about autism. It was actually embarrassing when he thought back to the first time they'd met. He'd been convinced she was playing games, but she'd probably had no idea he was flirting with her. All the times she hadn't laughed at his jokes she probably hadn't realised they were jokes … or that she was supposed to laugh. When he thought back on all of his encounters with her, he saw everything in a different light.

"I think you're worrying about nothing," his mum said. "It doesn't sound as though she's stupid or anything. I'm sure she knew what she was doing when she married you."

"I don't know how I should act around her now. I like her and I thought we were friends, kind of. But now it all feels weird."

"Just be her friend." His mum rubbed his back. "That's all you can do."

"Thanks." He kissed his mum's cheek, feeling better after the chat.

"Have you got much planned for while you're home?" his mum asked.

"No. I'll catch up with Liam and Allie but they're not back until the end of the week."

When Liam invited Fraser to the pub for lunch on Friday, he assumed Allie would be there too, but she was busy with her family. He tried not to take it personally. He had a couple of weeks to catch up with her.

"I'm happy to get away from her for a bit, to be honest." Liam glanced around furtively. "Living together is pretty intense, and now she's arranged the next two weeks with us doing everything together and splitting our time between each other's families. I could do with a break."

"From Allie?" Fraser asked, his voice rising slightly. The two of them had got together when they were fifteen and had been inseparable ever since. It was almost as though they'd morphed into one person.

"Living together isn't as easy as I'd thought. I can't do anything without telling her. You wouldn't believe the stick I get from my mates when I have to call and tell her I'm going for drinks after lectures."

"You two are fine though, right?"

"Yeah. I love her. It's all okay. Just a bit stifling at times. I watch the other lads playing the field and sometimes I feel as though I'm missing out." He shook his head. "Ignore me. I'll just live vicariously through you. Tell me about your exploits. I bet you had a wild first term."

"There's definitely been a lot of partying."

"I want to hear about the women. It'll probably be the only time I get to hang out with you without Allie around, so you should fill me in now to avoid her disapproving looks. It drives me mad when she gets on her high horse about you sleeping around."

"There hasn't actually been a lot of that going on."

Liam gave his shoulder a playful shove. "Don't tell me you've found someone to tie you down?"

"No. I guess it's just true what they say about marriage killing your sex life."

"Did something happen with you and Scarlett?"

"No." Fraser grinned, amused that Liam couldn't grasp the concept of there being no romantic attachments in his life. "There hasn't been anyone."

"There must have been a few one-night stands at least."

"Mate!" Fraser glared at him. "There's been no one. Nothing."

"So you haven't …?"

"No!"

"Since before you started uni?"

"Since before I got married."

"Why?" He shook his head. "I don't understand."

"I haven't met anyone I've been interested in. And I wouldn't take anyone back to our place in case Scarlett was there."

"I thought you said she was always away at the weekends."

"She is, but it'd feel weird anyway. Not that it matters since there was no one I felt like taking home."

"What's happened to you?" Liam asked.

Fraser shrugged and took a swig of his pint, glancing around the familiar pub to check for anyone he knew.

"How is it living with Scarlett?" Liam asked.

"Not quite what I expected." Fraser had spent a lot of time that week reading blogs by autistic people and listening to podcasts about autism. He was desperate to know all he could, but the more he found out the more confused he was. He couldn't shake the feeling that he'd done something morally wrong when he'd married Scarlett. The fact that he'd had no idea she was autistic was little comfort.

"In what way?" Liam asked when Fraser drifted into a daydream.

"She's autistic. I just found out and I don't know what to think."

"Wow," he said flatly.

"Yeah. I should have seen it earlier. It seems obvious now, but I honestly had no idea. I just thought she was a bit quirky."

"I only met her briefly," Liam mused. "I guess she did seem a little awkward, but I thought she was just nervous about marrying a guy she barely knew."

"I spoke to my parents about it. They think that if she's competent enough to have her own publishing company, then she's capable of making her own decisions about marriage."

Liam was staring at him. "She has her own publishing company?"

"Haven't I told you about that?"

He shook his head. "I remember you saying that was her plan for after uni."

"She's already going ahead with it." He smiled widely. "It's pretty amazing everything she's managing to do. She's studying and writing books and working in her aunt's cafe and now she's setting up a publishing company. Clearly being autistic isn't holding her back."

"Yeah." Liam didn't sound impressed.

"What's that look for?" Fraser asked.

"I just wonder … how is it possible for her to do all that stuff?"

"She doesn't seem to have any social life, but I'm not sure that's really a sacrifice. I don't think she likes to socialise."

"No, but I mean *seriously*. What eighteen-year-old sets up their own publishing company?"

"She's doing it with her two best friends …" As he said it, Fraser heard how ridiculous it sounded.

"It's an impressive story," Liam said. "And I'm not saying it's not true but …"

"But what?"

"Have you actually seen any evidence of any of it? Have you met her friends or seen anything official to do with her business?"

"No, but …" Nausea swept up from his stomach and he wondered if he was the biggest idiot on the planet. And the most gullible person ever.

"If she has a publishing company, there'll be a website." Liam had his phone in his hand and began tapping away. "What's the name of it?"

"Hope Cove Press. They're based in Hope Cove."

He raised an eyebrow. "That's imaginative."

"Scarlett wanted to call it Scarlett Ink but her friends vetoed that idea."

"I can't find anything about it." His eyes scanned the phone screen. "There's no website and no social media presence."

"They're only just starting up so maybe they just haven't done that yet." He caught the pity in Liam's eyes and hoped that everything she'd told him hadn't been a fantasy.

"Do you think she might be delusional?" Liam asked.

Fraser dropped his head to his hands and pushed his palms into his eyes. "No. But I also lived with her for months without realising she's autistic, so I'm not sure about anything any more."

"What are you going to do?"

He took a deep breath. "I'm going to drive to Hope Cove and find out."

CHAPTER 10

It was years since Fraser had been to Hope Cove. He was struck by a wave of nostalgia when he stepped out of the car. The screech of seagulls drifted on strong gusts of salty air as he strolled towards the cafe. Across the road, the freezing wind lifted sand into frenzied swirls on the beach.

Thankfully, there was only one cafe in the village so he didn't have to search. The warmth enveloped him as he stepped inside. Except for a couple in the corner, the place was empty.

"Hello!" An older lady with rosy cheeks walked out from a room at the back. "What can I get you?"

"I'm looking for Scarlett … I think she works here?"

The woman looked at him closely. "She does. Not today though."

"Usually just on Sundays," he said, wanting to prove he knew Scarlett and wasn't some creepy stalker. "But she said she'd be working more over the holidays so I thought I might catch her. I don't suppose you know where I can find her? I'd call her but she's a nightmare when it comes to answering her phone." He'd tried calling to check she wasn't upset after the party, but as usual she hadn't answered.

"Tell me about it," the woman said, seeming to relax. "She's my niece and she won't even answer the phone to me most of the time."

"So you're Verity? She's talked about you. I'm Fraser …" He trailed off as it occurred to him that he didn't know what Scarlett had said to her aunt about their arrangement.

"Do you go to uni with Scarlett?" she asked.

"Yes. And she's talked about you and the cafe so much that I thought I'd check it out since I was in the area."

"That's nice." She smiled warmly. "She's upstairs. Go up and find her. Just through the back here … knock on the door at the top of the stairs."

"Thanks." He slipped behind the counter, following her directions. It was only after he'd knocked on the door that he noticed the shiny silver plaque with *Hope Cove Press* engraved on it. The smile spread slowly across his face.

He was still grinning to himself when a well-put-together woman answered the door. She was probably around forty and looked at him in surprise.

"Hello," she said after a moment.

"Hi." He raised a hand to point at the sign on the door. "I think I have the right place."

Her eyes roamed over him appraisingly. He was wearing his favourite blue Ralph Lauren shirt and he had the impression she was the sort of person who'd appreciate a well-tailored shirt. "You were looking for Hope Cove Press?" she asked.

He pushed his hair aside when it fell towards his eye. "Yeah. I wasn't sure it actually existed. That's cool, though."

"What can I help you with?"

"I'm looking for Scarlett. She works here, right?"

"Yes. She's a co-owner."

So she wasn't delusional. All the times she'd excitedly talked about her publishing company hadn't just been her own little fantasy. The relief made his smile even wider. "I didn't know if she was having me on about that. Sometimes it's hard to tell with Scarlett."

"That's true. Sorry, who are you?"

He dragged his teeth along his bottom lip, trying to decide how to answer as he realised once again that he had no idea what Scarlett had told people about him – or if she'd said anything at all. "Fraser," he said simply and extended his hand.

"Lizzie," she replied. "How do you know Scarlett?"

Again, he wasn't sure how to answer. She hadn't reacted when he introduced himself, so he presumed Scarlett hadn't mentioned him. "We both go to uni in Exeter," he said after a pause. "I'd like to say we're friends, but she'd probably say acquaintances. If she was feeling generous."

"It sounds as though you know her well."

"I'm not sure about that." He glanced over her shoulder. "Is she here?"

"Yes. Sorry." She stood aside and motioned for him to come in. "Just down the hall."

Scarlett groaned when she set eyes on him. "Are you kidding me? You've decided you don't annoy me enough in term time so you thought you'd stalk me over the holidays too?"

He laughed at the fire in her eyes as she glared at him. "I'm not stalking you. I came to visit. There's a big difference."

"I didn't invite you, and I'm sure I've never given you the address. You've tracked me down and turned up unannounced. It definitely feels like stalking."

She was cute when she was annoyed, and he struggled to take his eyes off her. "I wanted to see you," he said eventually. The desire to tease her was too strong and he flashed a boyish grin. If she hadn't told anyone about them being married he could really have some fun. "After all you are my—"

"Study partner," she screeched, cutting him off as he'd known she would. "He's my study partner." Her cheeks flushed adorably as she looked at Lizzie and the other woman, who he assumed was Emily. "We study together sometimes." She took his arm, apparently intent on marching him back towards the door, but he held his ground. "We agreed to have a break from studying over Christmas, so you should leave now. We were in the middle of a very important business meeting and you've barged in and interrupted us."

"Sorry," Fraser said to the two women on the couch.

They both told him it was fine and didn't appear bothered by the interruption. In fact, they seemed fairly amused.

"This place is really great," he said, glancing around. "I thought you might be messing with me about the publishing company."

"Why would I say it if it wasn't true?" Scarlett asked. "And why exactly was it so unbelievable?"

"It wasn't." He was actually quite annoyed with himself for doubting her. "I believed it when you said you were going to do it after uni. It's kind of amazing that you're already going ahead with it."

"Whatever," she said, shaking her head. "Can you please leave?"

He took a step towards the door, then hesitated, thinking of the last time he'd seen her. "I wanted to apologise for the other day and check you were okay after the party. I'm sorry you were upset."

"I wasn't upset. I was annoyed. Like I'm annoyed now. Please go away."

He took a step away from her before pausing again. Teasing her was too much fun and he couldn't resist. "If you're around at all over the holidays, maybe we could get together for some extra *studying*." He winked at her and was rewarded with the fiery flash in her eyes.

Quickly, he made a dash for the door, with Scarlett following after him, mumbling about how annoying he was. It was surprisingly satisfying when she slammed the door behind him.

The relief he felt was almost palpable. She definitely wasn't some delicate little flower who needed protecting, and the niggling idea that he'd done something wrong by marrying her vanished completely.

CHAPTER 11

On the first day of university in the new year, Fraser walked down the stairs in a fog of sleep. He could feel his hair sticking up at odd angles and dragged his hands through it in an attempt to smooth it down.

"Are you off to uni?" he asked Scarlett. She was standing at the front door with a raincoat on and her backpack on one shoulder.

She didn't turn around. "Yes. But it's raining. I'm going to get wet."

"Where's your car?"

"Outside the house."

"Just run to it then. You're not going to get that wet."

"I'm not going in the car. I always walk to uni."

"Why?" He stared at her, trying to figure out what was going through her head.

Glancing back, she shot him a look of impatience. "There's lots of traffic in the mornings. And I might not be able to find a parking space. If I can't find a space, what do I do? I can't leave the car if there's nowhere to park it."

"That's why they have a car park."

"Sometimes the car park gets full. There aren't enough spaces for everyone."

"So you always walk to uni? Just in case the car park is full?"

"Yes!" she said, as though it was obvious and completely reasonable.

As she opened the door, the sound of the rain battering the pavement filled the hallway. Scarlett adjusted the strap of her backpack and seemed to be psyching herself up to step outside.

"Do you want a lift?" he asked.

"What?"

"I can drive you to uni if you want."

"My lectures are on a different campus to yours."

"I don't have lectures until later. I can drop you off. You can't walk there in this weather." He pushed his feet into a pair of trainers and grabbed a hoodie from the rack, pulling it over his head.

After a quick dash to the car, they closed the doors in unison, dulling the noise of the rain. Fraser pushed his wet hair off his face with both hands, then glanced down at the damp patches on his hoodie. He exchanged an amused smile with Scarlett as they clicked their seatbelts on.

"What did you do over Christmas?" he asked as he pulled away, raising his voice over the drumming of the rain on the roof.

"Not much. Hung out with Lizzie and Emily and helped Auntie Verity in the cafe."

"Were you working at your publishing company too?" he asked, smiling as he thought back to visiting her.

"Yes. A bit."

"It was cool to see the place." He tapped his fingers against the steering wheel as he slowed at the traffic lights.

"You shouldn't have come there."

"If you'd have answered my calls I could have apologised

over the phone, then I wouldn't have had to turn up on your doorstep."

"It wasn't you who called me mental, so you didn't need to apologise."

He grimaced. "Simon shouldn't have said that. He was drunk and being a dick."

Scarlett didn't respond but dropped her gaze to her hands in her lap.

"It was nice to see the cafe anyway and meet Verity and Lizzie and Emily."

Her head shot up and anger flashed in her eyes. "I had to tell them who you were. And everyone asked so many questions."

"Did you tell them we were married?"

"I told Emily and Lizzie. Not Auntie Verity. I told her I was living with you, but she freaked out so much that I decided not to tell her we're married."

"I can't believe you hadn't told anyone before."

"It's a weird thing to explain."

"Tell me about it." He chuckled. "My mum cried when I told her."

"You told your parents?" She stared at him with wide eyes.

"Yes. And they keep asking when they'll get to meet their daughter-in-law."

"I hope you told them never!"

"Yeah, I suspected that might be your reply."

The car crawled through standing water, following the line of traffic until they stopped again for the next set of traffic lights. It would usually only take ten minutes to reach the campus, but the traffic and weather conditions meant it took almost twice that.

"Which building is your lecture in?" he asked, slowing as he reached Streatham campus.

"Queen's Building. But you can drop me anywhere."

"May as well get you as close to the door as possible." He continued a little way before stopping outside the grey building. "You shouldn't get too wet from here. The rain seems to be easing too." Leaning over the steering wheel, he peered through the windshield. It was definitely letting up.

She pulled her hood up, then reached for the door handle. "Thanks for driving me."

"You're welcome." He peeked around her hood. "What are husbands for, hey?"

She blinked a couple of times. "Generally, procreation. But in my case, a husband is for getting a student loan. Not for getting lifts to lectures."

He burst out laughing. "You're pretty funny sometimes."

There was a splash as she stepped out of the car and into a puddle. "Bye," she shouted behind her then scurried towards the building.

Aside from the rain, Scarlett's first day back at uni was pleasantly uneventful. During the two-hour break between lectures, she hid away in a quiet corner of the library. Instead of getting on with her assigned reading for uni, she pored over a psychological thriller which would be among the first books published by Hope Cove Press. It was the third time she was reading it. Since she'd be very involved with marketing and advertising, she felt she should know the books inside out.

The rain had completely stopped for her walk home that afternoon. At four thirty on the dot, she arrived back at the semi-detached house on Margaret Road. Her heart rate increased as she rooted in the front pocket of her backpack for the door key. Maybe she'd put it in the other pocket by mistake. As she rummaged, she thought back to packing her bag that morning. Putting her keys in was something she did on autopilot, so the fact that she didn't have any recollection of doing it didn't mean much.

Eventually, she gave up and pressed the doorbell. Fraser's car was nowhere in sight but he could've parked it somewhere else. It was probably the only time she'd ever hoped he was at home. Mostly, she wished for the opposite.

He'd be back soon anyway, she told herself, sinking to sit on the doorstep and refusing to think about the fact that he usually didn't arrive home until late in the evening and often not until after she was in bed.

Pulling her laptop out, she continued reading the thriller until the battery died. When hunger niggled at her, she walked to the shop on the corner and bought two bags of Monster Munch. She would have liked a drink but was aware of the fact that she had no access to toilet facilities until Fraser got home. Hesitantly, she typed out a message, asking when he'd be home, then stared at the phone for a while but got no reply.

The stone doorstep was cold and uncomfortable, so she interspersed sitting with walking up and down the short front path. She told herself he'd probably be home by seven, then eight, then nine. Shivering on the doorstep, she pulled her knees up and hugged them to her chest. When she checked her phone, she saw that Fraser hadn't even read her message. She should just call him. If she told him she was locked out, he'd probably come home and let her in. Her heart rate increased as her finger hovered over the dial button. Phone calls always made her panicky and she generally avoided them. After taking a deep breath, she tapped the button and frowned as the screen went black. The battery was dead.

Dropping her head to her knees, she wondered if she'd freeze to death if she spent all night outside.

~

Fraser was waiting to be served at the student bar on campus when he checked his phone. The message from Scarlett was a surprise. She almost never messaged him. It had come through ages ago, but he hadn't checked his phone. All she asked was when he'd be home. He tapped out a quick reply asking if she was okay, then tried calling her when the message didn't go through. The phone went straight to voicemail.

"What can I get you?" the barman asked.

He glanced back at his teammates, most of whom were drunk or well on the way to being. "Nothing," he muttered before walking towards the exit.

Abandoning his car on campus, he walked home, wondering why Scarlett had wanted to know when he'd be back. At the house he swayed a little as he approached the front door, then muttered a few swear words when he almost fell over something on the doorstep.

"What the hell?" he said loudly when he realised it was a some*one* rather than a some*thing*.

Scarlett jolted awake, sending her phone crashing out of her hand.

"What are you doing?" Fraser asked, as she scrabbled to retrieve it.

"I forgot my keys," she said through chattering teeth.

"So that's why you messaged me?"

She nodded as she stood up, looking stiff and cold. "You didn't reply."

"I didn't see your message until a bit ago. You should have called."

"I don't like speaking on the phone. I kept thinking you'd be back soon. And then my phone battery died." She was trembling and he hurried to open the door.

"What would you have done if I didn't come home?" He pushed the door open and gestured for her to go ahead of him. When she didn't reply, he shook his head and closed the door heavily behind him. "You could have frozen to death."

"Maybe," she murmured.

"Scarlett!" he said fiercely, annoyed that she didn't seem to be taking it seriously. "You should have called me. It's not normal to sit on the doorstep in the freezing cold." He let out a frustrated growl. After a long day and probably a couple too many beers, he really didn't need this. "You're so weird," he muttered.

As she hurried up the stairs, a sinking feeling hit his stomach and he called out to her. She didn't turn back, and he heard the lock on the bathroom door click a second later.

The buzz of alcohol in his system fizzled away as he made a cup of tea and took it upstairs. There was no reply when he knocked on Scarlett's door.

"Can I come in?" he asked while inching the door open.

"I suppose so." She was sitting at her desk with her pyjamas and a hoodie on. Her laptop was open in front of her with a message on the screen that it was installing updates.

"Sorry I said you were weird."

She kept her focus on the computer screen and didn't respond.

"I brought you a cup of tea." He set the mug on the desk. "You must be freezing. How long were you out there?"

She checked her phone, which was charging beside her laptop. "About five and a half hours. But I went to the shop to buy crisps for dinner, so that took a bit of time."

He shoved his hands into the pockets of his jeans. "I don't understand why you didn't just call me. I would have come and let you in." When she didn't reply, he pointed at the steaming mug. "Drink that. It'll warm you up."

She peered into the cup. "It's the wrong colour."

"What?"

"I don't like it like that."

He rolled his eyes. "It's a cup of tea. It'll warm you up."

"You put too much milk in it."

After inhaling steadily through his nose, he picked up the mug and took a sip. "There. Now there's less milk."

"There's less everything," Scarlett said. "The ratio is still the same."

"You couldn't possibly just say thanks, could you?"

"For drinking a mouthful of my tea?"

"No!" He laughed and wandered to the door. "For *making* you a cup of tea. At least hold it to warm your hands."

She slipped her hand through the handle, then brought it to her chest and held it there.

"You should probably go to bed soon," Fraser said. "You'll end up getting sick after spending so long in the cold."

"I've got work to do. I have a presentation next week and I need to be prepared. I hate presentations."

"Everyone does," he said with a hand on the doorframe.

"Do they?"

He thought about it. "Most people."

"Good." Her lips twitched to a satisfied smile.

CHAPTER 12

After Fraser had told her that everyone hated making presentations, Scarlett felt a lot calmer. Knowing that her nerves weren't abnormal was a comfort. Unfortunately it didn't stop her from being stressed on the day.

Standing up in front of the class, she reminded herself that the presentation would only last fifteen minutes. In fifteen minutes it would all be over. If her heart exploded – which it felt like it might – it would be over even sooner. Wiping her sweaty palms on her leggings, she tried to ignore the fact that everyone was watching her.

"Whenever you're ready, Scarlett," the lecturer, Paula Hillard, said.

The words blurred on the index cards in her hands. She was supposed to use them as a prompt but not read directly from them. When she'd practiced in her bedroom, Scarlett had managed to recite the whole thing from memory. But she hadn't had a room full of people staring at her.

Blinking the cards into focus, she began to give her overview of medieval literature. Once she got going, it was easy to speak without looking at her index cards. One of the tables near to her had a yellow smiley face sticker halfway up the leg, so she focused on that to avoid the urge to look at her notes.

Before she'd got very far, she was interrupted by Professor Hillard saying her name. From the volume and the accompanying giggles around the room, Scarlett suspected it wasn't the first time she'd said her name.

"Could you slow down a little?" the lecturer said with a reassuring smile. She had bright red lipstick which was smudged slightly on her top lip. It was off-putting. As was being interrupted in the middle of her presentation.

"I don't know where I was." Scarlett's eyes darted over the first index card and then the next.

"I think you were about to say something about *Beowulf*," the professor said.

"Yes." Scarlett lifted her chin, this time focusing her gaze all the way to the back of the room and out of the window to the car park beyond. She tried to speak slower but was desperate to get to the end.

At last it was over. And her heart hadn't exploded, so that was a positive.

The sudden hush in the room highlighted the ensuing giggles from a couple of girls at the back of the class. When one of them snorted loudly, the sound seemed to echo around the room.

Scarlett was desperate to dart back to her seat, but the torture wasn't quite over. At the end of the presentation there were five minutes for questions.

"Does anyone have any questions for Scarlett?" Professor Hillard asked brightly.

Whispers rippled around the room but no one directed any of their chatter at Scarlett. When she braved dragging her gaze up from her shoes, she caught the eye of the dainty Chinese girl who was grinning at her from the front row. She'd worked with Mingmei in group discussions a few times and she was about the happiest person Scarlett had ever met. For a moment, Scarlett thought she was going to ask a question, but she just stared at her with her wide smile and bright eyes. Beside her, Carolyn waved to draw Scarlett's attention. She was a mature student who was overweight and constantly had sweat patches around her armpits. When Scarlett looked at her, she tugged at the hem of her T-shirt so it sat smoothly over her vast stomach. The action exposed a damp stripe of sweat across her middle.

"I'd love to hear your personal opinion on the writing from this period. Is there anything you find particularly interesting or enjoyable in the works from the medieval period?"

Scarlett shook her head. "No. I think it's all really boring."

Silence fell for a moment before the lecturer spoke.

"Well done, Scarlett," she said, nodding towards her empty seat. Scarlett scurried back there, breathing a sigh of relief that it was over. Richard was up next. He was one of only a handful of men on the course. Scarlett barely registered his presentation, apart from the fact that he got more questions than she had.

"You talked so fast," Mingmei said in her cheerful voice at the end of class.

Scarlett put her index cards in her backpack. "I had a lot to say."

"Yes!" She laughed. "You said a lot. And *so* fast! It was very funny."

"It wasn't supposed to be funny," Scarlett said.

As everyone filed out of the room, Professor Hillard approached Scarlett and invited her to a personal tutoring session in her office in half an hour. She had a feeling that wasn't a good sign.

~

"How do you feel your presentation went?" Professor Hillard asked from behind the desk in her office.

"Okay, I think." Scarlett's eyes darted around the clutter in the room, from the piles of papers, to a selection of framed photos of a little boy and girl.

"I think it's an area you need to work on. You spoke so quickly that it was difficult to understand what you were saying. There wasn't a chance for the audience to digest your points."

"It's a broad subject and I had a lot to say."

"Part of the exercise was being able to pick out key points to give a short overview. That's a skill you need to practice. You also failed to engage your audience. When you're addressing them, you need to look at them."

"I didn't know that." Scarlett had her backpack on her lap and hugged it to her chest. She should have known it really. It was one of the things her mum had always gone on about.

"The question and answer part didn't go well either ..."

She snapped her head up. "I answered the question. It's not my fault I only got one."

"Getting the answer right isn't the point. The questions are a chance for you to show further knowledge of the subject. Even if you're not a fan of the work from the period, you could give more insightful thoughts on why you don't like it."

"Okay," Scarlett replied meekly.

Professor Hillard folded her hands in her lap. "I've noticed you also don't participate in class much."

"I haven't missed any classes," Scarlet said in a rush. "I'm always there and I listen and take notes. And I hand assignments in on time."

"Yes. But part of your grade comes from class participation. You need to be able to discuss the topics we're working on and engage with your lecturers and the other students."

"I'm not good at that," Scarlett admitted.

"Do you take part in any extra-curricular activities at uni?"

"No. I don't have time. I have my studying, and I work in a cafe on Sundays. I also work for a publishing company, so that takes up time."

"Are you doing work experience at a publishing house?" the lecturer asked, sitting up straighter.

"No. I'm co-owner. It was actually all my idea, but Lizzie

and Emily are running it at the moment because I have a lot on. I still help though."

Professor Hillard squeezed her eyes closed as she gave a small shake of the head. "You're co-owner of a publishing company?"

"Yes." When the lecturer stared at her, Scarlett had the impression she was supposed to say more. "It's called Hope Cove Press. You can look us up if you want." She pointed to the laptop on the desk. "The website is up and running now. My picture is on there with Lizzie's and Emily's. We're only just starting up, so we haven't published any books yet but we will soon."

"That's impressive." She peered at the website on her laptop. After a moment, she turned back to Scarlett. "I'm a little concerned that you're not making time for social activities. Do you have many friends?"

"Lizzie and Emily." She pointed to the computer. "I think Jack's my friend too. He's married to Emily. But he might just be nice to me because I'm Emily's friend. I'm not sure."

"But these people aren't your age?"

"No. They're old. Lizzie's married with two kids and she's pregnant again. Emily's married. She's a writer."

"So you don't have any friends your own age?"

"No. Well, there's Perry. He's eight in human years, which is probably about fifty or so in dog years. Either way, he's not my age."

"And he's a dog?" Professor Hillard asked slowly.

"Yes." Scarlett's index finger began to tap against her thumb. As soon as she noticed, she balled her hand into a fist and clamped it against her backpack. "I don't know why I mentioned the dog. I say weird things sometimes when I'm nervous."

"You don't need to be nervous." Professor Hillard smiled at her. "If you need extra help with your studies, you can always ask. You can come to me or any of your lecturers. There are also student support services. If you speak to someone there, they could point you to further resources to help you in any way you need."

"Do you mean because I'm dyslexic? Because I have software on my computer that helps me with that. And I get someone to proofread my assignments." Her eyes snapped up. "That's not cheating, is it?"

"No. That's sensible. It's great that you're finding ways to manage the dyslexia. There's no problem with your coursework. I just wonder whether you might find some time for social activities. The drama club maybe? That could be a real benefit for you."

Scarlett almost laughed. Drama club was her idea of hell. "I'll think about it."

"Great." Professor Hillard pushed her chair back as she stood. "And feel free to come by if there's anything else I can help with."

"Thanks," Scarlett muttered before making a quick exit.

~

When Fraser arrived home that Thursday evening Scarlett was pacing the kitchen.

"Hi," he said, sliding the pizza box onto the table.

"You're not usually home so early."

Moving around her, he opened the fridge and took out a can of Coke, then offered Scarlett one. When she shook her head in reply, he took a seat. "I was supposed to be playing five-a-side, but the pitch was double booked so it was cancelled. Thought I'd binge on carbs instead. Do you want a slice?"

She shrugged and leaned against the counter.

"How was your day?" he asked through a mouthful of pizza.

"Crap."

He licked a string of cheese from his bottom lip. "How come?"

"I had a presentation. I don't like presentations."

"Didn't it go well?"

"Not really, no."

"Don't worry. These things usually seem worse in your head. I always panic afterwards about some word that I tripped over, but I don't think anyone else really notices."

"Everyone laughed." She bit her lip when her chin trembled.

Fraser paused with the crust of pizza halfway to his mouth. "What?"

"Everyone laughed at me. Then I had a meeting with the lecturer and she said I'd talked too fast and hadn't looked at the audience. And that I didn't answer the question well."

"What was the question?"

"Someone asked me what I thought of medieval literature. I said I don't like it, but apparently that wasn't a good answer."

Fraser wanted to say something sympathetic, but he could imagine her bluntly stating her opinion and had to suppress a grin at the thought of it.

"Then the lecturer asked if I had friends and I told her about Perry, so now she'll think I'm crazy."

"Who's Perry?"

"My aunt's boyfriend's dog."

Fraser put a hand over his mouth to hide his smile. He thought she'd be offended but the corners of her mouth twitched upwards.

"You have friends though, don't you?" he asked.

"Yes. Emily and Lizzie. But apparently they don't count because they're not my age. So I panicked and mentioned Perry. And I could feel that it was the wrong thing to say, but sometimes the words just fall out of my mouth. I can't believe I told her how old the dog is."

Fraser thumped at his chest as he choked. "Did you tell her in dog years or human?"

"Both!" She joined his laughter and her features relaxed. "It's not funny really," she said as her smile fell away. "Sometimes I feel as though I get everything wrong. This is why my mum said I shouldn't go to uni. It wasn't really the dyslexia – it's everything else."

He felt his forehead wrinkle to a frown. "What do you mean?"

"I'm weird, like you said."

"You're not weird. I shouldn't have said that."

"It's true though." She paused, looking thoughtful. "I'm not like other people."

His mouth felt suddenly dry and he swigged at the Coke. If she confided in him about being autistic, he was fairly sure he'd say the wrong thing. "Like … Do you mean …" He opened and closed his mouth a few times but didn't get any further with his sentence. Giving up, he pushed a chair out from the table with his foot and tipped his head at it. "Sit down before you give me neck ache."

She slumped into the chair. "Like the other day when I was locked out. I don't know why I didn't call you. Anyone else would have done, but my brain doesn't always work like other people's. There are lots of things I find difficult that are easy for everyone else."

"Like not being able to look people in the eyes?" Fraser asked hesitantly.

"I can look people in the eyes." She glared at him to make her point. "I just don't like it, so I don't. But that seems to make people uncomfortable. Or so my mum always said."

"Do you ever speak to your parents?"

"Not much. I saw them at Verity's place at Christmas. We don't get on and I'm fine with hardly seeing them. I'm still annoyed that they wouldn't pay for uni. But today I thought maybe they were right about me not being cut out for university. I could quit."

"Quit your course?"

"Yes. I wanted to do the course so I could have a publishing company one day. People take you seriously if you have a degree. But I already have the publishing company. I could quit uni and go and work with Lizzie and Emily."

"You can't quit uni. After everything you went through to get this far, you can't quit now."

"If I quit now, I wouldn't end up in so much debt. And we could get a divorce so I could stop worrying about that."

"About what?"

Scarlett stretched her neck and stared at the ceiling. "Max said that getting married for a loan is fraud."

"Who's Max?"

"Lizzie's husband. He used to be a lawyer. He thinks we could get into trouble."

"Is he going to report us?"

"No. But you told your friends, and they seem to think it's a big joke."

He licked a drop of tomato sauce from his thumb. "I told three of the lads when I was drunk. But I told them to keep quiet about it. It's fine."

"It won't be fine if I get arrested for fraud."

"You're not going to get arrested! All we did was get married for a student loan. Which you'll have to pay back. It's not as though we stole from anyone."

"Everything feels too difficult."

"That's because you had a bad day. You can't quit your degree over a presentation that went wrong."

"It's not just that. Weren't you listening to me?"

"Yes. I get that it's difficult. But I think you can do it if you stick at it."

"Now you sound like Emily. She told me I can do anything I want, but I'm starting to think she's pretty naive."

"She sounds wise." He nudged the pizza box towards her. "Can you help me eat this? I ordered too much. And I'm currently taking a module on nutrition so I feel pretty guilty about eating so much crap."

"You study nutrition?" she asked as she picked up a slice that was thick with cheese.

"Yeah."

"That's interesting."

He nodded. "I like how varied the course is. We do modules on psychology and anatomy, bioenergetics …"

"I don't even know what that is." She looked confused. "I thought you studied sports."

"Exercise and Sport Sciences," he corrected her. "What did you think, that I could spend three years playing sport and they'd give me a degree?"

From the way her cheeks pinked, it was clear that was exactly what she'd thought.

"What do you want to do after uni?" she asked, in an obvious attempt to move the conversation on.

"I don't know."

"What's your dream job?"

His lips twitched at the corners and he stifled a smile. "I don't want to say."

"Why?"

"Because it's stupid."

"Tell me."

He debated whether or not to tell her. "Professional footballer."

"Are you serious?" She smiled widely. "That's the dream job of an eight-year-old."

"I told you it was stupid. It's also not possible."

"I thought you were good at football."

"Not good enough to play professionally."

"Just practice more."

"I tried but it didn't help. I decided to get a degree instead. It keeps my parents happy, and maybe I can be a fitness coach to professional footballers or something." He shoved the pizza box closer to her again. "Can you please do a better job of helping me eat this?"

She took another slice and bit into it, chewing slowly. "I was wondering about something," she said, seeming unsure of herself. "Why did you agree to marry me?"

The question took him by surprise. "What?"

"I needed to get married to get a loan, but why did *you* do it? I never really understood."

He swallowed hard, remembering how attracted to her he'd been when he first met her. That wasn't the reason, though, more of a contributing factor. As was his argument with Allie and phone conversation with Monique that had left him filled with self-loathing. Then there was the fact that she only had two friends, but that would be difficult to explain. "I felt bad that you couldn't go to uni," he said, giving her a slither of truth. "And I was pretty shocked that your parents wouldn't help you. If you look at getting married as a bit of paperwork, it really wasn't such a big deal."

"So you did it to help me?"

He nodded firmly.

"You wanted to help me even though you didn't know me?" She sounded as though she didn't believe a word of it.

"Yeah. Don't look at me like that! I might have been crazy and impulsive, but so were you."

"So you're saying we're both crazy?" She smiled at him over the pizza box.

"It certainly seems like it."

CHAPTER 13

On Sunday, Verity spent the morning complaining to Scarlett, about the cafe being too quiet in the winter months. Since the weather was miserable and it didn't seem as though there'd be many customers, she left Scarlett alone in the afternoon. Half an hour before closing time, she sat playing Candy Crush in the empty cafe and hoped no more customers would arrive. At the sound of the door opening, she sighed heavily, then gave a slow smile when she saw who it was. Emily held the door while Lizzie pushed the empty buggy in.

"Where are the girls?" Scarlett asked.

"Max and Jack have taken them for a run around on the beach," Lizzie replied. "We thought we'd come and have a coffee in peace. I doubt they'll be far behind us though. It's freezing."

"I bet I look like Rudolf," Emily said, touching her nose. "My nose is like ice."

"Your cheeks are bright red too," Scarlett said.

Once she'd given them both coffees, she ducked upstairs to get her laptop.

"I made adverts for the first book release. This should be enough for all the social media posts and anything else you want to use them for. I made a book trailer too. A lot of publishers use them."

"Wow," Lizzie said as she watched the short video with excerpts and teasers about the book. "You've been busy. We only talked about this yesterday."

"I did it last night."

"When do you sleep?" Emily asked. "You must be so busy with uni work. We only said you could do some promotional stuff if you had time. Don't kill yourself trying to do everything."

She sat down with them. "It's my business too. Just because I'm at uni doesn't mean I can't help. And if it gets too much, I can drop out of uni and work with you full-time."

"Don't do that," Lizzie said forcefully. "You need to get your degree. We agreed to build the business up slowly because we all have other projects to work on. You have uni and Emily has her books. I have my regular editing clients who I've already made commitments to. Not to mention the fact that I'll need to take time off when this little one arrives." She put a hand on her stomach, which was still completely flat. The baby wasn't due until the end of the summer.

Scarlett glanced through the window. On the beach she could just make out Jack chasing the girls around. "I think it would be easier for me to live here and focus on the publishing company."

"You can't quit your degree after all you went through to get to uni," Emily said sternly.

"That's what Fraser said."

Lizzie's eyes lit up. "Have you been hanging out with him?"

"A bit. He shared his pizza with me." She stared at a wisp of steam coming off Lizzie's coffee. "And I found out why he agreed to marry me."

"Tell us then!" Emily said eagerly.

"Pity," she said.

Lizzie's features fell serious. "What?"

"He felt sorry for me. When I told him my parents wouldn't pay for uni, he felt sorry for me and wanted to help me."

Emily and Lizzie looked at each other, then shook their heads in unison.

"Why are you looking at me as though you don't believe me?" Scarlett asked. "That's what he said."

"He was lying." Emily took a sip of her coffee.

"How do you know?" Scarlett asked in confusion.

"It just doesn't ring true," Lizzie answered. "No guy would marry a woman he doesn't know out of the goodness of his heart."

"That's what he *said.* And I don't think he was lying."

"It might have been partly true," Emily said. "But I guess he also fancied you."

Scarlett sighed. "It's annoying how you have to turn everything into a romantic drama."

Lizzie drummed her nails on the side of her mug. "I think there's more to it. He must have some other reason."

"Maybe it was my personality," Scarlett said, turning her attention out of the window again.

"What?" Emily said, her voice slightly squeaky.

"Maybe he married me because of my sparkling personality." After managing to keep a straight face for a moment, she turned to Emily and Lizzie. Both of them were peering into their coffees while nodding slowly. Scarlett cracked up laughing. "That was a joke, but well done for not laughing."

Lizzie's face broke into a wide smile while Emily continued to look serious.

"I think you've got a great personality," she said, sounding flustered. "It might be an acquired taste, that's all."

The door opened and Jack burst in with Phoebe in his arms. Grinning, Scarlett moved over to them.

"Hi!" she said, taking Phoebe and giving her a hug. Max came in with Maya and closed the door behind him. Once Jack had taken his coat off, he hugged Scarlett, pressing his cold cheek against hers until she pushed him away.

"I haven't seen you for ages," he said.

"It hasn't been that long."

"It feels like it," he said, grinning at her.

Max took the girls' coats and hung them on the rack by the door. "I presume you three ladies have been talking about us while we weren't here," he said as he sat beside Lizzie. Phoebe climbed onto his lap and banged on the table.

"Do you really think we have nothing better to talk about?" Lizzie said, rolling her eyes.

"There *is* nothing better to talk about," Jack said, swinging Maya up in the air when she ran at his legs.

Scarlett wandered back to the counter to make hot chocolate for Jack and the twins. Jack liked cream and marshmallows on top, which Scarlett thought was pretty childlike. Max drank coffee. "We were actually talking about how my personality is an acquired taste," she said over the whir of the coffee machine.

"I'm a fan," Jack said immediately. "And I have very good taste."

"He does," Emily said with a cheeky grin.

"How's uni?" Max asked her.

The disastrous presentation sprang to mind, but she didn't want to share that. "Difficult. I keep thinking about quitting."

"Stick at it," Emily said. "You can achieve anything if you persevere."

Scarlett loaded the drinks onto a tray and took them to the table. "That's nice advice, but I'm starting to think that you live in a dreamland. You make everything into a romantic story, but it's not like that in the real world."

They all seemed very amused as Scarlett set the drinks out.

"That's my fault," Jack said, shuffling his chair closer to Emily and draping an arm around her shoulders. "Being married to me makes life feel like a fairy tale."

"Idiot," Emily said affectionately and gave him a quick kiss.

"How's it going with your husband?" Max said as Scarlett pulled up a chair to sit with them.

"Emily and Lizzie think he's a liar," she replied flatly.

"We didn't say that," Lizzie said. "Just that maybe he didn't tell you the whole truth."

Jack scooped the mini marshmallows out of his cup with a spoon and popped them in his mouth. "Everyone lies. Even married couples."

"Do they?" Emily said, looking at him accusingly.

He gave a smug smile. "Do you remember this morning when you said you were going to make me breakfast in bed?"

"That wasn't a lie! I meant it when I said it."

"The fact that *I* ended up making breakfast certainly made it seem like a lie."

"I got side-tracked with an idea for a scene in my book. If I didn't write it down, I'd have forgotten it."

"Okay," Jack said. "What about the other day when I asked if you thought I'd put weight on over Christmas … were you honest in your reply?"

"You do look as though you've put weight on," Scarlett said.

"See!" Jack beamed. "Scarlett's always honest."

"I hate liars," she said. Emily and Lizzie laughed as though she'd made a joke.

"If you're trying to claim you don't lie," Lizzie said, "I'd like to point out that Verity has no idea you're married."

"Withholding information isn't lying."

"It's very close," Emily argued. "And what about all the times you tell us that you can't publish your books yet because the third one isn't finished?"

"It *isn't* finished," Scarlett said adamantly.

"Oh, come on!" Lizzie shook her head. "We don't believe it. Just admit you're nervous about publishing your books."

"I *am* nervous." Actually, she was terrified. It had been hard enough asking Emily and Lizzie to read her books; the thought of anyone in the world being able to read them was horrifying.

That wouldn't stop her, though. "But book three really isn't finished. I'm stuck and I can't figure out how to end it."

"Do you want us to read what you've got so we can brainstorm ideas?" Lizzie suggested.

"No." Scarlett checked the time, then went to lock the door and switch the sign to closed. "I think I know what the end should be, I just can't get it quite right. And I don't have a lot of time at the moment."

"It all sounds like excuses," Lizzie said.

Jack gulped at his hot chocolate then wiped his top lip. "Leave her alone. The books will be published whenever Scarlett is ready. Don't pressure her."

Emily leaned her head on his shoulder. "It's not pressure. It's gentle encouragement."

"Like how I'm going to gently encourage you to go home soon," Scarlett said.

"Can't we have an after-hours party in the cafe?" Jack jumped up and went behind the counter. His eyes sparkled as he switched the radio on. "Who's up for a dance party?"

"Probably just you," Emily said.

Max raised an eyebrow. "I think you've overdone it on the sugar again, Jack."

"You guys don't know how to have fun!" Going back to the table, he lifted Maya from Lizzie's lap and danced around with her on his hip, making her giggle loudly.

Phoebe tugged on Scarlett's hand until she lifted her into her arms. Dancing around the cafe was pretty silly, but it made her laugh and was a good way to put off the drive back to Exeter.

CHAPTER 14

Scarlett was walking out of the kitchen when Fraser arrived home on Friday. He was deep in thought and didn't notice her until she spoke.

"Did you win a football match or something?" she asked.

"What?"

"You're smiling as though something amazing happened."

"I'm just happy it's Friday. I have plans to play video games all evening."

"Are your friends coming over?"

"No. I need a break from people."

"I know that feeling," she murmured.

"Are you going to be annoyed if I take over the living room?" He dropped his bag in the hallway. "I assumed you'd be going back to your aunt's place, but I can relocate to my room if I'm in your way."

"I'm going back to Hope Cove."

That was what he'd thought. He'd also never seen her in the living room. At least when he was at home, she stuck to her bedroom. Crouching to his bag, he opened the side pocket and pulled out a computer game.

Scarlett peered down at it. "Is that what I think it is?"

"It's just this space adventure game." Automatically, he hid it beside his leg.

"Space Crusading?"

"You know it?"

"Yes." She reached out and took it from him. "I love it."

He smiled at the delight in her eyes as she gazed at the box. "I had a phase when I was completely addicted to it," he told her. "My mum gave it to charity with a load of stuff and I was so annoyed with her. I just found it in a bargain bin at the games shop and thought I'd revisit it. I'm worried it's not as awesome as I remember."

"I can't believe you've got it. When I was fourteen I was pretty addicted to it. It's my favourite game ever." She handed the game back, then followed him into the living room.

"I don't think I've ever met anyone who's heard of it. It was made by this really small indie developer."

She perched on the arm of the couch. "I read that it was created by two guys in their basement."

"I'm seriously nervous that it's not as good as I remember," he said, sliding the disc into the console.

They locked eyes and grinned at each other as the familiar music began to play on the menu screen.

"I even love the music," she said, pressing a hand to her chest.

"Me too. I feel like I'm thirteen again. I played it obsessively for weeks. My mum would go crazy, shouting at me to come out of my room to eat. I'd totally lose track of everything else."

"Like you were in the game," she said, knowingly.

"Yeah! It was like I was living it. I don't even know why I love it so much. Whenever I try to describe it to anyone, it sounds lame."

As he scrolled through the menu screens, Scarlett moved to sit beside him on the couch. "I have to work on Sunday."

"In the cafe?"

"Yeah. I have to work every Sunday because I need the money."

He nodded, but was focused on the screen and wasn't really listening to her.

"Usually, I go back for the whole weekend because I prefer it to being here."

"Hmm." He swiped through the characters in their space-suits, then stopped abruptly. "*Usually?*"

"I don't have to. I was going to go back tonight because I have nothing better to do." She looked him right in the eyes and gave him a lop-sided smile.

His lips tugged upwards. "Are you suggesting a two-player?"

"I never get to play video games any more."

He laughed at the pleading in her eyes. Then he put a hand beside his face like a screen between them. "I thought you were supposed to have a problem with eye contact. Stop looking at me with your big, sad eyes. This is my alone time."

"Please," she said seriously.

He really had been looking forward to an evening on his own. Apparently that wasn't going to happen. As he stood, he growled in mock annoyance. After pulling out a second controller from the drawer under the TV, he gently threw it to Scarlett, then watched in shock as she raised her arms to her face and drew her knees towards her chest. The controller hit her elbow and tumbled to the floor.

"I can't catch," she said as she reached down for it. "Don't ever throw things to me."

"Good to know." He smiled in amusement and sat down again. "So who's your favourite character?"

"Ophelia."

He rolled his eyes. "Of course!"

"She's the best one," Scarlett said, beaming at the controller in her hands.

"I'm getting a cup of tea," Scarlett said, pausing the game for a second time that evening. In the first break, Fraser had made them toasted cheese sandwiches.

"I might have to go to bed soon," he said, yawning. After craving some time alone, it had actually been fun to hang out with Scarlett. He didn't have to make any effort around her, so it had been a relaxed evening.

"No!" she hissed. "We only just made it to the monkey planet. We can't stop now."

"We could sleep and play again tomorrow."

"Just a bit longer," she pleaded.

When she gazed at him with wide eyes, it was pretty hard to say no. "Okay, fine. I'll have a cup of tea then too."

Scarlett paused in the doorway. She opened her mouth, then stopped.

"What's wrong?" he asked, twisting around to face her.

"Should I make you a cup of tea?"

"Yeah, please."

"How do you like it?"

"However it comes."

"Right." She turned to leave then stopped again. "I'm not going to make it the way you make tea."

He squinted at her as he tried to figure out what she meant.

"You make tea with too much milk," she explained. "I'm not making it like that. It's offensive."

"To who?" he asked, amused.

"To tea. And people who drink tea properly, without destroying it with too much milk."

"However you make it will be fine."

"No. The way I make it will be perfect." She waltzed away to the kitchen and he leaned back on the couch, smiling to himself.

Five minutes later, she sat watching him sip at his steaming drink.

"I didn't expect Friday night to turn into a lesson on tea drinking," he said.

"Will you admit it's the best cup of tea you've ever tasted?"

"It's just tea. It doesn't taste much different to the way I make tea."

Slapping a hand across her forehead, Scarlett flopped back on the couch. "There's something wrong with your tastebuds. Maybe you should see a doctor."

Smiling, he set the mug on the coffee table and picked up the controller. "I really have to go to bed soon. It's one o'clock in the morning. You're ruining my plan for a weekend of detoxing and catching up on sleep."

"Do you go to parties every weekend?" she asked, reaching for her controller.

"Yeah. Pretty much. There's usually a party in the halls of residence, or we hit the bars and clubs. It gets a bit tiring after a while. But if you tell anyone I said that I'll deny it."

"Won't your friends be missing you?"

"I switched my phone off."

"When do you get your work done for uni?" she asked with her eyes on the TV. "You always seem to be playing sports or socialising."

He shrugged. "I go to the library between lectures. On Sundays I usually try and get something done. I just fit it in whenever I can."

"You're lucky that you don't have to work."

He wondered if that was a dig, but by the way she was so focused on the screen he decided she meant exactly what she'd said. From what he'd read about autism, he guessed she wasn't good at subtext. It was quite refreshing to be around someone who said exactly what they meant.

"Come on," she said, patting his leg and snapping him out of his trance. "Let's round up some monkeys."

"This game's kind of ridiculous," he remarked, his attention back on the screen.

"Don't you like it any more?"

"I love it. I'm just not sure why." He glanced at her, catching the look of rapt attention in her eyes and the hint of a smile at her lips. "My mum bought it for me one Christmas. I guess she just randomly picked out a game. I remember being disappointed because it wasn't anything I'd heard of."

"My parents wouldn't let me have a games console," Scarlett said, as their astronaut avatars ran through the forest. "So I used to play at my boyfriend's house. He had Space Crusading, but he didn't really like it. It annoyed him that I always wanted to play it."

"You had a boyfriend?"

"Yeah. No need to sound so surprised."

They were distracted by a bunch of monkeys on the screen and spent a while chasing them into cages for their removal to a different planet.

"I wasn't surprised that you had a boyfriend," Fraser finally said, when the game settled back to a calmer rhythm.

"Yes, you were."

"Okay. Maybe a little."

Scarlett kept her gaze on the screen and spoke quietly. "For most of secondary school I made a big effort to fit in. So believe it or not, I had quite a lot of friends … and a boyfriend."

"What happened?"

Scarlett concentrated on the game for a few minutes, and it seemed as though she wasn't going to answer.

"Something must have happened," he remarked as curiosity niggled at him. "You said you don't have friends now except the two women at the publishing company."

"Everything went wrong," she finally said. "My dog died right before I started my A-levels."

"Sorry," he muttered.

"I'd had Callie since I was five. She was the best dog in the world."

"My dog died a year ago," Fraser said, remembering the lovely golden retriever. "It's hard to lose a pet."

"Everyone thought I was being dramatic," she said, looking at him in earnest. "Nobody thought I should be so upset about a dog. I'd spent ages pretending to be someone else so I'd fit in, but I couldn't pretend not to be upset. And it made me realise that I didn't actually like any of my friends or my boyfriend. So I'd spent all that time and effort trying to fit in just so I could hang out with people who I didn't even like."

A lump had formed in Fraser's throat and he didn't know what to say. He wanted to say something to make her feel better, but emotional conversations made him uncomfortable. It was why he'd always avoided talking to Liam about his dad.

"So you stopped hanging out with them?" he asked gently.

She nodded, her eyes fixed on the controller in her hands. "I decided I didn't need friends. I focused on writing my books and didn't really care about anything else. I'd planned to go to uni because that seemed to be what everyone else my age was doing. But when I ditched my friends and went back to being my normal quirky self, my parents decided that university probably wouldn't be a good path for me."

"But you wanted to go anyway?"

"Not really. I was annoyed with them, but it was more on principle than because I actually cared about uni. I moved in with Auntie Verity to get away from my parents. Then I met Emily."

Fraser put his controller aside. "What happened with Emily?"

"She was nice to me." A slow smile pulled at her lips. "She was a writer so we had something in common. And she read my first book and told me I could publish it. She said I could do anything I wanted. Then I met Lizzie and she was lovely too." Her eyes sparkled as though she was remembering something funny. "It was the first time I'd had friends who I actually liked, so I was terrified they'd realise I was weird and not want to be friends with me. And because I was nervous I did some really stupid things … but they kept being friends with me anyway."

"What did you do?" he asked.

She shook her head and laughed. "I don't want to say."

"I promise I won't laugh."

She grimaced and seemed to be debating whether to say more. "Emily had been so kind and I wanted to do something for her in return. So I set up this book event in the cafe for the release of her book. I made flyers and put them up all around Hope Cove."

"That sounds like a nice thing to do."

"Yeah." Scarlett grimaced again. "But Auntie Verity told me it would have been a good idea to ask Emily first."

He pressed his lips together and stifled a laugh. "Oops!"

"You promised not to laugh," she reminded him.

He managed to keep his lips in a straight line. "I'm not laughing."

"I think you're laughing on the inside, so I'm not going to tell you about any of the other stupid things I've done. The point is, Emily and Lizzie never laugh at me, and they don't seem to care that I can be a bit odd. Lizzie even trusts me to look after her kids." She turned and caught him staring at her and he looked away quickly.

"Do you want to play some more?" she asked.

He'd happily have sat and chatted to her for longer, but she looked suddenly self-conscious as though she'd got carried away and said too much. After the intense conversation, he'd lost interest in the game. "I need to go to bed," he told her. "But maybe we could play again tomorrow."

~

Instead of going to bed, Scarlett got her laptop out and did some work on her novel, re-writing one scene and tweaking others. When she finally tried to sleep, she struggled to switch her thoughts off and replayed her conversations with Fraser that evening. She'd probably said too much, but it had been easy to talk to him. Somehow, she had the feeling that he understood her. A little bit, at least.

When the morning sunlight flooded into her room, she was wide awake and staring at the ceiling. She rarely bothered to close the curtains. Given how rare it was for her to be asleep when the sun rose, it didn't seem like something she needed to remember.

For a while she hung around on the landing, listening for sounds of Fraser being awake. When all was quiet she went down to make a coffee and pace the kitchen, occasionally looking overhead when she thought she heard the slightest sound. At nine, she contemplated knocking on his door to wake him up. Except his bedroom was off-limits and she didn't know if that included the door.

In the end she walked to the local shop to get ingredients for breakfast. Rashers of bacon were crackling in the pan when Fraser walked into the kitchen in a pair of jogging bottoms and his University of Exeter hoodie.

He lifted both arms above his head, yawning as he stretched. His top rose up to reveal taut skin at his midriff. "That smells amazing."

"I'm making bacon and eggs if you want some?" Fat popped in the pan and she shuffled the bacon around.

"Yes, please." He sat at the table and rocked his head from shoulder to shoulder as though he was still stiff. "Do you need any help?"

"No." She got plates out and began to divide the bacon between them, then added the scrambled eggs from the other pan. Setting them on the table, she went back for cutlery. "I was thinking we could have breakfast and then play video games," she said as she sat down.

Fraser rubbed sleep from his eyes, then gave her a quizzical look. "Did you cook bacon to wake me up?"

"Yes. It always wakes me up when Auntie Verity cooks bacon."

"You woke me up to play video games?"

"You said we could."

"Yeah, but you didn't have to wake me up. You could have played without me."

"Oh." She pushed eggs onto her fork. "I didn't know that."

"It doesn't matter. I'm quite happy to get a cooked breakfast." He grinned at her with a mouthful of bacon. "I can't play for long though. I've got an assignment I need to get on with, and I've got a football match later."

"Okay."

"How long have you been awake?" he asked.

"I don't know. Quite a while."

"You must have hardly slept."

"I don't think I need as much sleep as most people."

Fraser chewed slowly, then tapped his fork lightly against the edge of the plate. "Is that part of … your thing?"

"What thing?"

He swallowed even though she was fairly sure he didn't have any food in his mouth. "You know how you were saying that you're different …"

From the way he was talking, it was as though she'd told him she had superpowers. All she'd meant was that she didn't generally understand people and they didn't seem to understand her. "How long do most people sleep?" she asked.

"Seven to nine hours is considered optimal." He loaded up his fork. "It came up on my course recently."

"I definitely don't sleep for that long. Not all at once anyway. Which is handy because I get a lot of work done at night. It's probably my most productive time."

"So you never sleep all through the night?"

"Maybe sometimes. If I'm really tired." She put a mouthful of eggs in her mouth. "When I was a kid, Mum used to get so annoyed with me for not sleeping. She used to make me take melatonin but it didn't really help. I'd fall asleep easier but wouldn't stay asleep for long." She paused and loaded up her fork again. "Sorry. I'm talking too much." That seemed to be becoming a habit around Fraser.

"Your mum doesn't sound as though she has a lot of patience," he said softly.

"Not with me. I think pretty much everything about me annoys her." She pushed her plate away. "You can have the rest of my bacon if you want. I've had enough."

"Thanks." He took it with his fingers and ate it in one go. Then grinned at her. "Let's go and discover new planets."

CHAPTER 15

"Scarlett!" Emily barked the following Saturday morning.

"What?" She was standing by the living room window in the flat above the cafe, watching heavy rain fall over the deserted beach.

"I said your name three times. You were miles away."

"If I was miles away I'd never have heard you. I just wasn't listening."

"Do you have an opinion on these?" Emily held up a post-card-sized paper with gold lettering on it.

"I don't think it matters what I think of them, considering you've already ordered them."

"You weren't here," Lizzie said. "And we need to send out invitations for the launch party soon. We had to order them. I think they look good."

"Are you annoyed that we didn't run it by you?" Emily asked.

"No." Scarlett watched a raindrop trickle down the window-pane. "I don't care. There's just no point in you asking what I think now. Why do people ask for an opinion if they don't really want it?"

There was a short silence.

"Is everything okay with you?" Emily asked, walking over and touching Scarlett's arm.

"Yes." She moved to sit in the office chair at Lizzie's desk in the corner.

"Is uni okay?" Lizzie asked. "You're not still thinking of dropping out are you?"

"No. I want to get my degree. And it would be a bit stupid to quit after I went to so much effort to get there."

"Exactly." Emily smiled brightly. "You'll be glad you stuck at it when you have a degree."

"How is it living with Fraser?" Lizzie asked.

"Fine." She swivelled on the chair. "We played video games together last weekend."

"Cute!" Emily cooed.

Scarlett rolled her eyes. "It was video games not a candlelit dinner."

"It sounds romantic to me," Emily said. "It's nice that you're hanging out with him."

"It's okay." Scarlett continued to swing the chair from side to side. "The other week he drove me to uni so I wouldn't get wet in the rain."

"That was sweet of him," Emily said with an annoying dreamy look in her eyes.

"And when I locked myself out he made me a cup of tea because I'd been waiting on the doorstep and I was cold."

"He sounds lovely," Lizzie said.

"There was too much milk in the tea."

"He needs some training, that's all." Emily tucked a strand of hair behind her ear. "All husbands need a bit of training."

"You know I'm not really married to him, don't you? We have a piece of paper, that's all."

"The piece of paper means you're married," Emily said. "I keep thinking about it and it's really romantic to get married for a student loan."

"You think everything is romantic," Scarlett said. "That's why you write romance novels for a living."

"Do you really not fancy him? Even a little bit. He's very good looking."

"No." She planted her feet on the floor to stop the swaying.

"You look as though you're not sure that's true," Lizzie said, smiling.

"I like hanging out with him, that's all." At least that was all she was willing to admit to. Even if she did fancy him, the feeling was unlikely to be reciprocated.

"Maybe you should hang out with him more," Emily said. "You never know what might develop."

Scarlett frowned. "He's always busy. I don't see him much."

"You need to engineer ways to spend time with him," Emily said.

"How can I find ways to hang out with him when he's never at home?"

Emily's eyes lit up at the question. "You need to find a mutual interest."

"I did. Video games. But he doesn't have time for video games. He has a hectic social life, and he plays a lot of sport. He's on the football team."

"Could you take an interest in that? Go and watch one of his games maybe?"

"No," Lizzie groaned. "Don't do that. Just ask him out for a drink. Be casual."

Emily sighed. "I think he'd like it if you took an interest in his football games. But you could ask him out for a drink too."

"I have an idea," Lizzie said. "You can invite him to the launch party for the publishing company."

Scarlett slouched down in the chair. "You'd probably embarrass me."

"Emily might," Lizzie agreed with a smirk.

"I promise I'll be on my best behaviour," Emily said. "There'll be no matchmaking from me."

"He probably wouldn't want to come anyway."

Lizzie held out one of the invitations. "It can't hurt to ask."

"I'll think about it," Scarlett said, taking the invitation.

It was Friday afternoon before she saw Fraser, so she'd had plenty of time to mull over the idea of inviting him to the launch party. She'd come to the conclusion that if it came up in conversation it would be rude not to invite him. So she just needed to figure out a way to bring it up.

She wandered out of the kitchen and into the hallway when she heard him come in the front door, but he only called hello as he dashed up the stairs. Murmuring a pointless greeting, she returned to the kitchen. About a minute later, he thundered back down the stairs and dropped his sports bag before striding into the kitchen.

"I forgot my football kit this morning," he said as he opened the fridge. "We've got a game in an hour and I'm starving." He grabbed a block of cheddar and the butter, then reached for the loaf of sliced white bread.

Scarlett remembered Emily's advice about taking an interest in his football games. "Who are you playing against?"

"Just a friendly against the second team."

"Where do you play?"

"It's on one of the pitches at Streatham campus."

She didn't know anything about football so wasn't sure what else to say on the subject. "I haven't seen you all week," she remarked, taking a seat at the table.

"I've been pretty busy."

"Me too." She sat up straighter. "I've been organising a launch party for the publishing company with Lizzie and Emily. There's a lot to do."

"That's cool."

"Yeah. You could come if you want."

"What?" he mumbled through a mouthful of sandwich.

"To the launch party. I'm allowed to invite whoever I want."

"Oh, yeah maybe. When is it?"

"The weekend we finish for the Easter break."

"I'll try."

"Great." She shifted in her seat, watching as he took another bite of his sandwich. "I was thinking I should get more involved in uni life too. The social side, I mean."

"Good idea." He flashed her a brief smile and moved to the door.

Hopping up, she followed him into the hallway. "Maybe we could go out for a drink one night?"

"Sounds good." He swung his bag onto his shoulder.

"I heard some of the bars on campus are fun. Some people on my course were talking about going to the Ram Bar."

"Yeah, it's a laugh in there. We'll be there tonight after the match. It's always busy on Fridays."

"Maybe I could come and watch one of your matches sometime too. It'd be cool to see you play."

"Sure." He gave another quick smile as he picked up his car key. "I have to go. See ya."

The Ram Bar was always busy at the weekend and that particular Friday was no different. A hum of conversations filled the air. One section of the large room had been taken over by the football team, and Fraser rolled his eyes when one of the lads suggested a drinking game. He moved away from them as he caught sight of Bridget heading in his direction. She was cute and chirpy with glossy blonde hair and increasingly showed up in whichever bar the football team were in after a game or training.

"How was the game?" she asked after giving him a hug in greeting. They only knew each other from bumping into each other in the student bars, but they'd become pretty familiar.

Once or twice Fraser had thought about asking her on a date but wasn't sure he wanted to go there.

"You didn't come and watch?" he asked.

"God, no. It's bloody freezing standing around on the sidelines."

"It was a good match," he said with a smile. "We won."

"Score any goals?"

"One."

"The celebrating looks to be in full swing." She nodded to Simon, who was downing a pint of lager while the rest of the team cheered him on.

"It was only a friendly against the second team," Fraser said, watching beer dribble down Simon's chin as he finished the pint. Someone was timing how fast everyone could down a pint and he knew he'd get dragged over for a turn before too long. "How's everything with you?" he asked, turning his attention back to Bridget.

"Pretty good, thanks. Coursework is pretty full on at the moment so I'm looking forward to a break over Easter …" She continued, telling him about a trip to Italy that she had planned but he'd stopped paying attention. He could've sworn he saw Scarlett, but a group of lads had blocked his view. As he tried to focus on what Bridget was saying, his gaze kept drifting over her shoulder. Finally, a tall guy moved out of the way and he spotted Scarlett sitting at the bar, looking straight at him.

"I'm really sorry," he said, touching Bridget's elbow. "I just need to check on my housemate. Sorry. I'll be back in a minute." He was being rude, but it wasn't as though he could concentrate on the conversation with Scarlett staring at him.

"What are you doing here?" he asked when he reached her.

"You said we should have a drink together some time."

He dragged his hand through his hair and scratched the back of his head. "I didn't realise you meant tonight."

"I was going to go back to Hope Cove, but I thought I could

hang around so I could watch your match and have a drink with you."

"You were at the game?"

"Yeah. My toes went a bit numb but it was fun to watch." She put a hand on his arm and smiled widely. "You're really good. I saw you score the goal."

"Yeah." His mind whirred. He'd had no idea she'd been there. On dark winter evenings the floodlit pitch made it difficult to see who was spectating.

"Do you want to sit down?" she said, trailing her hand down his shirt sleeve and brushing her fingers over the back of his hand.

He perched on the stool beside her and took a swig of his beer.

She looked right into his eyes and beamed. "You said you're not good enough to play professionally but I really think you are."

"Trust me, I'm not." He glanced back at the football crowd who were chanting while another of the lads took a turn at chugging a pint. Bridget must have gone back to whichever friends she'd been with.

"Footballers all have great legs," Scarlett said, drawing his attention again.

He blinked a few times, wondering if he'd heard right. "What?" Why was she acting so strangely?

She leaned a little closer. "You look really good in shorts. Your legs are so muscly."

"Thanks." He'd thought he was used to her odd behaviour, but she was making him decidedly uncomfortable. They'd descended into silence when Simon came over.

"Don't think you can hide behind your wife. It's your turn to chug."

"I'll come in a minute," he said.

Brett appeared behind him and planted his hands heavily on

Fraser's shoulders. "What's the deal with that Bridget girl? Have you got dibs or is she fair game?"

"I'll be over in a minute," Fraser said, shrugging him off as he stood up.

From across the room, he could hear the rest of the team chanting his name. When Simon shoved him in that direction, it seemed pointless to resist. Someone passed him a pint of lager when he reached the table and he took a deep breath before putting it to his lips. It felt as though he was gulping endlessly before he finally reached the bottom of the glass.

He ignored the guy telling him his time and turned on his heel. Striding back across the bar, he cursed whoever's stupid idea the drinking games were. He'd felt Scarlett staring at him the whole time, and the look of disapproval on her face made him think of Allie. They were quite alike in their ability to make him feel like a crap human being with only a look.

"It's a drinking game," he said, in case it wasn't obvious. "It's easier to go along with it than to argue."

She didn't say anything for a moment and he put a hand on the bar to balance himself as the beer took immediate effect.

"It's really loud in here," she said, glancing around.

"It always gets rowdy in the student bars on the weekends."

She put a hand on his arm. "Do you want to go somewhere else? We could find somewhere quieter? Or hang out at home?"

He swallowed hard as she stroked his arm. "I have to hang out with the team. I really didn't think you were talking about tonight when you mentioned going for a drink."

"I thought it would be fun."

His head was pretty fuzzy after downing the beer, but he could have sworn she was fluttering her eyelashes. And why was she stroking his arm? He pulled away, irritated. "You shouldn't have just turned up. I have to go and hang out with my friends."

"I can wait here for you."

"No." He shook his head. "You can't sit and watch me all

evening. It's creepy." As her smile fell away, he felt a heaviness in his chest. "Sorry. But I can't hang out with you tonight."

"That's okay." She slipped off the stool. "We can go out another night. Somewhere quieter."

"Maybe. I don't know. Let's talk tomorrow."

Re-joining his teammates, Fraser had lost all enthusiasm for the evening.

"What was the ball and chain doing here?" Simon asked. "Come to check up on you?"

"Shut up," Fraser hissed. Simon rolled his eyes and wandered away.

"Hey!" Brett called to him. He was sitting at a table with a tray of shots in front of him. "Do you want one?"

"Yes." He sat down and knocked back a drink, then immediately reached for another. The alcohol did nothing to erase the image of Scarlett fluttering her eyelashes at him. It only served to make him more annoyed.

After snapping at a few of his teammates he called it a night and stumbled into a taxi to go home.

Groggily, he padded downstairs late the following morning and made himself a coffee, hoping it might soothe his pounding head. He was slouched at the kitchen table when he heard the creak of the stairs. He'd assumed Scarlett would have gone back to Hope Cove but apparently not.

"Morning," she said cheerfully. "How was the rest of your night?"

"Fine," he muttered.

"I don't know why your friends are obsessed with drinking beer as fast as possible. It's really stupid. And if you don't want to do it, why don't you just say so?"

He took a swig of his coffee. "You wouldn't understand."

"The way they talk about women is offensive too. Doesn't it annoy you?"

He pushed his palms to his temples, trying not to let her get to him. "I didn't invite you," he said through gritted teeth.

"What?"

"I didn't invite you out, so it's pretty rude of you to complain about my friends."

"Do you actually like them?"

"Yes." He gave a humourless laugh. "That's why they're my friends."

She tapped on the doorframe. "Do you want to play video games?"

"No," he snapped. "I don't want to play video games with you. I don't want you gate crashing my nights out. And I find it creepy that you showed up at my match."

Scarlett frowned. "I only wanted to see you play."

"But we're not friends." Standing, he took his mug to the sink. "We agreed we'd get married for the paperwork, so you could get your loan. We said we'd live together for three years and then get divorced. That's all I agreed to. I can't deal with anything else."

"You don't want to be friends?"

He took a deep breath. It seemed as though no matter what he did, he always ended up the bad guy. He'd done her a favour by marrying her, but he didn't want to spend his uni life feeling responsible for her. Especially not when she invaded his social life and acted so oddly.

"We're very different," he said slowly. "We have different lives and interests. I don't see how we'd ever really be friends."

Scarlett nodded and he was grateful that she hadn't burst into tears. He felt a churning in his gut nonetheless as she turned to leave. Marrying her had been a mistake. He hadn't even known her, so he should never have felt the need to help her. If she'd had to wait a year to start uni, so what? That wasn't his problem.

"Remember when you were saying about quitting your course?" he blurted out as she stepped into the hallway. "Did you think any more about it?"

"No," she said quietly. "I want to finish the course. It's hard but I think I can do it."

He stared at her back. "You might have been right about focusing on the publishing company. It makes sense. You don't even need a degree now, do you? And if you quit the course, we could get a divorce and you wouldn't have to worry about getting found out."

She stayed quiet for a moment and he had an inkling that she might agree with him. It was true, after all: she didn't actually need a degree. Maybe they could undo the mess they'd got themselves into and he could enjoy the rest of his time at uni.

Finally, she turned back to him, the defiance in her eyes telling him she wasn't going to let him off the hook. "I want to get my degree," she said firmly.

Fraser massaged his temples as his headache increased. "Fine. But we need to have more rules. You can't show up at my matches or when I'm out with friends. We live in the same house but that's all."

She nodded, and from the look on her face he was fairly sure she hated him enough that she wouldn't want to have anything to do with him anyway.

His stomach twisted as she walked away. He wished he hadn't upset her, but knew it was for the best in the long run.

CHAPTER 16

"You've been keeping a low profile," Jack said, wandering into the kitchen at the back of the cafe.

"Is it rude that I've skipped out?" Scarlett asked as she washed wine glasses. The launch party seemed to have gone well, and she'd been as sociable as she could until she completely ran out of energy and small talk.

"No." He picked up a tea towel and began drying the glasses on the draining board. "There are only a few people left and they seem to be the ones who took advantage of the free alcohol. Lizzie's been dropping hints that they should leave, but it's not working. It's the authors … I think they spend so much time hidden away that when they do go out they get a bit crazy."

"Not me," Scarlett said. "I'd rather stay hidden away all the time."

"I thought you'd have been the life and soul this evening. It's the official launch of the publishing company. It was all your idea."

"If you thought I'd be the life of the party I'm not sure you really know me at all."

He chuckled. "You must be proud of yourself though. It's all down to you."

"No, it's not. It was my idea but Lizzie and Emily have done most of the work."

"Are you annoyed with them for taking over?"

"Is that what Emily thinks?" As she dunked a glass, drops of water splashed onto her face.

"She was a bit worried, yeah."

"I'm not annoyed. It's good for me that they took over. There's a lot of stuff I'm not good at. I couldn't have organised a launch party, and they did the interview with the woman from the local paper. No way I could do that. Even talking to the authors is hard for me. Lizzie and Emily sound so professional. I'm sure most people think I'm the work experience girl or something. Which is fine by me."

"There's also stuff that you're good at that Lizzie and Emily are hopeless at."

"Yeah. I know. We all have strengths. And mine isn't listening to drunk authors drone on about their books at the end of the evening." She set the glass on the rack and reached for the next.

"I thought you might bring Fraser along so I can vet him. It hardly seems fair that Lizzie and Emily have met him and not me."

"You won't be meeting him." Another splash hit her nose as she dunked the glass too forcefully.

"That doesn't sound like things are going too well. Which is completely different to what Emily tells me."

She snorted a laugh. "Because Emily has invented a story where Fraser is madly in love with me. She might need to switch from writing romance to fantasy."

"Is it okay living with him though?"

"I guess so. I got a student loan thanks to him, and I get to live in a pretty nice student house very cheaply." She bit her lip as she suppressed a grin.

"What's funny about that?"

"Nothing. But I suspect the rent isn't cheap at all. I can't afford much and Fraser kept saying his parents would pay, which I said no to on principle. Then he came up with this story about how his dad is friends with the landlord so it's cheap." She raised her eyebrows at Jack. "Do you think people who rent out student houses give mates' rates that are about a third of what they could actually charge?"

"It's sounds a bit fishy," he agreed. "I take it you didn't quiz him too much?"

"No. All the places within my budget were awful. I don't really blame him for lying."

"Do you see much of him?"

"Not any more. We're just housemates. We ignore each other."

She'd been trying not to think about the disastrous night of his football game. Especially because she wasn't entirely clear about what had happened. When she'd spoken to him beforehand he'd definitely said they should hang out socially. She'd made a lot of effort too. While she'd been waiting in the bar after the game, she'd watched a girl flirting with another member of the football team and copied the way she'd acted. It hadn't gone down as well with Fraser though.

Now he didn't even want to be friends with her. She pushed the thought aside and concentrated on washing the glasses.

"You must be too busy to worry about boys anyway," Jack said. "It's amazing how you juggle so much."

"I'm very busy," she agreed.

"Any chance you might publish your own books soon, or are you sticking to publishing other people's books?"

"I'll publish my own too. One day. I'm not sure when." She stopped abruptly and turned to Jack. "I've been saying that for ages."

"So?"

"So I should do it. I don't want to be someone who just talks about doing something."

"You should do it then," Jack said.

"I'm going to." She slapped a wet hand against Jack's to high-five him.

Getting her own books ready to publish would mean that she'd have absolutely no spare time. So there'd be no time to worry about where she'd gone wrong with Fraser.

~

"How's your genius wife?" Liam asked, settling back in his chair in the corner of the Thorverton Arms on Easter Monday. For the past half hour, Fraser's conversation with Allie and Liam had revolved around uni and their respective courses, but he'd known it was only a matter of time before they asked about Scarlett.

He rolled his eyes. "She's not a genius."

"She has her own publishing company and a part-time job and is studying for a degree," Liam said.

"That just means she's busy. Not a genius."

"How's it going living with her?" Allie asked.

Picking up a spare beer mat, Fraser tapped it against the table as he debated how to answer. "It would definitely be better to live alone. But we agreed we'll stay out of each other's way from now on so hopefully it will be fine."

"Did something happen?" Allie asked. "Please tell me you didn't sleep with her and make things awkward?"

"No." He pushed the coaster aside. "I actually thought we might be friends, but then she went all weird on me."

"How so?" Liam asked.

"I think she fancies me."

"You think everyone fancies you," Allie said, giving him a friendly shove.

"That's not true." He raised an eyebrow. "Just most people."

"Did Scarlett make a move?" Liam asked.

"You could say that. She turned up to watch me play football, then came to the bar afterwards and did the whole giggly girlie routine – touching my arm and batting her eyelashes and laughing at nothing in particular."

"That's strange," Allie mused. "When we met her she didn't seem like that type at all."

Fraser nodded. "She wasn't like that before. Which is why I thought we could be friends. But I can't be friends with her if she fancies me. That's going to get awkward fast. So I told her we were housemates and that was all."

"It sounds as though things are already awkward," Allie said.

Fraser shrugged. "I think I've nipped it in the bud. I was pretty clear."

"Was she upset?"

He paused to take a swig of his pint. "She didn't say much, but I got that impression. What was I supposed to do, though?"

"I think you did the right thing," Allie said sympathetically. "You can't let her think something might happen if you're not interested in her. I'm assuming you're not interested?"

"No. I liked hanging out with her, but I don't want anything more than friendship."

"Why?" Liam asked. "Because she's autistic?"

"It's not that." He wasn't entirely sure that was true. The autism made him nervous, but he supposed if he really liked her, it wouldn't stop him. "I just don't think of her like that."

"You did when you first met her," Liam pointed out. "And I find it highly suspicious that she's the only girl you talk about these days."

"That's true," Allie said, catching a drop of condensation as it ran down the side of her glass. "Is there really no one you're interested in?"

"There's this one girl, Bridget, who hangs around quite a bit. She keeps hinting that we should go out just the two of us."

"Are you going to?" Liam asked.

"Maybe. I don't know."

"You don't exactly sound smitten." Allie took a sip of wine, a mischievous sparkle in her eyes. "I reckon you have a crush on Scarlett and you're in denial about it."

"I don't have a crush on Scarlett," he said firmly.

"That's the denial talking," Allie said. "You seem different since you met her. Calmer."

"I think that has more to do with not living with my annoying parents any more."

"Your parents are great." Allie clicked her tongue. "It's definitely Scarlett. Can you just admit that you have a thing for your wife?"

"Can we not refer to her as my wife? I don't have a thing for Scarlett. She's my housemate. That's it." Leaning back in his chair, he folded his arms across his chest. "I'm probably going to ask Bridget out."

Allie rolled her eyes. "Denial, denial, denial!"

CHAPTER 17

The summer term passed in a haze of studying and football and parties. Fraser went on one date with Bridget before deciding life was easier without romantic complications. He ignored the voice in the back of his head that told him the reason he was avoiding romantic entanglements was because he was married. It had occurred to him while he was out with Bridget that any relationship would either involve him lying a lot or explaining that he had a wife. That would be an interesting conversation.

He hardly saw anything of Scarlett that term. They exchanged polite greetings when they encountered each other but nothing more. Soon the first year would be over and Scarlett would go back to Hope Cove for the summer, leaving Fraser with the house to himself.

Two weeks before the end of term he was sitting on his bed, scrolling through social media on his phone, when a knock came at his door.

"Yeah?" he called.

"I have a question," Scarlett said, her voice sounding strained.

"Come in."

The door opened but she stayed on the threshold, shifting her weight from foot to foot.

"What's up?" he asked.

"I made a mistake and I'm trying to fix it but sometimes I get things backwards." She pushed her palm to her forehead. "Sometimes I think I'm not supposed to do something but then I find out it's fine. So I'm confused."

"You and me both," he said, swinging his legs off the bed as he sat up. "Explain the problem and maybe I can help." He'd been happy with their recent arrangement of living together without any other expectations, but when she knocked on his door asking for help he was hardly going to send her away.

She took a few steps onto the landing, then came back to the door, talking fast. "I got the dates mixed up for my assignment. I thought I had to hand it in next week but I have to hand it in tomorrow. It's finished but no one has proofread it. Usually I give my assignments to Lizzie or Emily to read because I'm dyslexic and I make a lot of mistakes. So I need to get one of them to read it for me, but Lizzie said once that I shouldn't call after ten o'clock unless it's an emergency. It's only quarter past ten so I don't know if it would be okay. And I think this is an emergency, but I don't know if it has to be life-threatening for it to be an emergency…"

"Scarlett!" He held a hand up. "Slow down."

Tears shone in her eyes. "Can you just tell me if it's okay to call Lizzie now or not?"

"You probably shouldn't. She has small kids, right?"

"Yes, and she's pregnant."

"I wouldn't call so late."

She bobbed her head repeatedly. "If I call her in the morning it will be too late. I have to hand the assignment in before midday."

"How long is it?"

"About 2,000 words. It's a short story for my creative writing class."

"I guess I can look over it, if you want?"

She stopped pacing and finally met his eye. "You can proofread it?"

"Yeah."

Her eyes rolled upwards and she seemed to be deep in thought. "You might not like it. It's a short story involving the main characters from my books."

"Does it matter if I like it? I thought you just want someone to proofread it, not critique it."

"Yes. I do. But it might be boring for you. And I don't usually let anyone other than Lizzie and Emily read what I write."

"I thought you wanted to publish your books one day? You might need to get over the fear of people reading your stuff."

"I'll just hand it in as it is," she said huffily. "The marks for this year aren't counted towards the final grade anyway, so if I get a bad mark it doesn't matter."

Fraser rubbed his hands over his face as she strode out of the room. It was much easier when they ignored each other. "Scarlett!" he shouted. "Email it to me and I can read through it now. I'll just look for mistakes and not comment on the story or anything."

He half expected her to ignore him, but his phone beeped with a new email a moment later. Moving to his desk, he opened the document on his laptop.

"I emailed it to you," Scarlett said, appearing in the doorway again.

"I've got it."

"Can I come in?"

"Yes," he said with a curt nod.

"I don't know if you'll enjoy it." She hovered behind him. "It's probably not really your thing. And short stories are difficult. You don't have a lot of time for world-building or to give a good sense of the characters in a way that makes the reader care about them. I guess that's the point of the assignment."

He glanced up at her. "I thought you only wanted me to check your spelling and stuff."

"Yes. Please. It shouldn't take too long."

"It would probably be quicker if you weren't standing over me."

"Sorry," she said, taking a few steps away. When he looked up again, she was gazing at his bookshelf. She ran a finger over the spines, then stopped abruptly. Fraser grimaced as she tapped the book about autism. She'd never talked about it directly and had only danced around the subject.

"You cover a lot of interesting stuff on your course," she finally said as her finger continued to graze over the books. He breathed a sigh of relief that she hadn't commented on the books about autism. He'd read up on it to try to understand her better, but she might find that a bit odd. Or maybe she'd appreciate the gesture and try to be friends with him again. Either way, it was better not to broach the subject.

"If you want me to read this, it would be easier if you left me alone," he said.

"Oh, okay. Let me know when you've finished."

Once she'd left it didn't take him long to read the document. Reaching the end, he sat staring at the screen for a couple of minutes, then realised he hadn't done a great job of proofreading and went through it more carefully. After making the corrections, he sent the document back to her, then wandered to her room. The door was wide open and she sat in the middle of the bed, chewing on her thumbnail.

"I only found a few mistakes," he said, making her head shoot up to look at him. "I fixed them and highlighted them so you can see what I did."

"Thank you." She pulled her laptop onto her knees and opened it up.

Fraser turned to leave, then hesitated. "You didn't want me to comment on the story or anything, right?"

"No." She looked at him with eyes full of uncertainty.

"Okay." He rocked on his heels. "It's really good, though."

"You think so?" she asked in a rush.

He nodded. "I had to read it twice because the first time I was too engrossed to look for mistakes. It's really great."

"I was thinking I could put it on my website as a teaser for the books."

"It definitely made me want to read more."

She pressed her lips together but her eyes sparkled. "I'm going to publish the first book in September."

As their eyes locked, he smiled widely, then left her alone.

~

When he came in from uni the following afternoon, Fraser heard movement in the living room and went to the doorway to look in. Scarlett stood in the middle of the room with her hands behind her back.

"Did you hand your assignment in?" he asked.

"Yes. Thanks for your help with it."

"You're welcome. Not that you really needed any help."

She gave a nervous smile and slipped past him.

"You don't have to clear out of the living room on my account." He'd never seen her in the living room before and had a horrible feeling that she might feel she shouldn't be there when he was around. Surely she didn't disappear to her room whenever she thought he was coming home.

"It's okay. I've got some stuff to do. And I'll probably head back to Hope Cove soon."

He watched her set off up the stairs. "I'm going out again in a bit anyway. If you want to watch TV go ahead."

"I wasn't watching TV," she said, stopping on the stairs.

"What were you doing then?" he asked, confused by why she seemed so cagey.

Her shoulders sagged. "Okay, I was watching TV. But it's the first time. I promise."

"The first time you've watched TV?" he asked slowly.

"No. The first time I've watched *your* TV."

He looked towards the living room, then back up at Scarlett. "You never watch TV in the living room?"

"No. Just today because I handed my final assignment in for the year so I thought I'd do something fun, and there's this TV series I keep hearing about but it's only on Netflix and I don't have Netflix. I'm sorry. I shouldn't have watched. Especially not without asking."

A lump formed in his throat and he cast his gaze down, unable to look at her.

"Are you upset with me?" she asked.

He shook his head and inhaled deeply. "Have you really spent a year thinking you can't watch TV in the living room?"

"It's your TV. All the stuff in the living room is yours so I thought I shouldn't."

"But I told you that you can use the games console," he said.

"I didn't know if you just meant that one time. And then you said we aren't friends so I definitely thought I couldn't use your stuff."

"Of course you can use it." What kind of monster did she think he was that he wouldn't let her watch the TV? "If you weren't sure you should have asked."

"Sorry." Her eyes darted upwards. "I didn't know. I always get stuff like that wrong."

"It's fine," he said gently. "I didn't mean to snap. I should have made it clear when we moved in. You can use any of the stuff in the living room. Any time. Okay?"

Her eyes stayed fixed on the ceiling. "I can't afford to pay."

"Why would you have to pay?"

"Because Netflix costs money and if I watch then I should pay, but I don't have much money."

Fraser's throat burned as he thought about the rent money she was paying that was sitting in his account. He'd much rather she kept it, but he knew she'd refuse if he mentioned it. She'd probably also be annoyed if she found out it wasn't actually going towards the rent. He'd stick to his plan and find a way to give it back to her when they finished uni.

"My parents pay for the Netflix account. It doesn't make any difference if you watch it." He tried to meet her eye but she wouldn't look at him. "Why don't you carry on watching now? I'm going out so you'll have the place to yourself."

"I should probably get back to Hope Cove."

"Please stay and watch. I feel bad that you thought you couldn't."

"So you'll feel better if I watch Netflix for the evening?"

He caught the gentle twitch of her lips and smiled back at her. "Yes."

"I suppose I could then." Slowly, she walked back down the stairs.

"What are you watching?"

"This new series about vampires. I like anything to do with vampires."

"I think I've heard about it." He told her to enjoy it and went upstairs.

As he got ready to go out, his mind refused to focus on anything other than the fact that Scarlett had spent the whole time they'd been living together thinking she wasn't allowed to hang out in the living room. It was a stark reminder of how much more difficult life was for her. On top of everything else she had to deal with, she'd also had him telling her he didn't want anything to do with her and spending months pretending she didn't exist. All because of his stupid ego.

The hum of the TV drifted from the living room when he returned downstairs. Instead of going straight out, he went to the kitchen and flicked the kettle on.

Scarlett moved her head in his direction when he walked into the living room but didn't take her eyes from the TV.

"I'm going out now," he said. "But I made you a cup of tea."

She whipped her gaze up to him as he set it on the coffee table. “Thank you.”

“You’re welcome. I tried not to put too much milk in, but it’s probably not up to your standards.” She gave him a quick smile, then shifted her attention back to the TV. He’d intended to apologise for the way he’d treated her, but she didn’t seem keen on the interruption.

The cup of tea was clearly an apology anyway.

CHAPTER 18

Scarlett worked at the cafe five days a week over the summer. Whenever she felt as though she'd reached her limit of holidaymakers with their odd accents and loud kids, she reminded herself that if Fraser hadn't agreed to marry her, she'd have been working in the cafe all year and not just the summer. And if her mum had got her way, it would be a permanent situation. The money she earned over the summer would also mean that she wouldn't be in so much debt when she finished uni.

Spending the majority of the summer indoors suited her too. A heatwave hit in August and she found it stifling. When she wasn't in the cafe, she hid away in the flat working half-heartedly on the third novel of her series and getting the first book ready to publish. She also did some work for the publishing company and tried to get ahead with her reading for the second year of uni.

She'd hoped to earn extra cash babysitting for Lizzie's girls too, but with Lizzie being heavily pregnant she wasn't keen to go out much. Sometimes Scarlett would take the twins to the park when she felt like getting out of the flat. She hadn't seen them for a couple of weeks when Max messaged her one evening in late August to say that the baby was on its way and could she come and stay over with the girls while they went to the hospital.

It wasn't the first time she'd stayed over at their place and she knew the girls' routines, so it was pretty easy. Lizzie and Max always complained that they got up too early, but Scarlett was an early bird anyway so she was up and dressed and drinking a coffee before they woke. After breakfast she took them out to play in the garden, filling the padding pool so they could have a splash around.

Max arrived home late in the morning. His hair was a mess and there was stubble along his jaw when he stepped out of the backdoor and called hello.

"Did Lizzie have the baby?" Scarlett asked.

"Yes." He beamed as he wandered over to the patio table where Scarlett was sitting. "A perfect little boy. They're both doing well." Pulling out his phone, he pressed buttons before handing it to Scarlett.

"He's cute," she said, looking at the photo then scrolling to the next. "What's his name?"

"Nathan." He scooped Phoebe up as she ran at him. "You've got a little brother," he told her.

"Where is he?" she asked.

"At the hospital with Mummy. We can visit them later. Do you want to see a photo?" He took his phone back and sat with Phoebe on his lap as he showed her. Maya came over to see too, but they lost interest quickly and went back to play in the paddling pool. "Have they been good?" Max asked Scarlett.

"Yes. They're easy."

He leaned back in the chair and yawned. "They're always better behaved for you."

"Because they like me more," she said, then remembered to smile when he stared at her.

He chuckled, then turned to the back door at the sound of voices.

"There you all are!" Lizzie's sister, Josie, stepped outside with her baby on her hip. She gave a little squeal as she moved to hug Max. "A nephew! I'm so excited. Lizzie said I can't go to the hospital until after the girls have met their brother, but I don't know what to do with myself so we thought we'd come over here and see what was happening."

"I only just got back from the hospital," Max said. "Scarlett's been looking after the girls."

Josie's husband, Sam, wandered out from the kitchen and shook Max's hand as he congratulated him. "I put a load of baby clothes in the hallway, but a lot of it's pink."

Max smiled. "I warned Lizzie it might be a good idea to know the sex ahead of time but she insisted she wanted it to be a surprise."

"Boys can wear pink," Scarlett said.

Max shrugged. "At least until he's old enough to complain."

"I brought beers too," Sam said.

Max checked his watch. "How is it midday already? I'd love a drink, but I've got to drive back to the hospital later. And I didn't sleep last night so I'd probably have three sips and pass out."

Josie bounced the chubby baby on her hip, then patted Max's shoulder. "Go and sleep for a while. We can watch the girls."

"Thanks. I'll take you up on that."

"I have to go," Scarlett said. "I told Verity I'd help in the cafe when you got back."

"Thanks so much for looking after the girls," Max said.

"I hear you're releasing one of your books soon," Josie said, as Scarlett smiled at the baby.

"Yes. At the end of September."

"It's so exciting. I can't wait to read it."

Scarlett forced herself to smile despite the discomfort in her stomach. The closer it got to publication day, the more she worried it was a big mistake. She'd sent early copies out to bloggers and reviewers the previous week and panicked whenever she thought that people were actually reading it. And not only that, but they'd be writing reviews to share their opinion with the world. Maybe she should have stuck to publishing other people's books.

"Are you going to have a release party?" Josie asked.

"No, I don't think so."

"Really? Because Lizzie mentioned that there'd be some sort of celebration. And when I spoke to Tara she was talking about hosting an event in the bookshop. Has she spoken to you about it?"

"She emailed me," Scarlett said, feeling a pang of guilt that she hadn't responded to Lizzie's friend. "But I haven't decided what I want to do yet. There definitely won't be a party."

Josie rubbed Scarlett's arm. "You should do something to celebrate."

"Josie likes any excuse for a party," Max said.

She gave him a playful shove. "It's a big achievement, and I think Scarlett should revel in it! I'm keen to help you celebrate. Just let me know the plan and I'll be there."

"Thanks." Scarlett gave the baby's hand a shake when she reached out to her, then said goodbye. She'd just picked up her bag in the hallway when Max called after her.

"How much do we owe you?" he said with his wallet in his hand.

She shook her head. "You don't have to pay me."

"Don't be silly. You were here all night."

"It was a favour," she said.

"Are you sure?"

"Yes." She smiled and put a hand on the door handle. "I'll just charge you more next time."

"Thanks again. You're a lifesaver."

"I didn't save anyone's life."

He tilted his head and looked slightly confused. "It was really good of you to look after the girls. We never worry when you're looking after them."

A lump formed in her throat and she couldn't think of

anything to say. "Congratulations on the baby," she finally said. "Tell Lizzie I said congratulations."

"I will." He rocked on his feet, then took a step forward and wrapped her in a hug.

Scarlett tensed slightly. She didn't mind hugs if it was someone she knew well. But even though she knew Max pretty well, she felt a little uncomfortable.

"Sorry," he said, stepping back. "You don't like hugs, do you?"

"It's fine." She scrabbled to open the door and called goodbye over her shoulder as she hurried along the front path.

~

When Scarlett arrived back at the house on the Sunday before term started, it was almost exactly three months since Fraser had seen her. They hadn't had any contact over the summer. He'd thought of messaging her a few times but wasn't sure what he'd say. There was no real reason for them to be in contact outside of term time.

"How was your summer?" he asked as she dragged her suitcase along the hallway. On Friday he'd done a big clean of the house, but she didn't seem to notice.

"It was fine."

"What did you do?"

"Mostly worked." She tilted her chin upwards as she appeared to mull it over. "Yeah, just worked really. The cafe was busy with holidaymakers. Then I was working on my books and the publishing stuff."

"Wow." He shoved his hands in his pockets and felt completely embarrassed by his summer. What had he even done with all the time? He'd had a few days in Manchester with Allie and Liam, and a week in Spain with a couple of his uni friends, but that didn't add up to three months. There'd been plenty of nights out and lazy days playing video games and watching TV, but that felt pretty pathetic when Scarlett had spent all summer working. Thankfully she didn't ask about it, just pulled her case to the stairs.

"Can you manage?" he asked. "I can carry it up if you want?"

"It's not that heavy." She heaved it up the first step, then stopped and met his gaze. "Thank you."

"You're welcome …" An offer to carry her bag didn't warrant much gratitude, so he was a little confused by the way she was looking at him so intently.

"Not for that. I meant for helping me with uni."

He still wasn't sure what she was talking about. "When I helped with your assignment?"

"No." Her eyes shifted to her feet. "Thanks for marrying me. I think you hate living with me, and—"

He cut her off. "I don't hate it."

"But you could've lived with friends or in halls …"

"It's really fine."

"Will you shut up for a minute!" she snapped.

"Sorry."

"When I was working in the cafe over the summer I realised that even if I'd worked there for a year, I'd still have struggled to pay for uni, and maybe I'd never have ended up going. And I'm really glad I get to go to uni and not work in the cafe all the time. I think it's probably quite rubbish for you, but I appreciate you helping me. I know we're not friends, but I just wanted you to know that."

Fraser's mouth was dry and he swallowed hard as Scarlett lugged the case up the stairs. It didn't seem as though she was expecting a reply.

"You're welcome," he finally muttered, before retreating to the living room and falling onto the couch. Staring at the ceiling, he reflected again on how Scarlett's ability to make him feel like crap was rivalled only by Allie's.

He still wasn't even sure what had happened that night she'd come to watch his football match and turned up at the bar to flirt with him. He'd panicked that her feelings for him were something more than platonic, but she'd probably never even fancied him. There was really no reason why they couldn't be friends.

The trouble was, they seemed to have become pros at living together while barely seeing each other. He didn't see her for the following two weeks. A few times when he'd heard her moving around in her room, he'd knocked and said he was making a cuppa if she wanted one, but she'd very firmly declined. There was a chance that was to do with his poor tea-making skills, but most likely she just didn't want anything to do with him.

On Friday he'd dashed home after football to get changed for a night out and was all set to walk out of the door again when he noticed Scarlett's phone vibrating on the table in the hallway where they kept their keys. When the phone stopped ringing, the screen lit up with multiple missed calls and messages, plus a load of social media notifications. He picked it up and ran up the stairs.

Scarlett didn't respond when he knocked on her door.

"Are you in there?" he shouted. "You left your phone downstairs and it keeps ringing."

There was no answer.

"I'm coming in." Slowly, he opened the door. Scarlett was lying on her bed, her eyes trained on the ceiling. It took a moment to register the tears trickling down the side of her face. Automatically, he stepped into the room. "Are you okay?"

"Yes." She didn't move.

"Your phone's ringing," he stated, holding it out as it began to hum.

Sitting up, she took the phone and hit the button to reject the call from Lizzie before dropping it beside her legs and lying down again. "Thanks," she murmured.

"What's wrong?"

She shook her head in reply.

"Someone's obviously keen to get hold of you," he said as

the phone began to buzz again. "At least let them know you're okay."

"Just go away," she whispered.

Instinctively, he picked up the phone and swiped a finger across the screen before moving it to his ear. "Hello?"

"Is Scarlett there?" the puzzled voice asked.

"Yeah. Hang on."

"Why did you do that?" Scarlett hissed as he thrust the phone at her.

"It's Lizzie. She wants to talk to you."

"Tell her I'm ill and I'll call her tomorrow."

"*Are* you ill?"

"No, but you know how to lie, don't you?"

His eyes flicked to the phone. "She can hear you!"

"You don't need to say anything then." She flopped back onto the bed. "Just end the call and leave me alone."

"Sorry," Fraser said into the phone. "I guess she'll get back to you sometime."

"Is she okay?" Lizzie asked.

"I'm not entirely sure," he said, causing Scarlett to glare at him.

"Her book published today," Lizzie said. "She was supposed to be coming to Hope Cove for a celebration in the pub, but she's ignoring everyone's calls and messages."

"I think she's okay," he said.

Lizzie sighed. "Can you please tell her that I said congratulations on the book release and ask her to get in touch when she feels up to it."

"Yeah, sure." He ended the call and relayed the message to Scarlett. She didn't even acknowledge that she'd heard him. "Lizzie said you were supposed to be going to Hope Cove tonight to celebrate. Are you going?"

"It was Lizzie and Emily's idea," she said flatly. "I never wanted a party."

Fraser hovered for a moment, then sank onto the edge of the bed. "Are you going to meet them?"

"No."

"Why not?"

"I don't feel like it."

"It's really great that you released a book," he said softly. "Don't you want to celebrate?"

"Do I look like I want to celebrate?" she snapped.

"No. You look upset. Did something happen?"

She used her sleeve to wipe tears from her face. "Can you please go away?"

"If you tell me what's wrong, I'll go away."

"Nothing's wrong. I just want everyone to leave me alone. I published the book and now I don't want to think about it. But Emily wants me to go on social media and reply to comments about the book release. And I sent the book to bloggers and reviewers so I'm supposed to share anything they've posted online and interact with readers. But I don't want to. And I don't want to go to the pub with them. I just want to be left alone."

"You put in so much work," Fraser said. "You should celebrate. At least see what people are saying online. That'll be fun."

"No. It won't." She manoeuvred around Fraser to get off the bed. "You need to go away. We have rules, remember? You're not supposed to be in my bedroom. We live together but we don't have anything else to do with each other. You're not allowed to interfere in my life." She pulled on his arm and marched him to the door. "You have no right to answer my phone, or ask me about my life, or be in my bedroom."

As she closed the door on him, he stood dumbfounded in the hallway until his phone vibrated in his pocket. He was supposed to be meeting the football team for dinner at a burger place before hitting the bars. Simon was asking where he was and if they should wait for him to order food. He fired off a message saying he'd catch them up later, then strode into his room, opening up his laptop as he sat at his desk.

It didn't take long to find what he was looking for. The website for Hope Cove Press directed him to their social media sites, which led him to Scarlett's pages. He spent a few minutes reading some of the posts about her book then moved back to her door.

"The reviews are really good," he called to her. "Mostly five stars and a few four stars. Lots of bloggers and reviewers have posted about it." He continued reading through the posts even though Scarlett didn't reply. "There's one blogger absolutely raving about it. She says you're her new favourite author and she needs to know when the next book will be released."

The door opened and Scarlett stood staring at him. "Really?"

"Yeah." He walked in and sat on her bed, resting the laptop on his knees. "This is awesome – a bookshop posted photos of a display of your book. They have it as their pick of the week."

"No way," Scarlett said, dropping beside him.

"Look." He turned the screen to her.

"Oh, that's Tara's bookshop. She only did that because she knows me."

"Do you know all of these bloggers and reviewers?" he asked, scrolling through the posts.

"No." She frowned. "Did anyone say anything bad?"

He shook his head. "They're all great from what I can see."

"Did anyone mention that I'm dyslexic?"

"Why would they?"

"I thought someone might say that dyslexic people shouldn't be writers."

"I thought your friend edited the book. How would anyone even know you're dyslexic?"

"Maybe it's obvious. I thought people might be able to tell."

He gave her a sad smile. "You're a great writer."

"Thank you." She moved to her desk and opened up her own laptop. "I should reply to these comments. It looks rude if I don't."

"People will probably assume you're too busy celebrating to

reply." He walked over and put a hand on her shoulder. "Congratulations. It's really amazing that you published a book."

"Thank you," she whispered as he walked away.

He stopped in the doorway. "You really can't publish a book and not do anything to celebrate."

"Watch me," she said without looking at him.

He checked his phone, which showed another message from Simon telling him to hurry up and come out because he needed a wingman. It in no way encouraged him to move any faster. After pondering his options for the evening, he moved back into Scarlett's room and grinned at her.

"I have an idea of how you can celebrate."

CHAPTER 19

"I don't like surprises," Scarlett said, not sure why she hadn't protested more against Fraser's idea to take her out and celebrate. She'd been determined to hide away in her room all evening, but after he'd forced her to read the book reviews she'd felt a burst of excitement. Now she was sitting in Fraser's car with no idea where they were going. All he'd said was that they needed to leave immediately to make it on time. Then he'd hustled her out of the door.

"I think you'll like this surprise," he said, glancing over at her.

"Are you sure I'm dressed appropriately?" she asked, looking down at her leggings and T-shirt with her soft, snuggly cardigan draped over the top.

"You look great."

"You're all dressed up," she pointed out, looking at his crisp blue shirt. "Did you have plans?"

"I'm supposed to be meeting some friends but I can join them later."

The car came to a stop at traffic lights and she briefly considered hopping out and running home. "Can you please tell me where we're going?"

"That would spoil the fun."

"Who's fun?"

"Mine. It's fun to watch you squirm!"

"Fine." She leaned back on the headrest as the car pulled away again. "Don't tell me. I don't even want to know."

"You're such a bad liar!"

"I know," she said, laughing. "And I *really* hate surprises."

"Maybe you'll guess before we get there. Then it won't be a surprise any more."

She stayed quiet, watching the buildings go by and trying to guess where they might be going.

"We're going out of Exeter," she finally said. It was the route she took every Friday. "You're not taking me to Hope Cove, are you? I told you I don't want to go out with Lizzie and Emily."

"No. Guess again!"

"This is the way I drive to Hope Cove. I don't know where else you'd take me."

"It's not as far as Hope Cove. I'm meeting people later, remember. I can't be too long."

Scarlett scratched her cheek and watched the road. As her phone beeped with notifications, she gave up on trying to figure out their destination and dived into replying to social media posts. With her head down she completely lost track of what direction they were going in. When she finally glanced up the road was lined with shops, but she had no clue where they were.

"Where on earth are we?" she asked as they stopped at traffic lights.

"You should really have guessed by now," he said.

"Should I?" There was nothing in view that gave Scarlett any hint of where they were. "I've never been here before in my life."

"Ha ha!" Fraser said dryly as the lights turned green.

"What's funny?"

"You must have been here. You're winding me up, right?"

"No."

Falling silent, he pulled the car over at the side of the road. "I don't know whether you're joking or whether I've got the wrong place."

"Where were you planning on taking me?"

He pointed. "Isn't that your friend's bookshop?"

"Are we in Newton Abbot?" Scarlett asked, taking in the cute bookshop with the eye-catching window display.

"Yes."

"I guess that's Tara's shop then. I've never been here before."

"I thought she was your friend."

"She's more of an acquaintance. She's friends with Lizzie and Max. Why are we here?"

"I need to buy a book and they have it in stock."

"No!" She whipped around to face him. "You're not buying my book."

His eyes sparkled with amusement. "I am."

"No, you're not allowed to buy it. And you're definitely not allowed to read it."

"Why not?"

"I don't want anyone reading it."

He laughed loudly. "Maybe you should have thought about that before you published it. But I'd also like to remind you that your reviews are brilliant."

"I can't go in the bookshop. It's embarrassing. Especially because Tara's been sending me emails and calling me and I haven't replied."

"Why?"

Ignoring him, she craned her neck to get a better look at the bookshop that she'd heard so much about. The window to the right of the door was filled with children's books. A cute little train ran around a track amidst them. The other window was a more sophisticated display of adult books cleverly perched in tree branches. As she stared at it, her breath caught in her throat and she put a hand to her mouth.

"What's wrong?" Fraser asked. "We can just go home again if you want …"

Scarlett didn't respond; she was already stepping out of the car. At the window she looked up at *her* book resting on a branch in the centre of the display. She was aware of Fraser standing quietly behind her.

"That's pretty awesome," he said, breaking the silence.

"Yeah," she agreed through the lump in her throat.

"I'm going in to buy your book."

Before Scarlett could protest, he moved to open the door. The bell tinkled and he turned back to her. "There are lots of copies of your book right inside the door. Are you sure you don't want to look?"

Her legs moved automatically, and she brushed past him as she stepped inside. At the end of the first row of shelves was a table with a stack of books neatly displayed alongside a framed picture of Scarlett and a couple of paragraphs about her. In another frame was Tara's handwritten review of the book.

"Can I help you?" Tara's voice called from the back of the shop.

"I want to buy this book by Scarlett Mercer," Fraser replied. "Is it any good?"

"It's fantastic. Just make sure you have a lot of time, because once you start it you won't want to put it down."

"Are you just saying that because you're friends with the author?" Fraser asked jokily.

Scarlett was caught up in reading the review, but in her peripheral vision, she was aware of Tara walking towards them.

"Definitely not," Tara said in a tone that made it clear she didn't appreciate Fraser's question. "I may be friends with the author but I'd never recommend a book unless I enjoyed it. How did you know I'm friends with …" She trailed off. "Scarlett?"

She turned and smiled. "Hi!"

"I don't know whether to hug you or throttle you. I've been calling you and I sent you like three emails. Did you get them?"

"Yeah."

"I have a stack of books for you to sign. And I wanted to throw you a release party. Or have a book reading or some sort of event. Why didn't you reply to my messages?"

"Because I don't want to do any of that stuff."

Tara stared at her for a moment. "You could have just said that."

"I was going to but you're quite pushy, so I thought I'd just ignore you."

"I'm not pushy!" Tara insisted. "Just forceful in my encouragement."

A burst of laughter came from behind her and her husband wandered over.

"Congratulations!" James said, kissing Scarlett's cheek. "We love the book."

"*You've* read it?"

"Yes."

"It seems as though I'm the only person who hasn't," Fraser said.

Tara leaned close to Scarlett. "Who's he?" she asked in a mock whisper.

"That's Fraser."

"Oh!" Tara's eyes lit up. "We've heard all about you."

James offered Fraser his hand and introduced himself, while Tara wasn't at all discreet about checking him out.

"Stop staring," Scarlett hissed.

"I'm trying to decide if he's as cute as I've heard," Tara said with a grin.

"He's not deaf," Scarlett said. "And you're really embarrassing."

"This is my revenge for you ignoring my calls and emails." She went to the table and collected up the books.

Scarlett curled her lip. "He only wants one."

"I know. But I want you to sign them. Can you fetch the others from the storeroom, James?"

"You've got more?" Scarlett asked, as they all moved towards the back of the shop.

"Yes. There's a local book club who are going to read it for their next meeting. I promised the copies would be signed, so I'd have come and tracked you down if you hadn't shown up."

"That's amazing," Fraser said.

"I'll tell you what's amazing," James said, walking out from a back room with a box in his arms. "That scene where Alissa pierces her own lip. That was intense."

Tara looked to Fraser. "Did Scarlett tell you she pierced her own lip for research?"

"No." Fraser's gaze fell to her piercing. "Seriously?"

"Yeah." She wasn't sure why everyone thought that was a big deal. "It's easier to write about if I know how it feels."

"It's a great scene," Tara agreed. "Made my stomach churn a little though."

"That's nothing. Wait until you read book two."

Tara bunched her shoulders up. "Speaking of which, when will we get a copy?"

"I'll release it next Easter."

"I'd like an early copy please," Tara said. "I need to know if Alissa and Matteo get together."

"I thought it was fantasy," Fraser remarked. "Not romance."

"It's not romance," James and Scarlett said at once.

"There's definitely a romantic element," Tara said, putting a hand to her heart as she fake swooned.

"Here." James handed Scarlett a pen. "Get signing."

"This is weird," Scarlett said, leaning on the counter as she scribbled her name in the first book.

Fraser pulled his phone out. "I need to get photos."

"Yes!" Tara handed her phone to Fraser. "You need to take a photo of the three of us for the wall." She gestured to the back wall, which was full of framed photos of Tara and James with various authors in the shop.

"I'd really rather not," Scarlett said.

"You have to." James stood next to her and put a copy of the book in her hands. "There's no getting out of it I'm afraid."

"Smile!" Tara said, tilting her head towards Scarlett's. "Try and look happy about the fact that you just published a book and everyone loves it!"

She forced a smile for the photo, then cracked up laughing when Fraser pulled a face at her.

"What's the plan for this evening?" Tara asked when Scarlett finished signing the books. "Lizzie was talking about drinks in Hope Cove …"

"I can't make it," Scarlett muttered.

"Why not?" Tara demanded.

"I'm probably going to be online all evening, chatting with bloggers and reviewers. And Fraser's got plans for the evening so we need to get back to Exeter now so he's not late."

"Maybe Fraser would like to change his plans and come and celebrate your book release instead," Tara said.

Scarlett rolled her eyes. "No. He wouldn't."

All eyes turned to Fraser. Scarlett glared at him, assuming he'd realise that she didn't want him to change his plans. His gaze flicked between her and Tara and he stifled a laugh.

"Your wife published her first book today," Tara said. "You have to celebrate with her."

James leaned towards her. "I don't think we're supposed to know about that."

"No!" Scarlett agreed. "You're not. Lizzie's got such a big mouth."

"It was Max actually," Tara said. "But we're getting off topic. Are you going to take your wife out for a drink or what?"

"This is why I didn't reply to your emails," Scarlett said. "You're pushy. We're leaving now." She pulled on Fraser's sleeve but he didn't budge.

"My plans are pretty casual," he said, looking her right in the eyes. "I could come for drinks in Hope Cove instead."

"I don't want you to change your plans. I was using your plans as an excuse to get me out of being sociable."

"I think we all realised that," Fraser said. "But we could go for a little while. I think you should do something to mark the occasion."

"He's right." Tara tapped away on her phone. "I'm rounding everyone up for drinks at the Anchor Inn."

"I don't want to go for long," Scarlett said to Fraser as they moved towards the door. Even though it would be people she knew well, being in a group made her uncomfortable. Especially as all the attention would be on her.

"We can leave whenever you want," Fraser said quietly.

"That would be *now!*"

"Whenever you want *after* everyone has congratulated you," he clarified. "You never know, you might even have a good time."

She frowned and turned back to Tara. "Thanks for ordering so many of the books. Sorry I didn't reply to your emails."

"Don't worry about it." Tara gave her a brief hug. "I'm really glad you called in."

"Thanks for signing the books," James said. "We'll see you shortly."

The bell over the door rang again as they left.

"Did you enjoy my surprise?" Fraser asked as they got back in the car.

"It was okay."

"Tara and James are cool."

"Yeah. I like them." Scarlett pulled the seatbelt around her. "We don't have to go to Hope Cove though. If you want to go out with your friends it's fine."

He was quiet for a moment. "I'd like to go out in Hope Cove with you. But if you really don't want to, I can take you home."

Scarlett felt a cool flutter in her chest. "We could just go for a little while," she said quietly.

"Good." He turned the engine on and pulled the car away.

Scarlett tried and failed to figure out what was going on in his head. "Why are you being nice to me?" she finally asked.

He gave her a sidelong glance. "Honestly?" She nodded and he pointed to his copy of her book, which he'd placed on the console between them. "I suspect that one day you're going to be really famous. I want to be able to tell people about the day you published your first book and we hung out for the evening."

While his attention was on the road, she gazed at his profile. After a moment, her lips shifted to a smile. "I feel as though I should warn you … when I'm famous I probably won't even remember your name."

His laughter bounced around the car and made her insides flutter.

CHAPTER 20

"I guess it's not like the pubs you're used to," Scarlett said as they walked into the Anchor Inn. "I've only been in a few times but it's not exactly a party scene. It'll be a boring Friday night for you."

"It's fine." He put a hand on her back to move her further into the room. "Stop worrying."

"I'm just warning you." She caught sight of Emily and Lizzie at a table close to the fire. Jack was with them too.

"We were panicking you weren't going to turn up," Lizzie said when they went over. "Tara said you'd definitely be here, but I thought we might end up celebrating without you."

"Fraser made me go to Tara's bookshop and sign books. Then she bullied us into coming here. I didn't actually want to."

Lizzie grinned up at Fraser. "Thanks for dragging her out."

"No problem. Nice to see you again."

"We haven't met," Jack said, reaching to shake Fraser's hand and introduce himself.

Max appeared beside Scarlett.

"*You're* here," she stated, frowning at him.

"Yep! No need to look so disappointed."

"Who's looking after the kids? You better not have left them with Dotty. She's definitely not capable of looking after a tiny baby." She flicked her gaze between Lizzie and Max.

"The kids are fine," Lizzie said. "Max's mum is staying with us for a few days. It's so nice to get out. It's the first time we've left Nathan."

"I'm not actually convinced my mum's a better choice than Dotty," Max said. "But I'm sure they'll be fine." He offered Fraser his hand as he introduced himself.

"Auntie Verity's here," Scarlett said, as she and Bill walked into the pub. She leaned close to Fraser, getting a waft of his aftershave. "Verity doesn't know about us. She thinks you're my housemate, that's all. Don't mention anything else."

"Okay."

"There you are!" Verity said, throwing her arms around Scarlett and squeezing hard. "Well done on publishing your first book. I'm so proud of you."

"Thank you. This is Fraser," she said awkwardly.

"We met in the cafe once," Verity said, then introduced Bill.

"This is Perry," Scarlett said, bending to stroke the friendly dog.

"I've heard about you." Fraser crouched down and stroked Perry's face. "You're gorgeous, aren't you?"

Scarlett caught Emily putting a hand to her heart and tilting her head to one side as she watched Fraser make a fuss of the dog.

"He's lovely," she mouthed to Scarlett, who rolled her eyes in reply.

"What's everyone drinking?" Jack asked.

"Get a couple of bottles of champagne," Verity said, looking to Jack. "My treat."

"Thank you," Scarlett said as Jack set off to the bar with Max following him. "Jack works here part-time," she told Fraser.

Once they all had glasses of champagne, Max offered to make a toast.

"Please don't," Scarlett said. "You'll only embarrass me." She took a swig of her drink, then glared at everyone around her. "Can you please just drink!"

There were chuckles and murmured congratulations as they raised their glasses in unison. Fraser clinked his glass against hers before taking a sip.

"Don't drink too much," Scarlett said. "You need to drive later."

"I know!" He smiled warmly. "I'm just having one glass, if that's okay with you?"

"I suppose it's okay."

"Scarlett!" Verity called. She was sitting at a small round table with Bill. "Come and sign this book for me please."

"I'll be back in a minute," she said to Fraser before moving to sit with Bill and Verity. After signing the book, she told Verity about the reviews and about her book being in the window display at Tara's bookshop. She was telling her about having her photo taken with Tara and James when Tara's high-pitched voice interrupted her.

"It seems as though you started the party without us," she said brightly. James was beside her and Josie and Sam were with them too. There was a lot of bustle as everyone greeted each other.

"I thought you couldn't make it," Emily said to Josie. "Who's looking after Annie?"

"Tara's mum volunteered to babysit. She's been really helpful."

Emily swayed slightly. "Is she still seeing the pub landlord?"

"Yes," Tara replied. "They're a bit sickening actually. She's very happy."

"That's so great," Emily gushed. "Everyone's in love. It's so wonderful."

"Are you drunk?" Josie asked, smiling.

"Nope," Emily insisted.

"She is!" Jack said. "It's great. I love drunk Emily. Until she starts vomiting, then she's a pain in the arse."

"One time!" Emily shook her head. "You'll never let me forget about that, will you?"

"Probably not," he said cheekily.

Amidst the bustle, Scarlett scanned around to check where Fraser was. He seemed at ease chatting with Max and flashed her a quick smile when she caught his eye.

"Amber's coming too," Josie said loudly. "So we'll have the whole gang. Scarlett, you need to publish books more often. I love having something to celebrate."

Scarlett smiled at her, then scanned their group again. "Oh, no," she groaned. "Emily's drunk and chatting to Fraser. She's going to embarrass me, isn't she?"

"I'd put money on it," Josie said brightly.

Amber and John arrived next. Scarlett didn't know them too well, but Amber was good friends with Tara and Josie. She always made an effort to chat to Scarlett when she saw her.

"We bought you a little present," Amber said, handing her a shiny gift bag. Scarlett peered inside at the notebook and pen set.

"Thank you," she said as Fraser appeared beside her.

"Do you mind if I borrow her for a minute?" he said to Amber, leading her away by her elbow.

"Are you bored?" she asked. "I feel as though I should stay a bit longer, but if you want to go I can stay and get someone to drive me back to Exeter on Sunday night. I think that'll be fine."

"I'm not bored. I just feel like having another drink. But then I won't be able to drive."

"I've only had a few sips of champagne so I guess I could drive. If you don't mind me driving your car? I should just warn you that I'm a pretty bad driver."

"You're not driving my car," he said with a wide smile. "But Emily was saying there's a couch at the offices for the publishing company … she suggested I could sleep there."

Scarlett snorted a laugh. "I'm sure she did! She's such a nightmare."

"What's that supposed to mean?"

"Nothing." Scarlett ignored Emily, who was beaming at her across the room and giving her a thumbs up.

"So can I sleep on the couch or what?"

"Yes."

"Great." He turned and nodded at Jack, who set off for the bar. "I'll see if he needs a hand. Do you want another drink?"

"No, I've still got a glass of champagne somewhere." As soon as Fraser walked away, she strode over to Emily.

"He's so cute," Emily cooed, leaning onto her arm. "Jack asked him if he wanted a beer and he said he had to check with you. You're like a proper married couple."

"Shut up," Scarlett hissed. "That's a secret, remember?"

"Sorry," she giggled. "I like him though."

"I approve of him too," Tara said, sidling over and jumping into the conversation. "And Lizzie's right; he's *really* cute."

"Why did you tell him he could stay over?" Scarlett asked Emily.

"Don't look at me like that." Emily laughed. "I just casually dropped it into the conversation. He seemed keen though."

"You're such a matchmaker," Tara said.

Emily lowered her voice. "I'd suggest you keep the heating off and claim you don't have any extra bedding. You can invite him to snuggle in with you to keep warm."

"I'm not doing that," Scarlett said adamantly.

Emily shrugged. "It works in my novels."

"I wouldn't want him in my bed anyway."

"Oh, come on," Tara said. "He's hot and he seems really sweet. It's obvious he likes you or he wouldn't spend a night with all of us." Her eyes shone with mischief. "Besides, you're married. Why not take advantage of that fact?"

"It's not that kind of marriage," Scarlett said, checking that Verity wasn't within hearing range. She wiped her clammy hands on her T-shirt as Fraser walked over to them with a pint in his hand.

"Did you get another bottle of champagne?" Emily asked Jack.

"No. There's still some on the table." He nodded to an ice bucket. "Besides, I think you've had enough."

"Don't be a spoilsport." Emily topped up her glass and Tara's. "I'm so happy you published your book," she said, touching Scarlett's arm. "In fact, I'm going to make a speech. I can't not."

"I'm fairly certain you could," Jack said.

"It's an important occasion." Emily held Jack's arm as she stepped onto a chair.

"She's really funny," Fraser said in Scarlett's ear.

"She's drunk. I've never seen her like this. Usually she's quiet and reserved."

"I haven't got anything to tap my glass with," Emily said loudly, tapping her fingers against her glass. "Everyone! I need everyone's attention."

Silence fell, not only with their group, but around the whole pub. Scarlett put a hand over her face and peeked out between her fingers.

"I just want to say …" Emily wobbled on the chair and Jack put a hand on her hip to steady her. "I just want to say that Scarlett published a book today." Her chin twitched and she put a hand to her chest. "I'm so proud." She looked down at Scarlett and tears filled her eyes. "And I'm so happy for you," she said, her voice turning to a squeaky whisper. "It's such an honour to be with you on this amazing journey."

As Scarlett winced, Fraser knocked his shoulder against hers, apparently amused by her discomfort.

"Thank you all for coming," Emily went on. "It's lovely that so many people are here to celebrate Scarlett's achievement."

"Jack!" Scarlett hissed. "Can you do something?"

He grinned as he reached up to Emily. "Hey, drunk lady! I think we get the point. Get down now before you fall down."

Emily draped an arm around his shoulders and hopped off the chair. "I'm not even that drunk. I'm just really happy. And a bit emotional."

Jack looked at Scarlett and held his glass up. "I think what Emily was trying to say is that we're very proud of you. Well done, Scarlett!"

"Thank you." Her cheeks felt as though they were on fire as everyone raised their glasses and toasted her.

"I might take you home," Jack said, pulling Emily close to him.

"No!" Emily said. "I'm having fun."

Jack nodded slowly. "You are now. But in about five minutes the room will start to spin and you'll tell me off for letting you drink too much."

"Probably," Emily agreed. She gave Scarlett a big hug, then turned to Fraser and tapped his chest. "It was so lovely to see you again. And don't forget, if there isn't a blanket, just cuddle up."

"What?" Fraser asked.

"Definitely time to leave," Jack said, directing Emily away from them.

"What was that all about?" Fraser asked.

Scarlett gulped at her champagne. "No idea. She's very drunk."

They stayed for another hour. Scarlett kept getting pulled into different conversations, while Fraser happily mingled. He had a long chat with Bill and Verity, then ended up standing at the bar with Max and James. He was more comfortable around her friends than she was.

When she'd had her fill of socialising, Scarlett moved to the men at the bar.

"This is so weird," Max said to her. "I know Fraser's dad. I worked for his company years ago. It's such a small world."

"I thought you used to be a lawyer." Scarlett knew Fraser's dad owned hotels, so she was slightly puzzled.

"I was. His company used our law firm." He looked to Fraser. "I remember your dad had photos of you and your sister on his desk. You were probably about five."

"You're really old," Scarlett remarked, rolling her eyes.

The bell rang for last orders and Fraser asked Scarlett if she wanted another drink.

She shook her head and told him she wanted to go.

"Are you drunk?" she asked when Fraser swayed outside of the pub.

"No. Well, maybe a bit." As they walked towards the beach a full moon bathed everything in a silver glow and the ripples on the water glistened. "It's really pretty here."

"Yeah." Scarlett watched him crane his neck to look up at the twinkling stars overhead.

"Did you tell Tara I'm cute?"

"No," she said quickly.

"Someone did."

"It wasn't me."

"Emily?" he asked, dropping his gaze to her.

She shook her head.

"Lizzie? Seriously? That's creepy. She's old."

"I know. But she's at that weird age where she still thinks she's young."

"How old is she?"

"Like forty," she said as they approached the cafe. "Or almost forty. I can't remember."

"Max is cool."

"Yeah. He's okay."

"Don't you like him?"

"I don't think he likes me," she confessed. "He looks at me

strangely sometimes. Like he can't figure me out. Probably because he's old."

"Maybe. I like him."

"You like everyone. Did you really have a good time? I thought you'd be bored."

"It was good," he said as they ascended the stairs to the flat. "Did you enjoy it?"

"Yeah." She opened up the door and led the way inside. "It was all right."

"Are you going to thank me for making you go out?"

"Thank you," she said, fairly insincerely as she went into the little kitchen off the living room and got them both a glass of water.

"You're different here," Fraser remarked.

Her stomach fluttered as he looked at her intently. "What do you mean?"

"You seem more relaxed around your friends and family."

"Everyone's different around their friends."

"I suppose so," he mused. "It was good to see you having fun."

Scarlett stepped away from him and pointed at the couch. "Should I help you pull it out to a bed? Or can you do it? It's pretty easy."

"I'll probably just sleep on it like that."

"Okay." The room felt increasingly small. "I'll get you a pillow and blanket." After fetching them from the wardrobe in her room, she dumped them on the couch. "If you get cold, just turn the heating up." She pointed to the radiator by the window and her cheeks burned again as she thought of Emily's comments about him sharing her bed. "The bathroom's there. The kitchen's there. That's all you need. Goodnight." Hurrying to her bedroom, she closed the door behind her. As she sank onto her bed, she was hit by the desire to go back out and chat to Fraser. That would be weird, though, considering she'd just run away from him.

Staying completely still, her senses were on high alert for any noise from the next room. At the sound of his footsteps she tensed, wondering if he might come to her room. The click of the bathroom door left her feeling oddly disappointed.

When his footsteps indicated he'd gone back to the living room, she wondered if he'd sleep in his clothes or maybe strip down to his underwear. Her heart rate skyrocketed and she moved to get changed into her pyjamas.

She reminded herself that Fraser always slept in the next room to her, and this was barely any different. Nevertheless, her mind wouldn't switch off, and she interspersed staring at the ceiling with checking the time on her phone. At two o'clock in the morning, she gave in to her restlessness and crept into the living room.

She slipped across to the kitchen without even glancing towards the couch. Fraser's quiet, shallow breaths indicated he was fast asleep, but she didn't dare peek at him. The light from the fridge lit up the kitchen. There was nothing in it but she left it open for the light as she moved to a cupboard and pulled out a packet of biscuits. Her crunching sounded loud in the stillness, and she put the packet back after she'd eaten a couple. Gently, she closed the fridge and moved to the doorway. The streetlights outside bathed the room in soft light.

Fraser was too long for the couch and one foot was propped on the arm while the other hung off the side with his foot on the ground. The blanket only covered his middle, and her eyes were drawn to his bare legs. He'd kept his T-shirt on but his jeans hung over the back of Lizzie's office chair in the corner.

Nervous that he might wake up, she dragged her gaze away from him and went back to bed.

CHAPTER 21

"It's convenient living above a cafe," Fraser said, pausing to take a swig of his coffee in between mouthfuls of bacon sandwich.

"Yeah," Scarlett agreed, watching a man with a fishing rod walk past the window of the cafe.

"You look tired. Didn't you sleep again?"

"I slept a bit. Alcohol tends to keep me awake. That's why I don't drink very often."

"I'm the opposite. It knocks me out. I don't think I stirred all night."

Scarlett took a bite of her toast as she thought about how peaceful he looked when he slept. Even though she'd only watched him for a moment, it felt creepy now.

"How's breakfast?" Verity asked, coming over and resting a hand on Scarlett's shoulder.

"Delicious," Fraser said as he swallowed his final bite.

"What are your plans for today?" Verity asked. "It's a bit blustery but I reckon these clouds are going to clear up soon. You could have a nice walk along the coast. Show Fraser a bit of the area."

"We need to get back to Exeter," Scarlett said.

Verity picked up their empty plates. "Are you going back today too?"

"I'll go with Fraser to get my car. I'll be back for my shift tomorrow."

"You could just stay. I'm sure Bill wouldn't mind driving you back to Exeter tomorrow."

"No. It's fine. Thanks for breakfast." She stood and pulled her jacket from the back of the chair.

"Have you got any plans for Wednesday?" Verity asked. "Bill and I thought we could come over to Exeter and take you out for dinner."

"No, thanks. I'll be busy with uni stuff." She pushed Fraser in the direction of the door.

"It was really nice to see you again," he called to Verity. Outside, he turned to Scarlett. "What's happening on Wednesday?"

"Nothing."

"It's your birthday, isn't it?"

"No."

"Liar."

"Whatever, let's go home."

He took a few steps then looked overhead. "I think Verity's right that the weather's going to clear up. We could go for a walk if you want."

"Don't you have stuff to do today?"

He checked his watch. "I have a match but it's not until three. There's loads of time."

"Let's just get back."

They were both quiet on the drive to Exeter. Scarlett was tired and didn't feel like talking. Back at the house, she trudged to the stairs, intent on lying down for a while before she drove back to Hope Cove.

"Scarlett?" Fraser called, making her stop on the third step.

"Yeah."

"I had a good time last night."

"That's nice." She managed two more steps before he called her name again. "What? I'm tired."

He put a hand on the bannister and looked suddenly lost for words. "I wanted to talk to you …"

"What about?"

"About the time you came and watched my game and then came to the bar."

Scarlett cringed at the reminder. She'd been hoping the subject would never come up again. "You don't have to worry. I'm not going to assume we're friends just because we hung out for one night. I promise I won't try and hang out with you."

"Wait," Fraser said as she took another couple of steps. "I wanted to apologise for being such a dick."

Turning, she sighed. "Which time?"

His features scrunched up. "What do you mean which time? How many times have there been?"

"Well, you leave your stinky sports clothes on the bathroom floor fairly often. And you leave damp towels lying around. Then there was the time you made me the worst cup of tea in the history of humankind." Finally, she let the corners of her mouth pull upwards.

He shook his head. "I'm trying to apologise and you're mocking me?"

"Okay. Go ahead. What did you want to apologise for?"

"Obviously for what I said after you came to the bar that night."

She wasn't sure why that would be obvious and didn't know how she was supposed to respond so she kept quiet.

"I said we weren't friends and I didn't want anything to do with you."

"Yeah. I know." She didn't need a reminder. She just wasn't sure why he was apologising for it.

"I'm sorry."

"Okay." She still didn't get it but shrugged and set off once again.

"Scarlett!" Fraser said impatiently.

"What?"

"It's difficult to have a conversation with you when you keep walking away."

"I thought the conversation was over."

"No."

She sank down to sit on the step halfway up the stairs. "What else did you want to say?"

"I wanted to say I'm sorry and I'd like it if we could be friends."

"I already have two friends. I don't need any more."

His smile lit up his face and he leaned on the banister as he grinned up at her.

"What's so funny?"

"You." He tilted his head. "You're so … I don't know …"

"Awesome?" she suggested jokily.

He nodded and his features turned serious. "You're pretty awesome. Can we please be friends?"

"I guess so. I'm not going to hang out with your friends though."

"That's okay."

"Can I go now?" she asked with mock impatience.

"Yes. But I feel as though I should tell you that judging by last night, I'm confident you have a lot more than two friends."

She smiled down at him. "Maybe."

Fraser usually played basketball with a guy from his course on Wednesday evenings, but he told him he couldn't make it that week and headed into town to go shopping after his afternoon lecture. Jewellery was usually his go-to gift for women. There were a couple of times he'd bought jewellery for Monique and he'd got the salesperson to choose for him. Monique had always been happy regardless, but he didn't suppose he'd have cared too much if she hadn't liked it.

He'd put more thought into Scarlett's present. Possibly more thought than he'd ever put into a gift. Which should have meant he was excited about giving it to her, but he was as nervous as hell. When you put a lot of effort into picking a gift, it mattered that the recipient liked it. As he walked into the house, he had a sinking feeling that he'd got it completely wrong. Maybe he should have gone to the jewellery shop and asked the shop assistant to choose something.

Along the hall, he could see Scarlett at the kitchen table, chatting on her phone. She didn't seem to have noticed him, so he could run up to his room and hide the present. He was fairly certain she wouldn't be expecting a gift from him. The card and cake would be enough. The card was stupid though. He'd chosen it as a joke, but Scarlett might not find it funny.

"Hi," she called, leaning back in her chair to look along the hallway.

His heart pounded. She'd have seen the bulky gift bag so he couldn't run away now. "Were you on the phone?" he said, hoping his jokey tone would hide his nerves. "It must be a special occasion!"

"It was Verity." She stared at him in confusion as he entered the kitchen with his hands full.

"Wishing you a happy birthday?"

"Yeah." She cocked her head. "I thought you had some sport thing on Wednesdays?"

"I usually play basketball, but I thought I'd come and eat cake with you instead." He slid the box on the table. "It's chocolate. I hope that's okay. Happy birthday!"

"You bought me a cake?" Obviously she hadn't been expecting *anything*, so the gift really might seem extravagant. It was too late to back out now though.

He held the bag out to her. "And a gift!"

She looked at it suspiciously as she took it from him. After pulling the large, wrapped gift from the bag, she scooted her chair away from the table and placed it on her lap.

"Wait," Fraser said, as she slid her fingers under the paper. "Open your card first." He held out a white envelope and she hastily tore it open while he waited with bated breath.

Scarlett immediately burst out laughing at the horrifically pink card with a picture of a jug of flowers on a table. The caption read "To my darling wife".

"You're such an idiot."

"It was the cheesiest card in the shop," he said, relieved that she found it funny.

She propped the card on the table and went back to opening her present while Fraser slipped onto the chair opposite.

"A blanket," she stated, running her hand over the soft blue material.

"It's weighted," he explained hesitantly. When he'd been researching autism, he'd read that sleep problems were common. He'd stumbled on a blog that suggested weighted blankets sometimes helped. But Scarlett probably already knew that. Why did he think he could solve a problem that she'd had all her life? She'd probably tried everything already. And if she had, she'd know how much weighted blankets cost and would freak out at him for spending so much. "I read that they're good for people with …" He trailed off, feeling like the world's biggest idiot.

Scarlett looked up at him expectantly. "What?"

Crap. Now he was about to upset her on her birthday. She never mentioned being autistic, so why did he think it was okay to bring it up? He really was a dick sometimes. "I read that they're good for people who don't sleep well," he said. "I thought maybe it would help. But if you don't like it I can return it. They probably don't help at all. It was a stupid idea."

"I like it," she whispered as she stroked the material in her lap. "Thank you."

He stood abruptly. "Do you want cake?"

"Okay." She opted for a small slice while Fraser took a huge slab.

"We could play video games if you don't have anything else planned for the evening," he suggested when Scarlett put the plates in the dishwasher.

She picked up her blanket. "I've got some work to get on with."

"On your birthday?"

"It's just another day. I'm not sure why everyone makes such a fuss about it. Thank you for the present though. And the cake."

"No problem," he muttered as she left. He tried not to be annoyed, but he'd changed his plans and now she didn't even want to hang out. Maybe she'd been offended by the blanket and was trying to get away from him. Or, knowing her, she actually *was* working on her birthday. He made a cup of tea, pausing before making one for Scarlett too.

"I don't mean to sound selfish," he said when he walked into her room with the drinks, "but I skipped basketball to hang out with you and you're choosing uni work over me."

"It's actually stuff for the publishing company."

"Even so, it can't be so urgent that you can't put it off for one evening."

"Just because *you* think people should go out and get drunk on their birthday doesn't mean I want to do the same. If I wanted to go out I'd have gone back to Hope Cove to see Lizzie and Emily. All I want to do is hang out in my room."

He chewed his bottom lip and looked thoughtful. "Okay."

"Okay, you'll leave me in peace?"

"Give me your laptop," he said, holding out his hands.

"Why?"

"Trust me."

"I don't think I do trust you." She passed him her laptop regardless and waited while he tapped away. Balancing the laptop on his forearm, he took her hand and pulled her up.

"You said you'd leave me alone," she reminded him.

"I will in a minute." He nodded to the bed. "Sit!"

"What am I, a dog?"

"Not a very well trained one," he said, giving her a playful nudge onto the bed. Once she sat down, he set the laptop in front of her.

"You logged into Netflix on my laptop?"

"Yes. You should do something nice on your birthday. The second season of that vampire show released this week. You can binge watch it in bed. That's got to be better than working." He picked her new blanket from the end of the bed and draped it over her, then went and got her mug from the desk.

"How are my tea-making skills coming on?" he asked as he set it on the bedside table.

"Improving," she said, glancing into the mug.

"Do you want me to leave you alone or am I allowed to watch with you?"

"It won't make much sense if you haven't watched the first season."

"I've seen it," he said. "Thought I'd better check what all the fuss was about."

"What did you think?"

"I like it."

She glanced around. "You can't sit on my bed. We have boundaries, remember?"

Smiling, he walked across the room and picked up her desk chair then set it down again right beside the bed. "Is that acceptable?"

"I suppose so." She reached to press play on the first episode, then hesitated. "Will your parents mind that you've logged onto the Netflix account on my laptop?"

"No."

Her finger hovered over the button on the laptop. "What do they think about us being married?"

"They're okay about it."

"I thought your mum cried when you told her."

"They were upset for about a minute. Then they were cool about it. Except they keep asking when they can meet you."

"I don't want to meet your parents," she said, looking slightly panicked.

"I know." He wasn't entirely sure why he was bothered by the fact that she so flatly refused. "What about your parents? Have they been in touch today?"

"Mum messaged me earlier to wish me happy birthday and to say that they'd come to the cafe on Sunday with my present. It'll be the first time I've seen them in ages."

"I can't imagine not being in regular contact with my parents." His mum could drive him crazy, but he couldn't comprehend the idea of his parents not being involved in his life.

"When I moved out it was a relief. No matter what I did, they disapproved, and it's not as though I was wild and rebellious. They just didn't understand me. It's exhausting being around them. If I see them a couple of times a year at Verity's place it's enough for me. I don't feel as though I'm losing anything."

"That's really sad."

"I've never had a good relationship with them so I can't imagine it being any other way." She hitched her shoulders. "Are we watching this or what?"

He smiled sadly. "Yeah."

She hit play and settled back on her pillows. By the middle of the second episode, Fraser was completely uncomfortable and shifted in the chair every few minutes. With a resigned sigh, Scarlett shuffled over, placing one of her pillows in the space she left on the bed. She patted it in what seemed to be an invitation for him to sit.

"Thanks," he said, moving over. He adjusted the pillow behind his back and stretched his legs out in front of him, crossing them at the ankles.

Occasionally he glanced at Scarlett, snuggled under her new

blanket. Her eyelids looked heavier and heavier until she finally drifted off.

Gently, he closed the laptop and fought the urge to stay and watch her sleep. He smiled at the thought of how much she'd shout at him if she caught him, then crept silently out of the room.

CHAPTER 22

The image of Scarlett sleeping haunted Fraser until he came to the conclusion he was losing his mind. He was out with the football crowd that Friday night and all he could think about was Scarlett. In the week since her birthday he'd hardly seen her. One night he'd skipped football training, thinking he'd coax her into playing video games with him, but she gave the usual excuse of having to work. Another evening he missed a night out in the hopes that she might want to do something with him, but she'd politely declined.

Zoning back into Simon in front of him, he realised he was still going on about some girl with large breasts at the other side of the pub. He really didn't want to be there. Scarlett would probably have gone back to Hope Cove given that it was Friday, but if she hadn't and was still at home she might take a break from working and hang out with him.

"What's up with you?" Simon asked, giving him a shove and breaking his trance.

"Nothing. I'm going to go home."

"It's Friday night!" He made it sound as though going home early was a crime.

"I'm not in the mood for drinking." Fraser set his almost

empty pint on a nearby table and said goodbye. He'd almost made it to the door when a woman stepped into his path. It took him a second to register it was Bridget. He'd only seen her a couple of times since their date, and never to speak to.

"How are you?" she asked.

"I'm good, thanks. How about you?"

"I'm fine. The workload's a bit tougher in the second year, but it's all okay."

"I'm finding the same." He was slightly embarrassed by the fact he couldn't remember what course she was taking. Teaching, he thought, but wasn't confident enough to mention it.

"You're not leaving already, are you?" she asked.

"Yeah. I'm not up for a big night."

"Shame. I was going to offer to buy you a drink. I think I owe you one."

It felt like a trap but he couldn't help but ask why.

"You insisted on buying the last time we went out." She stepped out of the way of someone walking behind her and ended up so close that she had a hand on his arm.

Her smile was warm and flirty. A voice in his head told him to run away but was quickly drowned out by another voice that told him she clearly still fancied him and he should probably stay and have a drink with her. Maybe the reason why he couldn't stop thinking about Scarlett was that he hadn't had sex for so long that it was literally driving him crazy. Bridget would probably provide a fix for that.

"I'll stay for another drink," he said, leading her towards the bar. "I can't let you pay though. It's definitely me who owes you a drink."

"How did you work that out?"

He stopped at the bar and turned to face her. "I completely fobbed you off after the last time we went out. I'm sorry."

"It's okay." Her cheeks pinked. "You said it was bad timing."

He nodded. "It wasn't anything against you. I promise."

"That's good to hear."

She ordered a gin and tonic and they moved to sit side by side in a quiet booth at the back of the pub, where she wittered away about her course and her placements for that year. He'd been right that she was training to be a teacher. Unfortunately, he quickly remembered why their first date hadn't gone so well. While she was attractive, she was also fairly boring. His mind wandered constantly and it was an effort to concentrate on what she was saying.

When a yawn came out of nowhere, he apologised profusely and gave her a story about how tiring it was juggling his football training with studying. It gave him a convenient excuse to go home.

"Maybe we could go out again sometime?" she suggested, her hand dropping to his thigh in an action that made him re-think whether he really want to go home or not.

"That would be good," he said automatically.

"I could come to your place one night. How about tomorrow?"

"No." He shook his head then felt bad at how crestfallen she looked. "Sorry. My place is no good because of my housemate."

"I don't think you've mentioned him."

"*Her*," he said sheepishly. If it scared her away it was probably a good thing.

"You live with a girl?"

"Yes. Scarlett. She's pretty cool."

"But she doesn't let you invite friends over?"

"It's not that she doesn't let me … I just choose not to bring people over. There were a couple of weird incidents. It's kind of a long story."

She looked up at him expectantly. "It sounds interesting."

Fraser glanced towards the door, then leaned back against the seat. "She's not great with people."

"How so?"

"She's socially awkward," he said with a smile. That was something of an understatement. "She's really great when you get to know her, but she doesn't let a lot of people get to know her. And I think most people find her so awkward that they either avoid her or make fun of her."

"That's horrible," Bridget said with wide eyes.

He nodded. "It's difficult because she's so hard to figure out … I did a lot of research on autism and I feel as though I understand her better."

Her eyes widened. "She's autistic but she's at uni?"

"Yeah. She's really intelligent. It's socially that she has problems. And she gets stressed easily I think. Which is why I don't invite people to the house any more."

"I totally understand." She rested her hand on his arm. "It's sweet of you to be so considerate."

The conversation flowed easily after that, though it never moved on from Scarlett. Obviously, he neglected to mention that they were married and gave some vague story about them meeting on the open day when Bridget asked how they'd ended up living together.

By the time he left the pub an hour later, he'd decided spending time with Bridget wasn't so bad. Over the following week, they exchanged a few messages and she invited him for dinner at her place the following Friday, mentioning that her housemates were both away for the weekend.

The subtext was pretty clear, but he still hesitated over whether or not to put condoms in his wallet before he left the house. She'd probably have some anyway, so not having any wouldn't work as an excuse. And why the hell was he looking for excuses not to sleep with her? Slipping the condoms into his wallet, he mumbled to himself about how he was losing his mind and was still muttering when he stepped out onto the landing and almost collided with Scarlett.

"Holy crap!" he shouted, making her wince. "I thought you were in Hope Cove. I called hello when I came home but you didn't reply."

"I said hi, but maybe I wasn't very loud. I was working."

"You're always working," he said, more gruffly than he'd intended.

"Not now," she said. "Do you wanna play video games or something?"

She really had impeccable timing. *Now* she wanted to hang out. After ignoring him for weeks, she suddenly had time when he was on his way to a date. It's not as though he could cancel at the last minute. Could he? He rolled his shirt sleeves back as he checked the time. "I'm going out," he told her. Tempting as it was to cancel, it would be pretty bad form. Bridget was cooking so she'd have gone to some effort. He could play video games with Scarlett another time.

"You've got something here," she said, indicating the side of his face. "Foam or something."

"Shaving cream," he said, wiping a hand along his jaw. When she shook her head, he tried again.

"Here …" She stepped forward and ran her thumb over his earlobe.

It felt like an electric shock and he stepped back so quickly that he crashed into the bannister rail.

"Sorry." She whipped her hand away and had that look as though she'd done something wrong but had no idea what. He hated that look. Especially because she hadn't done anything wrong. It was him. What the hell was going on with him?

"Are you going to Hope Cove this weekend?" he asked.

"Yes. But I might wait and go tomorrow morning. I'm going to carve pumpkins with Lizzie's kids tomorrow afternoon."

"Sounds fun."

"I love Halloween. There's a costume party next week in the student bar on campus. Are you going?"

"Probably not. I hate costume parties."

"I love dressing up." Her eyes sparkled as she smiled. "I already have my costume. I'm not sure whether to stay at home and wait for kids to come trick or treating or go to the party and check out the costumes."

He almost offered to go with her but pretty much everyone he knew would be at the Halloween party and he remembered what a nightmare it had been the last time she was around his uni mates. "I should get going," he said, putting an end to the conversation.

"Are you meeting the football team?"

Pausing at the top of the stairs, he contemplated what to say. It wasn't as though he had to hide the fact he was going on a date. In fact, it would probably be better if she knew. Sneaking around would make things awkward.

"I have a date," he said hesitantly. She didn't react and he wasn't sure why he'd thought she might.

"Is it a first date?"

"Erm … second really. We went out ages ago and I didn't think it was going to work out, but I thought I'd give it another go."

She smiled. "Where are you taking her?"

"I'm going to her place. She's cooking."

Her smile widened and it annoyed him immensely. "She must really like you then."

"I guess." He smoothed his shirt down. "I bought a new shirt. Does it look okay?"

"I guess so. It looks like all your other shirts."

Her lack of enthusiasm bothered him more than it should have done. "You could have just said it looked fine," he grumbled as he set off down the stairs.

"If you just wanted me to say it looked fine, why did you bother asking me?"

"I've got no idea."

"You asked for my opinion," she said. "Why do you seem annoyed with me?"

He shook his head, unable to come up with a reply. Why *was* he annoyed with her? "Have a good weekend," he said, then hurried down the stairs and banged the front door behind him.

The chatter in his head was constant as he made the twenty-minute walk to Bridget's house. What the heck was wrong with his shirt? It was expensive and well cut. He also had his favourite Rolex on. And a new pair of Nike trainers with his classic Levis. He looked good. He knew he looked good. Why the hell hadn't Scarlett thought so? And why did he even care what she thought?

Before he knew it he was standing outside Bridget's place and his thoughts were still all over the place. He really wasn't in the mood for the date. After taking a deep breath, he tapped the knocker on the middle of the door of the end-terrace house.

"Perfect timing!" Bridget said when she answered. As he stepped inside she kissed his cheek, then lingered by his neck. "You smell great." She beamed at him and ran a hand down his arm. "I love that shirt, too."

"Thanks." At least someone appreciated his dress sense. "I should have brought drinks or something…" He'd intended to pick something up on the way but had been too distracted to think about it.

"I have plenty," she said, moving to the kitchen. Steam was rising from whatever was bubbling on the hob and the table was already set. "I hope pasta is okay?"

"Great." He shoved his hands in his pockets, wishing he'd never agreed to the date. Especially not at her place. Drinks in a busy bar would have been a much safer option.

She got him a bottle of beer, then told him to take a seat while she finished cooking, keeping up a constant stream of chatter as she went. It was just as well she was good at conversation, because he was struggling to concentrate. All through dinner she went on and on, cheerfully telling him about her family and then about her course. Fraser nodded along and tried not to lose track of the conversation completely.

"You're a really good cook," he said, leaning back in the chair when he'd finished dessert of homemade apple crumble.

"It was all pretty basic," she said. "There's more if you want?"

"I'm stuffed, thanks."

She took the bowls to the sink, then got them both another beer. "Shall we move to the couch? It's comfier."

"Sure." He checked his watch as he followed her. "I can't stay too late. I've got a game tomorrow."

When they walked into the room at the back of the house, it turned out to be a bedroom and not the living room as he'd expected.

"I drew the short straw and got the downstairs bedroom," Bridget said.

"Isn't there a living room?"

"No. But the bedrooms are all a good size and the kitchen is pretty spacious too. It works okay." She bypassed the bed and drew the curtains, then took a seat on the two-seater sofa by the window.

Hesitantly, Fraser joined her and set his bottle on the low table in front of the couch.

"I'm really happy that I bumped into you last week," Bridget said, turning to sit sideways on the couch. Her leg rested against his.

"Me too." He took a few long gulps of his beer.

When he set the bottle down again, Bridget inched closer and rested her arm on his shoulder.

"You've got such great hair," she said, dragging her fingers through it.

"Thanks." His mind flashed to Scarlett asking if it annoyed him when it fell forwards. As Bridget trailed her fingers along his hairline, he thought of Scarlett touching his ear and how offended she'd looked when he'd pulled away so abruptly. He wondered if he'd upset her and whether she'd gone back to Hope Cove or if she was still at their place. He'd quite like to go home and find out.

Except he was on a date with an attractive woman who clearly fancied him. Why was he thinking of Scarlett? Clearly she didn't like him. Whenever he tried to hang out with her she fobbed him off, and when he'd mentioned going on a date she hadn't cared. He was being ridiculous. It was a case of wanting what you can't have. After all, when Scarlett had been openly flirting with him that night in the bar, he'd freaked out and hadn't wanted anything to do with her.

"Are you okay?" Bridget asked, breaking his thoughts.

"Yeah."

Her fingers teased the skin at the back of his neck as she leaned in to kiss him. It crossed his mind to stop her, but he told himself he was being stupid. Why would he stop a hot girl from kissing him?

She seemed oblivious to the fact that his heart wasn't in it and pushed her hands into his hair as she kissed him eagerly. Deftly, she undid the top button of his shirt.

"We probably shouldn't get carried away," he said, pulling back. "If I'm not on form for my match tomorrow, the coach will go crazy."

She smiled sheepishly. "Sorry."

"No worries." Had she really just apologised for trying to have sex with him? "I should get going and have an early night."

"Which pitch are you playing on tomorrow?" she asked. "I might stop by and watch."

"It's an away game." Thank goodness. "In Bristol. The team goes in the minibus."

"I bet that's a laugh."

At one time he'd have agreed, but the trips with the team weren't as much fun as they used to be. "It's all right."

"We should go out again sometime. Are you going to the Halloween party next weekend?"

"I'm not sure."

"We could go together?"

He ran a hand along his jaw. "I was thinking of going with Scarlett."

"Your housemate?"

"Yeah. She mentioned that she wanted to go, but she doesn't

have a lot of friends at uni so I thought I might keep her company."

"We could all hang out together," Bridget suggested. "I'd like to meet her."

He chewed on his bottom lip. "I don't think she'd like it." And *he* definitely wouldn't like it. "She struggles with meeting new people. We probably won't even stay long. She just wants to see people's costumes. I think she has a bit of an obsession with vampires." He smiled, knowing exactly what his costume was going to be.

"I keep thinking about her since you told me about her. It's so impressive how she manages with uni."

"She's amazing," Fraser said. "I've never met someone so driven. She just published her first book a few weeks ago. It's really good."

"When you said she was a writer I assumed it was a hobby."

"No. She started a publishing company with a couple of friends."

"Wow. How does she do all that and find time to study?"

"She doesn't have a social life." As he said it, he realised that she probably hadn't been making excuses when she said she had work to do. With everything she had going on, it made sense that she'd need to work every evening. He thought of her asking him to hang out tonight and wished he'd taken her up on it. "Anyway, I should get going," he said, standing abruptly. "Thanks a lot for dinner."

"You're welcome." She walked him to the door. "I had a really good time." When she stood on her toes and leaned in, he gave her a hasty peck before stepping away.

"I'll be in touch," he said.

"Let's get together again soon."

He nodded as he backed out of the door and called goodbye.

At the end of the road he flagged down a taxi and directed the driver to the house. The lights were all off when they pulled up, but that didn't mean anything. He paid the driver in a rush and hurried to the front door.

It was only ten so he didn't imagine she'd be asleep yet. He shouted hello as he took the stairs two at a time. There was no reply.

"Scarlett?" he called as he knocked on her door. Then he took a step back. What was he going to do if she was home? Ask her to play video games with him? Or tell her he'd go to the Halloween party with her? He shouted her name again, then moved towards the door. If she was asleep she was probably going to yell at him, but he didn't care.

The door handle clicked as he pressed it down. Light flooded in from the hallway, but there was no sign of her. Impulsively, he hit the light switch. With a heavy sigh he flicked the light off again before closing the door and wandering back to his own room.

It was probably a good thing she wasn't there. He'd been drinking and wasn't thinking clearly.

CHAPTER 23

On Saturday, Scarlett spent a messy afternoon carving pumpkins with Phoebe and Maya. She took them for a walk to the playground too, then hung around to have dinner at their place. After a busy few weeks of juggling uni assignments and work for the publishing company, she was happy to take a bit of time off. It would have been better if her plan to hang out with Fraser the previous evening had worked out but she didn't want to think about that. Instead, she focused on the bustle around Lizzie and Max's kitchen table as they ate.

"I could babysit tonight if you want to go out?" she offered while Max paced the kitchen with little Nathan, who'd started crying as soon as they sat down to eat. "I'm sure I'd be fine with Nathan."

"Thanks," Max said, through a yawn. "But I don't think either of us are fit for a night out. Between this one and Maya we've hardly slept in weeks."

"Doesn't Maya sleep well?"

"She used to," Lizzie said. "We think the new baby has unsettled her."

"You should get her a weighted blanket," Scarlett suggested. "I love mine. I sleep much better since I got it."

"A weighted blanket?" Max asked.

She nodded through a mouthful of pasta. "Fraser gave it to me for my birthday. He knows I don't sleep well and thought it might help." Scarlett glanced up in time to see Lizzie and Max exchanging a look.

Lizzie smiled at her. "I think it's just a phase with Maya."

"I've heard about those weighted blankets." Max jiggled Nathan in his arms and opened his mouth as though to say more but was interrupted by Lizzie standing up and offering to take the baby so he could eat.

"I still don't sleep brilliantly," Scarlett said. "But it's better than before."

"Tammy was telling us about them a while ago," Max said as he sat down. "The postwoman. Her eldest son is autistic and has ADD. They got one for him when he wasn't sleeping well."

Scarlett paused, chewing her food slowly. "Did it work?"

"She didn't think it made much difference, but they were desperate and trying everything."

"It feels nice anyway," Scarlett said.

Lizzie paced with the baby and glared at Max. "Your dinner will be stone cold if you don't eat it soon. And can you try and persuade Phoebe to eat? She's hardly touched her pasta."

Scarlett felt slightly sorry for Max. He was only chatting and Lizzie spoke to him as though he was a naughty kid.

"It was nice that Fraser bought me a present," she mused.

"Very thoughtful," Lizzie agreed.

"He's hard to figure out though." Scarlett's mind drifted to the previous evening when she'd touched his ear and he'd responded as though he was repulsed by her.

"Men are easy to figure out," Max said confidently.

"I think he's annoyed with me for not being enthusiastic when he asked if I liked his shirt."

Lizzie chuckled. "If a guy asks how he looks, you're just supposed to say they look good. They want an ego boost not an opinion."

After a moment Max shrugged. “She’s probably right.”

“Have you been hanging out with him a lot?” Lizzie asked.

“No. I’ve been busy with coursework.” She thought about the previous evening when he’d told her he was going on a date but decided she didn’t want to talk about that. If she could stop herself from thinking about it, that would be nice too. As she finished her food, she offered to hold Nathan, then walked into the living room with him to avoid any more questions about Fraser.

On Friday afternoon, Scarlett was just arriving home when Fraser pulled up outside the house.

“I hope this is enough,” she said, holding up a large bag of sweets. “I have no idea how many trick or treaters we’ll get.”

“Are you still up for going out?” he asked as he opened the front door. He’d told her on Monday that he’d be going to the Halloween party and said they could go together. She’d agreed but hadn’t been particularly enthusiastic.

“Yes. But we should get some trick or treaters before then. I’ve got a jack-o-lantern to put outside the door so kids know they can knock here.”

“You really get into Halloween, don’t you?”

“I love it.” She headed to the kitchen and emptied the sweets into a bowl. “Have you got a costume?” she asked over her shoulder.

“Yeah.” He leaned on the doorframe.

“Is it good? My costume’s really good. I don’t want to hang out with you at the party if you have some crappy costume.”

“I have a great costume.” He smiled brightly. “I presume you’re going as a vampire?”

“No way.” She waltzed past him and set off up the stairs. “A vampire’s a terrible costume. They just look like regular people.”

He followed her through the house. "What about Dracula and his cape?"

"I mean real vampires, not the cartoon kind."

"Oh, *real vampires!*"

"Yes." She laughed. "Everyone knows real vampires look like normal people until they get hungry and show their teeth."

"You make a good point. That would be a terrible costume."

"I mean they're super hot, of course."

"Every vampire I've met has been hot," Fraser said, his voice full of mirth.

"Get changed," she said at the door to her bedroom. "It's almost dark. The trick or treaters should start arriving soon."

He let Scarlett use the bathroom first, then had a shower and got dressed. When he was ready he went back downstairs, where he could hear Scarlett moving around the kitchen. He stopped in the doorway, swallowing a lump in his throat as he watched her lighting the candle in her jack-o-lantern.

His eyes trailed up her green and black striped tights and lingered on the black mini skirt. The tight green T-shirt highlighted her slender figure. When she turned and looked at him, the smoky eye make-up and black eyeliner made his breath catch. Her black lips matched her black nails, and she made a particularly striking witch.

"How long does the hair dye last?" he asked, smiling at the green streaks in her hair.

"Just until I wash it."

As the doorbell sounded she picked up the bowl of sweets and handed him the pumpkin as she rushed to the door. On opening it, she threw her head back and cackled an over-the-top laugh, then asked the group of schoolkids what they wanted in a theatrically wobbly voice. They beamed as they shouted trick or treat. While she handed out treats, she muttered spells, making them all laugh. Fraser couldn't take his eyes off her.

"You really love Halloween, don't you?" he asked, setting the pumpkin outside the door as the kids wandered away.

"It's my favourite day of the year." She peered up and down the road before they went back inside. "It's the one day I can be as weird as I want without worrying what people think. Halloween is the perfect day for anyone who's weird."

"You're not weird," he said quietly.

She shook her head and gave a quick shrug. "Where's your costume?"

"This is it." He held his arms out, showing off his black jeans and crisp white shirt with the sleeves rolled back. He'd slicked his hair back with gel too. "What do you think?"

She looked him up and down. "That's not a costume."

With a wicked grin, he curled his top lip to reveal long, pointed incisors. "Am I hot enough for a vampire?"

She laughed. "That's such a cheat. You can't go to the party like that."

"I think it's a great costume."

She moved past him and along the hall. "On a day when you can wear anything you want, why would you wear your normal clothes?"

"I don't like costumes," he said, following her through to the kitchen.

"You at least need some blood." She pulled a sharp knife from the stand and waved it at him. "Come here."

His heart quickened and he stepped backwards so fast he almost fell over a chair. "What are you doing?"

"A few drops down your chin would look awesome."

He stared at her. "What the hell are you doing with the knife?"

"We can get a few drops of blood from your hand. You'll barely even feel it."

"You're not cutting my hand. Are you crazy?"

She rolled her eyes. "You're such a wimp. We can do my hand instead." Turning, she put her hand over the sink and flicked the knife across her palm.

His heart hammered furiously as he dashed across the room.

He grabbed her hand at the same moment she dropped the knife into the sink and cracked up laughing.

"What the hell?" His shoulders sagged as he inspected her hand, which was completely unmarked. "You almost gave me a heart attack."

"I can't believe you're so gullible. Did you honestly think I'd cut myself just to enhance your costume?"

"It seemed like the sort of thing you might do."

He hadn't released her hand and was suddenly aware of their proximity. She didn't move away but gazed into his eyes. You'd never know she had a problem with eye contact. His breathing was out of whack after the adrenalin rush, and his eyes moved to her lips as he contemplated kissing her. She was staring at him so intensely that he was sure she wanted him to kiss her too.

"Your eyes," she whispered, her voice breaking the atmosphere. Taking half a step back, he released her hand and felt like a complete idiot. She wasn't gazing lovingly into his eyes. She was confused by the unnatural colour of them.

"Coloured contacts," he explained. "Do they look okay?"

"They look …" She swallowed hard and looked away. "Good," she said, stepping quickly around him. "I've got fake blood upstairs from last year. I'll get it."

When she returned, Fraser sat on a chair as instructed while she dripped fake blood down his chin. She put two fingers on his neck to stem the line of red dye before it hit his collar. He wondered if she could feel how fast his heart was beating under the warmth of her fingers.

"It would look good if the dye was on your shirt too," she said. "But I don't think you'd ever get it out, so you'd only ever be able to wear the shirt when you dress as a vampire."

"Often, then!" he joked.

Her fingers shifted slightly. "You're very warm for a vampire."

He moved so his knee rested against her leg. "And you're very hot for a witch."

She held his gaze for the briefest moment, then stepped away, leaving him with an ache in his chest.

"Go on then. Ruin my shirt if you must." Anything to get her close again.

"Are you sure?"

He nodded and she put a few drops on his collar and a line down his front. "You look good," she said, then moved to the door when the bell rang, giving Fraser a moment to catch his breath.

CHAPTER 24

Scarlett had often heard students talking about the Lemon Grove, the student-only club on campus, but it was the first time she'd been. It was loud and crowded and she was immediately captivated by the array of costumes; some elaborate and imaginative, some not so much.

"What the hell's that?" she asked, when Fraser returned from the bar and handed her a pint glass filled with red liquid. "I thought you were getting beers."

"They're putting red food colouring in the lager." He took a sip. "It tastes all right."

"That's stupid."

"Yes. But Halloween is stupid so it's fitting."

She pulled at her T-shirt and complained about the heat, then took a long swig of the beer, which thankfully tasted like regular lager.

A guy in his football kit shouted across the crowd to Fraser and raised an arm to wave.

"His terrible excuse for a costume makes yours look quite imaginative," Scarlett said as Fraser raised a hand in reply.

"Footballer was my second choice."

She glanced around. "If you want to go and hang out with

your friends, it's fine. I'll walk around and check out the costumes."

"I'll come with you. Lead the way."

She'd just set off across the room when Fraser tapped her on the shoulder and told her to follow him before setting off in the opposite direction.

"Where are we going?" she asked as she trailed after him. There was no way he could hear her over the music.

At the side of the room, he hurried up the steps of the raised platform and slipped onto a stool at an empty table.

"Well spotted," she said as she sat beside him. There weren't many tables, and the others were all taken.

"It's a perfect spot to watch people." He tapped the rim of his glass against hers and took a swig.

Finding herself distracted by the dazzling blue of his eyes, she only managed to nod in agreement, then gazed out over the sea of people, some of whom were dancing while others stood around chatting.

"I think the T-Rex is my favourite costume so far," Fraser said, leaning close to her.

"He must be so hot inside that thing. I bet he passes out before the end of the night."

"Probably. Which is your favourite?"

"I like the group of girls dressed as Ghostbusters."

"They're cool. Did you see the guy dressed as Donald Trump?"

"He'll probably end up getting punched by the end of the night. I really like the Incredible Hulk costume."

"I've noticed."

"What's that supposed to mean?"

"You can't take your eyes off him."

She felt her cheeks heating up. "It's a great costume."

"Yeah right! Admit you have a thing for muscly green guys!"

"Shut up." She knocked her shoulder against his. Fraser leaned his forearms on the table and ran his tongue along his shiny fang. "Where did you get those from?" Scarlett asked. "They're not the usual cheap plastic ones."

"I ordered them online. They came with adhesive to stick them to your teeth."

He curled his lip to give her a better look and she found herself wondering if he could still kiss with fangs. Snatching her gaze away, she went back to people-watching.

The bustle of people in costumes kept Scarlett thoroughly entertained. Keeping up a steady stream of chatter with Fraser made it all the more fun. If she'd have come alone she'd probably only have managed a few laps of the place to check out people's outfits and then left.

Now and then someone would call out to Fraser and shout a greeting or beckon him over, but he only smiled back and shook his head. Scarlett encouraged him to go and be sociable a couple of times, but he insisted he was happy where he was. There was a moment when he went to the bar for another beer that Scarlett wasn't sure if he'd come back. He laughed with his friends for a few minutes, then returned to her. She wondered what had happened to the girl he'd been on a second date with and if there'd been any more dates since then. The more beer she drank, the more she thought about it.

"Do you want another?" Fraser asked, when she finished her drink. He'd got through three in the time she'd managed one.

"No, thanks." She caught him glance over at the group of guys by the bar. "Why don't you go and hang out with your friends for a while?"

"No. I'm all right."

"I saw some girls from my course, so I might go and say hello to them. I want to walk around and check out the other rooms too."

"Shall we split up and meet back here later?"

"Okay."

"Great." He stood up when she did. "If I don't see you beforehand, shall I meet you back here in half an hour?"

She agreed and walked down the three steps from the raised platform, then turned back. "I'll see you later."

Fraser was fairly sure that Scarlett had no intention of talking to anyone on her course, but she seemed keen to get rid of him for a while, and it gave him an opportunity to speak to Bridget, who'd been eyeing him from the bar for the last ten minutes. He'd been panicking that she might come over and then wondered why he was so concerned by the idea.

Bridget beamed as she sidled up to him in her slinky black Catwoman costume. When she rested a hand at the waistband of his jeans, he automatically glanced over his shoulder. Scarlett was nowhere to be seen.

"How are you?" he asked.

"Great! There's such a good atmosphere tonight, isn't there?"

"Yeah."

"Your eyes look fantastic," she said, touching his jaw to bring his gaze to hers. "Has Scarlett left already?"

"No. She just went for a walk around."

"I wanted to come and say hello but I wasn't sure whether I should."

"It's probably best not to. She gets overwhelmed easily." Not that you'd have known it that night. She appeared completely at ease and was about as confident as he'd ever seen her.

"I'm happy I got to see you anyway." As she leaned in to kiss him, someone slapped him on the back. He was glad of the interruption.

"Where's your costume?" Brett asked. His Spiderman costume looked cheap and well worn.

Fraser grinned to show off his fangs, then took Bridget's hand and led her away from the crowd and into the adjoining room. Drum and bass played, and he was fairly sure Scarlett wouldn't venture in there. The air seemed to vibrate with the thudding of the music and fluorescent lights gave everything an unnatural glow.

"Where are you taking me?" Bridget asked, pulling on his arm to stop him.

"I wanted to get away from the football guys so I could talk to you." It probably wasn't the best time or place to let her down gently, but he didn't want to let things drag on with her thinking they were an item.

She giggled. "It's difficult to speak in here."

"True." You really had to shout to be heard.

"That's okay." Stepping closer, she hooked her arms around his neck and pressed her body against his. The catsuit was so tight it was almost as though she wasn't wearing anything.

He rested his hands at her hips, trying to discreetly push her away. "I should go and check on Scarlett."

"I'm sure she's fine." Lightly, she brushed her lips against his. "It's really sweet how much you worry about her."

"She doesn't have many friends." He glanced around. "I promised I'd hang out with her."

Bridget drew his attention with a hand on his cheek. "From what you've told me, she's perfectly capable of looking after herself."

"Yeah. I know… but …" *But what?* It was a bit harsh to say he was looking for an excuse to get away because he didn't want to kiss her. And that he actually *wanted* to hang out with Scarlett.

"I really have to go and find her," he shouted, but the music seemed to kick up a notch and he was fairly sure he was drowned out.

When she pulled on the back of his neck, he thought it was so she could hear him better, but the next thing he knew her lips were all over his and it took him a moment to peel her off.

"What's going on?" she asked, apparently only just getting the message that he wasn't into it.

He checked his watch. "I arranged to meet Scarlett and I don't want her to be waiting for me. I'm sorry. I have to go." Pulling away from her, he dashed back across the room and into the next one. His eyes scanned the crowd. It wasn't even time for them to meet up again yet but he needed to find her. He should never have agreed to split up in the first place.

When there was no sign of her, he ventured into the other room and did a lap of the dance floor. Still, he couldn't spot her so he headed back to their meeting point.

"Looking for your wife or your girlfriend?" Simon asked, stopping him with a hand on his arm. The football team were still scattered near the bar.

"What?"

"Are you seeing that Bridget girl?" He slurred as he spoke. "She was looking for you earlier, and Scarlett's just been here looking for you. I can almost understand the attraction tonight. She's looking hot."

"Where did she go?"

"I pointed her in the direction of the drum and bass room after I'd had a nice chat to her."

Fraser's hands formed fists and he forced himself to breathe deeply. "What did you say to her?"

"Nothing. I was just complimenting her outfit."

"If you've upset her I'll—"

"You'll what?" Simon seemed more amused than threatened. "I didn't upset her anyway. Just told her she looked good. Nothing wrong with that, is there?"

Pushing past Simon, he set off on another lap of the room, then went over to where he was supposed to meet Scarlett. He pulled his phone out and called her. Even if by some miracle she answered, he wouldn't be able to hear her. After holding the phone to his ear for a minute, he typed out a message asking where she was. He felt a momentary relief when a reply came through. She said she was on the way home and told him to enjoy the rest of his night.

There was no way he was going to enjoy himself. Not while he was wondering what Simon had said to her. And whether she'd seen him with Bridget.

After the heat of the club, being out in the fresh air was refreshing. He was about to set off towards the taxi rank when Bridget appeared beside him.

"Are you leaving?" she asked.

"Yes. I need to find Scarlett. I think Simon upset her. She went home."

"Do you want me to come?"

He shook his head in confusion. "What?"

"If she's upset, maybe she'd appreciate having a woman to talk to."

He got the impression she was genuinely concerned and not just looking for an excuse to come home with him. If she wasn't so bloody nice she'd be much easier to deal with. He could tell her to go away without feeling like a complete shit.

"Thanks for the offer, but I don't think it would help. She's probably fine, I just need to put my mind at ease."

She rubbed his shoulder. "Will you come back out later? It's still early."

"Probably not. I'm not actually a fan of Halloween. I only came out because Scarlett wanted to."

"Right." Her smile looked forced. "I see."

"I'm sorry. I need to go."

She bit her lower lip. "Will you give me a call?"

"Sure." He kissed her cheek and took off at a brisk pace.

As soon as he got home, he went to Scarlett's room. Light seeped out from under the door, and he was in such a hurry that he forgot to knock.

"I could have been getting changed," she snapped without turning around from her desk. She tapped away on her laptop in her pyjama bottoms and a hoodie.

"What?"

"Don't come into my room without knocking."

"Sorry. I was worried about you. I was looking all over for you."

"I messaged and told you I was on the way home. You didn't need to leave."

"I wanted to check you're okay. Simon said he'd seen you. He didn't upset you, did he?"

"The fact that you assume your friend would upset me might be a sign that you need new friends."

She made a good point, but he thought Simon was pretty harmless really. "He's not so bad," he said, moving further into the room. "He just says stupid things when he's drunk. Did he upset you?"

"He squeezed my arse. But it's exactly the sort of thing he'd do so it wasn't a massive surprise."

His jaw tightened and the action sent the stupid fake teeth digging into the inside of his mouth. "I'm sorry."

"Why? You didn't do anything."

It was driving him crazy that she wouldn't look at him. No matter where he stood, he couldn't get a good look at her face. "You could have told me you were leaving. I'd have come with you."

Scarlett paused and removed her fingers from the keyboard. Her thumb and forefingers on both hands tapped together repeatedly. Taking an audible breath, she clasped them in her lap.

"You looked like you were having a good time with your friend so I didn't want to disturb you."

So she had seen him with Bridget. The fact that she sounded jealous should have been a good thing, but he just felt like crap for upsetting her.

"Is she the one you're dating?" Scarlett asked.

"I've been on a couple of dates with her," he said.

"Does she know you're married?"

"No. Why?"

"Just wondering."

Fraser shoved his hands into his pockets. "Sorry," he whispered.

"You don't have to apologise to me. It's not as though we have any commitment to each other. We never said we wouldn't date anyone for three years."

"I know." He walked backwards and sank onto the bed, burying his face in his hands. "But I feel like crap. And I feel so guilty."

"You're lying to your girlfriend. I guess it's normal to feel guilty."

"She's not my girlfriend."

"Person you're dating then. Whatever you want to call it. How would you react if you were dating someone and then you found out they were married?"

"I don't think that's even the issue here."

She nestled her hands in the pocket of her hoodie. "What is the issue then?"

"My issue is that I think I've upset you."

Her gaze fell to the floor. "I'm not upset."

"Annoyed then? Are you annoyed because you think I'm seeing someone?"

"No."

"I don't believe you."

"If I'm annoyed it's because you're sitting on my bed when I want to go to sleep."

He stood up but didn't move any further. "Can you be honest with me? Because it seems as though you're angry with me because you think I have a girlfriend …"

"Well, I am your wife."

He suspected she was trying to make a joke, but the fact that she sounded bitter made it fall flat. "I've tried to be your friend, but I'm not sure that's working. Do you want more than that?"

She kept her eyes trained on the floor and shook her head. "I just wanted a student loan so I could get my degree. I don't want anything else from you. Apart from for you to get out of my room. I want to go to sleep." She checked her watch. "It's pretty early. You could go back to the party and hang out with your girlfriend."

"So you *are* annoyed about Bridget?"

"No." She threw her hands up. "I don't care. Just go away, please."

After a moment, he did as he was told. There was no way he was going back to the party though.

CHAPTER 25

Scarlett was effective in avoiding Fraser over the next week. If she could do an equally good job of putting the image of him snogging Catwoman out of her mind, she'd be much happier. She'd been enjoying the Halloween party up until that point and had thought Fraser was having fun with her too. As usual, she'd read the situation all wrong. Just because he seemed to like hanging out with her didn't mean he saw her as anything other than a friend. He'd been very open about the fact that he was dating someone, so Scarlett really shouldn't have got the wrong idea about his feelings for her.

Now she didn't even want to be friends with him. She got angry whenever she thought about him and she didn't have the time or energy to try and figure out why. It was easier to avoid him. She managed it well for a week, but then he caught her unawares on campus and she had no choice but to speak to him. She was on her way to the study hall and he was hanging around outside the building. If he hadn't already seen her, she'd have changed direction.

"Hey!" He sounded surprised, so at least he hadn't come looking for her. "Where've you been? You never seem to be at home. I messaged you a few times too."

"I've been working in the library or the study hall a lot. It's easier to concentrate." That was a lie; it was noisy and full of distractions. "I've got a lot of work on – coursework and lots of stuff with the publishing company. We're publishing a couple more books this month and we're on a big advertising drive to get Christmas sales."

"Sounds like you're snowed under."

"Yes."

He nodded and glanced around. "I'm meeting someone or I'd have suggested we grab a drink or dinner or something."

"I've got too much to do anyway."

"Maybe another time? I could buy you dinner. I feel as though you probably don't eat properly."

God, he was annoying. No wonder the very thought of him made her angry. She sighed heavily. "I'm perfectly capable of looking after myself, thanks."

"Yeah. I didn't mean it like that. I'd just like to catch up. Can you spare a couple of hours for me sometime?"

"I'm really busy." She went to step around him but stopped at the sight of a smiley girl walking out of the building. Scarlett recognised her instantly, even without her catsuit on and her tongue down Fraser's throat.

"Fraser!" she called before she reached them.

"Hi," he said as he turned around. Scarlett searched his features for signs of discomfort but he seemed at ease, if slightly morose. He certainly didn't look like a guy whose girlfriend had just come face to face with his wife. Or at least not one who was troubled by the fact.

Scarlett looked away when Catwoman kissed Fraser lightly on the lips.

"This is Scarlett," he said, before she could make a quick exit.

"Hi!" Catwoman smiled. She had annoyingly bouncy golden blonde hair. "I'm Bridget. It's great to finally meet you. Fraser's told me all about you."

"I highly doubt that," Scarlett muttered.

Bridget only smiled wider. "Fraser told me how much fun you two have living together. About how you like the same video games and have the same taste in TV shows. It must be great to share a house with someone you get on so well with. I share with two girls. It gets a bit crazy sometimes, especially when we're all fighting over the bathroom on a Friday night."

Scarlett stared at her. "I have to go. I've got work to get on with."

"Don't feel you have to rush off," Bridget said. "Fraser and I were just going to grab a bite to eat. You're welcome to join us. I'd love to get to know you better."

"You wouldn't," Scarlett said, curling her lip. "Trust me."

Bridget's smile fell away and Scarlett hurried into the building and up the stairs. Her usual table in the corner of the study room was free. She'd just opened her laptop when Fraser slid into the seat beside her.

"You didn't have to be rude," he whispered.

"I wasn't rude. It would have been rude to pretend to be nice to her and go out for a cosy dinner with you. If anyone is being rude it's you. How can you be in a relationship with someone and lie to them constantly?"

"I'm not in a relationship with her," he snapped. "And even if I was, you said it's fine for us to see other people, so I'm not sure why you're so pissed off with me."

"Please just go away. I thought you were going out for dinner."

"I am, but you seem to be avoiding me and I'd like to know why."

"Because you annoy me. I would have thought that was obvious."

"Whatever I've done, I'm sorry." His hand moved to hers and he ran his thumb over her knuckles.

"Stop it!" Quickly, she snatched her hand away and shoved her laptop back into her bag.

"Where are you going?" he asked, shooting out of his chair as she stood up.

"Leave me alone," she hissed over her shoulder as she hurried across the room.

In the hallway, he grabbed her elbow and pulled her to face him. "Please talk to me," he said, looking right into her eyes. "I want to know what's going on in your head. I hate the thought that you're upset because of me."

Tears filled her eyes and her throat felt so tight she wasn't sure she could speak. "I *am* upset because of you," she said.

He put a hand on her cheek and brushed her tears away. "I'm sorry."

"Don't touch me." She pushed his hand away and stepped to the edge of the corridor. "It confuses me when you touch me. Everything about you confuses me. Sometimes you want to hang out and sometimes you don't. Sometimes you're nice to me and sometimes you ignore me. And you say Bridget isn't your girlfriend but you kiss her on the lips … and I don't understand any of it. But I do understand that you're someone who plays games with people and I don't want you to play games with me." She looked at him through teary eyes. "I just want you to leave me alone. Please." She held his gaze, and the hurt in his eyes made her chest ache.

"I'm sorry," he whispered before he left.

CHAPTER 26

As much as it pained him, Fraser did what Scarlett asked and kept his distance. Any time he thought about trying to make amends, he remembered the look on her face in the study hall. Whether he'd meant to or not, he'd hurt her. Apparently Allie had been right; hurting people was just what he did. The best thing he could do for Scarlett was to stay away from her.

Considering how little he saw of her during the last weeks of term, it was surprising how alone he felt when she went back to Hope Cove for the Christmas holidays. His mum messaged and called him daily asking when he'd be home. Allie and Liam kept asking him the same. He'd definitely go back to Thorverton for Christmas; he just lacked the motivation to make any sort of a plan.

It was the Friday before Christmas when Allie and Liam turned up on his doorstep late in the morning.

"You look like crap," Allie said as she kissed his cheek.

"Thanks. Nice to see you too." He hugged Liam and led them into the living room.

Allie plonked herself on the couch. "You seriously need a shave. And clean clothes."

"I've been enjoying a relaxing break. I didn't realise you were going to turn up and tease me about it."

"I feel like you could have predicted the visit really," Liam said. "There's only so many times you can fob us off before we'll just come and track you down."

"I wanted to see your place too," Allie said, looking around the room. "It's nice."

"Yeah."

"Are you going to tell us why you're hiding out here?" she asked, leaning onto her knees.

"I'm not hiding out. I'm chilling out. As soon as I go home Mum will start nagging me about something, and Hattie will be her high-pitched annoying self."

"You *are* going home though? Because your mum will come and drag you back if you don't go soon."

"Yeah. I was thinking of going back today but you seem to have messed up my plans."

"I don't believe you had any plans. But I'd like you to shower and shave and come out for lunch with us."

"I can manage that." He was actually glad of the reason to get himself in gear. Hanging around the house on his own wasn't doing him any good.

"Can we have a nosey around?" Allie asked, trailing behind him when he left the room.

He gave them a quick tour of the house before he got ready to go out. They walked to the Mexican restaurant a couple of streets away and settled in a quiet corner for lunch.

"So what's new with you two?" Fraser asked. He exchanged messages with Liam frequently so he felt up-to-date, but it was always good to catch up in person.

"Nothing," Allie said on a sigh. "We're completely boring. We may as well talk about your life or we'll all be asleep before the food arrives."

Fraser's eyes darted between Allie and Liam. Beneath the jokey exterior, he got the impression there was more going on than they were letting on. Liam was always slightly drowned out by Allie but he was particularly quiet that day.

"There's not a lot going on with me either," he finally said, then shifted his focus to the menu.

"Liar!" Allie spat. "There's always something going on with you. What's the deal with that girl you were seeing?" She looked to Liam. "What was her name?"

"Bridget," Liam said.

Fraser shook his head. "I only went on a couple of dates with her."

"Then broke her heart?" Allie asked.

"No. We're still friends." He'd been meeting her to tell her he didn't think it would work out between them the day they'd bumped into Scarlett outside of the study hall. Bridget had taken the news surprisingly well. She still messaged him now and again, so maybe they *would* end up being friends.

Allie grinned. "Friends in the sense that she's hanging around in the hopes that you'll realise you're in love with her?"

"No!" Fraser huffed. At least he hoped not.

The waiter arrived to take their order. Fraser was glad of the reprieve in questions, but it didn't last long. As soon as they were alone again Allie barrelled on with her questions.

"How's things with Scarlett?"

"Fine, I suppose. We ignore each other."

"I thought you were getting on well," Liam said.

"We were … sort of. And now we're not."

Allie tilted her head. "So that's what the bad mood's all about?"

"I'm not in a bad mood," he said in a tone that didn't make it a very convincing statement.

"Oh, come on," Allie said. "You're moping around in the house on your own in Exeter instead of coming home. I knew there was something going on with you. What happened with Scarlett?"

"Nothing. I pissed her off and she asked me to stay away

from her so I have." He paused, wondering whether to say more or leave it at that. "Pretty much anyway."

"I have so many questions," Allie said. "Firstly, what did you do to piss her off? Secondly, what do you mean that you've *pretty much* stayed away from her?"

He blew out a breath, knowing he was probably about to get a lecture. "I was hanging out with her sometimes, and we were getting on pretty well, but she didn't like that I went on dates with Bridget …" He trailed off to let Allie get in a snarky comment but she just stared at him.

"Go on …" she instructed.

"She said that I'm the sort of person who plays games and she didn't want me playing games with her. She asked me to leave her alone."

"And you did?" Allie asked.

He nodded. "Pretty much."

"Which means?"

"It means that I spent the last month and a bit staying out of her way. I did exactly what she wanted. If I saw her I was polite and said hello. That was it. Except …" He leaned back in his chair. "I bought her a Christmas present."

"Is that bad?" Liam asked.

"Yes! Because she accused me of playing games and I'm still doing it."

"I'm slightly lost," Allie said.

"I bought her a gift so she'd have to talk to me. It's manipulative. If someone asks you to leave them alone, you shouldn't buy them a gift."

"What did you buy her?" Allie asked.

"Just a pen. And it wasn't as though I had some evil scheme … I was in town looking at watches—"

Allie interrupted him. "What the hell is it with you and watches? How many do you own?"

"Shut up. Not the point. The point is, I was shopping and I started thinking about what Scarlett would like for Christmas.

She's a writer so a pen seemed fitting, but it's kind of boring … then I remembered that when she was setting up her publishing company she wanted a different business name than her friends so I got the pen engraved with the name she wanted."

Allie closed her eyes as she sighed. "Oh my God, Fraser."

"I know! I shouldn't have done it. I should've stayed away from her like she asked, but I couldn't help myself."

"It's a very thoughtful gift," Allie said, looking slightly pained.

"You can lecture me now," Fraser told her. "Tell me what a shit person I am. It's fine."

She shook her head and shuffled her chair closer to his before she wrapped her arms around him and squeezed him hard. Then she planted a big kiss on his cheek.

"What was that for?" Fraser asked, casting a bemused look at Liam, who shrugged.

"You actually care about her, don't you?"

"Of course I care about her. But obviously not that much or I'd leave her alone."

"No." Allie glared at him. "If you genuinely care about her that changes everything."

"It doesn't matter if I care about her. I mess women around and hurt them. I can't do that to Scarlett… she's …" He rubbed his hands over his face as he debated how to finish the sentence. She was brilliant and beautiful and funny and inspiring and perfect. "She's not someone I want to hurt."

"Then don't play games," Allie said. "Don't hurt her."

He shook his head. "Even *I* think I'm not good enough for her."

"Then be better," Allie said, glaring at him.

"I don't think it's possible for me to be good enough to deserve her."

"Oh God!" Liam groaned. "Bring the old Fraser back. This version is depressing."

"Sorry," Fraser said lightly.

“What did Scarlett think of the gift?” Allie asked.

“I don’t know. I gave it to her as she was leaving. She didn’t open it and was pissed off that I bought her a gift.” When she’d snapped at him, saying she didn’t have anything for him, he’d reassured her that it was only a pen. In reply, she’d picked an old biro from her desk and thrust it at him as she wished him a happy Christmas, then told him to get out of her room. “I thought she might have messaged but I haven’t heard anything from her since she left.” Automatically, he checked his phone.

“It’s not Christmas yet,” Allie pointed out. “Maybe she hasn’t opened it. She’ll probably call to say thanks on Christmas Day.”

“I doubt it.” She definitely wouldn’t call. If anything, she might message.

“I have a question,” Liam said, with a teasing grin. “Are you in love with your wife?”

“No,” Fraser said, but struggled to keep a straight face at the disbelieving looks he got in reply. “I’m not … stop laughing … it’s not even funny. And *I’m not.*” He reached out to shove them both. “Leave me alone!”

~

The more Scarlett tried not to think about Fraser, the more he invaded her mind. She’d been convinced that if they went back to ignoring each other, she’d be able to put him out of her thoughts and focus on everything else she had going on. It hadn’t worked, and the final weeks of the autumn term had been a slog to get through.

Essays were even more difficult when her brain only seemed to want to think about Fraser. She’d also had another presentation to make. At her lecturer’s prompting, she’d asked another member of her class to help by listening to it in advance. Carolyn still had a problem with excessive sweating, even in the colder weather, but she was kind and helpful. On the day of the presentation she'd sat at the front and made a few hand gestures to signal when Scarlett should slow down. She felt as though the presentation had gone okay, but she'd thought that about the first one too so it was hard to know.

When she went back to Hope Cove in December, she tried to keep busy. It wasn't difficult; when she wasn't working in the cafe, she was busy with getting ahead with her required reading for her course or working on publishing projects with Lizzie and Emily. After almost a year in operation, Hope Cove Press was ticking along nicely. The three of them had settled into their various roles. Scarlett stuck to the behind-the-scenes stuff of setting up and maintaining online marketing and advertising campaigns as well as keeping an eye on market trends and liaising with cover designers.

Even with so much going on, Fraser still managed to pop into her head with annoying regularity. On the Friday before Christmas she was sitting in the living room of the flat with Lizzie and Emily, discussing their plan for releases in the next few months. Lizzie had brought the baby with her, but he'd slept through their entire discussion.

They'd been chatting for a while when Scarlett was hit by an image of Fraser kissing Catwoman at the Halloween party. It was a thought that came back to her multiple times a day. He'd said they weren't together but she didn't believe him. She wondered whether they'd be seeing much of each other over Christmas. Maybe Bridget was at the house a lot now that Scarlett was out of the way. That thought annoyed her more than most.

The sound of Nathan crying broke Scarlett's thoughts and she immediately registered the look on Emily's face – as though she'd asked a question and was waiting for an answer. Next she noticed the incessant drumming of her thumb against each of her fingertips in turn. Both of her hands were doing it in unison.

Inhaling sharply, she balled her hands to fists.

"Are you okay?" Emily asked. Lizzie's eyes were on her too as she lifted the baby out of his pram.

"Yes." She looked at Emily's notepad on the table. "It makes sense to publish more books by Colin Creedy. They sell brilliantly and the reviews are great. Readers want more."

"Have you been sleeping okay?" Lizzie asked, ignoring the comment. "You look tired."

"I forgot …" She trailed off, having intended to say that she'd forgotten to bring her blanket with her but realising it would make her sound like a five-year-old. "I sleep okay," she said instead. A few times she'd been tempted to go back to Exeter for the blanket. Then she'd argued with the voice in her head that insisted it was only an excuse to see Fraser. Mostly, her decision not to return had been based on the thought that she might walk into a scene of domestic bliss with him and Bridget.

"Have you heard from Fraser?" Emily asked in an annoyingly soft tone.

"No."

"Did you ever open his gift?" Lizzie asked.

"No." Scarlett rolled her eyes, wishing she hadn't mentioned that.

"Why not?" Emily asked.

"Because it's not Christmas yet. Besides, he already told me it's a pen."

"But what kind of pen?" Emily mused with a dreamy look in her eyes. "I bet it's a fancy fountain pen or something. I'm sure it's not just any old pen. It's an 'I love you' pen."

Scarlett hadn't mentioned Bridget to anyone. A couple of times when Emily had been wittering on about how she was sure Fraser liked Scarlett, she'd opened her mouth to say that he'd been dating someone. But every time she'd thought about mentioning it, she hadn't managed to find the words. Emily would no doubt make a big drama of it and Scarlett didn't particularly want opinions on the matter.

"Are we finished here?" she asked. "I told Verity I'd help in the cafe over lunchtime."

As they both muttered it was fine, Scarlett scarpered. The cafe was quiet but she hung around anyway, only going back upstairs late in the afternoon once Emily and Lizzie had left, keen to avoid any more conversations about Fraser.

CHAPTER 27

As she'd done the previous year, Scarlett invited herself to stay at Lizzie and Max's place on Christmas Eve to avoid waking up on her own in the flat on Christmas morning. She babysat while they went out for drinks for a couple of hours. It was the first time she'd looked after all three of the kids, but it turned out to be easy. The girls were asleep before Lizzie and Max went out, and little Nathan fell asleep when Scarlett gave him a bottle.

It was fun to spend Christmas morning watching the twins open their presents. From there, she went over to Verity and Bill's place for lunch. Her parents joined them for a while in the afternoon, which put a damper on the day. Verity excitedly told them all about what Scarlett had been doing with her books and the publishing company and uni. They seemed pretty impressed but it only annoyed Scarlett. She didn't have a lot of time for people who needed a string of achievements to think well of a person. Especially not when the person was their daughter.

It left a bitter taste in her mouth when she set off back to the flat that evening. Thankfully she was looking after Perry the dog for a couple of nights while Verity and Bill were away visiting Bill's relatives.

She scratched the top of his head when they arrived back. The empty flat was depressing and she was glad that she at least had the dog for company. He followed her around as she got a drink and then unpacked her overnight bag.

On her desk, Fraser's gift seemed to taunt her. She picked it up and wandered to the couch with it.

"It's only a pen," she said to Perry, who sat at her feet looking up at her. "A token gift from one housemate to another. I'm a writer so a pen is a very unimaginative gift. He basically put no thought into it." She sank back into the couch cushions, fingering the ribbon on the box and contemplating opening it. It was Christmas so she really should, but she was worried about finding that it was just a plain old pen. Foolishly, she wanted Emily to be right that it was somehow sentimental and romantic.

She almost jumped out of her skin when her phone began to vibrate on the table. For a moment she stared at the screen, annoyed with Fraser for calling when he knew she hated speaking on the phone. Then her pulse quickened at the thought of speaking to him and she fumbled the phone, panicking that she wouldn't answer it in time.

"Hi," she said in a rush.

There was a short pause. "I thought you weren't going to answer. I was going to leave a message. Happy Christmas!"

The sound of his voice made her stomach quiver. "Happy Christmas," she replied weakly.

"How are you?"

"Fine."

In the silence, she cursed herself for sounding so uninterested.

"I was just thinking about you so I thought I'd call and say hi. I probably shouldn't have. Sorry to bother you."

Scarlett opened her mouth to speak but no words came.

"I'll let you get on, I just wanted to wish you a happy Christmas."

She panicked, not knowing what to say but not wanting the call to end. "Where are you?" she blurted out.

"At home. Our place, I mean. I was at my parents' house for a few days, but I got sick of my family so came back here this evening."

She nodded, then realised he couldn't see her and she needed to speak if she wanted to keep the call going. "I was at Lizzie's house this morning, then went to Verity and Bill's place. I just got back to the flat."

"Did you get any good presents?"

"Verity and Bill gave me a scarf. Emily gave me earrings and Lizzie gave me a set with shower gel and body lotion … I don't know if that means she thinks I smell."

Fraser's gentle laugh made her sit up straighter. Phone calls had their perks, she supposed.

"Surely someone bought you stationery?" he asked. "I thought you were a writer."

She switched the phone to speaker and balanced it on her knee as she pulled at the ribbon on the small box.

"What are you doing?" Fraser asked.

"Nothing."

"Nothing you want to tell me, more like. You sound as though you're moving around."

"I'm opening your present, if you must know." Lifting the lid, she stared at the ballpoint pen in deep red. It was engraved with the words 'Scarlett Ink'.

"What do you think?" he asked quietly.

Her smile stretched wide. "I think you don't listen to anything I say," she teased. "The publishing company is called Hope Cove Press."

"I think Scarlett Ink was a better name."

"Me too." She ran her finger over the engraving on the pen. "Thank you."

"You're welcome."

"What did you get for Christmas?"

"Oh, you know, the usual … a scarf and some bath products."

"You're such a liar. You can tell me about your rich-people gifts. I promise I won't roll my eyes."

"My parents got me a new laptop and golf clubs. My grandparents gave me money. My sister bought me a football shirt." He paused. "I definitely heard your eyes roll!"

She chuckled. "I thought I'd done it quietly."

"I forgot to tell you about the best present."

"What was it?"

"I got this really cool biro."

"Black or blue?"

"Blue. Writes like a dream. And the end is already chewed, which saves me a job!"

She cracked up laughing. "It sounds as though someone took a lot of time choosing the perfect gift."

"It made me feel very special."

You are, she thought. Hearing his voice made her heart ache. There were two more weeks before she went back to Exeter and it felt like forever.

"What are you doing this evening?" he asked.

Her heart rate increased again at the thought that he might suggest meeting up.

"I don't have any plans. How about you?"

"I have some wild ideas about a night in front of the TV. There's a new series that Liam was telling me about. It's a drama but set in space with a lot of geeky science stuff. You'd probably like it."

Her cheeks felt as though they were getting a workout from all the smiling. "You think I'm into geeky science stuff?"

"I know you are! Playing Space Crusading with you was like a science lesson."

"Space is pretty interesting," she said.

"You should watch the series too. Watch it now and it'll be like watching it together… If you want to?"

"Yeah, okay." She moved to her bedroom and turned back to Perry when she got to the doorway. "Come here," she said, patting her leg.

"To your place?" Fraser asked.

"Oh, no. I wasn't talking to you. I'm looking after Bill's dog."

"I thought you were talking to me."

Scarlett picked her laptop from her desk and moved to sit on the bed. "No," she said quietly, wondering if he'd sounded disappointed or if she'd imagined it. Surely she'd imagined it. It's not as though he'd drive an hour to come and watch TV with her.

"Fraser?" she whispered.

"Yeah."

"Have you been seeing Bridget a lot?" Her stomach churned as she waited for a reply.

There was a short silence. "No. We're still friends, but that's all. And she went to Italy for like a month over Christmas. She has family there."

Scarlett wasn't sure why she forced herself to keep a straight face. It wasn't as though there was anyone around to see her. "That's good. I mean it's nice for Bridget to spend a month in Italy."

"Yeah." He cleared his throat before he told her the name of the TV series. "Let's hang up and watch the first episode now and we can discuss it."

She ended the call and immediately found the series. It was edgy and gripping, with themes of black holes and relativity theory that satisfied her interest in physics.

A few times Scarlett smiled to herself, thinking of Fraser sprawled out on the couch watching it on the big TV. After forty-five minutes he messaged and asked her what she thought. She replied to say she was getting a cup of tea and changing into her pyjamas then going straight into the second episode. While she waited for the kettle to boil, he sent another message saying he was doing the same, then sent a photo of his cup of tea and a question about whether the colour of it was offensive. Laughing, she told him it looked acceptable.

The remainder of the evening was spent watching back-to-back episodes with an exchange of messages throughout.

At three o'clock in the morning they finished the final episode of the first series and wished each other goodnight. She didn't have her blanket but she slept better than she'd done in weeks.

~

The Anchor Inn was as busy as Scarlett had ever seen it on New Year's Eve. Thankfully Jack had reserved a table by the window away from the bustle of the bar. He and Emily had been to visit family in Oxford, so Scarlett hadn't seen them since before Christmas. She told them about spending Christmas with Lizzie and Max, then Verity and Bill. She didn't mention Fraser, though he was all she could think about.

Emily was telling her about visiting her old colleagues at Oxford Castle when Scarlett completely zoned out of the conversation.

"Can I ask your opinion on something?" she asked, cutting Emily off mid-sentence. Reaching into her bag, she pulled out the pen, which was tucked into a side pocket. Jack leaned in to look when Emily took it from her.

Emily blinked rapidly as she looked at Scarlett. "We talked about this. You agreed to Hope Cove Press. We can't change the business name now."

"Yeah. I know. That's the pen that Fraser gave me for Christmas."

Emily looked at it again and a smile spread over her face. "I told you it's an 'I love you' gift."

"A pen?" Jack asked, raising an eyebrow.

"It's engraved." Emily passed it to him. "With the business name Scarlett wanted. That's really sweet."

"He called me on Christmas Day, and we watched the same TV series and kept messaging about it. And every night since then we've been messaging and watching the same TV shows."

"That's so romantic," Emily said. "I told you he has a thing for you. You're obviously going to fall in love and live happily ever after."

Scarlett exchanged a look with Jack and rolled her eyes. "It's confusing. I can never figure out if he just thinks of me as a friend or what."

"He likes you more than just a friend," Jack said. "Emily might be a bit soppy, but there's no way he'd message you every day if he wasn't interested."

Taking the pen back, Scarlett stared at the engraving. "There was this girl he was going on dates with," she finally said. "I saw them kissing one night. Now he says they're just friends, but I still don't know what's going on between us. Sometimes I like hanging out with him and sometimes everything feels messy. Last term I told him I didn't want anything to do with him, but I didn't like it when I didn't see him either."

"Relationships are messy," Emily said. "Especially at the start."

"Yours isn't," she pointed out.

"Not now. But it was." She turned to Jack. "Wasn't it?"

"I guess you could say that."

"You must know this story," Emily said to Scarlett. "Jack was together with Josie and I was besotted with him for years before we got together. At one time I thought we could never be together."

"I don't think I knew that," Scarlett said. "So you had to wait until Jack realised he didn't like Josie any more and that he actually liked you?"

"Pretty much. And it took him years!"

Jack chuckled. "Hang on a minute. For one thing, I didn't just stop liking Josie ..."

"That's a little bit awkward!" Emily said with a smirk.

He draped an arm around her shoulders but looked at Scarlett. "I realised that Josie and I weren't right for each other. And I always liked Emily, I just didn't know she liked me and it was a bit awkward because she was my girlfriend's best friend."

"Poor Josie," Scarlett said, stifling a smile.

"It all worked out fine in the end," Emily said. "But the point is ... sometimes relationships are complicated and messy... and sometimes you feel as though you'd be better off if you'd never met the person." She flashed Jack a cheeky grin. "But if you get past all that, relationships can also be really great."

"I don't even know if I want to be more than friends with Fraser," she said.

Emily rolled her eyes. "How often do you think about him?"

"I don't know," Scarlett said, reaching for her glass and feeling as though she'd been caught out.

"You definitely want to be more than friends," Emily said with an annoyingly bright smile. "I can tell, even if *you* can't."

CHAPTER 28

Fraser had tried hard to leave Scarlett alone like she wanted, but he'd had a moment of weakness on Christmas Day and told himself that there was no harm in leaving her a quick voicemail to wish her a happy Christmas. He'd almost fallen off the couch when she'd answered and was even more shocked when she didn't tell him to go away and hang up on him.

Since then he'd been counting the days until she got back to Exeter and had been trying to convince himself that maybe things would work out and he'd manage not to break her heart. He could be good enough for her. He *would* be good enough for her.

After giving the house a thorough clean and tidy on the Sunday morning that Scarlett was due to come back, he spent most of the afternoon pacing around, too hyped up with nervous energy to settle to anything. He had the TV on but wasn't paying any attention to the sitcom when the sound of the front door jolted him from his trance. After holding himself back for the briefest moment, he took a deep breath and walked to the hallway.

"Hi," she said, dropping her bag to the floor.

His mouth was dry and he swallowed hard. "Welcome back!" He sounded like an idiot. "It's good to see you."

"You too," she murmured.

He took a step forward, almost head-butting her as he gave her the world's most awkward hug.

"How was the drive?" he said as she picked up her bag and moved to the stairs. Inwardly, he cringed. Next he'd be talking about the weather.

"Good. There wasn't a lot of traffic."

"That's good. Do you want me to help with your bag?"

"No. It's not heavy."

He rocked on the balls of his feet, not sure what to do. It wasn't exactly the reunion he'd been imagining. After a moment he set off up the stairs behind her.

"I cleaned," he said. "You'll be happy to know the bathroom floor isn't covered in my clothes."

She nodded. "Good."

"Are you hungry?" he asked as she walked into her room. "I could make us some dinner."

"Auntie Verity made me eat before I left. She thinks I don't eat properly so she was on a mission to feed me all holiday."

"My mum's the same," he said with a grin.

Dropping her bag on the bed, she ran a hand over the blanket that he'd given her. Then she moved to the window and looked out.

Fraser hovered in the doorway. "It keeps snowing but it never settles on the ground." He winced. Apparently spending so much time alone had affected his conversational skills.

She remained at the window, not saying anything.

"Maybe we could hang out this evening?" he said. "We have to find a new TV show to watch."

"I need to unpack. And I have to prepare for uni tomorrow."

He was glad she didn't turn, sure he hadn't managed to keep the disappointment from his features. "I should probably leave you to it then," he said quietly.

"Maybe we can do something another time," she said, whipping around and looking right at him.

"Sure. I'd like that."

"I have to be careful that I don't get behind with my work, that's all. I can't watch TV every night. But maybe on Friday …" She shook her head. "You're probably going out on Friday."

"We can do something on Friday," he said eagerly. "Hang out and watch TV or whatever you want."

"Okay." She smiled awkwardly and he returned it.

As he closed the door and left her to unpack, he shook his head. He wasn't sure why he was surprised that her return hadn't gone as he expected. Nothing was ever predictable with Scarlett.

As Fraser left her alone Scarlett put her hands over her face. She'd been so excited to see him and then she'd turned into a nervous wreck as soon as she set eyes on him. Speaking to him on the phone and in messages had been so easy, but it was as though her brain and mouth refused to cooperate when he was in front of her. Then she'd freaked out about spending time with him. What if she stayed in panic mode and acted all weird and mute and twitchy?

Falling backwards onto the bed, she felt utterly deflated. How did she think she could be in a relationship with him when she got so stressed by the thought of an evening watching TV with him? At least she hadn't completely brushed him off. He'd seemed keen to do something on Friday. Which meant she had until Friday to pull herself together.

It was a struggle to concentrate on anything else over the week, and she wondered whether it would be better if she and Fraser went back to ignoring each other. She had so much work to do and it was difficult to concentrate when all she could think about was him.

Maybe she should fob him off and say she didn't have time

on Friday after all. Except she really wanted to hang out with him. And it was ridiculous to be so nervous. She just had to remember to breathe … like Carolyn had told her when she'd been practising for the presentation. And all those things her mum used to tell her to do around people: make eye contact and smile and ask questions to keep the conversation going.

Why did she have to coach herself though? It was all so tiring.

Scarlett was thinking about Fraser again on Thursday afternoon when she walked out of Queen's Building after a lecture. She ignored the female voice that called her name. There were a few people on her course who she could chat to easily enough now, but she didn't socialise with any of them and she wasn't keen to start. On hearing her name for a second time, she realised she wasn't going to get away with pretending she hadn't heard and stopped to see who it was.

"Do you remember me?" the girl with flowing golden locks asked. "Fraser introduced us once. I'm Bridget."

"Hi," Scarlett said.

"Have you finished lectures for the day?"

"Yes."

"Me too. You study English, don't you?"

Scarlett nodded, and glanced around, trying to come up with a polite excuse to leave. If she couldn't come up with anything polite she'd probably just walk away.

"I'm doing teacher training. I love it, but I'm finding it pretty difficult now. The first year was a breeze."

Again, Scarlett nodded. Not speaking usually made people uncomfortable, and she hoped Bridget might make her own excuse to get away.

"Do you want to get a coffee?" she asked, clearly unperturbed by the one-sided conversation.

"I was about to go home," Scarlett said flatly.

"Oh, come on." Bridget linked her arm through Scarlett's. "It's my treat. I'd really like us to get to know each other." Scarlett stared down at their interwoven arms until Bridget withdrew. "Sorry. I'm being too pushy, aren't I? I've heard so much about you from Fraser that I feel as though I know you. I'd really like it if we could be friends."

"I already have two friends," Scarlett said. "I don't know how many more I can juggle."

When Bridget's bemused smile started to look painful, Scarlett forced the corners of her lips upwards.

"Oh! You were joking!" Bridget said, her shoulders relaxing. "Fraser said you have a very dry sense of humour."

"Did he?" Scarlett asked with a glimmer of interest.

"Yes. Gosh, he absolutely adores you. It's so sweet."

"I suppose I have time for a *quick* drink," Scarlett said.

"Great!" Bridget led the way and Scarlett fell into step beside her. "I've been wanting to get to know you, but Fraser said you're shy around new people. He outright told me I wasn't allowed around to your place because he was worried it would make you uncomfortable."

Scarlett wondered if that had more to do with Fraser not wanting Bridget to find out they were married than concern for Scarlett.

"Can I be completely honest with you?" Bridget said as they approached the cafe. "I was hoping you might be able to help me figure out what's going on with Fraser. He told me he just wants to be friends … but I really like him. Since you live with him I thought …"

"You thought being nice to me would be a good way to get close to Fraser?"

"I don't know whether you're joking again or if you're just very direct."

"I'm very direct."

"Oh, okay." She paused at the door to the cafe and pulled on the handle. "Yes, I suppose I did think that us being friends might help my relationship with Fraser, but I also really admire you."

Scarlett squinted at her. "Because I published a book?"

"Yes, the books. And the publishing company, and uni. I think it's so inspiring how much you've achieved. I can't imagine how hard it is for you, but Fraser's always saying how determined you are. It makes me feel a bit pathetic when I struggle with uni work. I think about you and how much you've overcome. What do you want to drink?"

Scarlett registered the server looking at them expectantly across the counter. "Tea, please."

As they collected the drinks and moved to a table, Scarlett wondered what exactly Fraser had said to Bridget. She supposed he thought she was a charity case because she didn't have her parents funding her education, but surely lots of people were in the same situation. It wasn't that much of a hardship.

"Don't you drink coffee?" Bridget asked when they were seated.

"Sometimes."

"Fraser said you have sleep problems. I guess coffee doesn't help."

"I don't have a sleep problem." She was beginning to feel unsettled by how much Fraser had told Bridget about her. "I don't need as much sleep as other people, but it's actually quite useful. I have more time for other stuff."

Bridget laughed. "So it's more like a superpower? It's great how you put a positive spin on it."

"It is what it is," Scarlett said with a shrug.

"That's such a good way to look at life." Bridget pushed her hair behind her shoulder and took a sip of her coffee. "Sometimes I think people who suffer through adversity have a much better outlook on life. Do you know what I mean?"

"Not really." She was talking in riddles and Scarlett was getting tired of the conversation. Her tea was still hot, otherwise she'd probably drink it in one go and leave.

"Do you get much extra help at uni?" Bridget asked. "Are there special allowances or something? I'm sure there must be."

"I don't know what you mean."

"Like extra support for students with disabilities." She winced as though she'd said the wrong thing. "You're supposed to say *disabled people* aren't you? Not people with disabilities. I'm sorry. I don't mean to offend. It's hard to know sometimes. Fraser's better with the terminology since he read up on it."

Scarlett struggled to keep up. Had Fraser told Bridget she was dyslexic? Because she didn't think it was that big of a deal. She certainly didn't consider herself disabled because of it.

"What did Fraser read up on?" she asked.

"Autism." Bridget bit down on her bottom lip. "I hope you don't mind that he told me. He wasn't gossiping or anything. He was only concerned."

Scarlett's hands gripped her mug tightly as a lump formed in her throat.

"It's one of the things I like about Fraser," Bridget went on. "He's so caring. I don't think many guys would be so supportive. Like at Halloween when he knew you didn't have anyone to go to the party with. It was so cute how he spent the whole evening hanging out with you. He completely freaked out when he lost you. I think he feels responsible because you live together."

Scarlett's blood was rushing in her ears. "I have to go home," she said, her legs seeming to move of their own accord.

"I haven't upset you, have I?" Bridget said. "I probably say the wrong thing sometimes but I don't mean to offend. I'm quite intrigued I suppose."

Scarlett picked her bag up from the floor. "Me too," she muttered, then walked briskly away.

CHAPTER 29

Scarlett jabbed repeatedly at the button on the pedestrian crossing. A woman waiting beside her tutted loudly, clearly unimpressed by her impatience. The walk home seemed to be taking far longer than usual. When the green man lit up, Scarlett hurried across the road. Then she broke into a run and didn't slow until she was on the front path at home. Breathing hard, she continued inside and up the stairs. As she sank onto the edge of the bed, she clutched the corner of the weighted blanket and twisted it in her fingers.

Quickly, she pulled her laptop from her bag and opened it on her knees. She typed weighted blanket into the search bar but didn't bother to explore any further. The fact that the search bar suggested *weighted blankets and autism* as a search term told her everything she needed to know.

"Fraser!" she shouted, leaving her room and heading to his. She was fairly sure he wouldn't be home yet but called out again before opening his bedroom door. The room was empty and she rocked on her heels before venturing inside. Standing in front of the bookshelf, she found what she was looking for immediately: two books on autism, tucked in among his uni textbooks. The first one looked clinical and not at all out of place with his other books. The second one was a memoir by a woman with autism.

Taking a few steps backwards, she lowered herself onto Fraser's bed, turning over the first book to read the description. She flicked quickly through the pages but couldn't bring herself to stop and read. Her stomach felt as though it had turned to stone and her thoughts raced so fast her head felt like it was spinning.

She tried closing her eyes to block everything out but her mind continued to race. Eventually, she placed the books on her lap and slowly tapped her thumbs against her forefingers, then her middle finger, ring finger and pinkie. She took a breath as she went back the other way and focused her attention on her fingers. Her mind quietened and she stayed there, tapping away until Fraser arrived home an hour later.

He stopped short in the doorway and inhaled a short sharp breath, then let out a gentle laugh. "You scared me."

She kept her eyes on her fingers. When Fraser sat beside her, she had a brief image of him slapping her hands like her mum used to do when she was little.

"What's wrong?" he asked gently.

Her fingers sped up before she forced herself to stop.

"Are these for your course?" she asked, touching the books at her lap. She was clinging to the tiny hope that she'd misunderstood Bridget. She often misread situations, so there was a chance she'd done that again.

"No."

"Why do you have them then?" she asked, unable to look at him.

"I wanted to understand better."

Tears burned the back of her eyes. "Understand *me?*"

"Yeah."

Her chest felt as though it was being crushed and her throat seemed to be closing up.

"What's going on?" Fraser asked.

"I spoke to Bridget today," she said, her eyes on the memoir.

On the cover, a butterfly flew among disorganised colours and shapes.

"How come?"

"She wants to be friends with me to get close to you."

"Sorry. I'll message her and tell her to back off."

"You told her I'm autistic?" Scarlett said through gritted teeth.

"I mentioned it," he said, putting his hand over hers. "It's not a big deal, is it? I know you don't talk about it, but maybe you should. It might be easier if you were more open about it."

Finally, she forced her gaze up to meet his. Her chest began to heave and she couldn't speak.

"What exactly did Bridget say?" he said, gently squeezing her hand. "Whatever it was, she wouldn't say anything purposely to hurt you."

"I'm … I'm not," Scarlett spluttered, the words burning in her throat. "I'm *not*."

"Not what?"

She pulled her hand from his and shot up from the bed, taking his books with her.

"Scarlett!" Fraser called as she reached the doorway. "What's going on? You're not *what*?"

She paused but didn't look back. "I'm not autistic." She was almost at her room when she heard Fraser swear to himself.

The weighted blanket that she'd become so attached to felt like an insult, and she slung it on the floor before she crawled onto the bed. A couple of minutes later she got up and retrieved it, snuggling under it with Fraser's books beside her. She didn't move when he rapped lightly on the doorframe.

"Can I come in?" He came and perched on the edge of the bed. "I don't know what to say," he whispered after a moment.

Finally, she pushed the blanket off her shoulder so she could look at him. "I had a test. When I was in primary school, my teacher thought there was something wrong with me. My parents argued with her, but before I started secondary school, they agreed to an evaluation." Her chin twitched and she fought back tears. "The psychologist said I was fine. I'm not autistic. The doctor said so."

"I'm sorry," Fraser murmured. "You told me you were different from other people and I misunderstood. I thought you were saying something else."

She sniffed. "I'm not autistic. Did you really think that? All this time?"

"I got it wrong," he said. "I'm sorry."

Scarlett chewed her bottom lip. "It doesn't matter."

"Do you want to come down and watch something? I can make us something to eat."

"I'm not hungry. I'm tired. I might sleep."

"That feels like you're trying to get rid of me."

"I am," she said, adjusting her head on the pillow.

"Do you want a cup of tea at least?"

"No."

"Give me a shout if you want anything," he said as he moved slowly towards the door.

He didn't close the door behind him and Scarlett couldn't muster the energy to do it herself. A couple of times throughout the evening she sensed him in the doorway, looking in at her. It was oddly comforting. Eventually the room fell into darkness.

She checked the time at midnight and again an hour later. At around two, she rolled over onto the books, which were still nestled under the blanket with her. She contemplated turning the lamp on to read them but couldn't bring herself to. Deep in her gut, she had a horrible feeling she couldn't face whatever was in their pages.

The room was light again when she jolted awake.

"Sorry," Fraser said, standing over her. "Do you need to get to lectures?"

Blinking, she reached for her phone and checked the time. "I'm late."

"I can drive you, if you want?"

"No. I'll go in later." Rolling over, she pulled the blanket tighter around her, hoping she'd be able to fall back to sleep. Being awake didn't feel good.

"I've got lectures all day," Fraser said. "And I've got football training afterwards but I should be home about 8 p.m. if you still want to hang out tonight."

It was Friday. Her conversation with Bridget had made her forget all about her plans to hang out with Fraser. She thought back to what Bridget had said about him feeling responsible for her. Was that why he was nice to her? Because he'd thought she was autistic?

She realised he was standing over her, waiting for a response.

"Goodbye," she said, just wanting him to leave.

"Are you okay?"

"Yes," she snapped. "I'm fine. Why do you keep bothering me?"

"Sorry. I'll see you later."

She waited for a while after she'd heard him leave the house, then reached for one of Fraser's books. Ignoring the fluttering feeling in her chest, she began to read. Tears blurred her eyes after only a couple of pages. Hastily, she wiped them away and focused on the words. Once she reached the end of the book, she picked up the memoir and skimmed through that. It was creepy how the writer seemed to have crawled inside her head and stolen her thoughts and feelings. She supposed it should have been comforting that maybe she wasn't quite as different as she'd thought. Or at least not the only one who was different.

From the books, she was led to various resources online. She read blogs and listened to a podcast until her stomach began to growl and she realised it was the middle of the afternoon and she hadn't eaten anything since lunchtime the previous day. After venturing to the kitchen for food, she continued her research. Finally, she took an online test. She took every online test she could find, ignoring the fact that they were all pretty much the same and all told her the same thing.

By the time Fraser arrived home, she was lying on her back on the bed, exhausted.

"How was your day?" he asked from the doorway.

"Okay," she replied, then wanted to laugh. It hadn't been okay at all. She wasn't sure what it had been, but certainly not okay.

"Are you going to Hope Cove this weekend?"

"No."

He moved further into the room. "How come?"

Scarlett cursed the tears that pooled in her eyes. Surely her tear ducts should be in need of a break by now.

"I can't go back there," she whispered.

"Why not?"

"Because they think I'm autistic too."

"Who?"

"Max and Lizzie. I don't know why I didn't realise. It's why Max looks at me like he can't figure me out. He was trying to decide if I was autistic."

"You don't know that."

"When you gave me the weighted blanket, Max was talking about their friend's autistic kid who has one. Lizzie clearly wanted him to shut up. I thought she was being mean and grumpy, but she just wanted him to drop the subject because she knew where he was going with it."

Fraser moved to take her hand. "Who cares what they think anyway? Who cares what anyone thinks?"

"*I* do." She turned her head towards him, enjoying the feel of his fingers against hers. "Do you really think I'm autistic?"

"You told me you're not. Why are you even asking me?"

"Because you've lived with me for eighteen months. The psychologist spent a few hours with me. I think you might be a better judge."

"I'm not a doctor. I don't know anything."

"You do!" She sat up and looked him in the eyes. "You said you wanted to understand better. You read books and researched it. Based on that, do you think I'm autistic?"

He swallowed hard. "Some of your traits are the same as someone with autism, but that doesn't necessarily mean anything."

"I took an online test and it said there was a strong likelihood that I have autism spectrum disorder."

"One online test can't be that reliable."

"I took seven."

He smiled sadly. "Do *you* think you're autistic?"

She nodded and hugged her knees as tears spilled down her cheeks.

When Fraser circled his arms around her, she moved her face to his chest. Her chest hurt and her throat burned as she cried quietly.

"You're okay," Fraser said. "Nothing's changed. Even if you are autistic, you're still the same person you were yesterday. It's not such a bad thing, is it?"

"I don't know," she sniffed. "I feel as though I don't know anything any more."

CHAPTER 30

Scarlett told Verity that she wouldn't be able to work in the cafe that weekend. She hadn't given her a reason, not sure what to say but not wanting to lie. When Verity replied to say it was fine and asked if everything was okay, Scarlett debated how to reply before eventually messaging to say she was okay. She'd spent most of her life feeling confused, but now she really couldn't get things straight in her head.

She tried to tell herself that she might not even be autistic. The psychologist had determined that she wasn't and Scarlett had believed that completely for the past nine years. If the psychologist had deemed she wasn't, then maybe she wasn't. But the more research she did, the more women she found who'd been misdiagnosed or undiagnosed as children.

She swung between being terrified of what it meant if she was autistic, and being comforted by the inspiring examples of autistic women she found online. Fraser had said she was still the same person no matter what, and she kept reminding herself of that. If she *was* autistic, it at least explained why she'd always felt so different to other people. And why she felt as though she constantly got things wrong when she was around other people.

On Sunday morning, Scarlett got sick of being in her room

and sick of her racing thoughts. She didn't know what she was supposed to do next. Should she go to the doctor? Try to get an official diagnosis? She wasn't sure what the point was. She'd managed fine until now without knowing.

Fraser stepped out of the living room as she walked down the stairs. He'd been at home all weekend and she wondered if he'd felt he had to hang around to look after her. He kept offering to make her food and cups of tea and inviting her to watch TV with him. She'd declined repeatedly and couldn't help but think about what Bridget had said about him spending time with her because he felt responsible for her.

"How are you?" he asked.

"I'm fine. I'm going to drive over to Hope Cove."

"I thought you weren't working this weekend?"

"I'm not, but I need to speak to someone. I thought I'd visit Lizzie and Emily."

A smile flashed on and off his face. "You can always talk to me, if you want."

"Thanks." She paused at the bottom of the stairs and pulled a sheet of paper from her backpack. "Maybe you could do me a favour?"

"Yes. Anything."

"Can you answer these questions about me?"

"What is it?" he asked, taking the paper.

"It's the autism test. I heard a woman on a podcast saying that as well as taking it herself, she got people close to her to answer the questions about her. I thought I'd do the same."

"Is that why you're going to Hope Cove?"

"Yes. I'm going to ask Lizzie and Emily to do the test for me, and maybe Auntie Verity. Anyone who knows me well. Then I feel like I'll know for sure. Will you answer the questions for me?"

He promised he would and she told him she'd see him later.

Driving made her thoughts race even more and she had to remind herself to concentrate on the road. She wasn't a great driver at the best of times. Maybe that was an autistic thing. Suddenly, so many parts of her life made more sense. As she reassessed her odd behaviours and struggles, it all seemed to fit perfectly with autism.

By the time she reached Hope Cove she wasn't sure she even needed to ask anyone to take the test. It seemed pretty obvious that she was autistic. She'd ask them anyway, because that was what she'd set out to do and she didn't like to back down when she'd started something.

"I thought you weren't coming today?" Verity said when she walked into the cafe. She'd just brought sandwiches to a couple sitting by the window. There were a few other customers too but it wasn't overly busy. "I got Tina to come in instead."

"I'm not here to work," Scarlett said. "I just need to talk to you."

"I'm a bit busy at the moment. Can it wait?"

Scarlett followed Verity to the counter, pulling the papers from her bag as she went. "I need to know if you think I'm autistic."

Verity's eyes widened as she stopped abruptly. "What did you say?"

"Do you think I'm autistic? I have this questionnaire for you to fill out about me to help me figure it out."

"Of course you're not autistic," Verity said quietly while glancing furtively around the cafe. "What a silly thing to say."

"Why is it a silly thing to say?"

"Because you're not. Why would you think that?"

"Because I'm different and I want to know why." She chewed on her lip. "Can you fill out the questionnaire please?"

Verity took Scarlett's arm and led her into the back. She put her head around the kitchen door and asked Tina if she could take over out the front for a little while. Then she marched Scarlett upstairs and into the flat.

"I only need you to fill out the form," Scarlett said, slumping on to the couch. "You don't need to make a big deal out if it."

"I'm not filling out this daft questionnaire." Verity stood in the middle of the room and held the papers up. "But I would like to know where all this nonsense is coming from."

"I don't think it's nonsense. Fraser thought I was autistic … and I think he's probably right."

Verity slid the papers onto the coffee table as she took a seat beside Scarlett. "You never did tell me how you met Fraser, and I don't know how you came to live with him. He seems like a nice lad, but if he's bullying you that's not okay."

Scarlett covered her face with her hands as she sank back on the couch. "He's not bullying me."

"Well, it's not a very nice thing to say to someone."

"Why? He wasn't being mean. He just thought I was autistic."

"But clearly you're not! You're studying at university and write books and you've done all this publishing company stuff with Lizzie and Emily. You wouldn't be able to do all that if you were autistic, would you?" She shook her head. "You're far too intelligent to be autistic."

"Lots of autistic people achieve all sorts of things," Scarlett said calmly. "Being autistic doesn't mean you're stupid. But I'm also not as intelligent as you make out, I just work hard." She tried to smile as she looked at Verity. "Have you really never thought there was something different about me?"

"You might be a bit eccentric but that's all. And that's not a bad thing. You're not autistic though. Do you remember when you were younger you had that teacher who thought there might be something wrong with you? Your mum took you for a test and you were fine."

Scarlett pushed at her piercing with her tongue. "There's this thing called masking, or camouflaging. It's where you hide your autism traits and act in the way that makes you seem neurotypical. Girls are often especially good at it. That's what I did." She paused and inhaled a steady breath. "Before I went for that assessment, Mum spent ages telling me exactly how I should act and what sort of things I should say. She made out that it was some important test that I wasn't allowed to fail. And I did what she said because I knew she'd be disappointed if I didn't. For once I thought I could make her proud of me. But just because I can convince a psychologist I'm not autistic doesn't mean I'm not autistic." She reached for the papers on the table. "Please can you do this for me?"

"I suppose so."

"I'm going to ask Lizzie and Emily to do it too." She scooped up her backpack as she headed for the door but paused and turned back. "There's something else I want to tell you."

"What?" Verity asked sadly.

"Fraser and I are married."

Verity rolled her eyes dramatically. "Have you been taking drugs or something? You're full of crazy talk today."

"No. The only way for me to get the student loan was to get married. Fraser agreed to help me out. That's why we're living together."

"I hope that's a joke."

She grimaced. "It's not. But you don't have to make a big deal out of it. I got my loan and Fraser turned out to be nice so it's really not so bad."

"Fraser is your husband?" she asked, closing her eyes briefly.

"Yes. But we just did it for the paperwork. It's not as though we're actually together." Again, Scarlett was reminded of Bridget's words about Fraser feeling he had to look after her. She didn't have enough headspace to think about that now.

"I presume your parents don't know?" Verity said wearily.

"No. And you probably shouldn't tell them." She continued to the door. "I'll come back later."

The five-minute walk to Lizzie's house gave Scarlett a bit of breathing space. A cool breeze rushed at her face and she kept her head up as she strode along the road.

The sound of the baby wailing hit her ears as she knocked on the door. Since it was unlocked, she let herself in then crouched to stroke Tilly when the dog trotted out from the kitchen. The noise of the TV and the girls squabbling drifted from the living room.

"Hi," Max said, walking towards her with Nathan in his arms. "I'm not sure I've ever been happier to see you. Any chance you could take the girls out for a walk?"

"I can't today."

"You can name your price. I honestly can't think of a number I wouldn't be okay with at this moment."

"Sorry. I just wanted to talk to Lizzie."

"She's having a shower. This little guy vomited in her hair."

"That's gross."

"Yeah. Is it anything I can help you with?"

She looked at the baby, who was bright red from screaming. "Maybe," she said, raising her voice over the noise. "Do you think I'm autistic?"

Max shifted Nathan onto his shoulder. "What?" he said, even though she'd said it loud and was certain he must have heard.

"Do you think I'm autistic?" she repeated, speaking slowly.

He bounced the baby and went slightly red himself. "I don't know. Why? Are you?"

"I think so, yeah. Fraser thought I was, and I looked into it and I think I am too. And I had the feeling that you already thought so. Because you look at me like I'm weird sometimes."

He patted Nathan on the back and shook his head. "I don't think you're weird."

"It doesn't matter if you do," she said, then opened her backpack and found the papers. "But can you and Lizzie fill out these questionnaires? It'll help me figure out if I'm autistic."

"Yeah. I guess so."

"Thanks." She let herself out again, then turned back on the path. "Can you do it today? I'm going back to Exeter later and I'd like to have all the results so I can analyse them."

"Sure." He ran his teeth over his bottom lip. "Are you okay?"

"Yes. I'm going to see Emily now. Bye."

He called goodbye as she sauntered away.

Scarlett had the papers in her hand when she knocked on Emily's door. Again, the door was unlocked, so she let herself in. Emily was walking down the stairs and Jack was shouting at the football on TV.

They all said hello at once and Scarlett thrust her papers at Emily.

"I need you to answer these questions to help me figure out if I'm autistic."

Emily's mouth fell open but she didn't say anything as her eyes flicked from Scarlett to the papers.

"It's not difficult," Scarlett said. "And it doesn't take long. You could do it now quickly."

Emily remained mute and Scarlett found the silence uncomfortable.

"Can I do it?" Jack asked, walking over to her. "I like doing quizzes."

"Yes." She handed him the paper and he went and sat at the dining table with it.

"Don't people usually get diagnosed with autism as a kid?" he asked.

"Not always. A lot of people don't get diagnosed until they're adults. Especially women. I had an evaluation as a kid and they said I wasn't autistic, but I think maybe they got it wrong."

Jack turned his attention to the questions in front of him. A playful grin spread over his face as he read a couple out loud. "Scarlett enjoys social interactions … Scarlett is good at chitchat …" He laughed. "It seems as though this isn't going to require too much thought."

"Jack!" Emily hissed. "Don't joke around. It's not funny."

"Sorry." He looked up at Scarlett. "I don't mean to make

light of it … but to be honest I already thought you were autistic."

"Really?" she asked, moving closer to him.

"Yes. It's not the sort of thing you can ask though."

Nodding, Scarlett raised her gaze to the ceiling, focusing on the smoke detector for a moment. "Can I ask you a question?"

"Yes," Jack replied.

"Are you nice to me because I'm Emily's friend or do you actually like me?"

"I like you."

"Even though you thought I was autistic?"

"Yep."

When she nodded again, tears fell down her cheeks.

"Do you want a hug?" Jack asked. "Or do you want me to get on with these questions?"

"Hug," she whispered, then heard the creak of his chair moving before his arms wrapped around her.

"Are you okay?" Emily asked, gently rubbing her back.

"Yes." Shuffling away from them, she wiped the tears from her cheeks. "Can you answer the questions now?"

"We'll answer the questions if you put the kettle on," Jack said.

Happy at the excuse to leave the room, she went to the kitchen. As she stood at the window watching small birds flitter from the bush to the tree, Emily's indecipherable whispers drifted through from the living room. Eventually the noise of the kettle drowned her out, and when it clicked off everything was silent. Scarlett took her time making coffees for Jack and Emily, then took them through. Jack was bent over the questionnaire, while Emily sat close beside him, dabbing at her eyes with a tissue.

"Did you answer the questions?" Scarlett asked, setting the drinks down.

"Yes," Emily sniffed.

"Why are you crying?"

"Because I'm worried about you. What happened that you suddenly think you're autistic?"

"Fraser thought that I'm autistic. He told a girl and then she mentioned it to me."

"Oh, Scarlett," she said on a sigh. "I'm sorry."

"I don't understand why you'd be sorry," Scarlett said.

"I'm sorry you're going through this. It must be very hard."

"I don't know," she mused. "I've been reading about autism and it all sounds like me. I'm not sure why I didn't realise before."

"Finished," Jack said, sliding the pen and paper over to her. "I hope I got a good score."

"Jack!" Emily gave him a stern look.

"What will you do with our answers?" Jack asked, ignoring her.

Scarlett scanned their papers. "I'll enter them into the online test that analyses the likelihood of autism."

"So anyone can take the test online?" he asked.

"Yes."

"And it's easy to find if I do an internet search?"

She nodded. "Are you going to take it yourself?"

"I wasn't thinking for me." He flashed a quick glance in Emily's direction.

Scarlett laughed but Emily didn't look at all amused as she glared at Jack.

"What?" he said, laughing. "You have to admit you have some traits!"

"Stop joking around," Emily said. "This is a big deal for Scarlett."

"It's okay," Scarlett said, not minding the jokes.

Jack's face fell serious as he looked at Scarlett. "I know it's a big deal for you. And if there's anything we can do to help, we will. I'm only joking around because I want you to know that it's not a big deal for me. It doesn't make any difference to me if you're autistic or not."

A lump formed in her throat. "Thank you."

"*Is* there anything we can do?" Emily asked.

"I don't think so."

"Any time you want to talk about it, you can."

"Thanks." Scarlett wasn't really sure what there was to talk about. They probably didn't even know anything about autism, so they wouldn't be able to help much.

"Didn't you make yourself a drink?" Jack asked, then took a sip of his coffee.

"No. I have to go now." She put the papers in her bag, then paused, thinking. "When Fraser thought I was autistic he bought some books on autism and read about it so he'd understand me better."

"That was nice of him," Emily said.

"Yes. Maybe you could do the same. I found some blogs that I like. I can send you the links and you could read them to learn about autism."

"We can definitely do that," Emily said, smiling.

"Okay. Good. I'll probably see you next weekend."

On the way back to the cafe, she stopped at Lizzie's place to pick up their questionnaires. When Lizzie asked if she could do anything, Scarlett told her to read the blogs too. That was all she could think of.

By the time she got back to Exeter she was tired but wanted to put everyone's answers into the online test. She'd skimmed over everyone's answers and already knew that they'd indicate she was autistic, but she wanted to do it anyway.

She'd just started up the stairs when Fraser called to her from the kitchen, asking if she wanted a cuppa.

"Yes, please," she called back, then headed back down to him.

"How did you get on in Hope Cove?" he asked, leaning against the counter as he waited for the kettle.

"Fine. I got everyone to fill in the questionnaire. Now I'm

going to find out what score everyone got, but I think I know what the verdict will be."

He smiled, then turned his attention back to the drinks.

"When did you first realise I'm autistic?" she asked, sitting at the table and watching him pour steaming water over the teabags.

"Some guy asked me if you were. He wasn't being mean, he just wondered. Then I did some research and everything clicked into place."

"So you didn't notice when we first met?"

"No. You seemed completely normal." He grimaced. "Sorry."

She shrugged and kept her expression neutral to hide the fact that she wanted to cry.

"When we started uni, you seemed different," Fraser said. "Like you were on edge all the time."

She thought back to the first term of uni. She'd definitely been on edge. "I moved in with a guy I barely knew. I was living in a new place and trying to figure out university life. It was pretty stressful. Didn't you find it difficult?"

"Not really. It was exciting. Living away from my parents was great, and I liked being free to do whatever I wanted without anyone breathing down my neck."

"I found it stressful."

"Maybe that's why I noticed your behaviour was a little odd. But I still just thought you had kind of a quirky personality. To be honest, until I did some research on autism I didn't know much about it."

"So you really had no inkling I might be autistic when we got married?"

"No. I wouldn't have married you if I'd have realised."

Scarlett cast her eyes downwards as her lungs felt as though they were being squeezed. On one of the autism blogs she'd read that, statistically speaking, not many autistic people got married.

At the time, she'd felt a pang of pride that she'd beaten the statistics, but now she was reminded that it was all fake.

"Did that sound mean?" he asked.

"No. I understand." She forced the corners of her mouth upwards as she took the cup of tea from him.

"I think I'd have felt I was taking advantage of you or something."

Nodding, she stood up, needing to get away from him. "That makes sense," she muttered.

It was exactly as Bridget had said: he felt sorry for her and felt a sense of responsibility towards her.

Stupidly, Scarlett had thought he felt something completely different.

CHAPTER 31

After spending the entire weekend obsessing about whether or not she was autistic and reading everything she could on the subject, Scarlett really needed to focus on her uni work to avoid falling behind. Her mind wouldn't focus though, and she found herself staring aimlessly at the laptop screen for most of Monday evening.

Since she was clearly wasting her time, she opened a browser and typed *autism and relationships* into the search bar. The articles she found about the difficulties autistic people have forming meaningful relationships were depressing, and she soon closed the browser again. Apparently her autistic characteristics would make romantic relationships or even dating a challenge.

That was stupid. She had her own publishing company and lived independently. When she looked at other people her age, she was sure she'd achieved far more than most of them. Autism hadn't stopped her from getting whatever she wanted before, and she wasn't about to let it get in the way now.

Setting up her profile on a dating app turned out to be relatively straightforward and soon she was sitting on her bed swiping through a bunch of guys' profiles. She forced herself to swipe right on a few of them, telling herself she shouldn't be picky. How much could you tell from a dating profile anyway? Hers certainly didn't give the full picture.

She was about to call it a day when a photo caught her attention. The guy was wearing a football jersey. It was the same colour as the one Fraser wore for his games. Zooming in on the logo, she realised it was the same team. Her thumb hovered as she wondered whether it would be weird to go on a date with someone Fraser knew. Maybe it would make him jealous. She was probably kidding herself, but the thought that it might annoy him was somehow appealing.

At a knock on her door, she panicked and swiped right before throwing the phone aside.

"Are you okay?" Fraser asked.

"Yes."

"I was going to ask if you want to watch TV but you look like you're about to go to bed."

"I am," she said quickly. "Goodnight."

"Night," he replied and gently closed the door.

When Scarlett settled down in bed, she imagined guys looking at her photo on the dating app and idly deciding whether to swipe left or right. She felt slightly sick and wasn't sure she even wanted anyone to swipe right. If she matched with someone she'd have to move onto the next phase of the plan, which was going on a date.

The thought of going on a date with a stranger bothered her throughout the following day. Repeatedly, she told herself she was probably worrying about nothing. They'd all swipe left and she'd never match with anyone.

Except when she arrived home from uni, she'd matched with three guys and had three messages. The first message was from someone called Theo who looked like a bodybuilder. Why on earth had she swiped right on him? That might have been an accident. His message was pretty direct: *Hey! Are you into anything kinky?*

A shiver ran down her spine and she deleted the message.

The next message was from a guy who was holding a puppy in his picture. It had been the dog that had made her swipe right, not the guy.

Hi Sexy his message read. *How do you feel about threesomes?*

Delete.

Was internet dating just for people looking to have sex with strangers? Or had she inadvertently written something in her biography that was sending out the wrong signal?

Clicking into the next message, she paused at the picture of the guy in the football strip. Swiping right on him probably hadn't been the best idea.

Curious, she clicked onto the message from Mike.

Hi he said. *I see we both go to Exeter uni. How are you enjoying uni life?*

She took a deep breath. He wasn't outright asking for sex so he'd scored a few points over the other guys. It was weird to think that he probably knew Fraser. They might even be friends, so Scarlett should delete the message and move on.

Another message popped up. *What are you studying?*

English she typed automatically. She liked straightforward questions where she didn't have to spend ages wondering how to reply.

Cool he wrote. *So you're at Streatham Campus? The grounds are pretty. Always nice for a stroll.*

Yes she replied. *I like to walk around there.*

The messages went back and forth for a few minutes, mundane stuff about uni that Scarlett felt comfortable chatting about. When he asked if she wanted to go out sometime, she hesitated, her fingers poised over the keypad. A simple exchange of messages over the internet was manageable, but going out and spending time alone with someone she didn't know was another story. She felt queasy at the thought of sitting in a bar or restaurant and having a one-on-one conversation with someone she didn't know.

Taking a deep breath, she reminded herself she was part owner of a business, and she juggled that with working at the cafe and studying for her degree. She'd also married a guy she barely knew and moved in with him. She could definitely manage a date.

I'd like that, she replied, telling herself it wasn't a complete lie.

Great. How about Thursday evening?

That was soon, but she supposed it gave her less time to worry about it. *Okay. Where do you want to go?*

What's your ideal first date? he asked.

She should probably lie. What would a normal response be? Candlelit dinner, or maybe ice-skating or watching live music in a cosy bar? Did people actually do those things or was it just in films? She realised she was taking too long to reply when Mike sent another message.

Be honest. I can't promise anything but it's a good thing to know anyway.

Scarlett thought about what she'd really like to do on a date. An image of playing video games with Fraser sprang to mind, followed closely by the memory of her birthday when they'd lain side by side on her bed, relaxing and binge-watching Netflix.

Hesitantly, she typed a response.

My ideal evening would be to watch Netflix and chill. She tensed as she waited for a reply.

When his message came it simply said, *Wow.*

"Wow?" Scarlett mouthed as she stared at the phone. What did that mean? Was he shocked at how boring she was?

She breathed a sigh of relief when another message came through.

I wish all women were as direct as you. If you know what you want you may as well just say so, right?

She smiled as she typed, *Yes. I always think so.*

Well, I have Netflix. He added a winky face emoji, which

confused Scarlett slightly. But a lot of things confused her so she decided to put aside her tendency to overthink. *How about you come to my place on Thursday evening?* he asked.

Okay, she typed. *I hope we like the same shows.* Feeling brave, she added a winky face.

He replied with a row of smiley faces and told her he couldn't wait. Flopping back on the bed, Scarlett felt very pleased with herself. It was only a few messages but she had a good feeling about Mike.

If he liked women who could say exactly what they wanted, she suspected they were going to get on very well.

Fraser was still reeling from the fact that Scarlett didn't have an autism diagnosis. After the research he'd done, it never occurred to him that she might not be autistic, or that she was unaware of it. He felt horribly guilty that Bridget had been the one to mention it and couldn't quite imagine how Scarlett had felt. As with everything, she seemed to be taking it in her stride.

She'd been upset, of course, and he'd tried to be supportive and let her know he was around if she needed him while also being careful not to crowd her. He'd felt as though they were getting closer, but now she was back to declining every invitation to hang out. As much as he told himself not to take it personally, he couldn't help but feel rejected. He just needed to be patient, he told himself. She wasn't in a place to get into a relationship and it would be wrong of him to force the issue.

When he arrived home from football training on Thursday evening, Scarlett was walking down the stairs. Instead of her usual black leggings, she was wearing jeans and a blue T-shirt. He didn't remember seeing her in jeans before. Looking closer, he decided they were actually leggings that looked like jeans. Still, she looked good.

"Hi!" he called, when he realised she was in a trance and

hadn't noticed him. "I'm going to collapse in front of the TV for the evening if you want to join me?"

"I'm going out."

He felt his brow wrinkle. "Where are you going?"

"I have a date," she said, taking her coat from the rack and putting it on.

Puzzled, it took him a moment to speak. "Who with?"

"Some guy I matched with on a dating app."

Fraser could have taken a punch in the stomach and wouldn't have felt more winded. As he watched her put her shoes on, he fought for words. When he finally spoke, his voice came out slightly croaky. "Are you sure that's a good idea?"

"To go on a date?"

"To go on a date with some guy you met on the internet."

"It's what people do."

"Yeah, I know but …" His heart raced and he didn't have time to contemplate if it was because he was concerned or jealous. He suspected both.

"But you don't think I should?" she asked frostily. "Because I'm autistic and not capable of a relationship?"

"No. I don't think that."

"Then why are you being weird about me going on a date?"

He dragged his teeth along his bottom lip. "I'm worried about your safety, that's all. Where are you meeting him?"

Glancing at her watch, she moved towards the door. "I have to go."

"Make sure you meet him somewhere public," Fraser called as she slammed the door behind her.

Crap, had he really just said that? It was what his mum said to Hattie when she was going on dates. The urge to dash out of the door and stop her was fairly overwhelming. She was his wife, so it would be totally fine for him to tell her he didn't want her to go on dates. Except he'd been on dates himself so that excuse wouldn't really wash.

Trudging to the living room, he sank onto the couch and

dropped his head into his hands. It was going to be a long evening.

Arriving a couple of minutes early, Scarlett loitered outside the halls of residence for a moment before pressing the bell. Mike buzzed her into the building and told her he'd come down to meet her. Automatically, she wiped her shoes on the coarse mat inside the door.

"Hi!" The dark-haired guy looked exactly like he did in the photos, except now he was wearing a green polo shirt with a logo on the breast pocket. It looked like something Fraser would wear. "Did you find the place okay?" he asked, kissing her cheek.

"Yes. I followed the map on my phone."

"Can you imagine life before mobile phones and Google Maps?" He tipped his head to indicate she should follow and set off up the stairs. "It blows my mind thinking about it."

Not knowing how to respond, she kept quiet.

"Have you been in these halls before?" he asked, turning to look back at her.

"No."

"They're pretty new. Just built a few years ago."

"They look nice," she said. "It must be convenient to live on campus."

"Did you live on campus in your first year?" He held the door on the second floor and she stepped into the corridor.

"No. I always lived in a house."

"That's cool. Do you have nice housemates?"

"Yeah."

"I bet that's fun then." He stopped at the first door. "This is my place," he said as he led the way inside. "I thought about moving off campus, but I really like it here. And like you say, it's very convenient. I can roll out of bed ten minutes before lectures."

Scarlett stopped to look around the small room. A single bed was against one wall, and a chest of drawers sat at the end of it with a TV on top, angled to face the bed. Against the opposite wall was a wardrobe and a desk. She presumed the door between them was a bathroom.

Wandering to the window, she looked down on a courtyard with gravel paths and a couple of benches.

"Do you have a kitchen?"

"There's a shared one down the hall. I don't do a lot of cooking though. The canteen food is decent and I eat a lot of takeaways."

"That's not good for you," she mumbled.

"I do a lot of sport," he said, patting his stomach. "I like to think that cancels the junk out."

"I don't think it does." She was fairly sure Fraser would back her up. He knew about that stuff.

"What do you want to drink?" He opened a small fridge in the corner, which she hadn't noticed. "I've got beer or wine."

She would have preferred a cup of tea, but since that didn't seem to be an option she asked for wine.

"I haven't got wine glasses," he said as he unscrewed the top and poured it into a tumbler. "I've seen they sometimes serve it like this in restaurants these days. I think it's trendy. Probably an Italian thing or something." He handed it to her. "Pretend you're in a restaurant."

"There aren't any tables," she said, then wished she hadn't when he gave her a funny look.

After a second he grinned. "In that way it's even better than a restaurant…" He walked over and sat on the bed with his back against the headboard, then patted the space beside him. "It's much comfier than a restaurant."

After taking a swig of wine, she set the glass on the bedside table and sat down. "What do you want to watch?"

"I'm quite happy watching you," he said.

The way he was staring at her made her uncomfortable. "Where's the remote?"

"I dunno." He looked around, then leaned around her and exchanged his beer bottle for the remote. He switched the TV on and handed it to her. "You choose."

"I really like programmes about vampires," she said, scrolling through the TV shows. "Or anything set in space." She wouldn't choose something set in space though – it would feel wrong without Fraser. "I heard this crime drama is pretty good. Shall I put it on?"

"Whatever turns you on," he said with his eyes on her rather than the TV.

"If it's no good we can choose something else." She put it on, then turned and smiled at Mike before leaning back against the headboard.

They'd only been watching for a few minutes when Mike leaned close to her. She discreetly shuffled over to give him space. When he moved too, she ended up at an odd angle leaning over the edge of the bed.

"I'm not really comfortable," she told him.

"Sorry. We could scoot down if you want?" He moved to lie on the bed.

"That might be better," she agreed, moving onto her back and propping her head on the pillow.

"I'm really happy we matched," he said, turning on his side to look at her. "I usually don't have a lot of luck on those apps, but I really liked your messages."

"Thanks." Discreetly, she pushed his hand away when his fingers crept under the hem of her T-shirt.

"You're really hot." He was so close that his breath tickled her cheek and she got a whiff of beer. "Usually women post pictures of themselves looking amazing and then they're totally ugly."

She gave him a sidelong glance. "You look nice too," she said, hoping he'd shut up and watch the programme.

"I'm glad you think so." His lips trailed along her cheek and landed at the corner of her mouth.

"What are you doing?" she asked.

"Kissing you. You're very kissable."

"I can't concentrate on the TV when you're doing that."

"Maybe give up on the TV then," he suggested.

Before she knew what was going on, his lips covered hers and he pushed his hand up her top. It felt as though her heart stopped for a moment, then began to pummel her ribs.

"Wait," she whispered, turning her head away from him.

"Don't worry," he said, breathing hard against her neck. "I've got condoms."

As he shifted his weight on top of her she pressed her hands against his chest but he was too heavy for her to move. "Get off me."

"You wanna go on top?" he asked, pulling his T-shirt over his head as he moved off her.

"No." She jumped off the bed, relieved at not being pinned under him any more.

He laughed and stood up, placing a hand at her waist. "Don't get all shy now. You were totally up for it in your messages."

"No, I …" She was drowned out when his lips landed heavily on hers. "Stop!" she said, pushing him off and backing away until she hit the wall.

"What's wrong?" He stepped slowly towards her and she froze to the spot.

"I don't like it," she said, her voice shaking.

"But you said you want to Netflix and chill."

"Yes. But I don't want you to kiss me."

"I'm confused." Smiling, he took a step towards her.

With her back flush against the wall there was nowhere for her to go. Instinctively, she balled her right hand to a fist and took a step forwards as she swung. She yelped as her knuckles made contact with his mouth.

Mike stumbled backwards, stunned. "What the hell was that?" he growled, touching his top lip, which dripped with bright red blood.

"I told you to stop," she said, looking at her knuckle and wondering if it was his blood or hers. It throbbed, and the shearing pain made her think it was cut.

"You got my tooth!" He put his thumb to his front tooth as though checking if it was wobbly.

"You shouldn't have touched me," Scarlett said. "I asked you to stop."

"You said you were up for it. What the hell was I supposed to think? You can't go around telling guys you want to have sex with them and then punching them because they come on too strong."

"I didn't tell you I wanted to have sex with you," she said, her breathing ragged and uneven.

He stared at her. "Yes. You did!"

"I don't think I did," she whispered as a drop of blood dripped down his chin and splattered on the carpet. "You're bleeding."

He held his hand in front of his mouth. "Just get out."

She fumbled the handle before finally opening the door and fleeing. By the time she reached the stairs, her vision was blurred with tears and her legs felt like jelly. She was on the bottom step when she stumbled. Her hands hit the coarse bristles of the doormat while her right knee slammed onto the floor. The mat was sunken and the metal edge around it dug into her kneecap. Blood seeped through the thin material of her trousers.

After a couple of heaving breaths, she dragged herself up and limped outside.

CHAPTER 32

Fraser was idly clicking the remote, looking for something to watch, when he heard the front door. It was less than an hour since Scarlett had left and he'd been anticipating waiting for her for ages yet. The date obviously hadn't gone well. Or maybe she'd changed her mind and hadn't even met the guy. She could also have forgotten something and would leave again immediately.

"Hi," he said, stepping into the hallway.

Scarlett was already on the stairs and didn't seem to have heard him. She was hunched over, but from a glimpse at the side of her face he could have sworn she was crying.

"Hi," he called again, but she only moved quicker. A moment later her bedroom door clicked shut.

His heart was hammering and he shot up the stairs on a rush of adrenalin.

"Scarlett!" he shouted at her door. "Are you all right?"

"Yes." Her voice was muffled and he was sure she was crying. "I'm going to bed. Night."

After hesitating for a moment, he opened the door, then stopped short at the sight of her on the bed in only her underwear and T-shirt. She groped for her blanket and pulled it over her, but not before he caught the streak of blood on her leg.

"Are you okay?"

"Yes." She kept her head down, avoiding eye contact.

"What happened?"

"Nothing."

"Are you crying?"

She shook her head, but her eyes betrayed her by producing more tears.

"Tell me what happened," he said, sinking onto the bed.

As she tried to speak she just cried more. Fraser's chest tightened and he circled his arms around her, drawing her close.

"I don't know what I did," she said between short, sharp breaths. "I don't know what I said but he thought …"

"He thought what?" he asked, pulling back to look right at her.

"He thought I wanted to have sex with him." She pushed her face into his chest while Fraser felt every muscle in his body tense.

"Where were you?" he asked quietly.

"At his place in the student halls. That was stupid, wasn't it? You said to meet him somewhere public."

"It's not your fault," Fraser said, running a hand over her hair as his stomach twisted to a knot. "Did he hurt you?"

"Yes," she sniffed.

He felt physically sick and held her tighter as he tried to figure out what to do.

After a moment she pulled away and held her hand out. The knuckle had a small cut on it. "He kept kissing me and he had his hands on me. I thought he wasn't going to stop."

Fraser took her hand to inspect it. "You punched him?"

"Yes. He stopped then."

A wave of relief washed over him. "Good."

"Is it? I made his lip bleed."

"You didn't do anything wrong." Gently, he pushed her hair

behind her shoulder and wiped a tear from her cheek. "What happened to your knee?"

"I tripped on the stairs trying to get away quickly."

"Let me see."

She shook her head. "I don't have any trousers on."

"I'm only going to look at your knee." He stood to release the corner of the blanket he was sitting on and she carefully moved it so just her lower leg was sticking out.

"Ouch." He put a hand below the wound and moved her leg to look at it at a different angle. "I can clean it up for you."

"It's fine," she said, pulling away from him.

"It needs cleaning up. Wait there." He walked out and returned a few minutes later with a damp cloth, a tube of antiseptic cream and a box of plasters. Slowly, he cleaned the cut and patched her up. Once he was finished with her knee he did the same for her knuckle.

"Thank you."

"You're welcome. I'm going to get you a cup of tea."

She didn't argue and looked so tired that he was surprised to find her still awake when he returned.

"I don't understand what happened," she said, looking at him searchingly.

"You went on a date with a creep. You didn't do anything wrong."

Sitting up against the headboard, she took the tea from him. "But he said I'd been asking for it."

"Because he's a creep. They all say that."

"Really? Because he said I'd written in the message that I wanted to have sex with him, but I didn't say that. I don't understand why he thinks I did." Putting her mug aside, she picked up her phone and went into the messages.

"Do you want me to read them?" he offered.

"No." Angling the phone away from him, she scanned the messages. "I didn't write anything about wanting to have sex with him. We just talked about uni. Then he asked what I wanted to do tonight and I said chill out and watch Netflix. That's all that I messaged him. Nothing else."

Fraser winced.

"What did I say wrong?" she asked in a rush.

"Nothing." He puffed his cheeks out as he exhaled. "Did you say chill out and watch Netflix or Netflix and chill?"

She pressed her lips together. "What difference does it make?"

"Netflix and chill means sex," he told her sheepishly.

Scarlett stared at him, confusion wrinkling her features. "No, it doesn't. How can it mean sex? It means relax and watch Netflix. Like we do."

"I don't know why it means sex, but it does."

She shook her head firmly. "That doesn't make sense. Chill means relax. It can also mean cool, but it doesn't mean sex."

"It's stupid," Fraser said. "I don't know where it came from."

Scarlett looked away. "I suppose this proves that I'm not capable of being in a relationship."

"Who said that?"

"The internet." She sank down the bed and pulled the blanket up to her chin.

"The internet is wrong a lot of the time," Fraser said. "It was just one bad date."

"I get everything wrong," she sniffed. "No one will ever want to be in a relationship with me."

"They will," he said gently.

"No they won't. You said you wouldn't have married me if you'd known I was autistic."

He sighed loudly, hoping that wasn't what had spurred her into internet dating. "It came out wrong. I didn't mean it like that. I just think that if I'd known you were autistic I'd have felt as though I was taking advantage of you somehow."

"So you think because I'm autistic I can't make my own decisions?"

He shook his head. "That's not what I meant."

"What did you mean?"

"I don't know… but it doesn't matter. If I could go back in time … knowing what I know now … I'd do it again."

She locked eyes with him. "Really?"

"Yes. I'm glad we got married." The smile spread slowly over his face. "It was completely stupid. But I don't regret it. Uni life would've been incredibly boring if I hadn't met you."

"I'm not boring," she said, managing a smile.

"Definitely not." He pushed a strand of hair from her face. "Do you want me to leave you to sleep?"

She shrugged. "You probably have better things to do than sit here with me."

"As it happens, I don't. I can stay until you fall asleep, if you want?"

"Okay." She moved over and he lay on his back beside her.

He was desperate to slip his arms around her and hold her while she fell asleep, but she'd had enough unwanted advances and he didn't want to freak her out, so he kept his distance and listened to the sound of her breathing as he waited for her to fall asleep.

When he woke he blinked his eyes open and squinted at his watch. He genuinely hadn't meant to stay in Scarlett's bed all night, but he couldn't quite manage to feel bad about it. Beside him, Scarlett's hair splayed around her on the pillow and her features were relaxed in sleep. She'd moved closer to him, lying on her side with one leg hooked over his. The bare skin of her ankle felt hot against his.

"If you're watching me sleep it's creepy," she said, softly batting her eyes open.

"Apparently you attract creeps," he replied, his voice raspy with sleep.

She stared at him. "You're not a creep."

The alarm on his phone sounded and broke the atmosphere. "Was I snoring a lot?" he asked, silencing the alarm.

"No. You don't snore."

"Good. Sorry, I didn't intend to sleep here."

"It doesn't matter."

Sitting up, he ran his hands through his hair. He needed to shower and get to uni, but extracting himself from Scarlett's bed was going to take a lot of willpower.

"Are you all right?" she asked.

He shook his head, knowing the image of her looking serene against the pillow would stay burned in his memory. "I need to tell you something, but I'm worried it will make you uncomfortable."

She looked thoughtful, almost nervous. "Just tell me."

"Yesterday when you said no one would ever want to be in a relationship with you … you were wrong."

"I can't even manage one date," she said, shifting her head on the pillow.

"You just picked the wrong person." He lay down again, his body facing hers. As his heart rate increased, he hooked his little finger around hers. "You could have asked me if you wanted to go on a date."

"I wanted to go on a proper date and find someone who's attracted to me, not go out with someone who thinks I'm a charity case."

His brows drew together. "I've never thought that."

"Bridget said you only hang out with me because you feel sorry for me, and you feel you have to look after me."

"That's not true at all."

"She made it sound as though you think I'm delicate and need someone to look after me."

He couldn't help but smile. "You're part owner of a publishing company. You write and publish books and work in a cafe. And you do all that on top of your uni work. You're one of the strongest people I know."

"So you've never felt you have to look after me? Don't lie to me."

He licked his lips. "I *want* to look after you … but that's different to thinking you *need* me to. I hang out with you because I like hanging out with you, not out of any sense of duty. And I would really like to go on a date with you."

"Really?"

He laughed. "I've asked you every day for about the last two weeks."

"You ask me to watch TV or play video games."

He nodded. "I know it's not very romantic, but I thought it's what you'd want to do. I'll happily take you out for dinner if you'd prefer."

"No." She grimaced then looked at him seriously. "I didn't know how you felt about me."

"I thought I'd made it obvious at Christmas, but then with all the autism stuff I was worried it was bad timing. There's a lot for you to process and I don't want to make things more complicated for you."

"I only went on the date yesterday because I thought you just saw me as a friend, and I wanted to prove to myself that I could handle a relationship … but now my head feels like a big mess."

He fought the urge to lean over and kiss her. "I don't want to push you into anything you're not ready for. But whenever you feel like giving dating another go, can I be first in line?"

"Yes." She squeezed his finger, then released it.

"I need to get to uni." Mostly he needed to get out of her bed before he did something to completely negate all his chivalrous intentions. "How's your knee, by the way?" he asked as he stood up.

"It feels a bit bruised and stiff but it'll be fine when I get moving."

"Do you want me to drive you to uni?"

"No, thanks." She sat up and looked at him in a way that made him stop in his tracks. "Maybe we could play video games tonight or watch TV? If you're not busy."

He smiled widely. "I'll be home around eight."

CHAPTER 33

Scarlett heard the front door opening and closing when Fraser arrived home that evening. The thought of spending the evening with him had been a pleasant distraction throughout the day when her mind drifted to the events of the previous evening. After hearing his footsteps on the stairs she expected him to appear in her doorway, but she only caught a glimpse of him as he passed.

"Hi," she called, moving to the hallway.

He stopped at his door with his back to her. "Hi."

"How was your day?"

"Erm … okay. I guess."

"Would you rather play video games or watch TV? Either is fine with me."

"I actually remembered I have an assignment I need to write. Sorry." He still didn't look at her, but at least that meant he couldn't see her disappointment. "Are you going to Hope Cove this weekend?"

"Tomorrow probably."

"Okay. Have a good time." He pushed the door open and stepped inside.

"I don't understand you," she blurted out, before he could

close the door on her. "Sometimes I feel as though you're my best friend in the world. Then it seems as though you don't want anything to do with me. It's really confusing."

His shoulders sagged. "I'm sorry. I just have work to do."

"Do you think I'm so stupid that I'd believe that? It's Friday night. I'm sure you can't have anything that urgent. You won't even look at me."

There was a brief pause before he turned around. He kept his head lowered for a moment, then looked up at her. His left eyelid was blue and the skin around it puffy and swollen.

She took a couple of steps forwards. "What happened?"

"I had a bit of an accident at football training. It's not so bad. Probably worse than it looks."

"What kind of accident?" she asked, peering at his bloodshot eye. When he didn't reply, she suspected it wasn't an accident at all. "Tell me! Did you get in a fight?"

"No. But I take it you know that the guy you went out with last night is on my football team? That's why you didn't want me to look at the messages?"

She nodded. "I was hoping you wouldn't find out."

"I overheard him talking about his date before the game."

"What happened?"

"I might have been playing slightly aggressively. When I went in for a particularly dirty tackle, I ended up with his elbow in my eye."

"You were trying to injure him and injured yourself instead?"

"Yep."

"That's embarrassing." She walked away and headed for the stairs.

"I know … Where are you going?"

"To get ice for your eye."

"Thanks," he said as she walked down the stairs.

When she returned with a load of ice cubes wrapped in a tea towel, Fraser was in his room, sitting on the edge of the bed.

"Does it hurt?" she asked, standing beside him and gently touching the skin around his eye.

"It does when you poke it," he said with a grin. "Why are you doing that?"

"I see people do it on TV shows. I think it's to check if your cheekbone is broken."

"It's not, but I imagine if any of the bones in my face were broken, you prodding them would be pretty uncomfortable."

"Sorry." She moved the ice pack to his eye, making him wince. "So your day wasn't really so great?"

"It wasn't brilliant," he admitted. "I also saw Bridget and it was really awkward."

"What did she say?"

"She asked if I wanted to go out sometime and was being all flirty."

"I thought you'd told her you didn't like her in that way."

"I did, but she didn't seem to get it."

"You didn't agree to go out with her again, did you?"

"No. Of course not." The way he looked at her made her self-conscious. "How was your day?"

"Fine. Completely uneventful compared to yours. It was just a normal day."

He smiled lightly. "That sounds nice."

"How long do you need to keep ice on an injury?"

"About twenty minutes."

"That's pretty long," she said, the proximity to him making her heart race.

"How's your knee?" Gently, he touched the back of her leg.

"Fine," she whispered, but his touch seemed to turn both of her legs to jelly, and without really knowing what she was doing she sank onto his knee.

"How about your hand?" He took her fingers in his and looked down at the plaster across her knuckle.

"It's okay. Do you definitely need this on for twenty minutes?" she asked, indicating the ice pack.

"Probably not." He pulled it away from his face. "Do you really see me as your best friend?"

"Yes," she mumbled, then swallowed hard when he took her hand again.

"You're my best friend too. Which is kind of surprising."

She couldn't help but smile at the amusement in his voice. "Why? Because I'm so weird?"

He nodded, making her laugh. "I like your weirdness."

As far as compliments went, it was probably the best she'd ever had. Automatically, she reached to push his hair from his face when it fell forwards. "Doesn't that annoy you?"

"Nope." He gave a small shake of the head so his hair fell forwards again. "But it clearly annoys you."

"Yes." She pushed it out of the way, her fingers grazing across his temple as she did. Her heart rate soared as she lightly kissed the red skin beneath his bruised eye. When she tried to move away, he caught the side of her face and looked deep into her eyes. "Sorry," she said, getting up from his lap. "I shouldn't have …"

"It's fine." He reached for her hand but she shuffled backwards.

"I have some stuff to do … I should probably get on with it."

He nodded solemnly. "An urgent assignment that you need to write on a Friday night?"

"Yes. Exactly."

"I thought we were going to hang out."

Her eyebrows pulled together. "I can't. I'm too confused. Yesterday, I thought you didn't like me and I was on a date with someone else and today … I don't really know what's going on today but I'm freaking out and I'd rather do that on my own. If you don't mind."

"Okay. Don't freak out too much though. Everything's fine, isn't it?"

"I think so. I just need to … think."

He nodded and flashed her a sad smile before she turned and walked away.

"We were just talking about you," Lizzie said when Scarlett walked into the flat above the cafe the following morning. It seemed more and more like an office space, but she still thought of it as Verity's flat.

"It's rude to talk about people behind their backs," she said, joining Emily on the couch.

"Only if you're being mean," Emily said.

Scarlett removed a cushion from behind her and leaned back. "It's a bit sad that you have nothing better to talk about than me."

Lizzie swivelled in her chair and reached into the pram beside her to adjust Nathan's blanket. "We were discussing your books. Is everything set up for the release of book two?"

"Yes." She was fairly sure they knew that. Scarlett was unlikely to forget the publishing tasks for her own book.

"How's book three coming along?" Emily asked.

"It's almost finished, I think."

Lizzie pushed the pram back and forth as the baby made a few pathetic attempts at crying. "As soon as you release book two, readers will start asking for the next book. It would be good to set a date."

"I know," Scarlett said. "I'm working on it. But you can't rush creativity. And I do have a few other things going on as well."

"We know," Lizzie said calmly. "How is everything? Are you going to get an official autism diagnosis?" She shook her head. "Sorry. Am I supposed to say autism spectrum disorder instead of autism? I read about it but I found the terminology a bit confusing."

"Me too," Scarlett said. "The official diagnosis would be

autism spectrum disorder, which I find weird because it doesn't feel like a disorder to me. I like the idea of a spectrum though. It makes me think of a colour wheel with all the different autistic traits."

Lizzie nodded. "So will you get a diagnosis?"

"I don't think so. I'm pretty certain I'm autistic but I'm not sure why I need a doctor to confirm it. I found lots of people online who identify as autistic without getting an official diagnosis."

"Maybe you'd be able to access some sort of support services if you had a diagnosis?" Emily said.

Scarlett rolled her head against the back of the couch. "I'm fine though, and seeing doctors would be stressful. I have too much going on at the moment. I need to focus on the books and uni."

Lizzie smiled at her. "If there's anything we can do to help just let us know."

"Thanks." Scarlett folded her arms across her chest. "I suppose there is something you could help me with …"

Emily turned to face her. "What is it?"

"I don't know what to do about Fraser."

"What's going on now?" Lizzie asked.

"We almost kissed. At least I think we did. He got in some sort of scuffle with this guy who I went on a date with and ended up with a black eye. And then we had this moment …"

"You went on a date?" Emily asked.

"Yes! Don't look so surprised. I matched with a guy on a dating app and met up with him. It was a disaster."

"And Fraser got in a fight with him?" Lizzie asked, leaning forward in her chair.

"Not really. They're on the same football team and there was some dirty tackle that went wrong or something. Fraser got all macho I guess."

"He definitely likes you then if he was upset about you going on a date." Emily picked up her notepad from the coffee table and scribbled something in it. "Tell us about the almost kiss …"

"There's not much to tell. We just had this moment. But then I panicked and said I had an assignment to get on with." Distracted, she looked suspiciously at Emily's notebook. "What did you write in that?"

"Just something I needed to add to my shopping list. Why?"

Lizzie grinned. "Are you taking notes on Scarlett's love life so you can turn it into a novel?"

"No," Emily screeched. "Of course not."

"It'd make a pretty boring novel," Scarlett said.

"I think it'd make a great book, but I honestly wasn't. It's only my shopping list."

"That might be more believable if you ever did any shopping."

Emily glared at Lizzie. "What's that supposed to mean?"

"It means we all know Jack does the shopping and cooking and cleaning at your house."

"You sound jealous," Emily said, amused.

"I *am*. Not that I can complain about Max. He definitely does his share. It's the three kids who don't pull their weight."

"I'm going to cook a nice dinner for Jack tonight." Emily opened her notebook and showed them the shopping list as proof. "It'll probably go wrong but at least I can say I tried."

Scarlett had drifted into a daydream. "Do you know what Netflix and chill means?" she asked.

"Yes," Emily said, seeming a little confused by the question. "Jack and I do it every Friday night."

Lizzie burst out laughing and almost fell off her chair.

"I don't know why it's so funny," Emily said. "I realise we lead the sad life of a married couple but that's what we are. Jack always laughs too. The other week when I was telling Tara about our Friday night routine, she and Jack thought it was hysterical. James kept telling them not to be so immature, so I assume he's also happy to Netflix and chill at the weekend."

"Oh, god." Lizzie wiped a tear from the corner of her eye. "I don't know whether we should break it to you. We're going to get Jack into trouble."

"What are you talking about?" Emily asked.

Scarlett grimaced. "It actually means sex."

"No, it doesn't." Emily screwed her nose up. "Why would it mean sex?"

"I don't know. But it does."

Lizzie nodded. "You're not so boring after all, if your Friday night routine is some quality time with Jack with Netflix in the background."

"Are you serious?" Emily asked with wide eyes.

Scarlett and Lizzie nodded in unison.

"I'm going to kill Jack! I'm actually going to kill him. He let me keep thinking it was some innocent saying." Emily covered her face with her hands. "I was in the shop the other week and I told the women on the till that I was getting snacks for an evening of Netflix and chill!"

Scarlett felt herself relax as she laughed.

"I'm so embarrassed." Emily's face was set in a frown as she picked up her notebook and drew a big cross through her shopping list. "It looks like Jack will be cooking for the foreseeable future." Snapping the book shut, she stood up. "If you'd like to say a final goodbye to Jack you should call him now. I'll talk to you later."

"You're supposed to be telling me what to do about Fraser," Scarlett complained.

Emily cast a glance over her shoulder as she marched towards the door. "Kiss him. Obviously!"

"Poor Jack," Lizzie said, when the door closed behind Emily. "I almost feel as though I should call him and give him a heads up."

"He should have told her what it means," Scarlett mused.

"Yeah. It's pretty funny though."

"At least I'm not the only one who didn't know what it

meant. I thought it was one of those things I missed because I'm autistic."

"Everyone struggles in life," Lizzie said kindly. "Don't be so hard on yourself."

"It's frustrating. The more I try and make sense of things, the more confused I get."

"Are we talking about Fraser?" Lizzie asked.

"I was talking about life in general. But Fraser is confusing too."

Lizzie stood and peered into the pram, adjusting Nathan's blanket. "I think Emily's right – you just need to kiss him. Then see what happens."

Scarlett sat up straighter, her attention drawn to a loose thread on the carpet. "I'm scared of what happens from there," she admitted. "I've never been in a proper relationship before. I don't know how."

"That's quite a funny statement considering you're married."

Scarlett rolled her eyes. "It's not a real marriage."

"I know. But as far as relationships go, I don't think anyone really knows what they're doing. If you care about each other you'll figure it out." She rocked the pram. "I think I'll take him for a walk and leave you to work on book three."

"I'm going to get it finished soon," she replied determinedly. "If it's rubbish you'll tell me, right? You wouldn't let me publish it if it was bad."

"Of course not. But it won't be rubbish. And I want you to hurry up because I'm dying to read it."

CHAPTER 34

Taking out his anger at Mike on the football pitch hadn't been Fraser's finest moment, but when he'd heard him laughing about the girl who didn't know what Netflix and chill meant, he'd seen red. Given that he'd pretty much stopped socialising with the team, he was already feeling some tension with his teammates. His aggression during training hadn't gone down well with anyone.

When he apologised to Mike before the game on Saturday, he'd made sure the rest of the team were around to witness it. He definitely wasn't flavour of the month, but going out for drinks with them after the game seemed to smooth things over a little.

Scarlett was on his mind constantly. After he'd told her how he felt, he was determined to take things at her pace. As much as it felt like torture, he wouldn't risk rushing her into anything and messing it up.

On Sunday evening, he called hello from the living room when he heard her arrive home but purposely didn't go out to greet her. If she wanted to hang out it was up to her. The last thing he wanted was for her to feel uncomfortable in her own home.

She wandered in and looked at the screen while he continued

with the car racing game he was playing. "You don't go out so much these days."

"That's because I'm snowed under with uni assignments." He paused the game and turned to her with a cheeky grin.

"It looks like you're really keeping on top of that uni work," she said mockingly.

"How was your weekend?"

"Good. I was very productive. I got a lot done on my novel yesterday and worked in the cafe today."

"If you're trying to make me feel lazy, you're succeeding."

"Have you done any work this weekend, or have you been playing video games the whole time?"

"I did some work," he said.

"Haven't you been out at all?"

"I had football yesterday and went for a couple of drinks after. Didn't stay long though." He pointed at his eye. "I'm feeling a bit self-conscious now that my good looks have been destroyed."

"Good point." She turned to leave again. "Do you want a cup of tea?"

"Yeah, please. But you were supposed to reassure me that I still look good!"

"I'm fairly sure you know that," she called over her shoulder as she walked out.

Returning with tea, she lingered, and he wondered whether she'd stay around or make an excuse and disappear to her room for the evening.

"Do you want a game?" he asked casually, holding out a controller.

"Okay."

After a couple of games she relaxed and joked around with him. He had to remind himself almost constantly not to lean over and kiss her. He needed to go at her pace. For now, they were just two best friends hanging out. Which was actually pretty great.

Scarlett loved her time with Fraser. They fell into a routine of spending an hour or so watching TV or playing video games in the evening before each going off to their own rooms to study. Everything felt easy. At least for a few days. Then the relief that Fraser wasn't pressuring her for anything more than friendship was replaced by concern at the fact that he hadn't tried to kiss her.

When things had felt like they might be heating up between them she'd got scared, but when he backed off it was even more terrifying. He'd said that whenever she was ready to date, he'd be waiting. But she sort of thought that hanging out and playing video games was her version of dating. Maybe she should go with Emily and Lizzie's advice of kissing him and seeing what happened.

She was contemplating just that as she walked out of her lecture on Thursday afternoon.

When a voice called out to her, she went with her usual tactic of pretending not to hear and hoping they'd lose interest. Unfortunately, the voice came again, accompanied by a hand tugging on her elbow.

"Didn't you hear me?" Bridget asked when Scarlett turned around.

"I was daydreaming." It wasn't a complete lie – she'd been happily imagining kissing Fraser.

"I do that too sometimes," she said. "Get completely lost in thought and lose track of everything around me."

Scarlett forced herself to smile but it felt like a grimace. How did people smile on demand and make it look natural?

"Do you want to get a coffee?" Bridget asked. "Or a tea? You prefer tea, don't you?"

"Yes. But I haven't got time today. I have to study."

"Oh, right. Of course." Her smile fell and she put a hand on Scarlett's arm again. "Could you maybe spare ten minutes? I know I shouldn't drag you into it, but I wanted to pick your brains about Fraser. He told me he just wanted to be friends but now he's not even replying to my messages. I was hoping he just needed some space and maybe we could try again, but I don't know what to do."

"I don't think I can help," Scarlett muttered.

"Please," Bridget said. "Just ten minutes. My friends keep telling me to get over it and move on. No one understands."

Scarlett could relate to having no one understand you and felt a pang of sympathy for Bridget. "We could get a drink," she said hesitantly. "Just a quick one though."

"If I'm completely honest," Bridget said once they were settled in the cafe, "he was always distant but I kept hoping we'd get past that. I felt as though there was something going on with him and it was bad timing, but now I'm not sure."

Scarlett blew on her tea and took a sip.

"Sometimes he was so sweet and lovely," Bridget said with a faraway look. "And then he seemed as though he'd rather be somewhere else. It sounds stupid because we only went out a few times, but I really fell for him. I kept thinking it would just take time for things to develop, but then he said he didn't see it going anywhere."

"Sorry." Scarlett wished she hadn't agreed to hang out with Bridget. She was hopeless at advice.

"Do you think it's something I did? Maybe I was too intense."

"Possibly. Or maybe he just didn't like you very much." Scarlett could tell by Bridget's face that she'd said the wrong thing. People didn't like the truth. "Sorry," she said as Bridget wiped tears from the corners of her eyes.

"It's fine. I appreciate you being honest. Do you think that's the problem?"

"Yes. He thinks you're really nice. But he just sees you as a friend."

"I'm pathetic," Bridget sniffed. "I need to get over it, but it's hard when I can't stop thinking about him. He's so lovely."

"Yes," Scarlett agreed. "He is."

She was wondering if it would be okay to leave yet when a tall figure approached the table. Inwardly she groaned at the sight of Fraser's friend Simon.

"Is this an 'I hate Fraser' club?" he asked with a smirk.

"No." Bridget sat up straighter. "Why would you think that?"

"It's just a bit odd to find his wife hanging out with the woman he was dating," he said with a shrug. "And if you did have an 'I hate Fraser' club, I'd be tempted to join. He's been pretty annoying recently. Like he thinks he's better than everyone or something."

Scarlett's heart was pounding furiously and she didn't know what to say. Apparently Bridget was having the same problem as she stared up at Simon.

"Maybe it's juggling two women that's stressing him out," he went on. "You'd think that since you two clearly get on, it would be a nice arrangement for him. I guess the reality of two women doesn't live up to the fantasy. Anyway, I'll leave you to continue comparing notes or whatever it is you were doing."

"What did he say?" Bridget asked slowly, her eyes on Simon's back as he walked away. Scarlett glanced at her backpack on the floor, wondering if she could grab it and bolt. She could feel Bridget's gaze searing into her before she even looked up. "What was he saying about Fraser having a wife?"

"It's sort of a weird story," Scarlett said, her voice uneven.

"Fraser's married?" Bridget asked, blinking rapidly. "You're Fraser's wife? That can't be right." She laughed but didn't really seem amused. "It is a joke, isn't it?"

"No. But it's probably not how he made it sound. We're married, but not really."

"That doesn't make any sense," Bridget said. "Surely you're either married or you're not?"

"Legally, yes, we're married. But we're not really together. I couldn't get a student loan so Fraser agreed to marry me to help me out. It was a favour. So, he really is lovely."

Bridget's eyes widened and she put a hand over her mouth. "I've heard this story around campus, but I thought it was one of those urban myths. You're saying it really happened? And it was you and Fraser?"

"Yeah." She smiled at the thought of being an urban myth but that seemed to make Bridget angry.

"When I was going on dates with him, he was married?" she said, louder than Scarlett would have liked.

"We're not really together," Scarlett said again. "It's all fake."

"He lied to me. You both lied to me."

"I didn't lie. You didn't ask me, so I never lied about it."

"Why on earth would I ask you if you were married to the guy I'd been telling you I liked?"

"It's not really my fault you like him. Or that he didn't tell you he was married."

Tears rolled down Bridget's face as she stood up. "Were you laughing at me the whole time? You two are sick."

"We weren't laughing at you," Scarlett said. "Fraser thinks you're nice. I think so too." She wasn't sure Bridget heard the last bit as she'd already stormed away.

Not wanting to leave the cafe immediately for fear that Bridget was somewhere outside, Scarlett hung around and finished her tea before venturing out. She hoped Fraser would be at home so she could tell him what had happened.

Halfway home she impatiently prodded the button for the pedestrian crossing, then gave up on it and pulled out her phone while she waited for the lights to change. It turned to green at the same time as she pressed dial on Fraser's number.

"Are you at home?" she asked, hurrying across the road.

"Yeah. But I'm in the middle of something. I'll call you back in a bit."

"No, wait," she said in a panic. "I need to tell you something. It's important."

"I already know. I'll talk to you later."

She swore as she pushed the phone into her pocket and picked up her pace. At home, she could hear raised voices as she put the key in the lock. Part of her wanted to backtrack and hide out somewhere until Bridget left, but maybe together they could convince her that the marriage wasn't real and Fraser hadn't intended to hurt her.

Creeping into the hallway, she placed her bag at the foot of the stairs and ventured towards the living room.

"You're awful," Bridget shouted. "You led me on and treated me like dirt. And you're making a mockery of marriage. How could you get married to someone you didn't even know? All to cheat your way into money that you're not eligible for. It's disgusting."

"I'm sorry," Fraser said, sitting on the couch with his head bowed and his hands pushed into his hair. "I should never have agreed to go out with you."

"I suppose I should have realised! All you ever wanted to talk about was *her*."

"He didn't mean to hurt you," Scarlett said, making her presence known.

Bridget wiped at her cheeks with her sleeves. "I don't even fully understand. Are you really autistic or was that all part of your lies?"

Scarlett shook her head slowly. "I'm not sure." From the way Fraser winced, she suspected she'd said the wrong thing.

"I can't believe you two," Bridget spluttered. "What's wrong with you?"

"I'm probably autistic," Scarlett said, making Fraser wince again. Maybe she should just keep her mouth shut.

Bridget strode past Scarlett. "You can't get married for a loan. It's wrong. I've got a good mind to report you."

"Wait!" Fraser called, standing and following her. "I really am sorry."

The front door slammed behind her.

Scarlett walked further into the living room and sank onto the couch. "Simon told her," she explained when Fraser came back in.

He nodded as though he already knew. "How come you were with Bridget anyway?"

"Because she asked me to hang out and she's hard to say no to. Now I feel bad because I quite like her."

"You don't need to feel bad. It was me who messed up."

"Do you think she's going to report us?"

"I don't think so," Fraser said, sitting beside her. "She's hurt and angry but she's not spiteful."

"What will happen if she reports us?"

"I imagine we'd get kicked out of uni."

Scarlett sat up straight. "I can't get kicked out of uni. I'm more than halfway through the course. It would be such a waste."

"She'd also have to prove it," Fraser said.

"I don't think it would take much detective work to figure out our marriage isn't real. The only people who know we're married know it's a fake."

"That's true." He glanced up at her. "What do you want to do about it?"

"What do you mean?"

"I mean we can carry on as we are and hope Bridget doesn't say anything, or we can make people believe we're married. We'd have a better chance of getting away with it if Bridget does decide to say something."

Scarlett hesitated while she mulled it over. Or at least pretended to mull it over. "I suppose it would be better if we act as though we're in a relationship."

"I think so too," he said with a small smile. "We need to be seen together and act like a couple in public. People need to know we're married. We can say it was an impulsive thing but we're very happy."

"What about Bridget? Do people know you were dating her? Because if they do, they're going to think it's very strange that you're married."

"I can say we were having a rough patch and thought we were going to split up but now we've sorted things out. Married couples have their ups and downs. It doesn't mean it's not a real marriage."

"No. What makes it not a real marriage is the fact that it's not a real marriage!"

He laughed. "You're going to have to stop saying stuff like that. We'll need to be convincing. Do you think you can manage it?"

"Yes."

"Good. So you'll have dinner on the table when I get home from now on?"

She rolled her eyes. "It's only when we're in public, remember?"

"Damn." He grinned at her. "Do you want to come and watch me play football tomorrow night?"

"No. I did that once before and it was awful."

"Because you didn't tell me you were coming. This time you're invited."

"I still don't want to come. It's boring. Plus, it's February; I'll freeze to death."

"Please," he said with a hint of a pout.

"I suppose I can come for a bit. I'm not coming for all of it though. I'd die of boredom, if not from the cold."

"We should probably start wearing our wedding rings too," he said.

She nodded her agreement and felt a tingle of excitement spread through her.

CHAPTER 35

Resorting to faking a relationship was pretty desperate, but at that point Fraser would do anything to get closer to Scarlett. She'd seemed keen to make their marriage appear real, so it wasn't as though he'd pushed her into it. Plus, there was a chance that Bridget had been serious about her threat to report them. It was probably only a very slim chance, but there was no harm in covering their tracks just in case.

Finally, he'd be able to kiss Scarlett. It would have been better if it didn't feel so contrived, but if he waited for her to move their relationship on, he suspected he'd be waiting a long time. As much as he wanted to be patient, the reality of it was frustrating to say the least.

During the first half of the football match, he glanced at the sidelines repeatedly but couldn't see Scarlett. He'd just scored a goal in the second half when he happened to catch sight of her clapping and grinning at him. He played harder after that, though he was fairly sure she wouldn't have a clue if he played well or not. Trying to impress her with his football skills was unlikely to be effective.

When the whistle blew for full time, he flashed her a smile before getting caught in the bustle of his teammates congratulating each other. It was only a friendly game but they'd played well.

By the time he looked for Scarlett again, she'd vanished. Scanning the area, he saw her walking across the car park and set off after her. The studs of his football boots clicked on the concrete of the car park as he called out to her.

"Where are you going?" he asked, only stopping when he'd completely invaded her personal space. He rested a hand at her waist, his heart rate increasing with the thrill of being able to touch her.

"I was going to go home."

"Do you want to come for a quick drink in the Ram Bar?"

"With your teammates? Not really, no."

He smiled. "I'll re-phrase … Will you please come for a drink? The whole point of you coming to the match is so that people see us together."

"I suppose I can. I definitely don't *want* to."

"I'll be with you the whole time," he said.

"Are you going in the bar like that?" she asked, looking him up and down.

"No. I need to have a shower and change. But I'll be really quick and then I won't leave your side. I promise."

"I don't want to go in the bar on my own. I'll go for a walk and meet you once you've changed."

He glanced behind him, then back to Scarlett. "Can I kiss you?"

"What?"

"If we want people to think we're married we need to act like it. Married couples would usually—"

She cut him off, lifting onto her toes to brush her lips against his. It caught him by surprise and his pounding heart seemed to stop dead. Her hands crept up his neck and into his hair as she kissed him.

With her eyes closed, he swore she'd never looked so beautiful. Slowly, she batted them open as she pulled away. When she took a step back, he took one forward and cupped her cheek as he moved his face back to hers, probing her mouth with his tongue as a jolt of desire hit deep in his gut.

He had to force himself to stop. This time she didn't step back but kept her face close to his, her breath sweeping over his cheek and leaving him longing for more.

"I'll send you a message after I've changed," he whispered, wishing they could skip the bar and go home instead. He wanted to be alone with her, not surrounded by his obnoxious teammates.

She tilted her head and gave him a soft peck before she moved away.

As Scarlett walked away from Fraser, her insides were fluttering so much that she felt slightly nauseous. Her legs had gone all wobbly and she didn't dare look back in case it caused her to trip over.

She couldn't stop grinning as she strolled around the grounds of the campus. Considering they were only faking a relationship, it felt very real. It was actually pretty perfect. There was no need for her to freak out, since it wasn't real. She didn't have to worry about messing things up. Surely even she was capable of a fake relationship.

Eventually, she headed towards the Ram Bar and found a bench nearby. It was cold and uncomfortable and she hoped Fraser wouldn't take long.

"Where've you been?" he asked when he appeared beside her ten minutes later.

"I went for a walk around campus. I told you that's what I was doing?"

He sat beside her. "And I told you I'd message you when I was ready. You could have looked at your phone."

"Oh. Sorry."

"It's fine." His lips twitched upwards. "I thought you might have ditched me and gone home."

"No. Just sitting here on the world's most uncomfortable bench."

With a hand on her back, he gently nudged her off the bench, then slid along and pulled her back down on his lap. "Is that better?"

"Yeah," she mumbled, slightly dazed by the way her heart raced.

"Are the guys from my team still hanging around up there?" He tipped his head behind him.

"Yeah."

He nodded. "Maybe I should kiss you again then?"

"You should probably stop asking and just do it. It'll seem a bit weird if someone overhears you asking to kiss me."

"Good point." His arms tightened around her waist, drawing her close as their lips met.

"Are they still there?" he asked when he drew back slightly.

She glanced at the building and nodded vaguely. No one was around, but someone could appear at any moment. It wouldn't hurt to keep kissing for a while. This time he pushed his hand into her hair, and the tips of his fingers massaged the back of her head as he kissed her with an intensity that made her whole body tingle.

"I suppose we should go inside," Fraser said, breathing hard when he finally pulled away.

"I guess so." She stroked the soft hair at the back of his neck. "I don't want to stay for long though. And what should I do if I see Mike?"

"It'll be fine, I promise." He held her hand as they walked up to the building, then kept hold of it as they made their way to the bar. It was busy, with a hum of chatter in the air.

Fraser ordered the drinks and had a brief chat with the barman about the football game.

"Let's see if we can find a table," he said, then set off through the crowd.

Scarlett followed close behind him, slipping her hand into his when he reached back. "Don't you want to hang out with the team?"

"Not really." He pulled out a chair for her at a table at the far side of the room, then sat close beside her.

"Do you just want your friends to see us together but not hang out with them?"

He put a hand on her knee and leaned into her. "Not because I'm embarrassed by you," he said as though reading her mind. "It's more that I'm embarrassed by them. Some of them at least. When they're all together they're a bit full on."

"I'm not complaining." She relaxed knowing she wasn't expected to be sociable.

He gave her a reassuring smile, followed by a lingering kiss. "You're a very good kisser," he whispered.

"You too," she mumbled, hoping her cheeks weren't bright red.

A lanky guy with a shaved head appeared, slapping Fraser on the back before taking a seat.

"Good game tonight," he said.

"Thanks. I don't think you've met Scarlett." He tipped his head towards her. "My wife."

He offered her his hand and she shook it weakly. "I'm Wayne. I didn't know you were married."

"We split up for a while because he cheated on me," Scarlett said, then tried not to laugh as Fraser choked on his beer.

Wayne's eyes widened. "Oh, right."

"Obviously I won't let him forget it for a while," Scarlett added. "But I think we'll be fine if he can learn to behave himself."

Fraser draped an arm around her shoulders. "In my defence it was more of a flirtation than anything."

"Aren't you supposed to be trying to get back into my good books?" she replied with a mischievous smile.

He rolled his eyes. "Yes, darling. Sorry, darling."

She burst out laughing and gave him a gentle shove away from her. After asking where the toilets were she left them to chat.

She was walking back across the room when she caught sight of Mike standing directly in her path.

"Hi," he said, as he approached her.

Her gaze fell to his scruffy blue trainers. "Hi."

"I wanted to say sorry about the other night. I think it was a misunderstanding."

"I thought it meant chill out and watch Netflix," she said.

"Yeah. I realised that eventually. I really am sorry."

"It's okay. I'm sorry I punched you."

"Fraser wasn't happy with me either. I had no idea you two were together. To be fair, you were on a dating app so it seemed as though you were single." He paused and blew out a breath. "It's kind of weird to agree to go on a date with someone if you're not single."

"I wanted to get back at Fraser for cheating on me."

"Fair enough."

Fraser appeared through the crowd and slipped an arm around Scarlett's waist. "You better not be trying anything with my wife again."

"Your *wife?*" Mike asked.

"Yeah."

"He wasn't trying anything," Scarlett said to Fraser. "I was just saying how I went on the date with him to get back at you for cheating on me."

"You're really loving that story this evening, aren't you?"

"You two are married?" Mike asked.

"Yes," they said at once.

"Aren't you a bit young to be married?"

"Yes," Scarlett replied. "It was impulsive. And obviously

Fraser was too immature to understand the rules of marriage, because he cheated on me."

"It was a mild flirtation," Fraser said through gritted teeth as he gently pushed his fingers into her ribs, making her laugh and squirm to get away from him.

"I know it was more than flirting!" Scarlett said, as Fraser clamped both arms around her waist to stop her moving further away.

"I thought we were putting it behind us." He pressed his lips to hers so she couldn't tease him any more.

"You two need to get a room," Mike said, before wandering away.

Scarlett pulled back from Fraser. "You can't kiss me when someone's standing with us."

"You said I didn't need to ask permission. Plus, it got rid of him."

"Did you kiss me to get rid of him?"

"Yes. Partly." Smiling, he kissed her again. "Do you want to go home?"

She nodded, then followed as he went around saying goodbye to a few people.

"Haven't you got your car?" she asked as they wandered through campus.

"No." He was still holding her hand, and she wondered how long it would be until he let go. "I thought we might have a few drinks so I got a lift over here."

"You could have stayed longer if you wanted. You didn't have to leave because of me."

"I didn't really feel like it." He cast her a sidelong glance. "Especially since you were smearing my reputation by telling everyone I cheated on you."

"Well, how else do we explain the fact that you were dating Bridget? And I'm sure it was your idea to say that."

"No! I suggested we say we were separated at the time and were free to see other people."

"Oh. I might have got confused. I should have said that."

"Too late now. You've painted me as a villain."

"Sorry," she said when he fell silent.

"I was only joking." He squeezed her hand. "You know I only went out with Bridget a couple of times, don't you? Other times she tagged along when I was out with the team."

"If you say so."

"I didn't sleep with her."

She felt a sudden lightness in her stomach. "Really?"

"Yes."

He continued to hold her hand but he went quiet again.

"Are you annoyed with me?" she finally asked.

"No. Why?"

"I don't know. I just thought maybe you were."

"I'm not." It seemed as though he wasn't going to say any more and Scarlett had resigned herself for a quiet walk home when he spoke again. "I know you were only joking about me cheating on you, but whenever I was with Bridget that was kind of how it felt."

Since she had no idea what to say, she squeezed his hand and they continued in silence. They were almost home when Fraser spoke again.

"I have a question for you and I think I know what the answer will be but I'll ask anyway …" He hesitated and looked at her uncertainly. "How would you feel about meeting my parents?"

She pulled her hand from his and buried her hands in her pockets. "I don't want to."

"That's what I thought. And if you really don't want to it's fine, but if we need to convince anyone this is a real marriage my parents would back us up. It would be easier for them to do that if they'd met you."

"Your parents would lie for us?"

"Of course. They definitely wouldn't want me to get kicked

out of uni." He pulled his keys out and opened the front door. "Will you at least think about it? They're nice. You'd like them."

"They wouldn't like me though." Slipping her coat off, she hung it on the rack. "If they met me they'd probably want people to think it's a fake marriage."

"Don't be daft. They'd like you. And I already told them about you, so they'd know what to expect."

"You told them I'm autistic?"

"Yeah." He grimaced as though he was concerned he'd said the wrong thing. "When I first thought you were autistic, I kind of freaked out and spoke to them about it."

"What did they say?"

"They said I should be a friend to you."

"That was nice."

"Yeah. So will you meet them?"

"I'll think about it," she said, then walked upstairs, wishing him goodnight as she went.

CHAPTER 36

When Scarlett arrived in Hope Cove on Saturday morning, Lizzie and Emily were in the flat, sitting at opposite ends of the couch, each with their laptop on their knees.

"I'm glad you're here," Scarlett said. "I need to talk to you both."

"We're busy," Lizzie told her without looking up from the computer screen. "It'll have to wait."

Scarlett took her bag into her bedroom. It was pretty rude of them not to speak to her. Especially because most of the time she thought they talked too much, but now that she really wanted to chat to them, they couldn't spare her a few minutes. They could at least tell her whether they'd got the manuscript for her latest book. She'd emailed it to both of them late the previous evening but neither of them had replied. After a few minutes she walked back into the living room.

"Fraser and I kissed," she said, standing in front of them with her hands on her hips.

They closed their laptops in unison.

"Tell us everything," Emily said.

Scarlett told them about Bridget finding out about their fake marriage and how she said she might report them.

"So Fraser thought it would be a good idea to make people believe we're married in case she really does report us," she explained.

Emily chuckled. "Of course he did!"

"What's that supposed to mean?" Scarlett asked, glaring at her.

"It means the guy is clearly in love with you. Anyway, tell us about the kiss! All the details please."

"I went to watch him play football and afterwards he came over and we kissed." Scarlett's stomach did a flip as she replayed it in her head. "Then we went to the bar and we kissed a few more times. Fraser thinks we should make sure we're seen together and that people know we're married."

"I'm sure he does," Emily said with an annoying smirk.

"In case there's an investigation or something," Scarlett clarified.

Emily pressed her lips together. "Oh, of course."

"He also asked me if I'd meet his parents."

"In case you get investigated?" Lizzie asked, flashing Emily a quick smile.

"Yes." Scarlett sighed. "Why are you both grinning as though it's hilarious?"

"It's not funny," Emily said. "It's adorable. He must really be smitten if he wants you to meet his parents."

Scarlett hesitated, thinking of Fraser telling her he wanted to go on a date with her. Hopefully one day there would be more between them, but for now they were only pretending. "He just doesn't want to get kicked off his course."

"Yeah, right," Lizzie said. "Who is this girl even going to report you to?"

"I don't know," Scarlett said. She hadn't given it much thought.

"Not the police," Emily said. "They've got better stuff to deal with. If she tells the loan company, I'm not sure if they'll really care. You're going to have to pay the loan back, so it's not as though you've stolen anything."

"She could tell the university."

"But it's her word against yours," Lizzie said with a shrug. "And there's no way she can prove your marriage isn't real."

"No," Scarlett agreed. "But if anyone looks into it and finds out we got married a month after we met it looks pretty suspicious."

"Love at first sight," Emily insisted. "It happens all the time."

"No it doesn't," Scarlett said.

Lizzie grinned. "I don't think you have anything to worry about. You've managed to make Emily believe it's a real marriage even though she knows the truth."

"Emily lives in a dream world," Scarlett pointed out. "The people at the university probably aren't hopeless romantics like her."

"I like my dream world," Emily said. "Anyway, when are you meeting his parents?"

"Never. I said I'd think about it but I can't actually do it."

"Why not?" Emily asked in a whiney voice.

Scarlett rolled her eyes. "Do you seriously think that would go well?"

Lizzie made a poor attempt to cover her laughter with a cough. "I'm sure it would be fine."

"It'd be a disaster," Scarlett said.

"Can I get back to work now?" Lizzie asked. "I told Max I'd only be a few hours and I want to get as much done as I can."

"Fine!" Scarlett threw her hands up and headed back to the bedroom. "Don't worry about my problems! Clearly you have better things to do." She stopped abruptly and turned back. "By the way did you get an email from me? I sent the book to you both last night."

They wore matching smiles as they opened up their laptops again.

"No!" Scarlett snapped. "You better not be reading it here!"

"I can't read at home," Lizzie said. "It's a mad house."

Emily scooted back on the couch, shuffling to get comfy. "I got jealous that Lizzie was already reading it so I put my writing on hold and joined her."

"I don't want you to read it in front of me," Scarlett complained.

Lizzie made a shooing motion with her hand. "Go away then!"

~

On Monday, Scarlett was intent on spending the two-hour break between lectures in the study hall. As she shuffled out of her morning lecture amid the bustle of everyone chatting around her, she kept her head down and avoided looking at anyone. You'd think after eighteen months they'd have figured out that she didn't want to have lunch with them, but sometimes people still invited her to join them.

The voice that called out to her made her head shoot up.

"What are you doing here?" she asked Fraser.

"Nice to see you too," he said, drawing her away from the crowd to kiss her. "I thought I could take you for lunch."

"So that's why you were quizzing me about my schedule over breakfast?"

"Yes!"

"You could have just asked me."

"I thought if I surprised you there was less chance of you saying no."

"I've got my lunch with me. My plan was to get some studying in."

"You're the most studious person I know," he said, his hands resting on her hips. "Surely you can take an hour off. And you can eat your sandwiches in the food hall while you watch me eat a burger and chips!"

She relented and they set off hand in hand.

"Can you admit you'd rather eat a burger and chips than your cheese sandwich?" Fraser asked, after taking a large mouthful of his burger.

"Some people can't afford to spend money on eating out."

He stared at her. "You know I'd have bought you lunch, right? Tell me what you want and I'll get it."

"There's the principle as well," she said, shaking her head. "It's a waste to buy food when I have a perfectly good lunch here."

"I think we have different ideas about what constitutes a perfectly good lunch. At least take some of my chips."

"I'm okay."

"You're killing me. Give me half of your sandwich."

"Why?"

"Because then I can give you half my burger and I won't feel guilty for stuffing my face while you nibble on a crappy cheese sandwich."

"There's nothing wrong with my sandwich." She wondered why she was arguing when the burger looked so good. Passing him half of her sandwich, she smiled sweetly until he cut the burger and gave her half. "How did you do on the nutrition part of your course?" she asked.

"Is that your attempt at humour?" He grinned and shook his head. "I actually did really well. For example, I know that any unhealthy food consumed on a romantic date with your wife doesn't count."

"Have they done scientific studies on that?"

"If they haven't they should. Maybe I'll consider it for my dissertation."

"Is this your idea of a romantic date?" she asked, looking around the bustle of the food hall.

"I think it's romantic." He turned and straddled the bench,

pulling her close. "But maybe it's just being around you that makes me feel all lovey dovey."

She managed to keep a straight face for a moment, then burst out laughing. "That was really cheesy. If Emily needs helps writing her romance novels I'll tell her to call you."

"Stop being mean and kiss me!"

"You shouldn't make me laugh so much if you want me to kiss you."

"Fine," he said, sliding away from her. "I was only trying to save you from getting kicked out of uni, but if you don't want to kiss me, I'm happy to go back to my burger."

"You're an idiot," she said, pulling his face to hers and lightly kissing him. "And you taste like ketchup and coke."

"That might be the best compliment I've ever had!"

Scarlett took a bite of the burger, chewing slowly. "Do you think if Bridget was going to say something she'd have done it by now?"

"Maybe she has and there are spies out watching us."

"I can count eight potential spies in here," she joked as she scanned the room.

Fraser put a hand on her knee and his features turned serious. "Even if Bridget doesn't say anything, someone else might. I don't think it can hurt to make it known that we're married. Unless you really hate kissing me."

"It's not the worst thing in the world." A smile tugged at her lips. "The other day I dropped a can of soup on my bare foot and I'd say that was worse."

He looked at her in amusement. "Really?"

"Yeah. And one time my mum forced me to try eating fish even though I knew I hated it. That was worse too."

"It sounds as though you quite like kissing me."

"When you compare it to eating fish or dropping heavy objects on my big toe, yeah, it's not so bad."

He leaned in and kissed her again.

"Can I eat my burger before it goes cold?" she asked.

"The burger that you didn't even want?"

"I never said I didn't want it." She elbowed him away from her and took another bite.

Two girls from Scarlett's course gave her a quick wave before sitting at the next table. They were part of a group of four girls who Scarlett thought of as "the make-up gang". She wasn't sure how anyone had the time, money or energy for putting so much stuff on their faces.

Scarlett was aware of them glancing over while she chatted to Fraser and wasn't at all surprised when they came over after they'd finished their lunch.

"What did you think of the lecture this morning?" the blonde one asked. Scarlett couldn't remember either of their names.

"Pretty boring. I find the lecturer hard to follow."

"We were saying the same," the brunette said. "There's no intonation to her voice and it makes us sleepy after a while."

The blonde offered her hand to Fraser and introduced herself as Gemma. The darker one was called Bianca.

"We didn't know you had a boyfriend," Gemma said.

"We've never spoken," Scarlett pointed out, "so I'm not sure why you'd know anything about my relationship status."

"I'm actually her husband." Fraser nodded at the bench across the table. "Do you want to sit down?"

They didn't hesitate and Scarlett inwardly groaned. Why had he done that?

"You're married?" Gemma said in surprise.

Scarlett nodded, then craned her neck as someone else said hello.

"Hi," she replied, trying not to look directly at the sweat patches around Carolyn's armpits. Stepping out from behind her, Mingmei said a cheerful hello too.

"We thought we should arrange a time to work on our group presentation," Carolyn said. "But we can catch up with you later if you're busy now."

Fraser introduced himself, then offered them his space on the bench. "I'll leave you with your friends," he said to Scarlett. "I've got a lecture in a bit anyway."

She glared at him but he only smiled and gave her a quick kiss.

"Shall I cook dinner tonight or do you want to?" he asked.

"I can if you want. So long as you don't mind tinned soup."

His eyes sparkled. "Maybe I'll cook. See you later." He kissed her again and disappeared, leaving Scarlett to deal with a barrage of questions from her classmates.

CHAPTER 37

Scarlett followed her nose to the kitchen when she got home that evening.

"I didn't know you were really going to cook. I thought you just said that because there were people around."

"I did," Fraser said. "But then I thought it might be nice to cook."

She peered over his shoulder at the sausages in the pan. When he turned, she leaned forwards, intent on kissing him before remembering they weren't in public. Quickly, she took a step back.

"I don't know what you like to eat," Fraser said. "Aside from soup and cheese sandwiches and pasta."

"You know I like burger and chips too."

"I also know you hate fish. But I only learned that today. I suppose the more time we spend together, the more likely we could convince people this is a real marriage. If we ever need to." He took the pan off the heat and put the sausages on a couple of plates. "So do you like sausages?"

"Yes."

"And mashed potato and peas?"

"Yeah. I'm really hungry."

He handed her a plate of food and she moved to the table.

"I suppose this goes some way to making up for what you did today."

A small smile played at his lips as he sat opposite her. "What did I do?"

"As if you don't know! You left me with all those people. They asked me a load of questions and now they all want to be friends with me because I have a hot husband."

"You think I'm hot?" he said, picking up his cutlery.

"*I* don't." She felt her cheeks flush. "But apparently other people think so. And now all those people in my class will want to hang out with me."

"Is that so bad?"

"I don't have time for friends. And I don't have the energy for chatting about all the inane stuff they go on about."

"That's a bit sad. But at least people know about us now. Did you think any more about meeting my parents?"

"I don't want to."

He nodded and switched his attention to his food, not speaking again until he'd finished.

"Do you want to play video games?" he asked while he loaded the plates into the dishwasher.

"I've got work to do."

"Really?"

"Yes." She searched his features. "Do you think I'm lying?"

"Maybe. I don't know. You seem to work all the time. Surely you could take half an hour off."

"I really do have work to get on with. Don't you?"

He shrugged. "Nothing urgent."

She thanked him for dinner, then went upstairs and sat at her desk. Opening her laptop, she thought of the look on Fraser's face when she'd told him she couldn't play video games. Was he annoyed with her for having to work?

Thinking back on the conversation, it had been when she'd said she didn't want to meet his parents that he'd gone quiet on her. Why did he even want her to meet them? If she couldn't get on with her own parents, what hope did she have with anyone else's?

She hadn't heard from her own parents in ages and wondered if she should be bothered by the fact that they were only really in touch through Verity. Fraser had seemed shocked when she'd spoken to him about the situation, but she rarely even thought about them. If they couldn't accept her as she was, she didn't want them in her life. Not seeing each other seemed to suit them all, and being upset about the way things were wouldn't change anything.

With a frustrated sigh she gave herself a mental shake and focused on the research she had to do for her group project with Carolyn and Mingmei.

Emily messaged on Wednesday afternoon to say she'd finished reading Scarlett's latest book and loved it. It should have eased Scarlett's fears, but Emily was generally positive about everything. And she could be lying. After the autism revelation, Scarlett suspected Lizzie and Emily might be worried about upsetting her and would tell her the book was great no matter what.

The following evening a message came from Lizzie saying that she really enjoyed it too and looked forward to discussing it with her. Apparently she had a couple of suggestions for tightening up the ending. That wasn't exactly scathing criticism, but Scarlett's self-doubt kicked in and before long she was sure that Lizzie thought the ending was terrible and was trying to be polite about it.

On Friday afternoon, she messaged Verity and told her she had a lot of uni work so wouldn't be able to work on Sunday. It wasn't a complete lie, but it wasn't really the truth either. She just didn't want to face Emily and Lizzie's comments on her book, so avoiding Hope Cove for the weekend seemed the best plan. And if she was entirely honest, she hoped she might spend some time with Fraser. She'd only seen him in passing since they'd had dinner on Tuesday, and the desire to hang out with him was building by the day.

He usually played football on Friday evening so she didn't expect him to be home before eight, but she hoped he might skip out on the pub after the game in favour of a night in front of the TV.

Weirdly, he called her around seven. As usual, her heart pounded at the sight of the incoming call and she didn't manage to answer before it stopped ringing. She was about to call him back when a message came through. He was going out for dinner with some people from his course and asked if she wanted to join.

Scarlett stared at the phone as she pondered the question. The thought of spending time with Fraser made her stomach flutter, but dinner with a group of people she didn't know filled her with dread. She also had questions: Where were they going? What kind of food would it be? Would she meet them there? Was it within walking distance?

She was contemplating how to whittle the questions down to a short message when her phone beeped again.

Pizza place in town, Fraser had written. *I can pick you up in ten minutes*.

She was fairly impressed that he'd managed to answer most of her questions without even being asked and typed a reply that simply said *okay*.

At the sound of a car horn just over ten minutes later, Scarlett went outside. When she slipped into the passenger seat, Fraser leaned towards her. Automatically, she moved to kiss him. They both stopped when they were inches apart and drew back abruptly.

Fraser checked the rear-view mirror before pulling away. "How was your day?"

"Fine. I'm not going back to Hope Cove this weekend, by the way."

"How come?"

"I don't feel like it. I've got a couple of assignments I need to get on with so I told Auntie Verity I can't work on Sunday." She reminded herself it was only a slight twist of the truth. She did have assignments to work on after all. "Are the people on your course nice?" she asked, changing the subject. "I don't usually like having dinner with people I don't know."

"They're really cool," he said, flashing her a reassuring smile before concentrating on the road. "I'm glad you're coming."

"The restaurant isn't expensive, is it? I don't have much money."

"No. But I'll pay. Don't worry about it."

"I can pay," she said. "As long as it's not some fancy, expensive place."

"Students don't generally hang out at fancy restaurants," he told her.

"Even rich students like you?"

He laughed. "Even me."

In the restaurant, Fraser went around the table introducing her to everyone. There were about ten of them and she lost track after the first two. She sat between Fraser and a girl called Diane, who smiled widely at her when she sat down.

"I only just found out Fraser's married," she said, leaning close to Scarlett. "Bit of a dark horse, isn't he?"

"No. He's a blonde human." It was supposed to be a joke, but Diane didn't laugh.

"The pizzas are massive," Fraser said, opening the menu. He suggested they share a pizza and salad, then turned to chat to the guy next to him.

Scarlett gazed around, taking in the bustle of the packed restaurant. At the back of the room, a man in a white apron was sliding pizzas into a large stone oven.

"I love this place," Diane said, leaning in her direction. "Have you been here before?"

Scarlett frowned. "No. And I don't like places I don't know."

"I know what you mean. I have my favourite places that I go back to time and time again. Stick to what you know, I say!"

"Yes."

"Fraser said you're studying English?"

"Yes."

"How's the course?"

"Good."

Diane nodded, then shifted in her seat to give the waiter room to set their drinks down. After taking a sip of her water, Scarlett moved her leg so it rested against Fraser's. He was engrossed in a conversation and she wasn't sure he'd even noticed her, but after a moment he reached across and slipped his hand into hers while still chatting away.

"Do you ever watch Fraser play football?" Diane asked.

Scarlett was mesmerised by Fraser's fingers intertwined with hers, and it took some effort to drag her gaze away from their hands. "I've been to a couple of games."

"He's really good, isn't he?"

"I saw him score two goals so I guess he must be okay. I don't understand football."

"Take it from me, he's really good. I play on the women's team."

"That's interesting," Scarlett said, feeling she ought to say something.

Diane smiled, then started talking to the girl at the other side of her.

"She's nice," Scarlett remarked when Fraser turned to her.

"Yeah." He ran his arm along the back of her chair and she leaned to kiss him.

"Are you having a good time?" he asked.

She nodded. She couldn't quite say she was enjoying herself, but being beside Fraser made it okay. "I was thinking about meeting your parents," she said. "Maybe we could visit them this weekend."

"Really? I thought you didn't want to."

"I know, but you seemed annoyed about it. I'd rather meet them and you not be annoyed with me."

"I wasn't annoyed. I was a bit disappointed I suppose. They want to meet you and I'd like you to meet them. I really think it will be fine."

"You would think that. Everything's easy for you."

His thumb stroked her shoulder. "That's not true."

"Well, I'll meet them anyway. If it all goes wrong it's your fault."

He grinned at her. "I already assumed that."

CHAPTER 38

Scarlett's fingers tapped quickly against her thumbs as they drove to Fraser's parents' house on Sunday. When she caught Fraser looking, she stopped.

"You don't have to worry," he said. "Everything will be fine. We'll have lunch and if you're uncomfortable we can leave again."

"I bet they think it's all my fault that you got married. And to make things worse I'm probably the worst person you could have married."

"That's not true. I can think of a few worse people." He gave her leg a quick squeeze and smiled at her.

"Was that a joke?" She shook her head. "Never mind. My point is they're going to hate me."

"I guarantee they won't."

"I'm starting to wish I'd gone back to Hope Cove and faced Emily and Lizzie," she muttered.

"Are you avoiding them?"

She stared out of the window. "Yes. They read my book and want to discuss it."

"It's good to get feedback, isn't it?"

"Sort of. It's also horrible."

"Is that the real reason you stayed in Exeter this weekend?" he asked lightly. "Did you lie to me?"

"No." She stifled a laugh. "I just told you a different truth. I did have coursework to do."

"I think you lied!"

Ignoring his smirk, she switched her attention back out of the window. "Where are we?"

"This is Thorverton."

"Is this where your parents live?" She looked around at what seemed to be the hub of the village. A small shop was housed in a Tudor-style building on one corner of the cross-roads. Opposite was a pub with picnic tables outside. Turning left, they passed a couple of thatched cottages before turning onto a narrow road bordered by hedges. "Did you grow up here?"

"Yes."

"It's very rural," she said, looking over the hedge to the rolling hills beyond.

"Yep," he agreed, then pulled into open gates and onto a long driveway.

"Oh God. Are we here already?" Beech trees lined the drive and a chestnut tree stood on a large expanse of green lawn. The house was a beautiful red brick building with a double garage beside it. "I knew they were rich. But they're *really* rich, aren't they?"

"Yes. So they probably also think you're a gold-digger."

"Shut up! I'm nervous and you're not helping."

"Sorry. Don't be nervous."

"That is such a stupid thing to say." She craned her neck to look up at the house. "Can we go home again now?"

"No." He opened the door and stepped out but Scarlett stayed put until he came around and physically pulled her out of the car.

"Are you going to drag me all the way inside?" she asked, chuckling.

"I was thinking I'd just pick you up and sling you over my shoulder."

"You wouldn't be able to lift me."

"Do you wanna bet?"

"No!" Laughing, she took a few steps away from him. "I think you have to be rich to bet on stuff, because you have to be prepared to lose. Which is only really an option if you have an excess. Although some might say that if you don't have much, you don't have much to lose."

"You're wittering," Fraser said, taking steps towards her.

"Because you've got a look on your face that makes me think you'd find it funny to lift me over your shoulder."

He flashed a crooked smile and darted forward, lifting her off the ground with ease.

"You're really annoying," she said, proud that she'd managed not to shriek when he'd slung her over his shoulder. "And I don't know why you're laughing. It's not funny."

"Make sure you don't laugh then," he said and began to turn in a circle.

"You're such an idiot. Stop it now!"

As he sped up, the laughter that bubbled out of her was beyond her control. Then she shrieked when he turned even faster.

"See!" He stopped and set her down. "You laughed. It was funny."

"I was laughing at the fact that I married such an idiot. It was one of those laugh or cry situations."

"It stopped you being so nervous anyway."

She couldn't argue with that. "I'm dizzy," she said, stumbling to one side. "I'm probably going to look drunk now, so I think it would have been better to seem nervous."

"Hello!" a sing-song voice called.

Disoriented, Scarlett swung around in a full circle before her gaze landed on the middle-aged couple standing at the door. She veered to the left as she tried to walk towards them. "I'm not drunk," she said. "I hardly ever drink alcohol. But I didn't want to come so we were joking about Fraser having to drag me inside and then he picked me up and swung me around."

Fraser chuckled as he took her elbow and led her in the right direction. "This is Scarlett."

She remembered to smile as Dominic and Tricia introduced themselves. Tricia had shoulder-length blonde hair, which must be where Fraser got it from. His dad's hair was brown and thinning on top. They were casually dressed and looked friendly enough.

"Come on in," Tricia said, leading the way inside.

Scarlett gazed around the spacious entrance hall with wooden floor. Plush maroon carpet ran up the centre of the wide staircase to the right. Scarlett assumed the variety of doors under the stairs were cupboards. Three more doors on the left were closed. Sunlight flooded in through a large round window above the front door and reflected off the ornate chandelier.

"Your house is massive," she said, then bit her lip. "I mean *nice.* Your house is really nice."

"Thank you," Tricia said. "Come through and I'll get you a drink."

A dining area at the back of the house separated a cosy living room from the large modern kitchen. Glass doors gave a fantastic view out over the garden. Scarlett wandered over and stared out while Fraser chatted to his parents about uni.

"How's your course going?" Tricia asked as she handed Scarlett a glass of water.

"It's okay." She had a niggling feeling she ought to say more, but the more she tried to think of something, the more her mind went blank.

"And you're surviving living with this one?" Dominic said, patting Fraser on the shoulder.

"Yes. He leaves his clothes on the bathroom floor, which is annoying."

"Sorry," Tricia said. "I tried to train him better but he seems to be a lost cause on that score."

"I don't know why it's so difficult to put them in the wash basket or back in his room." Scarlett caught Fraser rolling his eyes. "Otherwise I suppose he's all right to live with."

"Glad to hear it," Dominic said, then launched into asking her questions about where she'd grown up and about her parents.

"So you don't see them at all?" Tricia asked, her eyes narrowing.

"I saw them at Christmas at my aunt's house. But I don't visit them." She smiled even though the conversation made her uncomfortable.

"Are you hungry?" Tricia asked, then went to the kitchen without waiting for a reply. "It's all prepared so it won't take long."

The rest of them moved to sit at the dining table, which was already set. Fraser chatted to his dad about football, so Scarlett had some respite from having to speak.

They continued chatting away while Tricia brought out plates of food, placing them in front of them. Even the sight of the white fish made Scarlett's stomach clench and she looked away from it, trying her best to catch Fraser's eye to convey her panic.

"Tuck in," Tricia said brightly as she sat down.

Scarlett stared out through the glass doors, her eyes fixed on a couple of birds darting in and out of the hedgerow.

"Is everything okay?"

Scarlett presumed Tricia was talking to her but didn't shift her gaze to find out.

"Oh crap!" Fraser said. "You don't eat fish, do you?"

She shook her head and pushed the plate towards Fraser. "If you take the fish away I can eat the broccoli and rice."

"You're not a vegetarian, are you?" Tricia asked. "I did message Fraser and ask that."

"No. It's just fish. I always imagine the oily, slippery things, swimming in the disgusting salty, polluted seas. It makes me gag. Sorry," she said, when the table fell silent. "I just can't eat it. I like broccoli though." She stabbed a piece and smiled as she chewed.

"Sorry," Fraser said. "I should have checked what we were eating."

"It doesn't matter." Her heart raced and her hands felt shaky as they all looked at her. "Can you just talk about something else?"

Dominic cleared his throat. "Fraser said you write books?"

She would have preferred it if he'd chosen to talk about something that didn't involve her, but she nodded in reply as she stabbed another piece of broccoli and popped it in her mouth.

"When did you start writing?" Tricia asked.

"I started writing short stories when I was twelve and decided to write a novel when I was fifteen."

Dominic bobbed his head. "That's impressive. That's the one you've published?"

"Yes."

"She's about to publish another in a couple of weeks," Fraser said. "It's a trilogy. Fantasy."

"Hattie really enjoyed the first one," Tricia said.

Scarlett looked at Fraser in surprise. "Your sister read it?"

He swallowed his mouthful. "I gave it her for Christmas. She loved it."

"Where is she?" Scarlett asked.

"Out with friends." Tricia smiled warmly. "She's keen to meet you, but Fraser thought it might be a bit much the first time you visit."

"Hattie's a bit much any time," Fraser said, grinning.

"Maybe you can meet her next time you visit," Tricia suggested.

"Maybe." Scarlett was encouraged by the thought that she hadn't made such a bad impression that she wouldn't be invited again.

"I forgot to tell you," Fraser said to his dad. "One of Scarlett's friends in Hope Cove knows you. He said he used to work with you. Max …" He looked to Scarlett. "What's his last name?"

"Anderson."

Dominic chuckled. "I remember Max. We played golf together a few times. Nice guy. How do you know him?"

Scarlett explained that he was married to her friend, then answered his questions about Max's life.

"Isn't it a small world?" Dominic said happily.

"It is if you're rich," Scarlett said, pushing the remainder of the rice around her plate as she debated whether or not it had touched the fish. "If you can afford to travel, the world will seem much smaller."

As silence fell, Scarlett glanced at Fraser.

"Dad just meant because you both know Max."

"Oh, right. But you probably only remember him because he has money. If he'd have been the cleaner or something I doubt you'd remember him." She paused as Fraser's parents stared at her. "That's just a guess."

Tricia smiled and began to pick up the plates. "I've made rhubarb crumble for dessert. I hope you'll like that, Scarlett."

"I don't like rhubarb. I think it's pretty weird. I don't like the taste or the texture."

"Maybe next time you come I'll check what you like to eat first."

"Good idea," Scarlett said. "If you'd have made apple crumble it would have been fine. I like apples. If you have an apple, I can have that for dessert."

"I'm sure we have." Tricia nudged Dominic, who helped clear the plates and followed her into the kitchen.

"Are you okay?" Fraser asked while they were out of the room.

"I think so. Am I embarrassing you?"

"No."

"Found one!" Dominic said, walking back in with a rosy red apple in his hand. "Ready?" he said, then threw the apple without giving her chance to say that she wasn't ready.

Her whole body froze until the apple hit the side of her forehead, jerking her head back.

"Oh God!" Dominic cried. "I'm so sorry."

"She can't catch," Fraser said, his hand on Scarlett's elbow, pulling her to face him. "Are you okay?"

Tears filled her eyes and she gasped as she finally remembered to breathe. "I'm fine," she said shakily.

"I thought you'd catch it," Dominic said, rushing around the table. "I'm so sorry."

"It's fine," she whispered.

Fraser pushed her hair back and ran his thumb over the area. "It's a bit red. Does it hurt?"

"Do you need ice or something?" Dominic asked.

"No, it's fine."

"I really am sorry," Dominic said, putting a hand on her shoulder.

"I said it's fine," she snapped, pushing past them and dashing to the entrance hall. She paced up and down, her fingers and thumbs tapping together in a frenzy.

"Scarlett?" Fraser said softly, appearing in front of her.

"I want to go home," she whispered.

"Do you want to sit down for a minute first?"

When she didn't reply, he took her hand and led her to the stairs, where she sat on the second step. Her fingers continued to work furiously on her lap.

"Sorry," she said, shoving her hands under her thighs as Fraser crouched in front of her.

"You don't need to apologise."

"I'm so embarrassed," she said, tears spilling down her cheeks. "This is why I didn't want to come. I don't know why I can't have a meal with your parents without embarrassing you."

"You didn't embarrass me."

"I don't know why I get so nervous. I hate it."

When she wiped her eyes with her sleeves, she saw the tears in Fraser's eyes too.

"I'm sorry," he said, squeezing her hand. "I didn't realise it would be so hard for you."

"Can we just go home, please?"

"Yes. But I promise I'm not embarrassed by you. I just wanted them to see you like I do."

She locked eyes with him and was surprised by how comfortable it felt. Eye contact had always been easier with Fraser. If she leaned forward a little, she could kiss him. She licked her lips and inched forwards.

"How's your head?" Tricia said, breaking the silence and making Scarlett pull back quickly.

"It's fine." She swallowed hard. "I'm sorry."

"Don't you apologise," she said kindly. "It was Dominic who almost knocked you out with an apple."

Scarlett laughed through her tears, then stood up when Fraser pulled on her hands.

"We're going to head off," he said. "I've got an assignment due tomorrow and I haven't even started it."

"Fraser!" his mum hissed. "How many times do I have to tell you not to leave everything until the last minute?"

"I've got all afternoon," he said. "And all night too if I need it."

She sighed and patted his shoulder. "There's some post for you on the table in the sitting room. I think it's all junk but have a look anyway."

Scarlett followed him to one of the doors opposite, partly because she didn't want to be left alone with his parents and partly because she wanted to see what a sitting room looked like.

After scooping the pile of post from a side table, Fraser sank onto the sumptuous green couch to flick through it. Scarlett was vaguely aware of the bookshelves covering every wall in the room as she moved to the shiny grand piano. Surely it would make more sense to refer to it as the piano room.

"Can you play?" she asked Fraser.

He glanced up. "No. I had lessons as a kid but it wasn't really my thing."

"Do *you* play?" Tricia asked from the doorway.

"I used to," Scarlett said. "The piano is probably the only thing I miss from my parents' house. Well the dog too, but she's dead, so I'd still miss her even if I was there."

"I didn't know you could play," Fraser said, tossing the post back onto the table.

"You're welcome to have a go if you want," Tricia said as Dominic appeared beside her.

Slowly, Scarlett lifted the fallboard to reveal the beautiful black and white keys. "I haven't played for two years."

"There's sheet music in the stool," Tricia told her. "I don't know if you'll know any of it, but you're welcome to have a go. It doesn't get played enough. I have a tinkle myself sometimes but I'm not very good."

Lifting the lid of the stool, Scarlett leafed through the various books and sheet music. At the bottom was a book of classical composers, the corners frayed and the pages yellowing.

"That belonged to my grandmother," Tricia said. "It's quite advanced – completely beyond me."

Scarlett opened it to a piece by Chopin and propped it on the stand. She closed her eyes for a moment, letting her fingers feel the keys. Then she looked at the notes on the page and began to play. It hadn't occurred to her just how much she'd missed playing until her fingers raced up and down and a warm tingle swept through her whole body.

It seemed like no time at all before she reached the end of the composition.

"Sorry," she said, turning to find Fraser and his parents staring at her. "I hit a wrong note at the start. I told you I haven't played for ages."

"That was …" Tricia opened and closed her mouth without saying any more.

"You're amazing," Fraser said, then laughed. "How didn't I know you were some sort of genius, professional pianist?"

"Because I'm not." She shifted on the stool. "I just like to play when I get the chance."

"You're welcome to come here and play anytime you want," Tricia said.

"Seriously?" Scarlett asked.

"Of course."

She looked excitedly back at the piano. "Can I play something else now?" At the murmurs of approval, she turned the page to a piece by Brahms and let her fingers loose on the keys.

CHAPTER 39

After spending two hours playing the piano, Scarlett was on a high and smiled to herself all the way home. On balance, she felt the visit had been fairly successful. At least once she'd discovered the piano. Fraser was quiet on the drive and walked straight up the stairs when they got back.

"Do you want to play video games?" she asked, not keen to break their time together.

"Can't," he said, rubbing his neck. "I've got an assignment to write."

"I thought you just said that as an excuse to leave."

"No." He turned at the top of the stairs. "I really have an assignment that's due in tomorrow."

"And you haven't even started it?" Scarlett automatically followed him up the stairs.

"Nope."

"Can you get it finished in time?"

"I can if you leave me to get on with it."

"Sorry," she said, hanging back at the doorway to her room.

He shook his head as he looked at her. "I'm sorry. I didn't mean to snap. I'm just tired and I've got a lot to do."

"We should have come home earlier." She'd ignored him

when he'd said they needed to leave. Caught up in playing the piano, she'd kept insisting on playing "just one more song". "Sorry," she said.

"It doesn't matter. I'm glad you had a good time." He closed the door softly behind him.

The following evening, Fraser apologised again for being grumpy with her and asked if she wanted to watch TV. She suspected he only asked out of guilt. Not that she would have let that stop her. It was the piles of work that stopped her.

On Tuesday evening she worked flat out too. It was the last assignment she had to hand in before the Easter break, so as soon as it was finished she could relax. Sort of. Realistically, she'd just switch to panicking about her upcoming book release. If she could stick to worrying about one thing at a time she could probably manage to get things done.

"Are you avoiding me?" Fraser asked on Wednesday evening, lingering in her bedroom doorway. He'd asked her if she wanted to hang out and she'd told him she didn't have time.

"No. Why?"

"Because after I snapped at you the other day, you're always busy. So I thought maybe you were just making excuses to avoid hanging out with me."

Scarlett blew out an audible breath. Her mind was strained enough by her coursework without Fraser creating drama.

"You think I'm using coursework as an excuse not to hang out with you?" she asked.

"Yeah. I do."

Her throat burned as she swung around on her chair. "Do you do well at uni?" she asked through gritted teeth.

His eyebrows shot up. "What?"

"Do you get good grades on your assignments?"

"Yes." He shrugged and shifted his weight.

"I don't," she said. "It takes me weeks to write my assignments. I have to read over my lecture notes several times. And the same with the required reading. Then I have to do extra research to make sure I understand properly. After I've written the assignment, I have to put it through a software that checks my spelling and grammar. And then I have my laptop read it aloud to pick out any other errors. After that I send it to Lizzie or Emily to read over for me."

Her throat tightened and she had to take a deep breath before she could continue. "I can't write an assignment in one evening. I have to work ten times harder than anyone else, and in the end I just do okay." Fraser was trying to get a word in but she just got louder. "I don't have time to explain to you why I can't hang out with you. And I don't have time to get upset about how unfair it is and how tired I am. If I fall behind, I'll never catch up. So please get out of my room and let me get on with it."

"I'm sorry," Fraser said. "I had no idea."

"Why would you?"

"Maybe I could help," he said.

"I don't need help. I have a system and it works fine. It just doesn't involve watching TV or playing video games." She tried to get back to work but couldn't concentrate with Fraser hovering in the doorway. "Please go away!" she growled.

After the door clicked behind him, it took Scarlett a while to focus on her assignment. She wasn't sure how much time had passed when the door opened. It took all of her self-control not to scream at Fraser to leave her alone, but he didn't even speak, just set a cup of tea and two slices of toast beside her and left again. She tried to thank him but couldn't manage to speak through the lump that swelled in her throat.

By midnight the following evening, the assignment was finished and she emailed it to Lizzie, who'd promised to keep a couple of hours free on Friday morning to read through it.

When she walked into the living room on Friday afternoon she was exhausted.

"Hi," she said, perching on the arm of the couch and looking at the RPG game that Fraser was involved in.

"Hey. How was uni?"

"Good. I handed my assignment in."

He nodded and paused the game. "Now you can have a break over Easter. When are you going back to Hope Cove?"

"I have to work tomorrow, but I thought I'd just drive back in the morning."

"Not much of a break then."

She shrugged. As well as the cafe, she also had work for the publishing company and her book release. "Sorry for shouting at you the other night," she said quietly.

"Don't worry about it. I had no idea how much work you put in. Sometimes you seem so confident and capable that I forget that …"

"That I'm not normal?"

"That you struggle with some things."

"When I told Auntie Verity I thought I was autistic, she said I couldn't be because I'm so intelligent. I had to explain to her that I just work harder than most people."

"The piano playing is impressive though," he said with a mischievous smile. "That's like *Rain Man* or something."

She laughed and dropped onto the couch beside him. "Considering you're supposed to be the intelligent one here, I spend a lot of time explaining stuff to you!"

"Here we go… is this where you tell me that your piano skills aren't that impressive? Because I've heard you play, so you can't argue that."

"I wasn't going to say that. But my talent isn't due to some sort of autistic genius. It's because I practised every single day for ten years. Often several hours a day."

"Are you serious?"

She rolled her eyes. "What did you think, that my parents sat me down at a piano one day and I could play like that?"

"No. But I thought... I don't know, that you were naturally talented and didn't have to work so hard at it."

"Wrong!" she said cheekily.

He smiled and glanced at the controller in his hand. "Do you want me to switch to two-player?"

"No, thanks. Do you mind if I watch you though?"

He told her it was fine and she stared at the man running around the jungle for a while before she eventually gave up on trying to keep her eyes open.

When she batted them open again, she was curled in a ball with her head resting on the arm of the couch.

"Morning, Sleeping Beauty," Fraser said when she shuffled to sit up.

"Is it morning?"

"No, I was joking. It's 9 p.m. You've been asleep for two hours."

She rolled her shoulders and squinted as her eyes got used to the dim light from the TV screen. Dragging her hands through her hair, she could feel it was all messed up.

"Don't laugh at me," she said, casting Fraser a stern look.

"I'm not laughing. You look very cute when you just wake up."

"My hair's crazy, isn't it?"

"Only a little bit." Shuffling closer to her, he took a section of her hair and moved it to the other side. "There. Perfect."

"I think it'll take a lot more than that to make my hair perfect."

"No." He gazed into her eyes. "You look perfect."

"Charmer," she whispered as he cupped her cheek with his hand. Their eyes locked for a moment before his lips brushed against hers. Her heart pounded and she forgot to breathe as he kissed her harder.

"What are you doing?" she murmured, finally pulling back.

"Kissing you."

"Yes, I know. But there's no one around?"

"I got sick of having to wait until there were people around before I kissed you."

"So it wasn't all fake when we were pretending before?"

His eyes widened. "No. I only really suggested we pretend to be in a relationship so I could kiss you. I sort of thought you'd have realised that."

"Lizzie and Emily thought that but I wasn't completely sure."

He pulled back. "Please tell me it wasn't all fake to you?"

"No." She slipped her arms around his neck. "I really liked pretending to be in a relationship with you."

He rubbed his nose against hers. "Can we stop pretending and just be in a relationship?"

"Yes." As she kissed him again, she ignored the flutter of anxiety in the pit of her stomach. A real relationship was almost no different to a fake one, she reassured herself. It didn't matter that she had no clue how to be in a relationship. It was like Lizzie said: if you cared about each other, you'd figure it out.

CHAPTER 40

Scarlett was relieved when Fraser asked to visit her in Hope Cove during the Easter holidays. The thought of not seeing him for four weeks hadn't felt good. As it was, she only had to wait until her day off on Tuesday. She worked at the cafe all weekend and was getting ready for another day of serving customers on Monday morning when Emily and Lizzie arrived at the flat.

"How's everything with Fraser?" Emily asked, perching on the arm of the couch beside Scarlett.

"Great." She twirled her wedding band. "We're not pretending any more so he's now my boyfriend."

Lizzie walked out of the kitchen with three mugs of coffee. "You realise most people start as boyfriend and girlfriend, then move to husband and wife? I think you might have got it backwards."

"Yeah, we did," she said happily.

Lizzie took a seat at her desk. "I'm glad we caught you this morning. I thought we could have a chat about book three before you head off to the cafe."

"We don't need to," Scarlett said, her jaw clenching. "You

said it was good, and I've already set the release date for the summer."

"It *is* good," Lizzie agreed. "But I wanted to discuss a possible tweak."

Scarlett groaned. "You said it was perfectly publishable as it is."

"We could just discuss it," Emily put in. "If you don't agree with the feedback, of course you can ignore it. It's your book. At least hear Lizzie's comments though."

From the glare that Lizzie shot at Emily, Scarlett was fairly certain they'd both agreed on the proposed changes. Emily just couldn't stand confrontation.

"I know what you're going to say," Scarlett said, folding her arms across her chest. "You think the ending isn't great. And I know it isn't perfect but I've re-written it loads of times. It's as good as I can make it, so it's going to have to do."

"Okay." Lizzie held her hands up. "Fine."

"Fine?" Emily frowned at Lizzie. "What do you mean *fine*?"

Lizzie's shoulders lifted. "You just said it's Scarlett's story and she can do what she wants with it."

"She can. But she at least needs to hear the feedback." She shook her head. "We wouldn't let any other author get away with not listening to the feedback. It doesn't even need much tweaking, but both Lizzie and I agree that it's lacking a sex scene."

Scarlett stared at her for a moment, then shifted her gaze to Lizzie, who was smiling to herself.

"A sex scene?" Scarlett repeated.

"It would make for a more satisfying conclusion," Lizzie said.

"It's not a romance book," Scarlett said, without much conviction. Even though she hadn't wanted to hear it, the feedback was spot on. The book did need a sex scene. She'd tried to write it a few times but came up blank.

Lizzie leaned forwards, resting her elbows on her knees.

"After all that Alissa and Matteo have been through, I think they deserve more than a quick peck at the end."

"All right," Scarlett conceded.

"So you'll write it?" Emily asked in surprise.

"I think it'd be better if *you* did," Scarlett said.

"What?"

"You could write it for me."

Emily shook her head in small sharp movements. "I can't write your book for you."

"Obviously! But you could write one scene. You're good at romantic stuff. I don't think I can write a sex scene."

"It doesn't need to be graphic," Lizzie told her. "In fact, I don't think it should be."

Emily nodded. "Focus on the emotions, rather than the act itself."

"I can't," Scarlett said, cringing. "It makes me uncomfortable."

"I'm sure you can if you try," Emily said. "Read a few sex scenes in other books and see how other writers handle it."

"You definitely won't write it for me?"

"No." Emily laughed. "Of course not."

Scarlett looked to Lizzie. "But you did say it would also be fine to leave the book as it is."

"Yes. If you really don't want to change it you can leave it. But it will be stronger if you round out Alissa and Matteo's relationship more."

"I'll think about it," Scarlett said, twisting her hands in her lap.

"We've not upset you, have we?" Lizzie said. "The book's brilliant. We both loved it."

"I'm not upset," she said, blowing on her coffee.

"Good." Lizzie sat up straighter. "What do you want to do to celebrate the release of book two tomorrow? Josie was asking if we're doing drinks in the pub again?"

"I don't know. Fraser's going to come over tomorrow."

"Maybe you'll want to stay in and have your own private celebration then?" Emily said, wiggling her eyebrows.

Scarlett felt her cheeks flush. Would Fraser be thinking the same as Emily? Was that why he wanted their relationship to be real now, so they'd have sex? Feeling jittery, she set her mug down.

"Why are relationships so complicated?" she asked as her heart beat erratically.

Emily's brows drew together. "I thought everything was good with you and Fraser?"

"Yes. I just find things confusing sometimes."

"Such as?" Lizzie asked.

Her face twitched and she stood up. "Lots of things. It doesn't matter."

"It's hard to give advice without knowing the problem," Emily said. "But I can tell you one thing … whenever I'm worried about something, talking to Jack always helps."

Scarlett stared at her, trying to figure out if that was a joke. "There's no way I'm asking Jack for relationship advice," she finally said.

Lizzie and Emily both laughed.

"You crack me up." Emily's coffee spilled as she chuckled and she shook a few drips from her hand. "You have the best sense of humour."

Scarlett forced herself to smile. "I better get down to the cafe," she said as she walked away.

It was already busy when she got downstairs, and she got straight to work serving customers. It was difficult to concentrate when her mind kept drifting to Fraser's impending visit. When they'd discussed it he'd mentioned staying overnight, so he probably was expecting them to have sex.

By the end of the day, her stomach was in knots from thinking about it. The excitement about seeing him had completely vanished.

Fraser wasn't sure how long he'd stay in Hope Cove. When he discussed it with Scarlett on the phone on Monday evening, she'd suggested it might be best if he just came for the day as she had a lot of work to do. He hadn't pushed the subject but packed enough clothes for a few days, hoping she might change her mind once he was there.

Stepping out of the shower on Tuesday morning, he frowned at the sound of someone pummelling on the front door. They were still banging away once he was dressed. He shouted at whoever it was to shut up as he descended the stairs.

Liam swore loudly and almost fell inside when Fraser opened the door.

"I thought you must be out," he said breathlessly.

"So you thought you'd beat the door down to get in?"

"Sorry. I just … I don't know what I'm doing. Can I come in?"

"Yeah." Fraser stepped aside. "I've tried to call you loads of times recently. I was starting to think you were ignoring me."

"Sorry. I'm a shit friend."

Fraser closed the door. "What's going on?"

"Everything's a mess." Liam walked to the living room and stood in the middle of the room, staring back at Fraser with pain in his eyes.

Fraser stood frozen to the spot. "Is it your dad?"

"Dad's fine." He moved to sit on the couch and buried his face in his hands. "Allie split up with me."

Fraser's eyebrows shot up and he swore under his breath. Then he moved to sit beside Liam, resting a hand between his shoulder blades. "What happened?"

"She said things weren't working any more. I think she might be seeing someone else."

"No way," Fraser said. "She wouldn't cheat on you."

He shrugged. "Maybe she didn't actually cheat, but I think there's someone else."

"I know you said living together was tough at first, but I thought everything was fine now."

"Things haven't been fine since we started uni. And the stupid thing is that I've thought about breaking things off loads of times … but it's Allie. I couldn't actually go through with it. When she said she'd had enough I was relieved."

"When was this?" Fraser asked.

"A few weeks ago. I was going to call you, but I couldn't face talking about it. I sort of thought that if I ignored it everything would be fine. But she moved out last week so I guess it's really happening."

"Shit," Fraser muttered.

"Her friend has a spare room so she's gone there."

Fraser blew out a breath. "I'm really sorry."

"I feel like a complete idiot." Liam gave a sad smile. "She's been driving me crazy for ages, but I missed her as soon as she left. I've just spent a week moping around the house on my own. She hasn't even been in touch. It's the weirdest thing. She's been such a massive part of my life for as long as I can remember. I literally don't remember a time when she wasn't in my life. I don't know what to do without her."

"I always thought of you two as the perfect couple," Fraser said. "I thought you'd be together forever."

"Me too."

"Do you think you can sort things out? Maybe you just need a break."

"I've no idea. And I'm not sure whether I want to get back together."

"But you said you miss her."

"I do. I'm gutted and I feel completely lost, but I don't know if it's because I'll miss her as a friend." His voice broke and he squeezed his eyes shut. "I can't imagine not being friends with her."

Fraser put an arm around his shoulders and drew him into a side hug. "You'll still be friends. You probably just need a bit of time to figure things out."

"I feel like crap," Liam said, leaning his head on Fraser's shoulder. "Is it okay if I hide out here for a few days?"

Inwardly, Fraser groaned. He was supposed to be on his way to Hope Cove. He could hardly ditch Liam though. He'd been a terrible friend when Liam's dad was ill. He couldn't let him down again.

"Yeah, of course."

"Thanks." Sitting up straighter, Liam dragged his hands through his hair. "It feels like forever since we just hung out. How about we binge watch all the Star Wars films?"

"Sounds great." Fraser tried his best to sound enthusiastic. "I just need to make a quick phone call. I was supposed to be meeting someone, but I can rearrange it."

"Sorry. Am I messing up your social life?"

"No, it's fine."

"I presume Scarlett isn't here?"

"She's in Hope Cove."

"How are things with you two?"

"Erm …" It would be a little tactless to tell him how great things were when he was in the midst of a breakup. "Everything's fine. It's all good."

"That's great. I'm really happy things are working out for you."

"Yeah. I'll be back in a minute. Make yourself at home."

He had a sinking feeling as he trudged upstairs to call Scarlett.

"I'm really sorry," he said, as soon as she answered the phone.

"What for?"

"Liam just turned up …"

"Who's Liam?"

He blinked a few times in quick succession. “My best mate. Liam and Allie were at our wedding.”

“Oh.”

“You should probably remember them since they were the only ones there.”

“I was a bit stressed. I don’t think I paid much attention.”

“Anyway. They’ve split up and Liam’s really upset. He just turned up here wanting to hang out.”

“So you can’t come to Hope Cove?”

“I really think I should stay and hang out with Liam. But I feel like crap. I was looking forward to visiting you.”

“If Liam’s upset, you should stay there,” she said briskly.

“Really?”

“Yes. It’s not a problem.”

He pushed his tongue against the inside of his cheek. “I thought you might be upset.”

“No, it’s fine.”

It hadn’t been the response he was expecting. “I don’t know how long Liam will stay. It might be a couple of days.”

“You can come over next time I have a day off,” she said.

“Yeah. Okay.” He tapped his finger against his front teeth. “Congratulations on the book release. How’s it going?”

“Good. The reviews are great. Everything’s going well.”

“That’s great. I should get back to Liam, but I’ll give you a call later.”

She told him to have fun and ended the call, leaving him wondering whether it was a good or bad thing that she genuinely didn’t seemed bothered that he’d cancelled on her.

CHAPTER 41

After his initial disappointment at postponing his trip to Hope Cove, Fraser enjoyed the time with Liam. They spent two full days watching films and playing video games. On the first night they had dinner in the local pub, then ordered a takeaway the next.

By Thursday, Fraser was desperate to ask how long Liam was planning on staying but stopped himself. He was going through a bad time and Fraser needed to be supportive, not push him out of the door.

"I have to say, I'm very surprised," Liam said, as they ate leftover pizza for breakfast in the middle of the morning. "I was fully expecting you to drag me out on some crazy drunken nights. I'm not sure if I'm disappointed or relieved."

"I did say we could go out if you wanted to."

"Not long ago you wouldn't have taken no for an answer. I take it this is Scarlett's influence?"

"Maybe," he said, unable to stop his smile.

"You really like her, don't you?"

"Yeah. I do."

"Will you see her over the holidays?"

Fraser bobbed his head ambiguously. "I'll probably drive down to Hope Cove one day."

"That's pretty vague."

"Just playing things by ear. I'll see what happens."

When Liam stopped with his pizza slice in front of his lips, Fraser could almost see him connecting the dots.

"Please tell me that wasn't what you were supposed to be doing on Tuesday?"

"It's fine. I explained the situation to Scarlett and she said it was fine."

Liam gave him a pitiful look. "You realise that when a woman says it's fine, it's not actually fine. Usually it's the opposite."

"I thought that, but I spoke to her again last night and she seemed" – he grimaced – "fine."

"You should have said something." Liam moved to the door with the pizza still in his hand. "Call Scarlett and tell her you'll come over today. I'm going to pack my stuff."

"Are you sure?"

He popped the rest of the pizza in his mouth. "Yes! One of us should have a love life that isn't a complete disaster."

Alone in the kitchen, Fraser pulled his phone out, then paced back and forth as he waited for Scarlett to answer. It took a little while, and he reminded himself that it was great progress that she answered the phone at all, and he should probably feel honoured that she did.

"I'm at work," she said briskly.

"Liam's leaving," he said, smiling into the phone. "I thought I'd drive down to Hope Cove today and stay for a few days …"

"That will be inconvenient since I'm working."

"When should I come then?"

"I don't know. Next week I suppose, when I have a day off. I'll call you later and let you know." She ended the call abruptly.

Fraser sank onto a chair and stared at the phone. Things definitely weren't fine.

"Fraser! Are you even listening?"

He snapped out of his trance and focused on his mum across the dinner table. Licking his wounds at his parents' place had seemed a good idea until about five minutes after he arrived. "What were you saying?"

"I asked when you're going to bring Scarlett over again?"

"I really want to meet her," Hattie said, beside him.

"She's busy," Fraser said. "She's working in the cafe and has a lot on with the publishing company and writing her next book."

"Maybe you two should take a leaf out of Scarlett's book," their dad said. "Find something productive to do instead of lazing around all the time."

"Don't start with this again," Hattie groaned. "I've heard enough about how great Scarlett is."

"She's ever so sweet," Tricia said. "Honestly, Hattie, you wouldn't believe how well she plays the piano. She told us she was out of practice and then sat down and played like a professional pianist."

Dominic nodded. "Absolutely incredible."

"You should see how cute she and Fraser are," Tricia said to Hattie. "They make such a lovely couple." She turned to Fraser. "Ask her to take a couple of days off. She works so hard; she must have earned a break."

"She can't. She's got too much on." Since she didn't even have time for him, he was fairly sure she wasn't going to make time for his family.

"It's really quite an achievement that she has her own publishing company," Dominic said, his fork scraping on his plate as he ate.

"You two should get summer jobs," Tricia said. "Maybe you can learn to support yourselves like Scarlett does."

Hattie put her cutlery down and pushed her plate away. "I'd

like to point out that she doesn't even pay her own rent. You pay for her, so you can't sit there and tell us how independent she is."

Fraser rolled his eyes as his mum launched into a rant about how hard Scarlett has to work to put herself through uni and that Hattie had no right to comment on the fact that they paid her rent.

He could have done without the reminder of Scarlett's money sitting in his account. Maybe he should transfer it back to her. She'd go crazy though. Better to wait until she graduated and find a way to give it back to her without telling her where the money came from.

The thought of graduating made his appetite disappear. In a year they'd be coming towards the end of their courses and he had no idea what that would mean for Scarlett and him. Would she still want to live with him? Maybe she'd want to divorce him and move back to Hope Cove. Judging by her current lack of enthusiasm for spending time with him, that was a definite possibility. He pushed his plate away, which put an end to his mum's lecture.

"What's wrong?" she asked, switching her attention to Fraser. "You've hardly touched your lasagne."

"I'm not hungry. I'll be in my room if you need me."

"You've been in your room all day," Tricia remarked. "You should get out and do something."

"I'm going to Hope Cove tomorrow," he said as he walked away. At least if Scarlett didn't come up with some excuse and tell him not to.

"I think it'd do you good to get a summer job before you start uni," he heard his mum saying to Hattie as he walked away, slowing his pace to listen to the conversation.

"Oh my god!" Hattie screeched. "I'm not getting some crappy job. Especially since the only reason you want me to is because of perfect-bloody-Scarlett."

"She sets a good example," their mum said firmly. "And she really is very sweet. You'll like her."

"If I ever get to meet her," Hattie said loudly. "Fraser, can you please bring my sister-in-law over sometime? I'd like to meet this super woman who seems to have taken my place as favourite child in this family."

His dad choked as he laughed. In normal circumstances Fraser would have indulged Hattie in some banter about which of them was the favourite, but he didn't have the energy and continued up to his room instead.

Checking his watch, he assumed Scarlett would have finished at the cafe and picked up his phone to call her.

"Is it still okay for me to come over tomorrow?" he asked, then held his breath as he waited for a reply.

There was a short pause. "Yes. You can only come for the day though because I have to work in the cafe on Wednesday."

"You're working in the cafe a lot. I thought you'd take two days off a week."

"I need the money," she said, sounding defensive. "And it gives Auntie Verity a break. I don't really like working with Tina but Verity appreciates it. And she's always been so nice to me that I like to help her out."

"Yeah, I know. I just miss you, that's all."

"I miss you too," she said quietly.

"Do you?" He sounded needy but he didn't care.

"Yeah."

He smiled as he stared out of the window. "I could always drive over this evening? That way we'd get more time together."

The silence wasn't a good sign.

"I have to work on my novel."

"Okay." He ignored the tightening of his ribs. "Did you ever talk to Lizzie about the book? Does she think it needs a lot of changes?"

"Erm ... She had one suggestion but I'm not sure I agree with her. I might leave it as it is."

"What was her suggestion?"

"It's difficult to explain. I have to go now. I'm very busy."

"I'll see you tomorrow then?"

She told him she would and said a curt goodbye.

Scarlett's sleep had been even more disturbed than usual while she'd been in Hope Cove. When Fraser was due to arrive she sipped a cup of coffee as she watched out of the window for him. When she saw him walking down the road she ducked away from the window, pacing the living room until he knocked at the door.

"Hi," she said when she opened the door, then frowned as he stepped inside. "Why have you got a bag with you?"

He dropped the backpack in the hallway. "I wasn't sure what we'd be doing this evening. I brought a change of clothes in case I ended up staying."

"I'm working tomorrow."

"Yeah. I know but I just thought …" He trailed off and followed her to the living room.

"We have to go out for the day," Scarlett said. "Lizzie and Emily will be coming over to work soon. I thought we could go for a walk and have a picnic." Actually, when they'd heard Fraser was coming, Lizzie and Emily had both insisted they'd work from home for the day to give them the flat to themselves. She just didn't feel like spending the day in the flat with him.

"That sounds good," he said, walking over and resting his hands at her waist. "It's nice to see you."

"It's nice to see you too," she said, feeling jittery as he pulled her close. Her breath hitched as he kissed her and her whole body felt tense. "We should go before Emily and Lizzie get here," she said as she pulled away. "Verity's making us a picnic."

She got her bag with the picnic blanket and they picked up the

food from Verity on the way out. Fraser chatted away as they ambled along the coastal path with the sun on their faces. After an hour they found a quiet stretch of beach and settled down on the blanket. Fraser took his shoes and socks off and sprawled out while Scarlett hugged her knees and stared at the waves rolling onto the shore.

"Are you annoyed with me?" Fraser asked, running a hand over her back.

"No." She turned to look at him. "Why?"

"I thought you might be upset with me for cancelling our plans to hang out with Liam."

"No." She'd been relieved when he'd called to say he couldn't make it. Except it had only delayed the issue and given her an extra week to worry about it. "I told you on the phone that it was fine."

"Yeah. But you don't exactly seem pleased to see me. You've been scowling since I arrived and you've barely spoken to me."

"Sorry. I am happy to see you, I just forget to smile sometimes when I'm tired. I probably forget to speak too."

"As long as you're not annoyed with me?"

"Liam's your best friend and he was upset. Of course you should have hung out with him. I told you lots of times it was fine."

He sat up and rested a hand at her waist. "Usually when a woman says something's fine they don't really mean it."

"I meant it," she replied. "Did you have a good time with Liam?"

"Yeah. It was good to catch up with him. I'm hoping he and Allie will sort things out." He paused and hooked her hair behind her ear as a strand blew across her face. "Are you okay? You seem tense."

That was an understatement. Every muscle in her body felt tight and she had a constant quiver of anxiety in her gut. "I'm really tired. I've been working a lot."

"Lie down." He stretched out again and patted the space beside him. "I make a good pillow."

She hesitated before cuddling up next to him and resting her head on his chest. The rise and fall of his ribs seemed to match the sound of the waves washing onto the shore, and the gentle thud of his heart against her ear soothed her. Slowly, she relaxed and gave in to the weight of her eyelids.

When she woke, she'd moved onto her other side with her cheek pressed against Fraser's bicep.

"Sorry," she said as she peeled herself off him.

"You really were tired. You went out like a light."

Wiping at the side of her mouth, she hoped she hadn't been drooling. "I'm not the best company, am I?"

"It's fine." He sat up and massaged his shoulder. "Are you feeling better?"

She nodded. Her nap had definitely revived her. The jitter of nerves had vanished and her head felt clearer. "Are you hungry?"

"Yes." He pulled her backpack over to her and she unpacked the picnic, opening a box of sandwiches and passing Fraser a bag of crisps. After fumbling with the packet, he straightened and flexed the fingers on his left hand, then tore at the crisp pack with his teeth.

"Are you okay?" Scarlett asked.

"Yeah." He wiggled his fingers. "You might have cut my circulation off a bit while you were asleep."

Her eyes widened. "You should have moved."

"It's all right. The feeling will come back in a minute. It seemed like you really needed sleep, so I didn't want to risk waking you."

Automatically, she put a hand on the back of his neck and moved to kiss him. Her stomach fluttered madly as she swept her tongue into his mouth. She savoured the taste of him and the feel of his lips against hers.

"So you *are* happy to see me?" he said when she finally pulled away.

"Yes." She gave him another quick peck. "Very. You're right that you make a good pillow."

"It's a talent I'm very proud of," he said, before reaching around her for a sandwich. "Are you going to take me exploring later?"

"Where do you want to go?"

"I'd quite like to have a wander further along the coast. If you're up for a walk?"

Her feet could have done with a rest after spending so much time standing around in the cafe, but she didn't like to say no to Fraser. They set off when they'd finished the picnic and walked for miles along the rugged coastal path. It was late in the afternoon when Scarlett convinced Fraser they should set off back. Her feet were throbbing by the time they got back to the flat.

"What do you want to do for dinner?" Fraser asked.

Scarlett had collapsed on the couch and couldn't muster the energy to move. If she'd been alone she'd have opted for toast or a sandwich but presumed Fraser would want something more substantial.

"I think there's probably pasta in the cupboard," she said, hoping he'd volunteer to make it.

"How about we go to the pub?" he suggested. "I'm starving after all that sea air and exercise."

"The food in the pub is expensive. And I'd really like to stay on the couch for the evening."

"We could just go for a little while," he said. "My treat. I'd really love a pint too."

"You have to drive home this evening," Scarlett reminded him.

He sat beside her and draped an arm around her shoulders. "If you're going to insist on throwing me out later, the least you can do is have dinner with me first."

Leaning into him, she nodded in resignation. As she rested

her head on his shoulder, all she wanted to do was sleep, but she could surely manage an hour in the pub.

Fraser shifted to kiss her. Her heart rate increased when he didn't pull away but continued with his slow, soft kisses. When his fingers slipped under her T-shirt and grazed over her bare skin she froze.

"Sorry," he said as he pulled back.

"It's fine." Standing, she took his hand to pull him up. "Let's go to the pub."

CHAPTER 42

Jack was working at the Anchor Inn that evening. He slipped into the booth with Scarlett and Fraser after they'd finished eating.

"What have you been up to today?" he asked.

"Scarlett's been showing me the sights," Fraser told him.

"We've walked miles." Scarlett rubbed at her neck. Relaxing in the flat would definitely have been her preferred plan for the evening.

"It's a beautiful area, isn't it?" Jack said, looking at Fraser.

"The views are amazing. Scarlett pointed out your house. It must be fantastic to live overlooking the sea."

"We haven't lived here for long," Jack said. "But I can't imagine the novelty will ever wear off. I often jog along the coast in the mornings."

"I'd say it's a bit different from jogging around Exeter."

"You should come for a run with me some time," Jack said. "I'll probably go tomorrow morning if you fancy it?"

Fraser looked questioningly at Scarlett.

"I have to work tomorrow," she said quickly. She'd thought she'd made it clear that he couldn't stay over. The only reason she was even working was because she'd taken an extra shift as an excuse for Fraser to only come for one day.

"Is it okay for me to stay tonight though?" he asked. "I can go for a run in the morning. Then drive home after that or find something to do while you're working."

She stared at the table, not having a good reason for him to leave that evening. "Lizzie and Emily will be working in the flat tomorrow so you'd have to stay out of their way."

"Let's swap numbers," Jack said, pulling his phone out. "You can give me a shout in the morning. I have to be at the pub to take a delivery at 10 a.m. so it'll need to be before that." He exchanged numbers with Fraser, then left them alone and got back to work.

"Would you rather I go back to Exeter tonight?" Fraser asked Scarlett.

"I don't mind," she said hesitantly. "But I can't take another day off tomorrow, and you can't be in the flat while Emily and Lizzie are working."

"I promise I won't get in anyone's way."

"Okay," she agreed. It was hard to say no when he smiled at her.

"That means I can have another beer if I don't need to drive." He slipped out of the booth. "Do you want anything?"

"I'd quite like to go home. I'm tired."

"Just one beer." He flashed her another smile and she nodded. At least it gave her time to figure out how to broach the issue of where he was going to sleep.

It ended up being almost two hours later when they finally left the pub. Jack joined them for a couple of drinks after his shift, and Fraser and he got chatting about football while Scarlett yawned repeatedly.

"I'm really tired," she complained when they walked back into the flat. "I need to go to bed."

Fraser slipped his hands around her waist and kissed her softly. When his hand roamed under her T-shirt, exploring the skin of her back, she wondered whether he'd misunderstood and thought she meant that she wanted them to go to bed *together*.

Hastily, she took a step back, wishing they were still in the comfortable realm of the fake relationship. Now that everything was real she felt completely out of her depth. "Was the couch comfy enough last time you slept on it or shall I show you how it pulls out to a bed?"

He glanced at it. "It's fine. I'll manage."

~

By lunchtime the following day, Scarlett was absolutely seething. After Fraser had got back from his run with Jack he'd nipped upstairs to get his things, but that had been two hours ago and there was still no sign of him. She'd specifically told him he couldn't hang out in the flat while Lizzie and Emily were working. If she'd had a break in customers she'd have gone up and told him to leave.

She was clearing a table by the window when he finally appeared. "What have you been doing?" she hissed.

"I had a shower, then got chatting to Emily and Lizzie."

"I told you not to get in the way when they're working."

"They insisted on making me a coffee, and they're really chatty. I couldn't get away."

"Where's your bag?" she asked, slightly distracted by the couple at the next table who were trying to get her attention. "I thought you were leaving?"

"I'm just going to go over to the pub to see Jack quickly. I have this project for uni next term where we have to find people to do personal training sessions with and make a fitness plan for them. I reckon Jack would be up for it."

"Whatever," she said, shaking her head. "I'm busy."

He gave her a quick kiss and told her he'd be back soon.

That turned out to be a lie. She didn't see him for the entire afternoon. By four o'clock her feet were throbbing and a headache was developing behind her eyes.

"You look shattered," Verity said when she came in at the end of the day. "Has Fraser gone back to Exeter?"

"I don't know where he is," she said wearily. "In the pub with Jack I guess."

When she took a tray of dishes to the kitchen, Lizzie and Emily were coming down from the flat. "We'll see you in a bit," Lizzie said cheerfully.

"Why will you?"

Emily smiled. "Barbecue at Lizzie's place. Didn't Fraser message you about it? He and Jack organised it with Max."

"I don't know anything about it," she mumbled and went back to work.

An hour later, she sank onto the couch in the flat and had just closed her eyes when Fraser sauntered in.

"Did you get my messages?" he asked.

"Only just." She glanced at the phone on the coffee table as he sat beside her. "I can't go to the barbecue."

"Why not? It'll be a laugh. Jack's keen to do the personal training with me and he thinks I'll be able to persuade Max to do it too. I'm even thinking about trying to rope Emily and Lizzie in. What do you think?"

Her feet were throbbing so intensely that she could feel it throughout her whole body. "I don't think Lizzie and Emily will do it." She also didn't care. "I can't go out tonight. You can go without me."

"No way. You have to come." He leaned in and nuzzled her neck until she finally managed a smile. "Please come. I don't want to go without you. We don't have to stay late."

"Okay," she relented, then rested her head on his shoulder until Fraser jumped up, saying they should leave already.

After being busy in the cafe all day Scarlett could've done with a shower and clean clothes, but the effort felt like too much.

"What were you doing all afternoon?" she asked Fraser when

they walked outside.

"Hung out at the pub. Then Jack took me to the lifeboat station and showed me around. He volunteers there, you know."

She nodded, then continued to nod along as he chatted all the way to Lizzie's place. The smell of smoke from the barbecue reached them at the front door, and they slipped around the side of the house and into the back garden to join everyone.

"I've heard a rumour you're looking for volunteers for personal training sessions," Max said to Fraser, a pair of tongs in his hand as he stood beside the grill. "I can tell you now I'm not interested."

Lizzie slipped her arms around his waist. "It's important to keep in shape at your age."

"Shut up about my age," he said, grinning at her.

"I need a few female volunteers too," Fraser said.

Lizzie's eyes widened. "Well don't look at me."

"Or me," Emily laughed when he turned to her.

"I think you should all do it." Fraser draped an arm around Scarlett's shoulders. "You too."

"There's no way *I'm* doing it." She moved away from him when Phoebe came and took her hand, leading her over to the table to show her the picture she'd been drawing.

"Let's all do it," Jack said enthusiastically.

Scarlett took a seat and watched the girls colouring while the adults joked about personal training sessions and Fraser did his best to get them all on board. It was difficult to keep up with the conversation as the pounding behind her eyes increased. Eventually, she went inside to get a glass of water.

From the kitchen window, she had a clear view of everyone laughing and chatting. The pounding in her head got worse, and when she turned the tap on the sound of the water felt like an attack on her ears. Switching it off again, she squeezed her eyes shut and tried to block out the hum of the dishwasher running beside her. Laughter from outside grew so loud it felt as though it was inside her head.

Her heart thumped and she leaned on the work surface as she tried to catch her breath. Her lungs felt constricted and the noise of the house only got louder. Hurriedly, she walked down the hallway and out of the front door. The sounds from the house were replaced by a piercing ringing. Pressing her hands against her ears didn't help, but she kept them there anyway. Tears poured down her face the whole way back to the flat.

By the time she reached the safety of her bedroom, she crumpled onto the bed, hyperventilating. There wasn't enough air in her lungs and her vision blurred while dizziness made her nauseous. The room spun and her body pulsated as her blood rushed furiously.

She had her eyes tight shut and her hands over her ears when she felt a hand on her shoulder.

"What's wrong?" Fraser's voice echoed in her head. "Scarlett!"

"Go away," she said, curling into a ball in an attempt to get away from him.

"What's wrong?" he asked again. Then again and again. The words reverberated around her skull.

The rushing of blood in her ears was excruciating and his voice only made it worse. "Go away. Just go away."

"I don't know what to do." He put his hand on her again and she hit out at him before scrabbling to the top corner of the bed.

"Leave me alone," she whimpered. "Leave me alone. Leave me alone." She repeated the words until eventually everything went blissfully dark.

~

The lamp beside the bed was on when she blinked her eyes open. Her heart was back in a regular rhythm and breathing no longer required effort. The room was exquisitely quiet as she sat up and checked her watch to find it was one o'clock in the morning.

At the doorway, she peered into the living room, which was

bathed in a gentle glow of light spilling from the kitchen. Fraser sat on the couch, his neck craned to look up at the ceiling. She thought he was asleep until her eyes adjusted to the dimness and saw that his eyes were wide open.

His gaze snapped to her as she moved into the room.

"I'm sorry," she said, stopping before she got too close to him.

He shook his head and held his hand out. "Don't apologise."

"I don't know what happened," she whispered, taking his hand and sitting with him.

He tilted his head, tears shining in his eyes. "You got overwhelmed and had a meltdown because I didn't listen when you said you didn't want to go out." Swallowing hard, he looked away from her.

"It's not your fault."

"I'm fairly sure it is. You didn't want to go to the pub last night and I coaxed you into it. Then you didn't want me to stay over and I did anyway. And I made you go to the barbecue when you didn't want to."

She ran her thumb back and forth across the back of his hand. "It's not that I didn't *want* to. But being around people takes a lot of energy for me, and when I've been working in the cafe all day I can't always manage anything else. Especially on days when the cafe's busy. I haven't been sleeping much either."

"I should have listened when you said you didn't want to go out."

"It's not as though you dragged me out of the door. I thought maybe I could manage it, but when we got there everything got too much."

"You scared me," he said. "I've never seen you like that. I didn't know what to do."

"I don't think there's anything you can do except give me space."

"I feel as though I should have known that going out was too much for you. I read so much about autism but it's like I never really understood. Maybe because it seems to affect you so mildly."

"I don't think it affects me mildly," she said. "I can just hide some of it so it only affects *you* mildly."

"I'm sorry."

"You don't have to apologise." She ran a hand through his hair. "I just don't know how we can be in a relationship when we're so different. You thrive on being sociable and I feel like people suck the life out of me."

"We'll figure it out." Lightly, he touched his lips to hers. "I messed up, but next time you say you can't go out, I'll know not to push you."

She snuggled into his chest when he relaxed back on the couch. "Did you manage to convince Lizzie and Emily to do your personal training thing?"

"They all reluctantly agreed." He rested his cheek against the top of her head. "I can tell them I can't do it if it's a problem for you. I don't want you to feel as though I'm intruding on your friendships."

"I'm glad you get on with everyone. And I think it's funny that you're getting them all to do the fitness stuff. I just didn't have the energy to laugh about it yesterday."

"I think it'll be fun to do it with them. And it means I can get ahead on an assignment for once."

"Your mum will be happy about that," she said through a yawn.

"You should go back to bed," Fraser said. "Is it possible for you to take more time off from the cafe? I'm worried you're completely exhausted."

"Maybe." She kissed his cheek, then headed back to her room. At the doorway, Fraser called out to her and she turned back.

"Can I sleep in your bed?"

Immediately, her heart began to pump faster.

"It doesn't matter," he said in a rush. "It was only a thought.

I'm leaving in the morning and I just thought … never mind."

Scarlett took a step into her room, then turned back. "I've never had sex before," she blurted out, louder than she'd intended. "I had a boyfriend at school but we mostly just played video games and kissed. So I don't know how to be in a proper relationship."

Fraser remained on the couch. "I was only thinking of sleeping. I wouldn't want you to do anything you're not comfortable with."

"So you'll sleep in my bed and we won't have sex?" she asked, her eyes on her feet.

"I can also just sleep on the couch if it makes you uncomfortable."

"I thought you'd want to have sex. That's why I haven't been sleeping … I was worrying about it."

"You could have spoken to me if you were worried. I presumed you might want to wait a while. That's fine."

"Really?"

"Yes. Now stop worrying and go and get some sleep."

"You can sleep in my bed," she said.

When they were settled under the covers, Scarlett shuffled onto her side to face him. "Why did you marry me?" she asked.

His fingers curled around hers. "I already told you. I felt bad that you couldn't go to uni."

"I don't believe that's the only reason."

The corners of his mouth twitched. "Okay, fine. I also fancied you."

"That's pretty obvious now." She beamed. "But it still seems weird that you'd marry someone just because they're hot and you feel a bit sorry for them."

He let out a gentle sigh. "I felt kind of drawn to you. Which sounds soppy and stupid, but it's true. I was also having a crisis. A few people told me that I was a crappy person and I took it to heart. Helping you felt like a way to redeem myself."

"I think you're a good person." She moved to kiss his cheek

before resting her head on the pillow with her face close to his. Sleep came easily and she didn't stir until dawn.

Watching Fraser sleep was a pleasant way to start the day, and she felt a vague sense of disappointment when he woke.

"I'm going to get up and leave straightaway," he said. "Give you some space."

"You don't need to rush off." She put a hand on his chest to stop him from moving. "I'm going to ask Verity if she can get someone to cover for me today."

"That's good, but I still think it's better if I get out of your hair."

"Maybe," she agreed. Having a day alone would probably be the best way for her to recharge. "I feel better though. I should have spoken to you earlier. I got it in my head that you'd break up with me if we didn't have sex."

"No." He slipped an arm behind her head. "Definitely not."

"Lizzie and Emily think I should add a sex scene into my book," she told him. "But I don't want to. The other books didn't have sex in them and the readers didn't complain, so I don't see why I need one in the third book."

"It's your book," he said. "Write it however you want."

"You're right." She looked beyond him at the bedside table. "Can you pass me my phone so I can message Verity."

He shifted to reach it. "If she can't find anyone to cover, maybe I could work for you today."

"Have you ever worked in a cafe before?"

"No, but I'm sure I'd figure it out. Plus, I'm kind of charming, so I can usually get away with anything."

"I'm sure Tina won't mind working," Scarlett said as she tapped out a message. "She's always complaining about me taking too many shifts." Setting the phone aside, she propped herself on her arm to look down at Fraser. "Have you ever had a job?"

"No." He winced. "And I don't need a lecture about that. Mum gives me enough grief."

CHAPTER 43

The weather turned wet and windy for the remainder of the Easter break, which meant a marked decline in customers at the cafe. It made life easier for Scarlett. Fraser cautiously checked it was okay to hang out with her on the days when he was in Hope Cove to work on everyone's fitness programmes, but made sure to give her space too. She was glad when it was time to get back to Exeter and into the rhythm of uni life again.

The final term of the second year was only seven weeks long, but it would require all Scarlett's focus and attention. She'd need to resist the urge to hang out with Fraser in the evenings. At the end of the second week she went to the library on Friday afternoon to go over her lecture notes, knowing that if she went straight home and found Fraser there she'd give up all thoughts of studying in favour of spending time with him. She was thinking about leaving when a curly-haired girl from her course slipped into the seat opposite her.

"We haven't met properly," she said with a nervous smile. "I'm Lindsey."

"Hi." Scarlett began to pack up her things. "I was just about to leave."

Lindsey grimaced. "I've been sitting over there for ages

trying to work up the nerve to talk to you. I almost spoke to you after the lecture today, but it felt weird with other people around."

"What do you want?" Scarlett had spent all week focusing on getting to Friday evening so she could hang out with Fraser, and she wasn't about to let anyone hold her up.

"Sorry. I'm probably going to come across as a crazy fan girl. I am, I suppose. Hopefully not crazy, but I'm a huge fan."

Scarlett shoved her laptop into her backpack. "What are you talking about?"

"Your books." Reaching into her bag, she pulled out both of Scarlett's published books. "I wondered if you could sign them for me ..."

Her head snapped up and she blinked a few times. "Yes. I can do that."

"I overheard you talking about your books once and I looked you up. Now I'm totally hooked. I can't wait for the third in the series."

"It'll be released in August," Scarlett said as she signed the first book.

"I'm so excited. I need to know if Alissa and Matteo finally get together."

Scarlett stopped with her pen poised over book two. "They're not romance books."

"I know. But the chemistry between the two of them is incredible." She bit her lip. "Please tell me they do actually get together? Have you already written it?"

"Yes. Do you really want me to tell you what happens? I don't think I should. You might put it on the internet or something."

Lindsey jutted her chin out slightly. "No," she said slowly. "I don't really want to know."

"Why did you ask then?" Scarlett wrote her name with a flourish and pushed the books across the table.

"I'm just so excited about the next book. There was that

gorgeous moment in book two when Alissa and Matteo were hiding out in the cave. I was sure they were going to do it."

"Do what?"

Lindsey let out a shriek of laughter. "Sleep together," she said, as though it was obvious. "That almost-kiss had my heart pounding." She opened the first book and smiled at the signature. "Thank you so much for this."

"You're welcome. I have to go now."

The walk home went quickly as Scarlett replayed the encounter in her head. Having a fan made her smile to herself, even if she had been a bit too fixated on the romantic elements.

"You look happy," Fraser said when she arrived home. He was in the kitchen, peering into the fridge.

"I had a good day. Someone asked me to sign my books."

"That's cool." He closed the fridge and slipped his arms around her waist as he kissed her. "Do you feel like a celebrity?"

"I don't know what that would feel like, and I suspect I wouldn't like to be a celebrity. It was pretty cool though."

As she kissed him again a shiver ran down her spine.

"Are you hungry?" he asked when they pulled apart. "I could order a takeaway."

"There's pasta," she said, moving to open a cupboard. "And pasta sauce."

"That's fairly boring."

"It's cheap. You shouldn't order takeaway so much."

Without further comment he got a saucepan and filled it with water. He sipped a beer and chatted about his week while he made the quick and easy dish.

They'd only just finished the pasta when he went in search of dessert, starting at the fridge then opening the cupboard above the kettle where he found a packet of chocolate chip cookies. "Why are you staring at me?" he asked, opening the biscuits as he sat back at the table.

"I didn't realise I was."

"You looked miles away." He took a bite and devoured half the cookie. "What were you thinking about?"

"Sex."

Fraser thumped his chest as he choked. The look on his face made Scarlett smile.

"Do you want to have sex with me?" she asked seriously.

He opened his mouth a couple of times before any words came out. "Do you mean in general? Or now?"

"I'm not sure." She picked up a cookie and inspected the unevenly spread chocolate chips. Until now she hadn't questioned whether or not he'd *want* to have sex with her.

"The answer's yes either way," he said. "But I thought you wanted to wait."

"I might have changed my mind about that."

He didn't seem as enthusiastic as she'd expected, and he scratched at his jaw before he spoke. "Are you sure? Because previously when I put my hand under your top you seemed really uncomfortable."

"Because I didn't want to have sex then, but now I think maybe we should."

"I wasn't trying to have sex with you," he said slowly. "Did you think that?"

"Yes." She felt heat sweep through her body and pool at her cheeks. "Anyway, I've been thinking about it, and since we're in a real relationship now I think we should have sex."

His forehead wrinkled. "We could, but it's not as though we have to."

"Do you fancy me?"

"Yes!" He laughed. "Of course I fancy you. It's not as though I don't *want* to. I just don't want you to feel any pressure if you're not ready."

"I don't feel any pressure. I'd like us to have sex tonight." She nodded, as much to convince herself as Fraser. "I think it will be helpful."

"Helpful?" he repeated, arching a lone eyebrow.

"Yes. The girl who wanted me to sign the books today was going on about the romance and how she'd been hoping the main characters have sex. Which is exactly what Lizzie and Emily said. So I think I should write a sex scene, and that will be easier if I've experienced it." When she looked at sex as research, it felt much less daunting.

Fraser was staring at her. "You want to have sex with me as research for your book?"

"Yes."

He pushed the heel of his hand into his forehead. "I can't have sex with you for book research."

"Why not?"

"Because…" He shook his head. "Are you serious?"

"Yeah. Is it a problem?"

"Yes!" He stood so abruptly that the chair almost toppled over. "I'm not going to sleep with you just so you can write a scene in your book."

"Why? I thought guys always liked sex. What does it matter what my motivation is?"

He pushed his hands into his hair. "If it's only for book research, you could have sex with anyone."

"Yes. I suppose so—"

"Thanks a lot!" he huffed, then strode out of the kitchen.

Scarlett rushed after him. "Wait! I don't understand why you're angry. I meant in theory I could have sex with anyone. I wouldn't, though."

"I can't have this conversation," Fraser said, taking the stairs two at a time so Scarlett had to run to keep up. "I thought I was used to your bizarre conversations, but this is a whole new level of weird."

"Stop!" Scarlett called as he reached his room, sure he was about to slam the door behind him. "I don't understand why you're so upset."

"Because you asked me to have sex with you for book research!"

"I know. But why is that bad?"

He stared at her impatiently.

"You can't be annoyed with me and not explain why," she snapped. "You know I don't always understand things like other people, so you have to explain it to me."

"No, I don't! You can't expect me to stop and explain things to you when I'm furious with you. It's not fair. I can't always look after you."

She turned away so he wouldn't see the tears that filled her eyes. "I don't want to have sex with you any more," she called as she walked away.

In her room she sank onto the edge of the bed, dropping her head to her hands and massaging her temples. What had she done wrong now? And how were they supposed to work things out if he wouldn't speak to her? Or did he want to split up? Was that why he didn't want to talk? Maybe he was never going to speak to her again. After a moment, she pulled out her phone.

She'd never called Jack before. The only reason she had his number was because he sometimes messaged looking for Emily when she was at the office and got caught up in her writing. For a while she just stared at the phone, then forced herself to press dial.

Jack greeted her cheerfully, as though they often spoke on the phone.

"I wondered if you could give me some advice," she said hesitantly.

"I'm just leaving work but sure … go ahead."

Scarlett scratched her collarbone. "Should I call back later or something?"

"No, it's okay. What's up?"

"I upset Fraser and I'm not sure what I said wrong. I thought you might know."

"What happened?"

She paused and pushed her tongue against her piercing. "I

asked him if he wanted to have sex with me. We haven't had sex yet and I thought we could do it this evening, but then I mentioned it would be good research because I need to write a sex scene in my book. He got really angry and upset. I don't understand why."

"Erm … right … okay …" Jack's voice was slightly squeaky and he coughed to clear his throat.

"Was it offensive for me to ask him to have sex for book research?"

"Not offensive," Jack said slowly. "But I can understand why he'd be upset."

"I thought guys always want sex."

"Not *always.*" He paused for a moment. "If you're in a relationship with someone and you care about them, sex is special. It's like an expression of your feelings …"

"So I'm supposed to want to have sex with him because I love him?"

"Well, yeah, or at least have feelings in that direction."

"Okay. That's helpful. Thanks."

"Just talk to him," Jack said. "I'm sure you'll sort things out."

"He stormed off and doesn't want to speak to me. Do you think that means he wants to split up?"

"I doubt it. If he's upset, he probably just needs time to calm down. Give him a while."

"How long? Later today or tomorrow or next week?"

"Later today. Just give him an hour or so."

That sounded about right. She'd give him an hour and then go and talk to him. "Thank you."

"No problem." There was a short pause and Scarlett wasn't sure if she was supposed to say something. "Don't take this the wrong way," Jack said, "but why did you call me and not Emily or Lizzie?"

She wasn't sure why he thought she might take that the wrong way. It was a straightforward question, so she wasn't even sure how else she could take it. "Emily told me to speak to you if I needed relationship advice."

"Did she?" His voice had gone squeaky again.

"Yes. She said whenever she's worried about something, talking to you always helps."

"Right … I suspect she meant that you should talk to the person you're in a relationship with, rather than me specifically."

As her stomach lurched, Scarlett moved the phone from her ear. Briefly, she contemplated hanging up, as though that might erase the conversation. Except she'd also have to avoid Jack for the rest of her life, and that probably wasn't realistic.

"Scarlett?"

"I'm sorry," she whispered, returning the phone to her ear.

"Don't be daft. It's fine."

"It's not." A lump swelled in her throat. "I shouldn't have called you, should I?"

"I don't mind. It might just be more comfortable for you to speak to another woman about this stuff. But you can also call me. We're friends."

She tried to breathe deeply but her chest was too tight. It seemed so obvious what Emily had meant now.

"Scarlett," Jack said firmly. "You don't need to be upset for calling me. Honestly, it's not a big deal."

"It is for me." Her breath hitched as she sniffed. "I get everything wrong."

"No, you don't."

"I do. I can't believe I called you. I'm so embarrassed."

"Don't be. It doesn't matter."

"I have to go," Scarlett said. "I'm sorry for calling you."

"You don't need to apologise. Are you okay? I'm worried about you now."

Scarlett took a shuddering breath. "I'm sorry," she said again and ended the call.

Immediately, she reached for her laptop. Her eyes blurred with tears as she typed *how to get an autism diagnosis* into the search bar. From there, she clicked from one link to another, constantly wiping tears from her face.

She didn't look up when the door handle clicked and Fraser appeared in the doorway.

"Sorry," he whispered.

"Do you want to break up with me?"

"No." He walked further into the room. "Of course not."

"In that case you can go back to your room and be angry with me. It's fine."

"Don't be like that. I shouldn't have said what I did about looking after you. I didn't mean it."

She folded her laptop shut. "You were right. You shouldn't have to look after me. I don't want you to."

"But I don't feel as though I have to look after you. I don't know why I said that. I just snapped."

"I want to get a diagnosis," she said, cursing her tear ducts as more tears came.

Fraser sank onto the edge of the bed and took her hand. "I thought you didn't see any point."

"I didn't. But now I do. If I have a diagnosis I can get help. Someone else can explain things to me instead of you."

"I don't mind explaining things to you. I should never have said that. Besides, all couples have arguments and misunderstandings. It's not just because you're autistic." He put his hand to her cheek. "I'm really sorry for what I said."

"It's okay." Shuffling closer to him, she circled her arms around his waist.

He kissed her hair. "Did you call Jack? He messaged and said you were upset and he was worried about you."

For a moment all she could do was bury her face in his shoulder. "Emily told me she always talks to Jack if she has a problem, and I thought she meant I should do the same."

"She probably meant you should talk to me."

"I know. But I didn't figure that out until after I'd told Jack what we'd talked about. I'm so embarrassed."

"I wouldn't worry about it." He smiled and gave a short shake of the head. "It might just make my personal training session with him slightly awkward next week."

She flopped back on the bed. "It's Emily's fault too. If she meant I should talk to you about my problems, why didn't she say that? If people said what they meant life would be much easier."

"That's true," he said, running his thumb over the back of her hand. "Do you really want to get a diagnosis?"

"Yes. I don't know if I can though."

"Why not?"

"I have to get a referral from a doctor." Her chin wobbled and she closed her eyes for a moment as she tried to get her emotions under control. "I don't have a doctor, and the one on campus only has a phone number to make an appointment …" She trailed off as her throat felt too thick to speak.

"I can call and make an appointment for you," Fraser said, lying down beside her.

"Thank you." She turned her head on the pillow. "I'm sorry I upset you."

He pushed her hair from her face. "If it weren't for the scene in the book, would you want to have sex with me?"

Her gaze flicked to the ceiling and she shook her head.

"That's what I thought," he said, slipping his arm under her head. "It's okay."

"Is it?"

His hesitation made her think it might not be.

"Let's talk about it another time," he said, then kissed her cheek.

CHAPTER 44

The cafe was busy on Sunday morning and Scarlett hardly had time to stop and think as she took orders and brought food out from the kitchen. A fine drizzle started to come down over lunchtime and the cafe got steadily quieter. It was almost four o'clock when Emily walked in. Scarlett felt a flutter of nerves, which settled when she realised Jack wasn't with her.

"I haven't missed Lizzie, have I?" Emily asked. "She said she'd call in with the girls after their walk."

"She hasn't been here," Scarlett replied, hovering by the table with her notepad. "Will Jack be joining you?"

Emily gave her a quizzical look. "No. He's working in the pub. Why?"

"Because I'm embarrassed and I don't want to see him."

"Why are you embarrassed?"

"Because it's embarrassing. You don't have to pretend it isn't."

"I have absolutely no idea what you're talking about," Emily said, scrunching her nose up.

"I'm talking about when I called and asked him for relationship advice."

"I don't know anything about you calling him, but I don't see why you'd need to be embarrassed about asking Jack for advice."

Scarlett stared at the floor. "Because it was sex stuff. I thought you'd told me I should ask Jack if I ever had relationship problems, but now I know you actually meant I should talk to Fraser."

"Oh."

"Yes. You should really have said I should talk to Fraser if that's what you meant."

Emily's brow creased. "Sorry. I thought you knew what I meant. But you don't need to be embarrassed about calling Jack. He won't care what you said to him – he'll only care if you avoid him because of it."

She managed a curt nod before the door burst open and Maya and Phoebe rushed in. Crouching as they ran at her, Scarlett caught them both in her arms and hugged them.

"I lured them out for a walk with the promise of hot chocolate and gingerbread men," Lizzie said, draping her jacket over the back of the chair.

When Lizzie and Emily ordered coffees, Scarlett glanced at the cakes in the display case. "Anything else?"

"No," they both said drearily.

"We're not allowed," Lizzie said. "Especially not in front of you."

"Why not?"

"Fraser called us both on Friday afternoon," Emily explained. "Checking how our week was and warning us not to celebrate a successful week of fitness by eating rubbish all weekend."

"It's a good job he's such a nice guy," Lizzie said. "It'd be easy to go off someone who calls you at the end of the week and ruins your plans for wine and chocolate on Friday evening."

"I'll get your coffees," Scarlett said, smiling.

When she returned, Emily caught her eye. "Do you still need advice or is everything okay now?"

"I still need advice." She cast a glance at the girls, who were munching on their gingerbread men and getting crumbs everywhere. "I can't talk about S-E-X in front of kids though."

Lizzie smiled gently. "The girls are too young to understand. We can talk in front of them."

After glancing into the back to check Verity wasn't about to walk in, Scarlett took a seat at the table. "I haven't had sex with Fraser," she said quietly. "And I don't know if I want to. He says it's fine not to, but I don't know if he's just being nice."

"You don't *have* to," Lizzie said slowly.

"You shouldn't if you don't feel ready," Emily added, then lowered her voice. "Have you *ever…*?"

Scarlett shook her head. "I've never had sex with anyone."

"If you're not ready," Lizzie said, "it's definitely okay to wait. I'm sure Fraser will understand."

"How do I know if I'm ready?"

"Do you *want* to sleep with him?" Emily asked.

She thought about it for a moment. "I don't know."

"How do you feel when you're doing other stuff?" Lizzie asked.

"What do you mean?"

"I mean when things are getting intimate … do you enjoy that?"

Scarlett thought about Fraser's hands under her T-shirt. "I panic about sex, so I don't have chance to notice if I enjoy it or not."

"Everyone's nervous about their first time," Emily said.

"Are they?" Scarlett asked, not sure she believed that. "I really don't like the thought of him seeing me naked. My body might be weird and I never knew it."

"That sounds like normal nerves," Emily said. "Everyone feels that way."

"Really?"

"Definitely," Lizzie agreed. "It's normal to be nervous. As

long as you're with the right person and you trust them, it'll be fine."

"I trust Fraser." Pausing, she watched Maya slurp her hot chocolate. "Do you actually like it?" she asked, forcing herself to look at Emily and then Lizzie.

"Sex?" Lizzie asked.

She nodded in reply.

"Yes!" Lizzie grinned. "It's great."

Emily took a sip of her coffee. "The first time can be nerve-racking, but once you get past that it's very enjoyable."

"Relax and let Fraser take the lead," Lizzie said, beaming. "He'll make sure you have a good time. I bet he's got a lot of stamina."

"Lizzie!" Emily shrieked. "Get that creepy smile off your face and stop fantasising about someone else's husband!"

"I wasn't," Lizzie insisted. "I was just thinking I'd quite like to be twenty again. And objectively speaking, Fraser's a pretty perfect specimen. He's all lean and toned – athletic but in a subtle way."

"You're twice his age!" Emily said. "You're a pervert!"

Scarlett laughed as she stood. "Thank you for the advice. It's quite handy having old friends sometimes."

"Hey!" Lizzie called affectionately as she walked away.

When she arrived home that evening, Scarlett was surprised to find Fraser at his desk, studying. On the drive home she'd decided she should ignore her nerves and have sex with him. And not for book research, but because it was part of being in a relationship.

The fact that Fraser had an assignment to work on was a relief, especially when she realised that all of her underwear was old and tatty. If she was going to let Fraser undress her, she should get some of the sexy kind of underwear that people wore in films. Or at least a matching knicker and bra set.

After her lecture on Monday, she walked into town and wandered around the lingerie section of a large department store. The middle-aged shop assistant helped her pick out a black knicker and bra set with a lace trim.

Fraser wasn't at home when she got back, which gave her time to have a shower and put her new underwear on. She put a T-shirt dress over the top and tried to get on with her course-work. It was hard to concentrate, partly due to nerves and partly due to the uncomfortable underwear, which made her squirm in the chair every few minutes.

When she heard Fraser shout hello, she went to the landing and watched him stride up the stairs in his football kit.

"Did you get my message about the doctor's appointment?" he asked, giving her a kiss on the cheek. "Next Tuesday. Is that okay?"

"Yes. Thanks for calling for me."

"No problem. How was your day?"

"Good. Do you want to hang out tonight or have you got work to do?"

"I handed my assignment in this afternoon. I need to jump in the shower, then I'm all yours."

When he disappeared into the bathroom, she went back to her room and sat on the edge of the bed, listening to the hum of the water gushing through the pipes. At the sound of his foot-steps in the hallway, she followed him into his room.

Drips fell from his hair and ran down his smooth chest, stop-ping at the towel around his waist. "Do you want to watch a film?" he asked.

"No." She walked towards him and trailed her fingertips over his chest.

He swallowed hard. "I just need to get dressed."

"I bought new underwear." Taking a step back she pulled her dress over her head and slung it across the chair by the desk.

"It looks good," he said quietly.

Stepping closer again, she pressed onto her toes to kiss him.

Her insides fluttered as his arms tightened around her waist, drawing her close. Her lips explored his as she moved her hands up to his neck and then into his hair. She kept hold of him as she took a couple of steps towards the bed.

"I thought you wanted to wait," he said, his breath hot on her lips.

"I'm nervous," she told him, sinking onto the bed and pulling him with her. "But Lizzie and Emily said everyone's nervous for their first time."

With an arm behind her back he moved her further up the bed and covered her body with his. The damp towel around his waist was uncomfortable against the skin of her thighs, but it was nothing compared to the way her new underwear bothered her.

"Are you okay?" Fraser asked, pressing up on an elbow to look down at her.

"My underwear's uncomfortable," she said, her shoulders writhing. "The back bit feels as though it's stabbing me."

Moving his weight off of her, he gently eased her shoulder off the bed, then reached behind her. There was a snapping sound before he held out a small rectangular piece of card.

"At least you're not cheap!"

She snatched at the price tag. "There's no wonder it was annoying me."

"I imagine it will feel better now." He ran his fingers over the lace edging of her bra, making her breath catch in her throat.

"I'm really nervous," she whispered, her voice hoarse.

"It's okay." His gaze met hers. "We can go slow."

She nodded and he brought his lips to hers, kissing her slowly. As his hand trailed over her ribs, she tensed causing her teeth to knock against his.

"Sorry."

"It's fine."

As Fraser's lips explored her neck and collarbone, Scarlett stared up at a fly which skittered along the ceiling. Aware of her arms laying limply beside her, she tried to move but got caught up with Fraser's arms.

"Sorry," she said again, not quite sure why her body so often seemed to be working against her.

"It's okay," he soothed, moving so his face hovered over hers. "Would you prefer it if we didn't do this now?"

"I'm just nervous," she said quickly, "but I'm sure it'll be fine once we get the first time over and done with."

He looked at her sadly and shook his head, before hauling himself up and out of bed.

"What are you doing?" Scarlett asked, averting her gaze as he removed his towel and pulled a pair of boxer shorts on.

"I don't think we should do this today," he said.

Scarlett's relief was only momentary, then she felt as though her lungs were being squeezed. "It's really okay. We can have sex."

He sat beside her, curling his hand around hers. "I can't sleep with you when you look terrified. And I also don't want our first time to be something that you want to be over and done with as quickly as possible."

"I didn't mean it like that," she said, her throat burning.

"I know. But I think the only reason you're considering having sex with me is because you feel you should, not because you actually want to."

She couldn't argue with him there. "I'm sorry. I just freak out because I don't know what I'm supposed to do."

"You don't have to know what to do." He lay beside her and draped an arm over her stomach. "We can take things slow and wait until you're comfortable. Okay?"

"Okay," she murmured before his lips brushed over hers. His hand roamed over her midriff, then began to explore the skin of her thigh. "Wait." She pushed at his shoulder. "I'm confused. Are we going to have sex now or not?"

He propped himself on his elbow. "No, but I thought we could play around a bit. If you don't want to it's fine."

"I don't know." She took a deep breath, trying to get her thoughts in order. "If we lie in bed in our underwear, kissing and stuff … isn't that frustrating for you?"

His smile lit up his face. "I've been feeling pretty frustrated by you since the day we met. I'm kind of used to it."

"Sorry."

"It's really not a problem," he said, brushing her hair from her face. "I'm very happy to lie here kissing you. And if I do something that makes you uncomfortable you can tell me to stop. At some point, when you feel ready, we'll have sex."

"How will I know when I'm ready? I don't even know what that means."

"When you want to do it," he said. "Not because you feel you should, but because you want to."

"Okay." She shifted her weight and entwined her legs with his. "Am I a really terrible girlfriend?"

He kissed her forehead. "No. You're a great girlfriend."

"I hate that you see me as fragile. I don't want you to feel as though you always have to look after me."

"I don't."

"Liar!"

He smiled. "I have never thought of you as fragile. I see you as brave and strong and fierce. But I also see how much you have to fight for things that most people take for granted. I want to make life easier for you, but half the time I feel as though I'm making things more difficult."

"You definitely make my life more complicated," she agreed. "But in a good way."

"I feel the same way about you," he said. "Now, can I get back to kissing you?"

"Yes." She let her fingers trail over his bare chest before snaking around his back and pulling him closer. With sex out of the equation she let herself relax and just enjoyed kissing him.

"What's funny?" he asked when she started giggling a little while later.

"My stomach's rumbling. Didn't you hear it?"

"I thought it was mine." He cupped her cheek as he planted a soft kiss on her nose. "Didn't you have dinner?"

"No. I was too nervous to eat."

"I'll make sandwiches." He sat up and perched on the edge of the bed. "Stay there. We can eat in bed. I bought triple choc chip cookies today. We can pig out."

Scarlett propped herself on her elbow. "Isn't it a bit hypocritical of you to eat so much rubbish while you give other people advice on healthy eating?"

He raised his eyebrows. "Don't tell Lizzie or Emily about my eating habits."

"I won't." She looked at him in earnest. "How come when you were enlisting people for personal training you didn't ask me?"

"I did but you said no."

"Lizzie and Emily said no to start with too, but you kind of bullied them into it."

"I guess I thought you'd never agree to it so there was no point in trying to convince you. Do you want to do it?"

"No. I only wondered whether it was because I'm autistic."

He lingered at the doorway, frowning. "I don't know what you mean."

"I don't either really. It doesn't matter. Do you still hang out with the guys from football?" she asked. Not that long ago he'd never have been at home on a Friday night.

He shook his head. "Not much. I'm thinking of quitting the team."

"Why?"

"It's not as much fun as it used to be. And I don't have as much time now. I'm already busy with the personal training. Next year I'll have even more going on." He laughed as her stomach growled again. "You really need to eat!"

"Stop chatting then," she said, grinning at him. "Feed me!"

CHAPTER 45

On Tuesday evening, Scarlett was at her desk working on an assignment on contemporary American literature when Fraser arrived home. She heard him moving around downstairs before he appeared in her room.

"How did it go with the doctor?" he asked, taking a seat on her bed. He'd wanted to go to her appointment with her but she'd insisted on going alone.

"Fine. I'd made a list of all the reasons why I think I'm autistic and showed her that. I also showed her the results from the autism tests I'd taken and the ones other people had taken for me."

"What did she say?"

"She was really nice. I thought she might say I'd already had one evaluation so I can't have another, but she agreed that it would be a good idea for me to get another one." She bit her lip as a lump formed in her throat.

Fraser walked over to her and squeezed her shoulders as he kissed the top of her head. "Are you okay?"

"Yeah. I'm relieved that she believed me. She referred me for an evaluation at an assessment centre, but she said there's a waiting list." She'd been expecting that but it was annoying nonetheless. "She said I can speak to the university's student support services even without a diagnosis, but I feel a bit weird about that."

"It might be helpful."

"I don't need help with uni life. I'm managing fine." She lifted his hand from her shoulder and kissed it. "At least when you don't distract me from my work!"

"Is that a hint for me to go away?"

"I've got loads of work to do." As much as she'd like to abandon it and spend the evening with him, she really couldn't afford to.

"Me too." He was at the doorway when he turned back. "Do you want to work out with me sometime?"

A snort erupted from her. "Exercise? No. Why?"

"Because yesterday you mentioned that I didn't try very hard to get you to do training sessions with me, so I wondered if you wanted to."

"I wasn't trying to make you feel bad. I actually liked that you know me well enough to know it's not something I'd want to do."

"I think it'd be good for you."

She shook her head, the thought of exercising making her heart beat erratically. "No thanks."

"But you don't do a lot of exercise, and it's important for your health. You also have a fairly poor diet. I could take you into the gym one day and we could work out a fitness and nutrition plan for you."

She tapped the end of her pen on her desk. "That's never going to happen."

"Why?"

"It doesn't matter why. Can you please leave me to get on with my work?"

"If I promise to shut up about it after, will you tell me why you're so against it? I'm curious."

She looked to the ceiling as she stretched her neck. "I've

never been good at sport and exercise. I found it stressful at school. The thought of walking into a gym makes me panicky. I wouldn't know what to wear or what I'm supposed to do. I'm also fairly sure I'd fall off a treadmill if you put me on one."

Fraser nodded slowly. "Thank you."

"For what?" she called after him.

"For explaining it to me. Get back to work!"

Over the next couple of weeks, they fell into a routine of eating dinner together and then settling down to uni work in the evening. Fraser had a lot of coursework, which meant Scarlett didn't have to feel guilty for neglecting him. Sometimes he'd come into her room and work sitting on her bed.

She'd almost forgotten he was in the room that Thursday evening until she turned and caught him staring at her.

"I've had an idea for my dissertation," he said.

"That's very organised. We've still got a few weeks left of the second year and you're already getting started on projects for next year."

"I've been thinking about it for a couple of weeks." Closing his laptop, he set it aside. "I've done some research and I spoke to my tutor about it today."

"What's the idea?"

He dragged his teeth along his bottom lip. "I want to study barriers to exercise and fitness for autistic people," he said hesitantly. "I got thinking about how you're so against the idea of exercise. When I looked into it, I found studies on exercise in children with autism but not much on adults." Pausing, he shuffled to the edge of the bed. "I've spent so much time studying the benefits of nutrition and exercise on health and well-being, but so much of it is inaccessible to autistic people."

Fraser's eyes sparkled when he talked so passionately, and Scarlett felt so much affection for him that a lump formed in her throat.

"Do you think it's a good idea?" he asked, dragging a hand through his hair and scratching the back of his head.

"Yes." She walked over and sat beside him. "I really like it."

"My tutor has a contact at a youth centre in Totnes. They run groups for autistic people, and he thinks they'll be able to put me in touch with people to interview for my research."

"You've been thinking about this a lot, haven't you?"

"I can't stop thinking about it. I'm also thinking of volunteering at the youth centre over the summer. See if I can run sports activities or something."

"Are you sure you'll have time?" she asked with a straight face. "I assumed you'd have a hectic schedule of playing video games and lazing around."

He bumped his shoulder against hers. "I might get a job as well. There's an Italian restaurant in town advertising for staff over the summer."

Scarlett's eyes widened. "Are you kidding?"

"No. If you're working all summer I may as well find something to occupy me."

The thought of spending the summer apart from him made her chest ache. "Can you make sure we have the same days off?"

"Yes." He gave her a quick kiss, then reached for his laptop again.

Taking it from him, she set it aside and put a hand on his neck as she kissed him. She closed her eyes and butterflies took flight in her stomach. For once, her mind seemed to still, and all she was aware of was his lips against hers and the warmth that radiated from him. She pulled him closer, wedging her body against his and pressing her fingers into the skin at the back of his neck.

He groaned against her lips, causing a shiver to run down her spine. Her breathing was loud and uneven as she was overcome with the need to be as close to him as possible. Her hands dropped to his waist, fumbling at his T-shirt before taking the hem and tugging it over his head. Next, she did the same with her own, then moulded herself against him as she kissed him urgently.

"What are you doing?" he murmured against her lips.

"I'm ready." Her hands explored the taut skin of his back as her lips devoured his.

Breathlessly, he took her face in his hands to stop her. "Are you sure?"

"Yes. I don't have the pretty underwear on though. Does that matter?"

"No." He caressed her cheek and kissed her excruciatingly slowly. "It doesn't matter at all."

~

With Scarlett's legs tangled around his, Fraser had no clue whether the trickle of sweat that ran down the inside of his knee came from her or him. Her head was nestled under his chin and her breath swept across his chest, tickling his skin. He'd have laughed and squirmed away, but he seemed to be paralysed in a state of utter bliss.

As his heart rate returned to a regular rhythm, Scarlett angled her face towards him, opening her mouth to speak, then closing it and settling back on his chest. He wanted to say something too, but his brain wasn't functioning and any words that came to mind felt wholly inadequate.

Instead, he stroked her hair and kissed her forehead, sinking further into the bed as his muscles relaxed.

"Now I understand why you were annoyed," Scarlett whispered, just as he felt himself slipping into sleep.

Stirred by her voice and her fingers tracing circles on his chest, he managed a quizzical groan.

"When you were upset because I suggested we have sex for book research … now I get it." She propped her chin on his shoulder. "It's special."

"Yes." He trailed a finger along her hairline, not sure

whether he was just out of practice when it came to pillow talk or if she'd completely addled his brain.

"I'm glad you stopped to talk to me on the bench that day," she murmured, her smile evident in the lilt of her voice. "And I'm glad you fancied me enough to marry me."

His voice felt thick when he finally managed to speak. "I think it was more to do with the fact that you only had two friends."

"What?" She shifted to look at him, a mixture of curiosity and concern in her features.

"Nothing."

She shook her head. "What do you mean?"

"Ignore me." He kissed her softly but the distraction tactic didn't work, and she pulled away, holding the bed covers to her chest as she sat up.

"So you didn't only feel sorry for me because I couldn't go to uni, but because I only had two friends? You must have thought I was a total charity case."

The post-coital drowsiness left him in an instant. If he didn't explain she'd make it all about her when it absolutely wasn't.

"I didn't feel sorry for you," he said, taking her hand and stroking her fingers. "I envied you."

She pursed her lips. "I remember it now … you laughed at me when I said I had two friends."

"I laughed because it sounded like a joke. But then I realised you were serious and I was jealous."

"Why would you be jealous of my lack of friends?"

"Because you didn't have a lack of friends. You had the kind of friendships that made you feel that you didn't need any other friends." His gaze dropped to her wedding band as he twirled it around her finger. "I used to only have two friends too."

Slowly, she lay beside him again, her face close to his on the pillow.

"Liam and Allie were my best friends since primary school," he went on, ignoring the tightness in his chest. "By the time we were teenagers they pretty much knew me better than I knew myself. Nothing could touch me and no one could hurt me because I had the two best friends in the world."

"They're still your friends, aren't they?"

"Yes. But it's not the same as it was."

"You went to different universities," she said. "When you don't see each other as much, things are bound to change."

"Going to uni wasn't the problem."

"What then?"

He licked his dry lips and pressed them together. "When we were fifteen, Allie and Liam ended up snogging at a party … I thought it was just a drunken thing, but then they got together. Allie came over to my place one day and sat me down for a chat … telling me how nothing was going to change and that they'd make sure they still included me in everything."

"That was nice of her."

He shrugged. "It wasn't very realistic. Of course everything changed. It wasn't the three of us any more, it was the two of them … and me. They didn't actually want me around most of the time. Plus, everything was completely awkward between Allie and me. She wasn't just my friend; she was my best friend's girlfriend. So I couldn't call her any more or hang out with her alone."

Pausing for a moment, he stroked her hair. "I realised that having two friends wasn't enough. So I made sure everyone liked me. I got invited to every party and I couldn't walk into a room without people falling over themselves to talk to me."

"That's my idea of hell," Scarlett said.

He interlaced his fingers with hers. "It was, but I told myself it was great and *I* was great, and I ignored the fact I only really wanted to hang out with Liam and Allie." Pausing, he looked deep into Scarlett's dusty blue eyes. "At the same time that I met you, Allie told me that she couldn't stand me and had this big rant about what a horrible person I was. And it pissed me off, because I knew she was right … and I hated that she had such a low opinion of me."

"So you married me to redeem yourself?"

He nodded. "And because someone who only had two friends was the sort of person I wanted to spend my time with."

Scarlett looked at him seriously, then pushed his hair off his face. "What I don't understand is how you got everyone to like you despite your dodgy haircut."

The laughter that burst from him took all his tension with it. "My hair's my best feature," he said, pulling her close.

"It's definitely not my favourite part of you," she said, her eyebrows raising suggestively.

"Really?" he said, feeling the tug of desire deep in his gut.

"Really," she replied, entwining her legs with his as she kissed him.

"You're totally going to add a sex scene in your book, aren't you?" he murmured against her lips.

"Probably," she said, beaming. "I'm feeling quite inspired."

CHAPTER 46

If she'd realised how distracting sex would be, Scarlett might have put it off until the end of term. Fraser had always occupied her mind a lot, but in those last weeks of term it was a struggle to concentrate on anything other than him.

When the summer break came around she worked five days a week in the cafe, then dropped down to four days when she realised it was too much for her. Mostly she spent her days off with Fraser, either in Exeter or Hope Cove. He was busy too, having taken the job at the Italian restaurant as well as volunteering a couple of mornings a week at the youth centre in Totnes.

Scarlett declined his invitations to go along with him. There was a group of autistic people who met up, and Fraser seemed to think Scarlett might like to join. She reminded him that she had enough friends and was insistent that she didn't need autistic friends. He'd looked amused when she'd said that, but he'd dropped the subject regardless.

The week before uni started up again, Verity insisted Scarlett take a week off to recharge before the start of term. She even gave her a summer bonus to make up for the lost pay that week.

After driving back to Exeter on Saturday afternoon, Scarlett felt a huge relief at being back there. Fraser had a shift at the restaurant but he'd said he wouldn't be late. When she got bored of waiting, she walked into town for some window shopping before heading towards the Italian restaurant.

The outside seating area was raised slightly, up a couple of steps. Scarlett paused when she saw Fraser serving a table of middle-aged women. From the discarded napkins and empty glasses, it seemed as though they'd finished their meal. All four of them beamed up at Fraser as he chatted. His white T-shirt showed off his tan and it was easy to see why he did so well for tips.

He'd just left the table of women and was about to walk back inside the restaurant when he glanced in Scarlett's direction. His smile came quickly and made her heart flutter. Changing his course, he hopped down the steps and practically crashed into her, kissing her hard.

"Have you come to pick me up from work?" he asked.

"I was bored of waiting for you. Are you nearly finished?"

"Yes. I'll be about five minutes." He rushed away again and Scarlett felt a buzz of pride when she caught a few customers looking her way.

"Where's your car?" she asked when Fraser returned.

"Not far away," he said, taking her hand. "What do you want to eat tonight?"

She gave him a sidelong glance. "Whatever you want."

"Indian food then," he said cheekily.

"Not that. But anything else."

"Chinese food?"

"Not that either."

"Mexican?"

"Well, no."

"Fish and chips?"

"Yeah, okay … no fish for me, obviously!"

"Obviously. Or we could get pizza like usual."

She squeezed his hand. "How much do my weird food issues bother you?"

"They don't," he said, then stopped to kiss her.

"I'm not sure I believe that …" She trailed off, distracted by a mannequin in the shop window. "That dress has pockets," she said, her eyes on the berry-coloured cotton dress.

"So?"

"It's hard to find dresses with pockets." She peered at the price tag hanging from the hem. "It's cheap too. If it's my size, I'm buying it." Setting off towards the door, she was met with resistance as Fraser kept hold of her hand and stayed rooted to the spot. "What's wrong?"

He looked up at the sign above the shop. "It's cheap because it's a charity shop."

"Yeah. I know. What's wrong with that?"

"The clothes are second-hand."

"So?" She set off again but he pulled her back.

"Are you really okay with shopping in a charity shop?"

"Yes." She looked him right in the eyes. "Most of my clothes are from charity shops. I can't afford to buy things new."

"You should have said. I'm happy to take you shopping."

Briefly, she raised her eyebrows, then decided it wasn't worth being offended. Snaking her arms around his neck, she screwed her nose up. "I thought I'd been doing an excellent job at beating the rich kid out of you, but I can see I've still got work to do …"

"I'm not being a snob … But you shouldn't have to buy clothes from charity shops."

"Why? I really don't see any problem with it. It's also good for the environment to buy second-hand stuff." Her lips twitched to a smile. "How about I give you a lesson in shopping?"

Ignoring his protests, she pulled him into the shop, giggling when he whispered in her ear about the smell. To be fair it was a little musty, but she ignored his pouting and moved for a closer look at the dress. Once the shop assistant had removed it from the mannequin they spent an amusing ten minutes browsing.

"Don't look so smug," Fraser said as they stepped back into the sunshine and fresh air.

"Oh, come on! I took you in a charity shop and you found something you liked. If this isn't a time to be smug, I don't know when is." She ran her hands down his new jacket, the black leather striking against his white T-shirt.

"I don't even like it that much." He wrapped his arms around her waist. "I only got it because you told me I look hot in it."

"I wouldn't get too used to me complimenting your looks. I like to keep you grounded." She gave him a quick peck. "But you love that jacket. I can tell by your face."

"I suppose it's all right."

As he released her, he turned and stopped dead.

"Bridget!" he said. "Hi."

"Hi." She flashed a quick smile at Fraser, then Scarlett.

"How are you?" Fraser asked.

"Fine, thank you." Swallowing hard, Bridget walked past them.

"Nice to see you," Fraser called.

"I don't think it was mutual," Scarlett said quietly, slipping her hand into Fraser's.

"No. That was really awkward."

CHAPTER 47

"Did you tell your mum we're bringing cake?" Scarlett asked Fraser over breakfast the following morning.

"Yeah. I messaged her yesterday. Did you bake it or Verity?"

Scarlett raised an eyebrow. "Verity. She was the one who said it would be polite to take something. Was it rude the last time we went and I didn't bring anything?" They'd been earlier in the summer and it had been a much more pleasant experience than the first time she'd met them.

"Yeah, really rude," Fraser said, then winced when Scarlett looked at him questioningly. "I was joking. They don't care whether you bring something or not, but they'll appreciate the cake."

They'd done coffee and cake last time too to avoid the awkwardness of a meal. "What time are we leaving?" Scarlett asked, munching on toast.

"I said we'd be there around two. But I need to drive down to Totnes beforehand. I forgot my laptop on Friday. You could come with me and then we can drive straight to my parents' house."

"No thanks!"

"Why not? It's boring driving all that way on my own. You can keep me company."

"I know what you're doing … trying to trick me into going to the youth centre. I'm not signing up for any autism social groups."

"I'm not trying to sign you up for anything," he said, smiling widely. "I only want you to keep me company for the drive. You can wait in the car. I promise I won't make you go inside."

"Isn't it like a forty-minute drive? That's pretty boring for me."

"You get the pleasure of my company." He took his plate to the dishwasher. "If you don't want to, I'll go on my own and pick you up afterwards."

"No, it's okay." She passed her plate for him to put in the dishwasher too. "I'll come. I'm definitely not going inside though."

"Thank you." He wrapped his arms around her and kissed her forehead.

"Is your sister going to be there this afternoon?" Scarlett asked.

"Yeah, I think so."

"I quite liked her when we were there last time."

"That's because you met her for about ten minutes and she was on her best behaviour. Just remember, if you get stressed you can always go and play the piano."

She gave him a playful shove. "I'm sure it will be fine."

"It's not often you're more confident than me about a social event."

~

The Community and Youth Centre in Totnes was a white-washed building at the edge of the town, with a car park in front and a playing field behind. Fraser had said he'd only be a few minutes, but it had been much longer than that already. Overhead, the clouds had broken and bright sunlight streamed through the windshield, making Scarlett squint. The stale air was becoming increasingly stuffy. Eventually, she stepped out of the car and wandered towards the double doors at the front of the building. Peering inside was unhelpful as all she could see was her own reflection in the glass.

She was reading the noticeboard when a cheerful voice said hello.

"Hi," Scarlett replied, keeping her eyes on the board as though she was engrossed in reading about the ethos of the place.

"Do you need any help with anything?"

"No."

"You're welcome to come in if you'd like to have a look around."

She shook her head. "I'm waiting for someone."

"Someone inside?" the woman asked. "Can I fetch them for you?"

Scarlett frowned as she turned to look at the woman. She had brown hair in tight curls and a pink glow to her nose and cheeks as though she'd been in the sun for too long.

"My boyfriend works here," she said. "He just nipped inside to get something."

She smiled brightly. "I work here too. Who's your boyfriend?"

"Fraser."

Her lips twitched before her smile faded. "Fraser's your boyfriend? Fraser Graham?"

"Yes."

"Oh …" She looked towards the doors and swallowed hard. "You're Fraser's girlfriend?"

"That's generally the way it works."

"I didn't know he had a girlfriend."

"I'm actually his wife," Scarlett said, slightly troubled by the fact that Fraser had worked there all summer and hadn't mentioned her existence.

The woman's cheeks puffed out before she exhaled loudly and slapped a hand over her heart. "You're Scarlett?"

"Yes."

"Oh my goodness!" The woman folded forwards and let out a weird little laugh. "Don't do that to me."

"What did I do?"

"You said you were Fraser's girlfriend … but I knew he was married." She put her hands at either side of her head and gave them a shake as her eyes bulged. "My mind went into overdrive, wondering if I was going to have to break it to you that he was married … and whether I'd have to track down his wife and let her know he was cheating on her. Not to mention my illusions of him being a nice guy were almost shattered."

"Sorry. Sometimes it's easier to say he's my boyfriend than get a load of comments about how I look too young to be married."

The woman grinned. "I suppose it's fine for a guy to have a wife *and* a girlfriend, as long as they're the same person!"

"He's my best friend too," Scarlett said.

"That's so sweet. I'm Bonnie, by the way." She glanced around. "Why did Fraser leave you out here? You could have gone inside."

"I didn't want to. He said he'd only be a few minutes."

"He'll have got chatting. Have you been inside before? I can give you a tour while you wait, if you'd like."

She shifted her weight, then automatically moved towards the door when Bonnie did. "I suppose I could."

After tapping onto a keypad, the door clicked and Bonnie pushed it open, then held it for Scarlett.

"See, there he is …" Bonnie pointed across the foyer towards a room with large windows where Fraser was leaning against a desk and talking to a bald-headed man. "Chatting to Ted in the office. Fraser's such a chatterbox. They both are, so he could be ages. Come and look at the art room …" She led the way into a large airy room with low cabinets under the windows and an array of artwork on the walls.

"It's all quiet this morning. Sundays generally are. We have some fantastic artists, though." After stepping back into the hallway, she led Scarlett to another large room with a pool table at one end and a bunch of mismatched, relaxed seating. Through a hatch in the wall was a bright white kitchen.

Bonnie called hello to a couple of teenage boys playing pool, then exited through a door at the other side of the room. "I'll show you the sports hall. That's where Fraser spends most of his time. He's so great with the kids. There are some kids who wouldn't even go near the sports hall until Fraser came along. He manages to get everyone involved."

She opened the door to a large hall at the side of the building with white lines marking a basketball court. Bonnie stepped inside, then put a hand in front of her mouth as she laughed. "There's this one girl who always refused to do any physical activities but Fraser was determined to involve her. He'd set up an obstacle course and one of the activities was hula hooping. This stroppy twelve-year-old told Fraser there was no way she'd ever be caught hula hooping and that it was for kids. Fraser told her it was fun no matter what age you were … and to prove it he picked up the hoop …" She beamed at Scarlett. "I don't know whether you know this about your husband, but he absolutely cannot hula hoop!"

"But he tried?" Scarlett asked, amused by the mental image.

"He was wiggling his hips and looked like a complete idiot. He had everyone in hysterics! Eventually, he declared that Fay was right and no one over the age of seven should ever go near a hula hoop. And he told her she'd have to advise him on the activities from then on."

"Does she?"

"Yes. She's very proud of her role as Fraser's advisor. Sometimes she even joins in."

"He really likes working here," Scarlett said.

"It's a great place. There's a lovely atmosphere." She tilted her head as she looked at Scarlett. "It's really good to finally meet you after Fraser's told me so much about you."

"I suppose he told you I'm autistic?" She frowned, feeling as though Bonnie would probably try to get her to come along to some group or other.

"Yes. He mentioned it."

When she didn't say any more, Scarlett shifted her weight. "He thinks I should join some of the groups here and meet other autistic people … but I don't want to. That's why I was waiting outside."

"It can be good to meet people who know what it's like to be autistic," Bonnie said, nodding. "But I can understand why you might not want to."

"I don't even have an official diagnosis," Scarlett told her. "And …" She stopped herself. What she'd wanted to say was that she probably wasn't as autistic as the people who came to the groups. She lived independently and went to uni and had a job. It was unlikely she'd fit in with the sort of people who went to special groups for autistic people.

"Fraser said you're trying to get a diagnosis," Bonnie said.

"Yes. I'm on a waiting list."

Bonnie rolled her eyes. "It's a nightmare trying to get a diagnosis as an adult. Having to wait for an appointment felt like torture to me. If they'd have given me an appointment for eighteen months' time, I'd have been fine. But they said they'd be in touch sometime and it might be around eighteen months. I couldn't cope with that."

"What did you need a diagnosis for?" Scarlett asked.

She raised her eyebrows. "Autism."

"You're autistic?"

"Yes."

Scarlett looked her up and down. "You don't seem very autistic."

"That can be a problem in itself. I am though! I got a diagnosis four years ago."

"How long did you have to wait for your appointment?"

"I didn't in the end. The waiting caused me too much stress, so I paid for a private assessment."

"I read about that," Scarlett said. "It's expensive, isn't it?"

"Yes, but for me it was worth it." She glanced around the echoey room. "Do you want to see the outdoor area?"

"I should probably find Fraser. We're going to his parents' house and I don't want to be late." She followed Bonnie back the way they'd come, gazing at the posters on the wall in the hallway. "Was it easy to get a diagnosis privately?"

"I wouldn't call it easy, but it was faster." She slowed her pace. "If you ever want to talk about it, Fraser has my number. You can message me any time. Don't call … I'm not great at answering the phone if I don't know the number. Or even if I do know, to be honest."

Scarlett murmured her thanks, then bit her lip to stop herself from smiling too widely.

"That's a lovely jacket," Fraser's mum remarked as Scarlett and Fraser stepped out of the patio doors to join his parents in the sunshine at the back of the house.

"Thanks," Fraser muttered, placing the cake on the table and avoiding eye contact with Scarlett.

"I bought it for him," she said. "From a charity shop. I was giving him a lesson on shopping on a budget."

With wide eyes, Tricia looked to her husband and then Fraser.

"Second-hand clothes are better for the environment," he muttered. "Who wants cake?"

As he began slicing it up, Scarlett glanced back into the house. "Is Hattie here?"

"She's supposed to be." Tricia picked up a flowery teapot and began to pour into dainty teacups. "But she had some sort of clothes crisis and had to go shopping. Hopefully she'll be back before you leave."

Dominic pulled his teacup in front of him. "How are you feeling about getting back to uni?" he asked, looking to Scarlett.

"I'm looking forward to it."

Tricia passed Scarlett a cup and saucer. "I can't believe it's your final year already. There'll be a bit more pressure now, I guess."

"There aren't as many lectures in the final year," Scarlett said. "Which will be easier for me. It's a lot of self-guided study, and I'll have more flexibility to choose which modules I want to take. For my dissertation, I can submit an extract of a novel. And I'll be able to publish the novel afterwards, which is a bonus. I'm also going to take a module in the principles of publishing … so I already know everything about that. I'll do a module in young adult literature and write a novel for that too."

"That sounds like a lot," Tricia said.

"It is. But it's everything I'm good at."

"Are *you* feeling as confident about the final year?" Dominic asked Fraser through a mouthful of cake.

He shook his head and swallowed his mouthful. "I think it's going to be full on. I'm glad I quit the football team – that takes some pressure off."

"Will you still help at the youth centre?" Tricia asked.

"I hope so. I've told them it'll depend on uni, but I should have time most weekends."

Scarlett ate her cake and zoned out of the conversation, looking over the garden and watching a bird hop along a tree branch nearby. When she focused on what they were saying, Fraser and his dad were talking about football.

She whispered to Tricia, asking if she could play the piano, then wandered back to the sitting room where she played uninterrupted for half an hour.

"Bloody hell, you're amazing!" a high-pitched voice said when she came to the end of the piece she was playing.

"Thanks." Scarlett turned on the velvet-covered stool to look at Hattie.

"They said you were good but I didn't realise quite how good. No wonder you're the golden child around here."

"What?"

"Never mind." She waved a hand. "Do you think you could help me with something?"

"Maybe."

Hattie beckoned her with a flick of her chin. In the entrance hall she picked up a load of shopping bags and set off up the stairs. "I need some advice on what to wear tonight. There's this guy Zach who I really like, and I know he'll be in the pub so I want to look hot."

"I'm probably not great at fashion advice."

Hattie closed the bedroom door behind them and immediately pulled her T-shirt over her head. "That can't be true. According to Mum you're perfect in every way, so I don't believe fashion advice isn't one of your skills."

As Hattie took her jeans off, Scarlett's gaze drifted around the room with the teal bedspread and matching curtains. A vanity table was littered with cosmetics, but the rest of the room was neat and tidy. "Did your mum really say I'm perfect?"

"Well, she didn't use the word, but you should hear her go on about you. We all joke that you're the favourite child these days."

Scarlett screwed her face up, trying to figure out if Hattie was joking.

"What do you think?" She tugged on the low neckline of the mini dress and pushed her boobs up. "It's not too slutty, is it?"

"I can see your bra," Scarlett pointed out. The flash of hot pink lace was impossible to miss.

"It's cute, isn't it?" Hattie walked over to a full-length mirror in the corner.

"If you pull the neckline up and move the straps you might be able to hide it."

Hattie put her hands on her hips. "Zach's going to be there. Having my bra straps on show is kind of the point. I want him to like me."

"You mean you want him to like your bra?"

She dropped a hip and pouted at the mirror. "You think it's too slutty, don't you?"

"I didn't say that, but ..." She trailed off when Hattie strode across the room. "Where are you going?"

"The wardrobe." A door led to a whole other room, full of shelves and hanging rails and racks of shoes.

"Does your mum really like me?" Scarlett asked, her mind unable to shift away from the comment.

"Are you kidding?" Hattie surveyed the shelves and spoke loudly. "She rambles on about how great you are and how brilliant it is that you have a job and pay for uni yourself." She threw a few outfits onto the bed. "One time I pointed out that you don't pay rent so you're not actually that self-sufficient and Mum bit my head off."

"What?" Scarlett muttered.

Hattie sighed. "I made a comment about how Mum and Dad pay your rent and that you don't actually contribute anything towards the house. Don't get me wrong, I don't care. I was just sick of hearing how brilliant you are. But Mum tore strips off me for even mentioning it."

Scarlett looked at her socks. There was a tiny hole in the big toe of the left one and a dot of pale skin contrasted against the black cotton. As she contemplated what to say, Fraser called her name.

Hattie threw the bedroom door open. "She's up here!"

"I better go," Scarlett said, shuffling past her and meeting Fraser on the stairs.

"What were you doing?" he asked.

"Helping Hattie choose an outfit for tonight."

"Is she being annoying?"

"No." Scarlett avoided looking at him and padded down the stairs. "I want to go home. I'm tired."

"You're okay, though?" he asked.

Scarlett remembered him telling her that women usually say they're fine even when they're not. At the bottom of the stairs she forced herself to look at him.

"I'm fine," she said with a tight smile.

CHAPTER 48

"You barely spoke on the way home," Fraser remarked, kicking his shoes off in the hallway. "What's going on?"

"Hattie confused me," Scarlett said.

"She confuses me most of the time too. I wouldn't worry about it."

She put a hand on his arm when he began to move away. "She thinks I don't pay any rent."

His features crinkled. "Ignore her."

"It made me wonder," she said loudly as he set off for the kitchen. "Do you pay the landlord from your account or do your parents pay it from theirs?"

He stopped but didn't look back. "My parents pay it."

"So you transfer my money to them?"

His shoulders lifted as he tensed.

"You don't give them my money, do you?" Scarlett asked quietly.

"They never wanted it," he said, turning around to her. "They were always happy to pay the full rent. I told you that."

"And I told you I wasn't happy for them to do that. You also lied to me about how much the rent was, didn't you?"

"Yes. Because all the places you could afford were awful."

"So, first you lied to me and then you stole from me?"

"I didn't steal from you. I have the money. I'll give it back. I was always going to give it back to you."

"I don't want it back. I gave it to you for the rent." She couldn't bear to look at Fraser and set off for the stairs to get away from him.

"My parents don't need the money," he said, following her. "It makes absolutely no difference to them. Just let me give it back to you."

Scarlett rushed to her bedroom, then spun around to him in the doorway. "It makes a difference to *me*. I don't want your parents paying my rent."

"You can be really pig-headed sometimes, you know? Why can't you let people help you?"

"I'm not pig-headed! I have principles. Something you wouldn't understand since you spent two years taking money from me and don't see why that's a problem."

He put an arm out to stop her from closing the door. "I know I shouldn't have taken your money. But I swear I was always going to give it back."

"Get out of my room," she said when he took a step towards her. "We have rules. You're not allowed in my bedroom without permission." Obviously the rules had been forgotten about recently. He'd slept in her room whenever she'd been there over the summer. His things were littered around as though it was his room too. But that didn't mean she couldn't kick him out when she wanted to.

He backed away until he was just outside the room. "Can we talk about this? Please."

"I don't want to talk to you," she said and closed the door.

Fraser spent the evening lying on his bed, staring at the ceiling. He tried to speak to Scarlett again but she told him in no uncertain terms to go away. He had two shifts at the restaurant that week and was signed up to help at the youth centre one afternoon, but otherwise he'd been looking forward to spending time with Scarlett.

For the first time ever he felt little enthusiasm for the sports activities at the youth centre on Monday, and his shift at the restaurant on Tuesday dragged on too. All of his attempts to speak to Scarlett failed. Whenever he knocked on her door she told him she wasn't ready to speak to him yet.

His feet were aching when his shift at the restaurant was drawing to an end on Wednesday. He had to keep reminding himself to smile at customers when smiling was the last thing he felt like doing. As he cleared a table outside, he had the feeling of being watched and straightened up to see a familiar face standing at the entrance. He hadn't seen Allie since Christmas. Occasionally they exchanged messages asking how each other were but that was all. His smile came easily as he went over to her.

Neither of them said anything as they embraced.

"I've missed you," he murmured into her hair.

"I've missed you too." She smiled as they broke apart. "I was in town and thought I'd come and see if the rumours were true … you actually got a job!"

"I'd like to say I'm a changed man, but sadly I don't think that's true." He nodded his acknowledgment to a couple who were trying to get his attention. "I'll be finished in about half an hour. Any chance you can hang around and have a drink with me after my shift?"

"I'd really like that."

He found her a spot at the bar inside and got her a drink while she waited for him. Then they wandered down the road making idle chit-chat until they found a pub with a beer garden at the back. The small talk continued until they were halfway through the second round of drinks.

"Have you seen much of Liam?" she asked, her voice ever-so-slightly high-pitched.

"No. He stayed in Manchester for most of the summer. I saw him a couple of times in July when he came home for a visit. We talk on the phone a fair bit."

She nodded. "How's he doing?"

"Okay, I think."

The silence that fell was loaded and they both took long swigs of their drinks.

"I hate that we're not friends any more," Allie said quietly.

"You could probably still be friends," Fraser said. "I guess it would be weird at first but you could give it a go."

"I meant you and me," she said, looking at him intently. "I knew that breaking up with Liam would mean losing you too, but I still hate it."

He stared at her for a moment. "You didn't lose me when you broke up with Liam."

"Oh, come on!" She laughed without humour. "I haven't seen you all year and your messages are infrequent and annoyingly polite. You can hardly describe that as friendship."

"I wouldn't," he agreed. "But it wasn't you splitting up with Liam that was the problem. It was you getting together with him."

She jutted her chin out. "What are you talking about?"

"We haven't really been friends for years. You're not seriously going to blame it on your breakup, are you?"

"Well, if you want to go that far back, I think we both know it was because you hit sixteen and decided you were too good for Liam and me!"

He let out a short sharp laugh. "Yeah, right! Like that's what happened!"

"It's true. You swaggered around parties, barely giving us the time of day."

"Because you didn't want to hang out with me," he said,

raising his voice and not caring that the people on the next table turned to look.

"Don't try and turn things around. When Liam and I got together we made every effort to include you still."

"Yeah, and you made it very clear that it *was* an effort. You invited me to things because you felt you should, not because you actually wanted me there."

"That's not true."

"It *is* true. And it's normal that you'd want it to just be the two of you … but I don't know why it never occurred to you that it made me feel like crap." He let out a breath, then stared into his pint.

"I'm sorry."

"It doesn't matter."

"It matters to me." She laid her hand over his. "I never knew you felt like that."

They descended into silence for a moment before Fraser found his voice.

"Haven't you been in touch with Liam at all?"

She shook her head and blinked rapidly as tears pooled in her eyes. "I totally messed up."

"How do you mean?"

"I miss him," she whispered as her face crumpled. "I miss him so much."

Fraser moved to sit beside her and enveloped her in a hug. "Call him," he said when she calmed down. "Tell him that."

"I'm scared he won't want to know. And I'm terrified of us trying to sort things out and hurting each other all over again. Maybe we're better off apart."

"I don't think that's true. You two were made for each other."

"When we were living together we couldn't stand each other, but as soon as I moved out I missed him."

"He said the same."

Her eyes sparkled with hope. "Really?"

"Yes. I think he's pretty miserable without you. Just call him. Meet for a drink and see what happens."

She gave a little laugh as she wiped tears from her cheeks. "I honestly never thought I'd be taking relationship advice from you."

"I'm probably not the best person to be giving it at the moment."

"I thought everything was great with Scarlett? I had a coffee with your mum yesterday and she does nothing but sing Scarlett's praises."

"Scarlett's great. I messed up, but I'm sure that won't come as a huge surprise to you."

"What happened?"

He gave her a brief rundown of the rent situation and tried to ignore her look of exasperation. "I know I was stupid," he said. "I just don't know how to fix it. She won't even speak to me."

"Where's the money now?" Allie asked.

"Still in my account." He cocked his head to one side, then pulled his phone out. "I should transfer it back to her. Why didn't I think of that? If I want her to believe I didn't take it for myself, I need to give it back." He opened his banking app but was stopped by Allie putting a hand on his arm.

"She doesn't want the money," she said, glaring at him as though that should be obvious.

"But she'd at least know I wasn't using her for financial gain."

"I don't think that's really what she's upset about. It's the fact that your parents think she hasn't been contributing to the rent." She stared at him as though the answer to how to fix everything should be obvious. "Give the money to your parents!"

"But it won't make any difference to them. It's not as though they think any less of her for not paying rent."

"No, but they'd probably think more of her if she did."

Fraser let out a low growl. "If I give the money to my parents I'll have to explain to them what I did."

"Yes." She nodded and pressed her lips together. "That's what you need to do. Then tell Scarlett that they have the money and you're sorry and you love her. She'll forgive you. I pretty much guarantee it."

"I'm fairly sure she'd run a mile if I tell her I love her, but the rest of your advice might not be too bad."

"You've never told her you love her?"

"Nope."

"You do love her though?"

"Yep." He went back into his banking app, then had to pause to calculate just how much rent Scarlett had paid before transferring it to his parents' account. "This better work. Otherwise I've just earned myself a massive lecture from my parents for no reason."

"At least you'll know you've done the right thing. And I'm sure Scarlett will forgive you."

"I'm not so sure. And sometimes I feel as though no matter how hard I try, I never quite measure up. She's probably counting the days until she can divorce me."

"Surely she could divorce you already if she really wanted to," Allie said idly.

"How do you mean?"

"Well, she got the loan. There's no reason you actually have to stay married until graduation, is there?"

"I suppose not." He finished his drink. "I'd offer to get you another, but I need to call my parents and then grovel to Scarlett."

"It was really good to see you," she said, leaning her head on his shoulder. "No matter what happens, can we keep in touch more?"

"Yes, please." He put an arm around her shoulders and kissed the top of her head.

The only good thing about being angry with Fraser was that Scarlett got a lot of work done in the three days that she wasn't speaking to him. She'd been working on a new novel, which she'd also use for her dissertation, so it felt doubly productive. Most of the time she managed to focus on that instead of her argument with Fraser, but now and then she found herself staring at the wall, running through the argument in her head. By Wednesday evening she was sick of being annoyed with him and waited for him to come home so she could speak to him. It was later than she expected when she heard the front door and then his footsteps on the stairs.

He gave a short rap on the door before opening it. She nodded when he asked if he could come in.

"I transferred the money to my parents," he said, taking a seat on the bed. "And I explained to them that you'd been paying the whole time." He caught her gaze. "I'm sorry."

She chewed her bottom lip. "I know you are."

"Do you think you might forgive me sometime then?"

"I think so. I'm glad you told your parents. But I also hate that you lied to me for two years."

He ran his hands down his face. "I can't do anything about that now. There's only so many times I can apologise. You can either forgive me or continue torturing me indefinitely."

"I'm annoyed with you."

"I know and I understand why. I messed up. I do that sometimes. I'll probably do it again."

"So I should just get used to it?"

"No! You should stop expecting me to be perfect, because I'm not. I never will be. I'll keep messing up, and if you can't forgive me you may as well divorce me now."

Scarlett closed her eyes as her stomach felt suddenly heavy. Occasionally she thought about the fact that they'd be divorced in less than a year, but mostly she refused to let her mind go there. Maybe Fraser was right and they should get it over and done with. She'd got the loan so they didn't really need to stay married until they graduated.

"I'll think about it," she said.

"About what? Whether you'll forgive me?"

"About whether I want to divorce you."

"You can't be serious?" he said, standing.

"I am serious. I need to think about it."

"I don't want us to get divorced."

She ignored the pain in her chest. Divorcing him now would be hard, but in a year it would be even more difficult. "I think it might be for the best," she said.

He stayed rooted to the spot for a moment, then walked slowly out of the room, closing the door behind him.

Hunger forced Scarlett out of her bedroom the following morning and she padded down to find Fraser sitting at the kitchen table with a pile of post in front of him and a plate containing two slices of toast.

"Morning," she said but he only stared at a letter in his hand and didn't reply.

Finally, he looked up at her. "What?"

"Aren't you even saying good morning to me now?"

"Morning," he murmured.

"What's wrong with your toast?"

"I lost my appetite."

"Is that a first for you?" she joked.

He didn't laugh as he pushed a chair out for her and told her to sit down.

"I need to get breakfast," she said. "I'm hungry."

"I got a letter from the university." He pushed an envelope towards her. "You got one too. I guess it's the same."

Slowly, she sat down. "What does it say?"

"I have to go to a meeting with the vice-chancellor of the

university on Monday afternoon, regarding an allegation that's been made about my relationship with you."

Scarlett tore open her letter and scanned the words. "Mine's the same," she whispered, barely hearing her own voice over the hammering of her heart. "Why?"

"I'd hazard a guess and say that's thanks to Bridget."

"Bridget wouldn't say anything. Not now. Maybe before, when she was upset, but not now."

"I swore to her that you and I weren't in a relationship, but when she saw us the other day it was obvious that we're together. She'll think I lied and we were together all along."

"She still wouldn't say anything."

"Well someone did."

"What's going to happen?"

"We'll go to the meeting and reassure them that the allegations are false and that the marriage is real. It'll be fine."

"If you really believed that you wouldn't have lost your appetite."

Picking up a slice of toast he took a bite and crunched noisily. "It'll be fine!" He pushed the plate to her, offering her the second slice, then stood up to put more bread in the toaster.

"Do you want to hang out today?" he asked when they finished breakfast.

"I've been working on a new novel and it's going well, so I think I'll get on with that."

He gave her a crooked smile and didn't comment as she left him alone again. Upstairs, she sat at her desk and stared at the laptop screen. After a few minutes she trudged back downstairs and joined Fraser in the living room.

"I'd like to hang out," she said, standing at the end of the couch. "But just as friends."

"How do you mean?"

"I mean I don't want to talk about the rent money or divorce or anything. I just want you to distract me because I'm scared

I'm going to get kicked out of uni next week and I don't want to sit in my room being scared on my own."

He reached for her hand and pulled her to sit beside him. "You're not going to get kicked out of uni."

"You don't know that."

"I'll do anything I can to make sure you don't."

"Thank you." Automatically, she kissed his lips.

"I thought we were just being friends today," he said with his face close to hers.

"I forgot."

He closed his eyes and kissed her again. "TV or video games?" he asked.

"Video games," she replied with a smile.

CHAPTER 49

Fraser had arranged to meet Scarlett before the meeting with the vice-chancellor. When he arrived she was pacing back and forth outside the building while tapping her thumbs against her fingers. Over the weekend he'd tried to reassure her that everything would be okay, but it clearly hadn't worked.

"Hey," he said as he approached her. "Why are you freaking out? I told you not to worry."

"I walked out halfway through my lecture this afternoon," she said, stopping and sitting on the low wall beside her. "There didn't seem much point in sitting through the lecture when I'm about to get kicked out of uni. I don't know how you think it's possible for me not to worry about this. Why are you so calm?"

He sat beside her, their legs touching. "I'm not."

"You seem it."

"I'm worried too, but I really think it will be fine. We'll just go in and tell them we're married and then we'll be on our way."

She set off pacing again. "I hate lying and I'm really bad at it."

Stepping in front of her, he rested his hands on her shoulders. "How about we tell part of the truth? And we avoid telling the whole truth."

"I'm too nervous. I'll say something stupid and get us both in trouble."

"I can do the talking."

She nodded and slipped her hand into his as they walked inside.

They only had to wait for a few minutes before the door to the vice-chancellor's office opened. The smartly dressed woman in a navy dress and blazer smiled warmly and beckoned them inside.

"I'm Georgia Sutcliffe," she said, shaking Fraser's hand and then Scarlett's. "Thanks for coming in. I'll try not to keep you for long."

Fraser took a seat on one of the chairs in front of the desk. When Scarlett sat beside him he tried to catch her eye, but her gaze was on her fingers tapping in her lap.

"I have to say this is a very unusual situation," Georgia said, smoothing her dress as she sat down. "I mentioned in my letter that we'd received a complaint about you. My first thought was that it was a prank or someone with a vendetta, but after looking into things I thought it best to hear your side." She tucked her neat blonde bob behind her ear. "The allegation is that you got married in order to obtain a student loan …" She was still smiling, but also looked slightly puzzled. "I looked at your files and found that you did get married very close to the start of university."

"It was a few months before actually," Scarlett muttered, her head still bent and her fingers still tapping. Fraser had to force himself not to put a hand over hers to still them.

"But it was around the time that you accepted your places on your courses and applied for a loan," Georgia said.

"We wanted to get married before we started university," Fraser said confidently.

Georgia's features were relaxed and friendly. "Was it a big wedding?"

"We couldn't afford a big do," Fraser replied.

Silence fell in the room as Georgia's attention switched to Scarlett, her gaze landing at her drumming fingers. "Is everything okay?"

Scarlett nodded but didn't look up.

"Did you enjoy your wedding day?" Georgia asked her.

All she had to do was say yes, but Fraser could almost see her internal struggle. When she raised her head, her cheeks were bright red and she swallowed hard.

"Is there a problem?" Georgia asked.

Fraser slipped his hand into Scarlett's and gave her a reassuring smile.

"I'm really nervous," she murmured.

"You don't need to be nervous," Georgia said. "I only need to know a bit about your relationship with Fraser."

"Fraser can tell you about it. He's better at talking than I am."

"I'd really like to hear from you," she said with a small smile. "Maybe you could tell me how you met Fraser?"

Scarlett looked to Fraser with so much pain in her eyes that it made him want to wrap his arms around her. "I'm sorry," she whispered.

"It's okay."

Georgia leaned her forearms onto her desk. "Scarlett, would you like to speak to me alone?"

"No," Scarlett said in a rush. "Fraser can tell you anything you want to know."

"I need to hear it from you," she said softly.

Fraser squeezed Scarlett's hand, aware of the fact that from the vice-chancellor's point of view their relationship might be starting to look more sinister than a marriage of convenience. "Just tell the truth," he said.

"But—"

"It doesn't matter." He brushed his thumb over the back of her hand. "Just tell the truth."

She lifted her chin to look at the vice-chancellor. "When I

met Fraser I was sitting on a bench on the university open day and he came over to talk to me. I didn't really like him …"

"Really?" Georgia asked, the corners of her mouth pulling upwards.

"Because of his hair mostly." Scarlett pointed and he couldn't help but smile.

"But your opinion of him must have changed quickly?" Georgia said.

Scarlett grimaced. "Not really."

"So how did you end up marrying him?"

"It's okay," Fraser said when she looked at him. "Tell her what happened."

"We were talking about uni." She bent her head again and spoke quietly. "And I told him I had to wait because I couldn't get a loan. I wasn't eligible for one because my parents could afford to pay but they wouldn't. They think I'm stupid because I'm dyslexic. But now I don't think it was the dyslexia that was the problem. It was probably because I'm autistic."

"You're autistic?" Georgia asked. "I didn't see anything about that in your file."

Pulling her hand from Fraser's, Scarlett tapped her fingers together, then pushed them under her thighs. "I don't have a diagnosis. I'm on the waiting list for an assessment. Anyway that's not the point. The point is that if you're married, the loan company doesn't check your parents' income. Fraser agreed to marry me so I could get the loan and go to uni."

Georgia ran her fingers along her collarbone. "I was convinced you'd tell me this was all a hoax. I have to say I'm slightly stunned."

Scarlett straightened her back. "When I applied for the loan, there wasn't anything to say you have to be married for love. We were legally married. That's all it asked on the form. I didn't lie. And why does the university care how I fund my course?"

"Normally we wouldn't be concerned about that," Georgia

said sadly. "But what you did goes against our code of ethics. If word of it were to get out it reflects badly on the university."

"Am I going to get thrown off my course?" Scarlett asked.

Georgia folded her hands in her lap. "At this point I'm at a bit of a loss as to the appropriate course of action. I'll have to discuss it with the university board members. For now, I will say I appreciate your honesty."

"I'm not good at lying," Scarlett said.

Fraser's heart was beating so fiercely, he was surprised the sound of it wasn't echoing around the room. He squeezed the bridge of his nose. "She didn't tell you the whole truth," he said, looking directly at Georgia.

"What are you talking about?" Scarlett asked.

"We got married for the loan," he said. "But that was two years ago. It wasn't a real marriage then, but it is now. To me, anyway." He paused and took a breath. "Scarlett is the most incredible person I've ever known. She amazes me every single day and I love her completely. I understand that you probably need to set an example, but if that's the case you can kick *me* out of uni. Just me. Let Scarlett finish her course."

"No!" Scarlett took his chin and turned him to face her. "That's not fair. It was me who needed the loan. You were only helping me."

He shook his head. "You should get your degree."

"Not if you don't get yours."

"Scarlett has to fight for everything," he told Georgia. "She works ten times harder than anyone else, and if anyone deserves to get a degree it's her."

Georgia looked at him sadly. "You seem like a sweet couple and I wish I could sweep this under the rug."

"Let's do that then," he said eagerly. "It's a real marriage now. That's all anyone needs to know."

"The trouble is that some people clearly know the truth of it. The person who complained threatened to go to the press if the university doesn't take disciplinary action. This is the sort of story the media loves. And it's not the sort of publicity the university is looking for."

Fraser dropped his head to his hands.

"I'll take this under advisement and get back to you as soon as I can," Georgia said. "You can continue with your courses for the time being."

By the time they walked out of the building, Fraser's blood was pumping furiously. "I'm going to kill her," he growled.

"Who?" Scarlett asked, hurrying to keep up with him.

"Bridget. Who else? I can't believe she'd do this. I know she was upset but I never thought she'd be so spiteful. Threatening to go to the press was about the worst thing she could do. The university will have to do something now."

"You don't even know it was Bridget," Scarlett said.

"Of course it was Bridget. And she's about to find out exactly what I think of her."

Scarlett grabbed at his arm and pulled roughly, forcing him to stop. "You're not going to talk to Bridget."

"I am, actually."

"No. You're not. Even if it was her, do you really think that going around and shouting at her is going to change anything?"

He stretched his neck and blew out a breath. "Maybe not. But maybe if I politely ask her what the hell she thinks she's playing at …"

"Take some deep breaths," Scarlett said, tugging on his collar to force him to look at her. "I don't like it when you get all wound up."

He touched his forehead to hers. "Sorry. I just don't want you to get expelled from uni."

"You tried your best. There's nothing else we can do. Just promise me you'll stay away from Bridget."

He couldn't do anything but agree when she looked at him with pleading in her eyes. After dropping a kiss on her forehead, they set off for the car.

Neither of them spoke much on the drive home, and Fraser complained of a headache and went to his room as soon as they got back. Scarlett went to her own room, hoping for sleep as she rested her head on her pillow.

Replaying the meeting in her head, her heart quickened as she felt the tension in the room all over again. How was it possible for Fraser to stay so calm through it all? And why couldn't she? Even thinking about it made her chest tight. They were definitely going to get kicked out of uni. Which wasn't actually so bad for her. At least she had the publishing company. What would Fraser do if he couldn't finish his degree?

Her mind went over the entire meeting again. Her heart fluttered when she thought of Fraser telling the vice-chancellor that it was a real marriage and he loved her. She just wasn't sure if it was the truth or if he'd said it to try to get them off the hook.

After lying on her bed for an hour she couldn't stand to be alone with her thoughts any longer and crossed the hall to knock on Fraser's door.

"Can I talk to you?" she asked, pushing the door open.

He nodded and shuffled over on the bed to make space but didn't sit up.

"You shouldn't have offered to take the blame," she said frostily. "I know it was nice of you, so I shouldn't be annoyed but I am. You always think you have to look after me but you don't. And if only one of us is going to get kicked out of uni it should be me. I already have a job lined up. I'm part owner of a publishing company."

"I'm well aware that you don't need me to look after you, but that doesn't stop me wanting to. It doesn't matter now anyway. All we can do is wait and see what they decide." He sighed loudly. "You should probably be prepared that we're going to get kicked out of uni. You'll end up with a loan to pay back and the last two years will have been a complete waste of time."

"That's not very positive." Scarlett lay down beside him. "But no matter what happens, I couldn't ever think of the last two years as a waste."

He turned on his side to look at her. "Really?"

"I wouldn't change anything."

"Me neither." He slipped an arm under her head and they spent a few minutes quietly cuddled up together.

"I keep thinking about the meeting," Scarlett said eventually. "You were so calm and confident and I was such a wreck. Anytime I get nervous, I fall apart. It's embarrassing."

"It's fine. The vice-chancellor was really nice. I think she was sympathetic."

"It made me wish I had a diagnosis. Whenever I tell people I'm autistic I almost feel as though I'm lying."

"Of course you're not lying."

"But a doctor said I'm not autistic, and I'm going around claiming that I am."

"We talked about this. The doctor didn't spend much time with you and you were masking the whole time."

"Yeah, I know. I'm just sick of waiting for the assessment. I could be on the waiting list for another year or longer. When I was talking to Bonnie at the youth centre she mentioned that she paid to go to a private clinic for an assessment and it was really fast. So I thought I might do the same."

"What do you need to do?"

"Choose a clinic and make an appointment. It seems to be straightforward. But it's expensive so I need to figure out how to get the money."

"If you want, I can ask my parents. They'd give you the money back for the rent."

"No," Scarlett said fiercely.

"I bet they wouldn't mind."

"*I* mind. Anyway, I thought I might ask my own parents."

Fraser pulled away slightly. "Do you really think they'd give you the money?"

"I think I could persuade them." She was sure they wouldn't be thrilled about her wanting to get an autism diagnosis, but if she spun the conversation the right way she might be able to convince them. "I thought I could tell them that if I have a diagnosis I might be able to get better."

Untangling himself from her, Fraser sat up. "You're not ill."

"I know, but if my parents think there's a possibility of me being fixed, they'll probably pay."

"No." Fraser's eyebrows drew together. "No way."

"What do you mean, no?"

"You can't do that. For a start, you don't need fixing. Also, what's happened to your principles? You wouldn't lie to the vice-chancellor but you're okay with lying to get money?"

"I don't want to. It just seems like the only option."

"It's not." He lay beside her again, wrapping his arms around her. "I'll see if I can work at the restaurant at the weekends and we'll save up the money. Please don't ask your parents."

"I don't want you to worry about getting the money. It's not your problem."

"We're married," he said, his face against her neck. "Your problems are my problems. But in this case it's not a problem, just a challenge. How much does it cost?"

"A couple of thousand."

He planted a soft kiss on her collarbone. "We'll figure it out."

Scarlett's eyelids grew heavier as she lay snuggled into Fraser's chest.

"You definitely don't need fixing," he whispered. "I like you just as you are."

She noticed he'd only said *like* and not love.

CHAPTER 50

Scarlett didn't have any lectures on Tuesday and probably wouldn't have gone to them if she did. After barely sleeping the previous night she spent the morning lazing in bed. Going to lectures didn't make much sense anyway since she'd probably be off the course soon.

When lunchtime approached she forced herself to eat, then ignored the desire to snuggle back in bed. If she was staying at home, she should work on her novel. Or at least try to.

Fraser seemed to be burying his head in the sand about the fact that it might be their last days at uni. Or maybe he was choosing to make the most of it. He carried on as usual, going to lectures and acting as though everything was normal.

On Thursday afternoon, he signalled his arrival home by banging the door shut behind him and shouting for Scarlett.

"What?" she asked, stepping out of her room and leaning over the bannister.

"Georgia Sutcliffe called me," he said, racing up the stairs.

Scarlett's entire body tensed. "What did she say?"

"Bridget took it back." He stopped in front of Scarlett with a massive grin on his face. "She told them that she made the whole thing up and since there's no complaint any more, the matter is being dropped."

"Thank goodness." Scarlett sighed as Fraser threw his arms around her. "So it really was Bridget who reported us?" she asked, pulling back.

"I don't know for definite. Georgia didn't name anyone, but I don't know who else it would have been."

"It could have been one of your friends." Her gut instinct was that it wasn't Bridget and she couldn't shake it. "Maybe Simon. Didn't you say he was grumpy about you quitting the football team?"

"Yeah, but he wouldn't be that petty. I'm sure it was Bridget."

"I don't think it was. I have a feeling. Do you know that some autistic people have really great instincts … like a sixth sense?"

"Are you serious?"

"Yeah. I read a social media post about it, and a load of autistic people commented that they agreed."

"Well, whether or not you have supernatural powers, we get to stay in uni."

"So this means I have to stop lazing around and get back into study mode?"

"I suppose it does." He gave her a lingering kiss. "But you could probably take this evening to celebrate not getting kicked out of uni."

"I think I might do that." Beaming, she slipped her arms around his neck and kissed him deeply. Her lips never left his as she took steps towards her bedroom.

~

The relief at being able to finish her degree made Scarlett grateful for every aspect of university life. If she'd had to leave it all behind, she'd even have missed the familiar faces on her course. On a rush of adrenalin she invited Carolyn and Mingmei to have lunch with her after the lecture on Friday. It was surprisingly pleasant to chat with them as they ate.

Arriving home late in the afternoon, she checked her emails to find one from someone called Miriam Croft. She worked for student support services and had been asked by the vice-chancellor to reach out to Scarlett to discuss any support they could offer her. Scarlett shook her head as she closed the email. She managed fine and didn't need any help. Pausing, she chewed her lip, then went back to the email and wrote a quick reply saying she'd like to meet with her sometime. It probably couldn't do any harm.

Fraser was later than she expected getting home that evening, and she was beginning to get impatient when the doorbell sounded. It wasn't like Fraser to forget his key and they didn't usually have visitors turning up unannounced. Quietly, she crept to the door and peeked through the spy hole, then hesitated before opening it.

"Hi," Bridget said, wringing her hands in front of her.

"Fraser isn't home yet," Scarlett said.

"I suspect that might be a good thing. I actually wanted to speak to you … if you've got a few minutes?"

Scarlett opened the door wider and gestured for her to come in. "How are you?" she asked, leading Bridget into the living room.

"Not great," she said as tears filled her eyes.

Scarlett raised her eyebrows, glancing out of the front window in the hopes that Fraser might be arriving home and could help her out with the situation. "Do you want to sit down?" she asked.

"I'm so sorry." Bridget sat at the edge of the couch and searched her pockets for a tissue. "You must hate me."

"No. I always thought you were nice."

She looked up, her eyes wide. "But I almost got you thrown off your course."

"That was you?" Scarlett asked, sitting at the other end of the couch. "Fraser thought it was, but I never really believed you'd do that."

"I can't believe I did it," she sniffed. "I hated myself as soon as I sent the letter. But when I saw you and Fraser the other week, you looked so happy. I thought you'd lied to me and I felt completely humiliated."

"We didn't lie to you. We really weren't together when Fraser went out with you."

"I think I knew that deep down. I really am sorry."

"It's okay. We didn't get kicked out so it's all fine."

"You're so sweet." She dabbed the tissue under her nose. "I thought you'd hate me."

"No. Fraser's not very happy with you though."

"He's got every right to be angry. I wanted to come and apologise at least. If there's anything I can do to make it up to you just say."

Scarlett thought for a moment. "Maybe you could help me figure something out …"

"What?"

"We had a meeting with the vice-chancellor of the university to discuss your complaint against us, and in the meeting Fraser said he loved me and that he sees it as a real marriage now. But I don't know if he meant it or if he just said it because he didn't want us to get kicked out of uni. And I'm not sure if I should ask him about it or not … I'm not good at this sort of thing."

"You're asking me for relationship advice?" Bridget said slowly.

"Yeah. You said if you could do anything you would…"

She shook her head and let out a gentle laugh. "If it was anyone else I'd swear they were trying to rub my nose in it, but you're not, are you?"

"I don't think so. I'm not actually sure what you mean."

"I'm probably not the best person to give relationship advice.

I've been single for a long time and seem to be slightly obsessed with a married man."

"That's not good," Scarlett said, making Bridget laugh again. "Do you mean Fraser?"

"Yes. I'm hoping I'll get over it one of these days. Anyway, to answer your question, I'd put money on the fact that he was telling the truth when he said he loves you."

"You're only guessing, though," Scarlett said. "You weren't even there, so it'd be hard for you to know."

"True. But the times I hung out with him, he always looked really happy when he was talking about you."

"Do you think I should ask him, or would that be weird?"

"I think it's fine to ask him."

"I also want to ask him about us getting a divorce … when we got married we agreed we'd get divorced when we graduated. But now I don't want to."

"I'm sure he feels the same way."

"But we agreed to get the divorce."

"If your relationship has changed since then, it makes sense that you'd change your mind about getting a divorce. You should speak to him about it." Standing, she shoved her crumpled tissue in her pocket. "Thanks for being so nice."

"You're welcome." She followed her to the front door. "We could be friends, if you want?"

"I'd like that." Bridget looked at her sadly. "I'm not sure it's a good idea at the moment, though, what with me having a crush on your husband."

"I didn't think about that. Maybe when you're over him."

"Maybe. Will you tell him I'm sorry?"

Scarlett promised she would, then closed the door behind Bridget. It was another half an hour before Fraser finally arrived home.

"You're late!" Scarlett called from the living room.

"Sorry." He wandered in and flopped onto the couch. "How was your day?"

"Interesting."

"Mine too," he said.

"Tell me about yours first."

His brow wrinkled as he looked at her. "I don't want you to be weird about this. I did something and I think you might not like it, but it's not a big deal and there's no need for you to be annoyed or upset about it, okay?"

"I don't know until you tell me … You're making me nervous."

"I sold my car."

She blinked a few times. "Why would you sell your car?"

"To get the money for your autism assessment."

She stared at him, not quite believing what she was hearing. "You *need* a car."

"I traded it in for a cheaper one. It's not a big deal."

It *was* a big deal because she knew how much he'd loved his car.

"You're not going to be stubborn about taking the money, are you?" he asked.

She shook her head and looked him in the eyes. "I love you."

"I love you too."

A smile tugged at her lips. "When you said you loved me in the meeting I didn't know if you were only saying it to convince the vice-chancellor it was a real marriage."

"No. It was the truth. I love you."

She moved closer and kissed him, then rested her cheek against his. "I don't want us to get a divorce."

"That's nice," he said, without enthusiasm. "It would have been nicer if you hadn't needed a week to think about it."

"I wasn't thinking about whether I wanted a divorce. I was thinking about whether it would be better to divorce you now or after graduation. But Bridget said that since our relationship has changed, maybe you wouldn't want to get a divorce at all. That would be my preference."

"You spoke to Bridget?"

"Yes. She came over to apologise for reporting us."

"I *knew* it was her." He grinned. "So you don't have a sixth sense after all?"

"Possibly not. But Bridget feels terrible. I told her not to worry about it … and then I asked her for relationship advice."

"That's weird."

"She thought so too, but she gives good advice."

He chuckled. "So you don't want to get divorced?"

"No. I don't think I'll make a very good wife, though. Just to warn you."

"You've been doing fine so far. We can just carry on as we are."

"For now … but one day you'll want a proper wife. Someone who can cook and who you're not embarrassed to be in public with."

"I'm not embarrassed by you," he said, hooking her hair behind her ear. "I love being married to you."

"Really? Because I worry that I'll get used to having you around and then you'll realise you'd rather be with someone else."

"I can't predict the future but I can't see that happening." He gave her a quick kiss. "Since we promised to be together till death do us part, I think we should try to stick to that."

She smiled widely. "I like that plan."

EPILOGUE

When the doorbell rang, Scarlett shouted for Fraser to answer it, then remembered he'd gone into town and she hadn't heard him come back yet. She grumbled about him taking so long as she hurried down the stairs.

Forcing a smile, she opened the door, then stepped back to allow Fraser's parents in.

"Happy Graduation Day!" Tricia said, bunching her shoulders up.

"Thanks."

"Are you excited?" Dominic asked.

"Not really. And Fraser went into town. I don't know why he had to go now. I needed him here to help me."

"I can help you get ready." Tricia handed a cake carrier to Dominic and told him to put it in the kitchen.

"Does Auntie Verity know you're bringing cake?" Scarlett asked. "Because she's organising the food for the party."

"Yes. I spoke to her. Between us, we have everything organised. Now, let's get you ready."

Scarlett looked down at her outfit. Admittedly the dress was the same style as she usually wore, but it was a new one. "I *am* ready."

"Good," Tricia said. "What did you need Fraser for?"

"Nothing." She moved and sat on the stairs. "I was just panicking about the stupid ceremony."

"I thought you'd been through everything with Miriam?"

"I'm just nervous." Though she'd probably be even more nervous if Miriam from student services hadn't spent the last two weeks reassuring her about everything.

"There's no need to be nervous. The ceremony will be over before you know it and you'll be back here celebrating with everyone."

"I didn't even want a party. You and Verity bullied me into it!"

"Yes. We did." Tricia sat beside her. "Because we're proud of you and want to make a fuss of the fact that you got your degree. You agreed to indulge us, remember?"

"Yeah. Okay. As long as you're not annoyed with me."

"Why would I be annoyed with you?"

"Because Fraser accepted the job at the youth centre. I thought you might be disappointed and blame me."

"I think youth work is an admiral career choice."

"It doesn't pay much," Scarlett pointed out.

"No. But it'll make him happy, which is the main thing." She bumped her shoulder against Scarlett's. "You bring out the best in him, so I'm grateful to you, not annoyed."

"That's good," she said quietly.

Tricia gave her hand a squeeze. "I'm going to see if Dominic's put the kettle on. Do you want a drink?"

"No. I'm going to paint my nails."

"What colour?"

"Scarlet. To match my dress!"

Tricia laughed. "I can do it for you if you want?"

"No thank you."

"Give me a shout if you need anything," Tricia said. "I'm sure Fraser will be back soon."

Scarlett was sitting at her desk, waiting for her nails to dry when Fraser finally appeared.

"Why did you need to go into town so urgently?" she asked, when he said hello from the doorway.

"I had to pick up champagne for the party. I bought you a load of balloons and flowers too."

"I hope you're joking." She blew on her nails and didn't turn around. "We can't afford balloons and flowers and champagne."

"True. It's actually cheap fizzy wine and a few balloons and crappy supermarket flowers. Is that acceptable?"

She smiled widely. "You've changed, Fraser Graham."

"I have indeed. But you'll need to look at me to see just how much."

She turned in her chair, then slapped a hand over her mouth. "What the hell happened to your hair?"

"I'm trying to impress a girl," he said, ruffling his cropped hair. "What do you think? You don't look very impressed so far."

"I have a confession to make," she said, walking over to him. "I actually liked your hair before."

He arched an eyebrow. "You've spent three years teasing me and making me feel self-conscious."

"That's a lie." She laughed and draped her arms around his shoulders. "You were never self-conscious about your hair."

"I could've been."

"I just enjoyed teasing you. I thought it was a good way to keep you grounded too."

"It worked. Don't you like it short?" He dipped his head to give her a better look.

"I like it." She trailed her fingers over the freshly cut hairs at the back of his neck. "But I don't really care that much about your hair. I just love you."

"I love you too." He kissed her slowly. "Emily's downstairs. We should get going soon. Miriam's meeting us there, right?"

"Yes." Scarlett was only allowed two guests at the ceremony, so she'd chosen Fraser and Emily. Miriam could go too since she worked for the university. Everyone else would come to the house for a celebration afterwards.

"You better get your cap and gown on," Fraser said.

"No. It's itchy and uncomfortable. I called Miriam earlier and she said to bring it with me and put it on at the last minute. She's also reserved seats for us at the end of a row and has made sure that I'll be one of the first to be awarded my certificate, so we'll be able to slip out after if I'm too stressed."

"Thank goodness," Fraser said. "I really don't want to sit through another two hours of people's names being read out while sitting on an uncomfortable chair in the cathedral."

"You didn't enjoy your ceremony, did you?" His had been a few days earlier.

"Not much. It was a good call for you to sit it out and let my parents go."

"Can you remind me why all we did to celebrate your degree was dinner with your parents while I get everyone making a big fuss?"

"Because you're worth making a fuss over." He hugged her tightly. "Now we need to get going. Have you got everything?"

She picked up her cap and gown and followed him downstairs, where Emily was waiting for them in a cute blue summer dress.

"I'm so excited," she said, beaming at Scarlett.

"I'm glad one of us is," she replied before they bustled out of the door.

Fraser was right about the ceremony being slightly tedious. The chairs were uncomfortable and it was hot inside the packed cathedral. As Miriam had suggested, they slipped out after Scarlett had been up to collect her degree.

"You're really embarrassing," she hissed, her eyes darting

between Fraser, Emily and Miriam when they stood outside the cathedral. "Who wolf whistled when they called my name?"

"Don't look at me!" Fraser said. "It was Emily."

Scarlett shook her head. "As if Emily can wolf whistle."

"I can actually." Emily beamed with pride. "Jack taught me."

"Why would Jack teach you to wolf whistle?"

"Because he was upset that he couldn't come to your ceremony and whistle to embarrass you, so he made me promise I'd do it for him."

Scarlett cracked up laughing. "Now I'm imagining you two sitting at home learning to whistle!"

"It was quite funny," Emily agreed.

"Stand in front of the cathedral," Miriam said. "I'll take your photo with your cap and gown on. Fraser, you get in too."

"Hurry up," Scarlett said as she smiled dutifully. "I want to take this stupid outfit off again."

"Do you want to wait until everyone else comes out so we can get some photos with your friends?" Miriam asked.

"No. Carolyn and Mingmei will come to our place later so I can get photos with them then."

"It's nice that they're coming," Emily remarked.

"Yes." Scarlett considered the two of them friends now and planned to stay in touch with them. "Mingmei is bringing her parents and Carolyn's husband is coming."

"It's going to be a houseful," Miriam said. "Shall we head back there now?"

Fraser checked his watch. "We could find a cafe and get a drink first. We're not in any rush."

Scarlett removed the bobby pins holding her cap in place and rubbed at her forehead when she removed the itchy material. "Going to a cafe's a waste of money. We can have a drink at home."

"Mum and Verity will still be getting the house ready for the party," Fraser said, taking her cap while she shrugged the gown off. "It'll give them more time to prepare."

Scarlett stopped dead and stared at him. "There aren't going to be any surprises, are there? I only agreed to the party if there were no surprises. I hate surprises."

"They just want to decorate the place a bit. You know what they're like."

"There really better not be any surprises," Scarlett grumbled as they set off for the nearest cafe.

"Chill out," Fraser said. "It's supposed to be a fun day."

"You know I hate it when you tell me to chill out. Miriam, didn't you have a word with him about that?"

"I did. He just does it to tease you. I've talked to him about that too, but he's a lost cause. Maybe you should divorce him?"

"And maybe I should make a complaint against you," Fraser said to Miriam. "You're a pest!"

"I'd like to point out that since Scarlett is officially no longer a student at the university, my role is now entirely unofficial. I'm only here as a friend."

"Damn it," Fraser said. "That means I'll have to start being nice to you."

Scarlett slowed her pace, contemplating how much would change now that university was over.

"We'll keep in touch," Miriam said, appearing beside her and seeming to read her mind. "And Bonnie at the youth centre will be a great mentor. She said you can message her whenever you need advice on something. And you can visit her at the youth centre too."

"That's a ploy to get me to go to the autism groups."

Miriam smiled. "I thought you went along the other week and it was fine."

"It was okay," she reluctantly agreed.

Fraser slung an arm around her shoulders. "She just won't admit to enjoying it because that would mean admitting I was right."

"I can understand why you wouldn't want to do that,"

Miriam said, grinning as they approached a cafe with outdoor seating.

Scarlett happily listened to the easy conversation between her three friends while they sipped refreshingly cool drinks.

"You're quiet," Fraser said when they arrived home.

"Conserving my energy," she replied as she opened the door. She expected the house to be a buzz of people, but it was all quiet. There were no obvious decorations either, though the living room door was closed, as was the kitchen door. "Where is everyone?" she asked Fraser.

"They're all here," Tricia answered, appearing from the kitchen and closing the door quickly behind her. "Apart from Allie and Liam," she said to Fraser. "Are they definitely coming?"

"Yes. Allie called earlier to say they're running late but they'll be here."

"I'm so glad they sorted things out," Tricia said.

Scarlett looked along the hall. "Did you shut everyone in the kitchen?" she asked in confusion. "Are Lizzie and Max here? And Jack?"

"Yes." Tricia smiled. "And the couple who own the book-shop … and another couple with a toddler. The kids are all playing out on the garden. I just wanted to get you on your own for a minute."

"I should probably go and say hello," Scarlett said, scratching at her neck. She'd just taken a step towards the kitchen when Fraser's hands landed on her shoulders, stopping her in her tracks.

"Mum and Dad bought you a graduation present," he said.

She swung around to him. "I said no surprises."

"It's my fault," Tricia said. "Fraser told me you didn't want any surprises but I insisted. If you don't like it you can blame me."

She bit her lip as she looked up at Fraser.

"It's just a gift," he said. "All you have to do is smile and say thank you."

"Come and look," Tricia said, leading her to the living room and gently pushing the door open.

Scarlett took a few steps into the room, then stopped.

"What do you think?" Tricia asked, hovering beside her.

"That's for me?" Scarlett asked. "*That's* the present?"

"Yes."

Her eyes were fixed on the polished black upright piano which fit neatly in the corner of the room.

"It's mine?" she whispered, the words barely audible.

"Yes." Tricia rubbed at her arm. "Happy graduation, sweetheart."

Scarlett moved and sank onto the couch as tears blurred her vision. Her chest heaved and her shoulders shook as sobs racked her body.

Fraser sat beside her and pulled her into his chest.

"Scarlett?" Tricia's voice was brittle beside her. "I thought you'd like it."

She opened her mouth but failed to formulate words and couldn't stop crying.

Miriam appeared and sat on the edge of the coffee table in front of her. "It's a good surprise, isn't it?"

"Yes," she said shakily. "It's the best surprise ever. I just can't stop crying."

"That's okay," Miriam said. "We're all crying."

Wiping at her cheeks, Scarlett saw the tears in Miriam's eyes, then looked back at Emily, who was hovering in the doorway with tears trickling down her face.

Fraser leant his head against Scarlett's. "I told you all you had to do was smile and say thanks! You never listen to me."

"Thank you," Scarlett said to Tricia.

"Do you like it?"

"I love it."

"I'm glad." Tricia kissed her cheek before Scarlett took a deep breath and moved to the piano.

Lifting the fallboard she gazed at the beautifully shiny black and white keys. "I really wish I hadn't agreed to a party now. I just want to sit and play for the afternoon, but I'm going to have to be sociable, aren't I?"

"I'm afraid so," Fraser said.

~

It was without a doubt the best party that Scarlett had ever been to. She enjoyed mingling and chatting to all of her favourite people.

By the time everyone left she was exhausted and headed upstairs with Fraser. He flopped straight onto her bed while she pulled a file out of her desk drawer to add her degree certificate to.

"I might frame these," she said, walking over to the bed with the file. "I'm not sure which certificate I'm most proud of, but I love them all."

"How many certificates have you got?"

She opened the file. "Marriage certificate…" She flicked the page. "Autism certificate … and now a degree certificate. It's a nice collection, isn't it?"

He nodded and sat up to look. "I didn't know they gave you a certificate when you got your diagnosis."

"They didn't. But I thought they should have done so I made one myself."

He chuckled and dropped a kiss on her shoulder. "I love you."

"Love you too." She took the file back to the desk. "Do you want to tell me what's bothering you?"

His cheek twitched. "How do you mean?"

"You've been worrying about something."

"No, I haven't."

She sat back beside him. "Liar!"

"I thought you were supposed to be bad at reading people?"

"Sometimes. You're pretty easy though. It annoys me that you help me with all my problems but don't share your problems with me."

"It's nothing. And today was for celebrating. I don't want to ruin the mood."

"Just tell me." She rested her head on his shoulder. "Please."

He blew out a breath. "Do you remember when I said we might not be able to afford to live here from September?"

"Yeah."

"Well. We definitely can't afford to keep living here. Not with what I'll be earning."

"I know that," she said. "It was pretty obvious."

"I thought I could find somewhere smaller, but we'll be on a tight budget and the cheap places aren't nice. I keep thinking I should look for a job that pays better."

She shook her head. "Don't do that. I already have the situation in hand."

"How do you mean?"

"I knew we'd have to move so I looked for places too."

"There's not much choice around here within our budget, is there?"

"No." She smiled brightly. "I've been working on a different plan. How would you feel about living in Hope Cove?"

He shrugged. "It would take the same amount of time to get to work as it does from here. But Hope Cove won't be cheaper. If anything, it's more expensive."

"Not if we live in Auntie Verity's flat."

"We can't. It's the offices for the publishing company. Lizzie and Emily work there."

"Yes. But I think I can kick them out."

He laughed. "You can't do that."

"I've been looking at alternative premises for the publishing company. I have a couple of options I can put to Lizzie and Emily. I think they'll go for it."

"Are you sure? I think they really love using the flat as an office."

"It's more important that we have a home. I've always loved the flat."

"I really like the idea. If you're sure it's not going to upset anyone, and if it's okay with Verity."

"Leave it to me," Scarlett said happily. "Don't you worry your pretty little head about it!"

He cracked up laughing, then raised an eyebrow. "You think I'm pretty?"

"Why do you think I married you?"

"I thought it was for money."

She kissed him softly. "That as well."

A NOTE FROM THE AUTHOR

When Scarlett first appeared in Verity's cafe back in the fifth Hope Cove book, I had no idea how significant her role would become. She was supposed to be a small side character, but wormed her way into the story in the way some characters insist on doing.

I'll be honest, it took me a long time (and a lot of requests from readers) to seriously consider giving Scarlett her own book. Though it hadn't been specifically mentioned, I always thought of Scarlett as autistic, and I wasn't sure that was something I was qualified to write about. I'm not autistic myself, and although I considered myself to have a reasonable awareness of neurodiversity (from both studying Disability Studies at Northumbria University, and having autistic friends), I still wasn't sure whether to go ahead with it.

Then I started to do some research. As I read blogs and social media posts by autistic people, I found myself more and more drawn to writing Scarlett's story.

A comment I've seen numerous times in the online autistic community is: "if you've met one autistic person, you've met one autistic person". That is to say that all autistic people are different, with different challenges and needs. Autism isn't just one thing and can look very different from person to person. Through Scarlett I wanted to draw attention to some of the challenges autistic people may face while also celebrating neurodiversity.

If you're interested in learning more about autism, you can find great information from autistic people online or in books.

I particularly enjoyed watching videos by @paigelayle and @neurodivergentrebel on Youtube and Instagram.

The Autism Podcast has a lot of fascinating interviews.

A couple of books I enjoyed are *Spectrum Women* (Barb Cook, Michelle Garnett et al.) and *I Think I Might Be Autistic* (Cynthia Kim).

For those of you wondering about further books in the Hope Cove series, I'm sorry to tell you that I don't have any more books planned.

Thank you so much for sticking with the series for eight books. I had no idea what I was getting into when I started writing this series. It's been challenging and fun, and I have learnt so much along the way. I continue to be touched by messages from readers who have taken this series and these characters to heart.

I'm so glad you fell in love with them as much as I did.

ALSO BY HANNAH ELLIS

<u>The Hope Cove Series</u>

The Cottage at Hope Cove (Book 1)

Escape to Oakbrook Farm (Book 2)

Summer at The Old Boathouse (Book 3)

Whispers at the Bluebell Inn (Book 4)

The House on Lavender Lane (Book 5)

The Bookshop of Hopes and Dreams (Book 6)

Winter Wishes in Hope Cove (Book 7)

There's Something about Scarlett (Book 8)

<u>The Loch Lannick Series</u>

Coming Home to the Loch (Book 1)

The Castle by the Loch (Book 2)

Fireworks over the Loch (Book 3)

The Cafe at the Loch (Book 4)

Secrets at the Loch (Book 5)

Surprises at the Loch (Book 6)

Finding Hope at the Loch (Book 7)

Fragile Hearts by the Loch (Book 8)

New Arrivals at the Loch (Book 9)

Always With You (Standalone novel)

<u>The Friends Like These Series</u>

Friends Like These (Book 1)

Christmas with Friends (Book 2)

My Kind of Perfect (Book 3)

A Friend in Need (Book 4)

The Lucy Mitchell Series

Beyond the Lens (Book 1)

Beneath These Stars (Book 2)

Hannah has also written a series of children's books aimed at 5-9 year olds under the pen name, Hannah Sparks.

Books in the Land of Stars series:

Where Dragons Fly (Book 1)

Where Stars Fall (Book 2)

Where Penguins Party (Book 3)

ABOUT THE AUTHOR

When she's not writing, Hannah enjoys spending time with her husband and kids. She loves to read and also enjoys yoga and jogging. And tea … she really loves a good cup of tea!

Hannah can be found online at the following places:

Facebook: @authorhannahellis

Instagram: @authorhannahellis

Twitter: @BooksEllis

Website: www.authorhannahellis.com

Feel free to contact Hannah at any of the above or email her at this address:

authorhannahellis@gmail.com

If you'd like to be kept up to date with news about Hannah's books you can sign up to her receive emails from her through her website:

www.authorhannahellis.com/newsletter

Printed in Dunstable, United Kingdom

72110191R00272